Timeless Desire

The wind ruffled Lucien's hair, but he stood motionless, his expression as intense as a physical touch. "I know how I feel. I love you—too much to give this up for the risks involved."

She had a sense of inevitability when he lifted his arms and she went into them. For a moment they simply held each other, afraid to let go. She listened to his heartbeat through his shirtfront, sighed when he nestled his lips in her hair...

Deepening violet tinged the sky. Even the gulls had quieted. Only the waves broke the solitary peace in either direction as far as the eye could see. They might have been in any time...hers or his, or another altogether...

D1293133

Beloved Captain

Jo Ann Simon

AVON
PUBLISHERS OF BARD, CAMELOT, DISCUS AND FLARE BOOKS

BELOVED CAPTAIN is an original publication of Avon Books. This work has never before appeared in book form. This work is a novel. Any similarity to actual persons or events is purely coincidental.

AVON BOOKS
A division of
The Hearst Corporation
105 Madison Avenue
New York, New York 10016

Copyright © 1988 by Jo Ann Simon
Published by arrangement with the author
Library of Congress Catalog Card Number: 87-91618
ISBN: 0-380-89771-7

First Avon Books Printing: January 1988

For Ian,
and for all my sailing friends

Prologue

Orange Street, Nantucket
January 1845

A single figure stood outlined in the pale winter-white light of the risng moon. He stood motionless, hands resting on the widow's walk railing in front of him. The slicing wind off Nantucket Bay whipped past. It dragged at his thick dark hair and lifted the heavy greatcoat away from his tall frame. He stared to the sea, his blue eyes narrowed on the horizon and a place beyond that only he could see. White wisps of vapor formed about his full, trimmed beard with each of his slow breaths, but he was impervious to the cold, just as he was impervious to the lights of Nantucket Town far below his rooftop perch.

On that cold and cloudless night, there were no observers to witness his silent vigil. Lucien Blythe alone relived the memories that brought a crippling pain. He alone suffered deep in his soul.

From somewhere below a clock chimed dimly. As a man pulling himself from a dream, he lifted his hands from the railing and started down the stairs into the house.

Chapter 1

Catherine Sternwood placed her hands on jean-covered hips and nodded in satisfaction. The last room in the house on Orange Street was clean. The antique tables in the spacious living room gleamed richly, as did the finish on the grand piano in the corner. The Chippendale sofa and wing chairs grouped before the fireplace had been brushed free of all dust. The oriental carpets had been vacuumed, the wood floors polished. The panes of the six windows in the long room twinkled. Each old oil painting on the walls was dusted and straightened; the brass sconces and candlesticks glowed.

Picking up her dustrag and can of polish, she started back across the front hall to the other downstairs rooms of the old house. Late afternoon light slanted through the glass-paned transom over the front door, brightening the square front hall with a hazy gold. Each step across the wide floorboards brought memories of the days she'd spent in the house as a child. In the small front parlor, tall bookshelves reached from floor to ceiling and were filled with old volumes collected by her grandparents—stories of the sea and whaling and the history of Nantucket. Beside the fireplace was a comfortable chair, and through the front windows was the familiar view of Orange Street. In the adjoining dining room her grandmother's collection of oriental blue and orange ginger jars was displayed atop the long sideboards, and centered beneath the pewter chandelier was the huge mahogany table where the whole family had gathered on holidays. So many warm and cherished memories.

When her grandmother had died nearly a year before and she'd learned she'd inherited the old house, Catherine's instinct had been to put it up for rent. She had too much to lose in leaving California—

friends, her interior design business, her lovely apartment overlooking the Pacific. Santa Barbara had been her home for over fifteen years. Nantucket had been a place to come and visit in the summer and on holidays. Of course, there were ties here, too. Her father had been born on the island, and she'd been born across Nantucket Sound in Falmouth, had lived in Massachusetts for fourteen years. Yet her real ties were in the West. She had no family left except her younger sister, Treasa, the sailor and wanderer. It had been nearly a year since they'd last seen each other and several months since Treasa's last brief letter postmarked in the south of France, where Treasa had been crewing on a yacht.

After their parents' deaths in an automobile accident seven years before, Catherine had tried to play substitute parent to her sister. Treasa hadn't been inclined to accept the advice or supervision of a sibling not much older than herself. There'd been continuing disagreements between them. Treasa rebelled against anything that smacked of authority or conformity, and the last few times Catherine had seen her sister, Treasa's drinking had become more of a problem. Escape seemed to be all Treasa wanted; escape from a world with which she couldn't cope.

Five years before, Treasa had sailed off on a yacht, and Catherine had turned her energies toward building up an interior design business. There'd been rough times, but Classics, her shop, was finally succeeding. She was making money—a lot of money. It had almost broken her heart to leave Classics in the hands of a trusted manager. Though she planned on opening a sister shop on Nantucket, where the wealthy summer people should prove a good clientele, she was uncertain about leaving the infant business she'd created. Would her manager, a young designer who had been her first employee, have the savvy about design that she did? Would the Classics reputation fade? She'd promised to give herself a year on Nantucket—a year to find out if the island was a place she wanted to stay. In that time, she'd keep in frequent touch with Santa Barbara. Still, she had grave doubts.

She walked on into the kitchen to put away her cleaning materials. That room in particular carried warm memories that brushed against Catherine's cheeks like a soft gust of wind. She could picture her grandmother's gray-haired form standing before the kitchen sink; could see her grandfather at the oilcloth-covered kitchen table, carving the turkey before it was brought into the boisterous Christmas gathering of friends and family. She remembered the summer mornings when her grandmother had taught her the intricacies of making tollhouse cookies and pies filled with early apples from the tree in the backyard.

Her grandparents had loved the place so, treating it like another child. They'd discovered the house when they were still a young couple, and though it was an historic home, it had been much neglected. They'd moved over from the mainland, and had done the restoration work themselves, carefully, authentically, with their own hands. When they were finished, the house looked much like it must have shortly after it had been built. Catherine supposed that was the ingredient that made the house so welcoming. Of course, the period antiques her grandparents had collected over the years appealed to and satisfied her own aesthetics, and they belonged in the house; they fit perfectly.

A sharp knock on the back door interrupted her from her musings. She looked through the screen to see a cheery, round, feminine face, framed by gray hair.

"Hope I'm not intruding," the woman smiled. "I thought I'd come over and say hello. I'm Marjorie Schmidt, your neighbor. Is it Catherine?"

"Yes, of course. I remember you, but it's been a long time. Come in."

As Catherine held the door, the older woman stepped through, setting a linen-towel-wrapped bundle on the kitchen table. It was obvious from Marjorie's attire that she wasn't your typical older lady next door. She was wearing a baggy pair of pants and what appeared to be one of her husband's cast-off dress shirts. Her feet were stuffed into a scruffy pair of Docksides, and her short, curly hair had been styled by a set of impatient fingers pulled briskly through the gray locks. Catherine vaguely remembered her grandmother mentioning Marjorie's eccentric but generous nature, and her mind that was often off on some intellectual tangent or other. Her unconventional manner had been one of the reasons she and Catherine's grandmother had become such good friends. "I just baked some bread," Marjorie added. "A little housewarming present for you."

"Why, thank you. How nice."

"Baking a weekly batch keeps me out of trouble—at least that's what my husband says." Marjorie's gray eyes twinkled behind wire-rimmed glasses. "I tend to get caught up in my projects and forget to cook altogether."

"How about a cup of coffee?" Catherine offered. "I was just making some."

"As long as it's no trouble, I'd love a little chat." Marjorie plopped down comfortably in one of the chairs at the square table. "How well I remember seeing you and your sister in the yard as toddlers . . . and now you're a lovely young woman. Time flies, or I'm just getting older than I'd like to think!"

Catherine chuckled as she filled the cups.

"I must say I felt the loss of your grandparents," Marjorie added quietly. "I liked them both so much—wonderful people."

"Yes . . . I'll miss them."

Marjorie took the cup Catherine offered her and looked up curiously. "Are you here to stay or just to sort out the house?"

Catherine slid into the opposite chair. "To stay—I hope."

"They'd be glad, but it's a big house for a single person. There aren't many unattached young people on the island off-season."

"I'd like to give it a try. When they left me the house, I think they hoped that I'd live here for a while, not rent it or put it up for sale. This place always meant more to me than it did my sister."

"Where is your sister?"

Catherine shook her head and absently traced her finger over the checked tablecloth. "Last I heard, she was in the south of France."

"Mmm, your grandmother told me something of the story. Will you be looking for work?"

"I'm an interior designer. I have a store out in California and plan on opening a small shop here."

"Good for you! I like a woman with spirit. There weren't many opportunities when I was your age, but I would have enjoyed a chance to do something all for myself, under my own steam. That's probably why I potter and get lost in so many projects now. I'll see what I can do to introduce you around. Evan and I have a good number of friends here."

"I'd appreciate it, but please don't feel you have to."

"Nonsense. It's the least I can do for the Sternwoods' granddaughter. You must have had quite a cleaning job to do with the house being closed up so long."

"It was worth it."

"You like antiques, I take it."

"Anything old, be it furniture or history."

"You've come to the right place. Anything on this island less than fifty years old is considered garish modern. Not that I'm complaining. It's just the way I want it, but young people don't always think that way. You know, this house goes back a good many years."

"I do know, and I wish I remembered more of the history."

"Your grandmother had quite a few of the old deeds."

"Did she?" Catherine's interest perked. "I'll have a look through their papers."

"Let me know what you find. One of my latest projects is gathering up information on the older island homes for the historical society—I chair one of the committees."

"That sounds like fun."

"It is—one of those projects that takes me off on tangents, as Evan would say." Marjorie winked, then glanced at her watch. "I should be going. I'm keeping you from your work."

"No rush."

"But time I started dinner." Marjorie finished off her coffee and rose. Catherine followed suit. Their hands met in a warm clasp. "I'm happy you're here," Marjorie said.

"So am I."

"Don't be a stranger. Stop by over at our place any time. I'm always looking for an excuse to keep me from housework." Marjorie headed to the door and pulled open the screen.

"Thanks for the bread!" Catherine called.

"Expect another loaf next week. Evan and I should both go on a diet."

Marjorie's cheerful essence lingered in the room as Catherine cleaned up the coffee cups and made herself a sandwich and soup for dinner. She was delighted to have renewed her acquaintance with her neighbor and, as she left the kitchen and followed the hallway to the front of the house, she wondered again about the old deeds Marjorie had mentioned. There certainly was history here. One could almost feel it. Why hadn't she paid more attention to her grandparents' stories?

Her hand glided up the shining banister as she climbed the stairs. Two bedrooms were to the right of the L-shaped upstairs hall—her grandparents' former bedroom to the rear, and a guest bedroom to the front. Another bedroom, with a connecting study, was to the left of the hall. That original master suite had always been Catherine's favorite. Comfortably proportioned, the bedroom had a fireplace toward the center of the house and two windows looking down on Orange Street. There was a masculine air to everything about the room, in its brass wall sconces and narrow bookcases at either side of the fireplace. A deep-toned oriental carpet covered the wide pine floorboards. The etchings and paintings on the walls were of tall-masted ships and roaring seas. The furniture was fine and well polished but had a certain sturdiness to its construction. Even the graceful leather wing chair by the fireplace spoke of a man having enjoyed its comfort by the warm fire with a good book on a stormy night.

The curtains at the windows had been one of her grandmother's treasures, found in an old trunk in the attic in amazingly good condition. From their design, her grandmother had judged them to be of English origin, handmade and over a hundred years old. As Catherine went to one of the windows and opened it, the breeze caught at the old lace, billowing it.

A long day, and her muscles ached from all the cleaning she'd done. She pinned her silver blond hair atop her head, took an embroidered blue silk kimono from the closet, and started toward the bathroom. The kimono had been a gift from one of her wealthy clients on the West Coast in thanks for a job well done. All of that seemed so far away now.

California. As she lay back in her scented bubble bath, she pictured the architecture, the scenery, the blue Pacific beating up against the mountainous coastline; and the smells—orange and lemon blossoms, desert sage and eucalyptus. She missed it already. Yet there were wonderful things about Nantucket, too. She couldn't go into this venture with a negative attitude.

Nantucket was an island full of heritage. It had been settled by American Indians, who were living there comfortably in tribal groups when the first English settlers arrived in the late sixteen hundreds—refugees from religious persecution in the Massachusetts Bay Colony. The American Indians suffered from their exposure to Europeans; their last representative died in the late eighteen hundreds. The Europeans prospered, however, farming the land, building their first settlement at Capaum and later moving to Sherburne. Then, because the land was so poor, they looked to the sea for income, and the whaling industry in Nantucket had its start. The Indians had taught the settlers how to whale off the beaches and in small boats. Later, as the coastal whales grew scarce, the islanders went farther afield. By the eighteen hundreds their well-constructed whaling vessels were traveling north into the waters of Greenland and around the Horn into the Pacific. Nantucket became a whaling capital second only to New Bedford. She prospered. Her docks overflowed. Her natives grew rich. Sea captains and company owners built substantial houses on upper Main Street and on Orange Street. First mates built farther down the hill to the harbor, on Union Street.

In the heyday of Nantucket in the mid-1800s, whalers and merchantmen had been docked, thickly abreast, along the wharves, their masts standing out against the skyline. So many majestic masts; so many furled sails waiting for the tide, coming over the bar, docking, unloading barrels of whale oil and other cargo—textiles, china, fine wines from Europe, spices and hemp from India, tea and carpets from the Orient.

From the rear upstairs windows of the house Catherine could look over the banks of her garden to the harbor. It was a beautiful view: Nantucket Sound in the distance, then the scalloped indentations of Coatue, no more than a long sand bar stretching from the Great Point to the harbor and enfolding the long bay of Nantucket Town. Then the harbor itself, its wharves pointing northeast away from the cluster of town.

Climbing from the bath thirty minutes later, she pulled the kimono tight about her. It fit her petite frame. She glanced in the mirror beside the armoire and felt taller than five foot two. Actually, it wasn't until she saw a photograph of herself in a group that she ever realized, by comparison, how tiny she was.

Her blond hair still pinned atop her head, she went back to the bedroom, then on impulse opened the connecting door to her grandfather's study.

There'd been evenings when she and her grandfather had stood together gazing down at the twinkling lights of town. The scents of the sea would fill the air and mingle with the perfume of the garden roses. Catherine walked across to those rear windows. The sun had just set, leaving a pinkish orange glow on the western horizon to mark its departure. On the table in front of the windows lay her grandfather's old spyglass, its brass finish badly in need of polishing. Catherine lifted it to her eye and peered through. A mist was slipping in over the harbor, wisping its fingers along the wharves where the great whalers and merchantmen had once docked. Now their former moorings were occupied by expensive modern sailing and motor yachts—several million dollars' worth within the sweep of the eye. The yachts arrived every summer from Palm Beach, the Caribbean, Hilton Head, to travel in the cooler climes of New England, sailing into the favored meccas of Nantucket, Newport, Block Island, Marblehead, and the Penobscot in Maine. For a few days they'd dock, and the owners would socialize with the other yachtsmen and the wealthy in their summer homes on Nantucket, then sail on again to another favored port.

Catherine replaced the telescope on the table and flicked on the green-glass-shaded lamp beside it. She was tired, but edgy from the many cups of coffee she'd drunk that afternoon.

There was a decanter of brandy and several glasses on one of the side tables. Dusting off a glass with her sleeve, she poured a bit of the amber liquid, then went to one of the comfortable leather chairs facing the empty hearth of the fireplace and sat down. There'd always been something special about this room—she'd sensed it even as a child. What was that special quality? Through the open windows came the scent of the sea and the muffled sounds of modern Nantucket, but the room did not feel modern. It was comfortable, relaxing, yet its atmosphere was slightly disturbing, too, as though something was supposed to happen in it—as if it were connected to her in a way she didn't understand.

Sipping her brandy, Catherine again studied the bookcases crammed with volumes of sea lore, the model merchantman on the fireplace mantel, the scrimshaw displayed behind the leaded glass doors of the desk top. She listened to the steady tick of the banjo wall clock beside the desk, which she'd rewound and reset that afternoon.

Selecting a book on Nantucket history from the volumes on the shelves, she eased back into the chair facing the fireplace. For several minutes she read, but she was tired, and her thoughts kept wandering. Closing her eyes, she leaned her head against the chair back. What would happen in her days ahead on Nantucket? Had her father and mother been alive to inherit instead, there would have been no cause for her to have left the West Coast. They would have kept the Nantucket house, if only as a second, vacation home. Even now Catherine clearly remembered her feeling of total disbelief when she'd received that personal visit at her dorm from Sergeant Juarez of the Los Angeles Police Department, who'd told her, as compassionately as possible, of the tractor-trailer that had lost its brakes and rammed into the back of her parents' car, sending them over an embankment to instant death.

That was all behind now—long behind.

Gradually her tired body gave in to its need for rest. She snuggled her head against the wing of the chair back and dozed.

Sometime later the musical chiming of the clock jarred her to alertness. Rubbing her eyes, she glanced over to its painted face. Ten o'clock. She'd been asleep for nearly three hours. Rising stiffly, she turned off the lamp and went through into her bedroom. The street lamp in front of the house cast enough light into the bedroom that she could see her way across to the old postered double bed. She turned down the covers, but before climbing in, she went to one of the windows and looked out.

The once cobbled street was now paved in asphalt, though the sidewalks were still the original brick. A car whizzed by, its radio vibrating with the blare of rock music turned to a deafening volume, so incongruous on the otherwise dignified length of Orange Street.

She reminisced over the nights when she'd stood before these same windows as a child, watching the street scene through the branches of the old elm outside. Tonight a group of laughing, chatting pedestrians passed on the sidewalk below. Another car slipped past. Her ear was attuned to the sound of downtown Nantucket only a few blocks away—the occasional horn, the waft of music from a night spot, the low hum of voices, the clopping of hoofbeats. Her ear grew more alert.

Hoofbeats? As she listened, they came up Orange Street.

She looked down the street. The streetlights no longer seemed so bright. They seemed mellower... like moonlight. The clopping, ringing noise of iron-shod hooves on cobbles was unmistakable. It wasn't her imagination. A horse was approaching. She could see it was a dark bay, trim, long-legged, and harnessed to a small closed carriage. Two brass lanterns fastened to its front glowed against its shining black paint and reflected the silhouette of the hatted driver on the raised front seat.

It seemed a bit more elegant than the standard tourist equipage. The carriage was a valuable antique in itself. The horse snorted, shook its shining, sleek head. The carriage began to slow, drawing close to the curb directly beneath her window.

The driver called out commandingly. The horse clattered its hooves on the cobbles, obviously unhappy to break away from its fast, measured trot, and gave out a few snorts as it came to a halt.

The carriage door cracked open and then swung wide. A long leg emerged from the darkness of the interior of the carriage. The leg was followed by an arm holding a decorative walking stick, then by the frame of a man attired in dark formal evening dress with top hat.

The man stood on the narrow sidewalk beside the carriage. He appeared tall, though it was difficult to tell accurately from her vantage point overhead. He wore white gloves; the same whiteness was reflected in the high collar about his neck. His head was averted as he closed the carriage door, but a moment later he turned, and as he looked up to the driver, the carriage lamp accentuated the planes of a strong-boned face above a full, groomed beard. White teeth flashed against tanned skin as he smiled.

"Well, Pierce, another dull evening. Perhaps I should have saved you the trip and walked home." He laughed. "See that Sarter has a good feed will you? He has been all about the island today."

"Aye, Captain. That I will, and good night to ye."

"What is left of it."

The driver lightly slapped the reins over the horse's back and moved forward, turning sharply into the drive at the side of the house.

For a moment the man in evening dress stood thoughtfully on the sidewalk, then, tucking his cane under his arm, he walked toward Catherine's front door. He went quickly up the two steps, lifted the brass knocker on the door, and rapped sharply. The sound echoed through the house, up to the bedroom window where Catherine stood staring.

She started across the room then stopped in her tracks as she heard the metallic grate of the bolt on the front door being thrown open from inside. The sound of the man's deep, British-accented voice was clear in Catherine's ears as it drifted up the stairwell from her front vestibule and into the bedroom.

"Good evening, Gladstone."

"Cap'n." The answering voice was equally as clear. "Let me take your hat. You had a pleasant evening?"

"Bearable. As I said to Pierce, I should have walked home to relieve my boredom. The business did not go as I expected, and the reception after was tedious. It seemed every match-making matron on the island was pushing an eligible daughter in my direction. Far better that I should have dealt with Quartermain over a desk in his office." There was a rattling sound as he dropped his cane into the stand beside the front door. "I don't mean to keep you up, Gladstone, but I have an intolerable headache. Perhaps one of your bromides?"

"I will prepare one for you, sir."

Catherine's hands had grown ice cold. Why was this man in her house? Who was he speaking to in the downstairs hall?

"Excellent," the deep voice continued.

"Shall I bring it up to your study?"

"No, here in the drawing room. I shall play a bit while I wait, then retire."

One set of footsteps retreated down the hall toward the kitchen; the other set seemed to move across the hall into the living room. In a moment Catherine heard the old grand piano in the corner by the front windows come to life. Mozart—one of his later works, and beautifully played.

For several moments Catherine stood frozen in shock, then she rushed out into the upstairs hall. The lovely piano music continued, lilting through the house. As she looked over the banister, down to the entry hall, she saw a dim light, as if from a candle or oil lamp, escaping from the open doorway of the living room. Nearly tripping over the hem of her kimono, she started down the stairs, clinging to the polished railing with both hands.

She was halfway down when suddenly all was quiet; deathly quiet. The hallway went dark, as did the living room beyond. The only illumination was that lent by the street lights outside the front windows. She rushed to the hall light switch. The ceiling fixture glowed, erasing the shadows from the corners. There was no one in the hall, and no signs or sounds of life coming from any other part of the house. She swung toward the front door. The bolt was firmly in place; the umbrella stand and hat rack beside the door were empty.

Despite the warm night, she was shaking. Cautiously she moved toward the living room, reached inside the doorway for the light switch. Two lamps glowed on, sending out sufficient brightness to show her that there was no one lurking in the room. The grand piano stood deserted, its keyboard covered by its folding wooden protector. Sliding farther into the room with her back against the wall, she picked up a brass poker from the nearby fireplace hearth, gripped it tightly in one hand, and slowly walked ahead, around the pieces of furniture grouped in front of the fireplace. Stealthily she stepped around each chair, then the couch. No crouching figures; no evidence of anyone hiding. Everything in the room was as she'd left it several hours before—freshly cleaned, each knickknack in place.

Poker still firmly in hand, she left the living room, switched on the lights in the hallway to the kitchen, and nervously followed the hall to the back of the house. She passed the door to the cellar. She hadn't the courage to explore there, but in any case, the door was bolted firmly shut from the hall. She put on the bright overhead kitchen light. The large room was empty, save for its original fixtures.

Turning on lights, until the whole house was blazing, she progressed through the dining room, into the front sitting room.

Was she losing her mind? She'd seen the man enter her house; had heard the voices and the sound of the piano distinctly. The horse and carriage pulling up before her door had been real—not a figment of her imagination.

The horse and carriage! She ran through to the back door of the kitchen and turned on the outside spot light. The small back garden was clearly outlined. The barn doors were closed; her Porsche was parked in front of them on the gravel drive.

For the moment forgetting her initial fright, she grabbed the flashlight from the kitchen windowsill and strode out the back door to the barn. The old wood creaked and grated across the gravel as she pulled the barn door outward. The beam of the flashlight penetrated into the darkness, glanced off the wood-beamed walls and the objects that were stored inside—the lawnmower, boxes of old newspapers, two pieces of broken lawn furniture. There was nothing remotely resembling a horse-drawn carriage; nor was there any sign of a horse in the old stall at the side of the barn, which was now cluttered with gardening tools. Even the stairway leading up to the long disused servants' quarters above was blocked by cartons that obviously hadn't been touched in months.

Frustrated, Catherine closed the barn doors and returned to the house, carefully double-locking the kitchen door behind her. Once again she went through every downstairs room, pausing beside the grand piano to stare down at the covered keyboard and the bench pushed well beneath. How could anyone have been playing the instrument only minutes before? Absently she reached down to slide the wood covering away from the keyboard. The cover wouldn't budge. It was locked. Of course—her grandmother had always locked the piano for some reason, hiding the key in the lift-seat bench.

With a chill racing down her spine, she nearly ran from the room, up the staircase. She checked every corner of her bedroom, then locked both bedroom doors. Yet, her bolted front door had proved no barrier to whoever had entered her house. Her heart pounding, she slid a side chair in front of each door. In the morning she would probably feel foolish. That night her fear was altogether too real.

Unable to consider sleep, she went to the front window again. A few cars were now parked under the elm tree along the curb. The street light cast a reassuring glow over them and the asphalt pavement of the street. The scene was so familiar and reassuringly mundane, but Catherine was far from comfortable. With frightening clarity she was recalling that when the carriage had pulled up at her door, the street had been cobbled, and there'd been no tree growing through the brick sidewalk in front of the house.

Chapter 2

Sheer exhaustion finally closed Catherine's eyes. She dozed off in the wing chair beside the fireplace, fire poker across her lap, an hour before dawn. She woke to bright sunlight, her neck and shoulders stiff. Rubbing her eyes, she felt the grittiness from lack of sleep, yet her mind was alert, recalling too swiftly and clearly the happenings of the evening before. In the morning light the facts she was recalling qseemed unreal, impossible. There had to be a logical explanation. She'd been exhausted the night before; her mind saturated with new experiences; and people *did* have dreams that seemed so real that upon waking, the dreamer was left in confusion.

Standing in the shower, letting the hot droplets beat against her skin, she told herself over and over it had been a dream—no more. By eight-thirty she was out of the house, striding down the brick sidewalk of Orange Street toward town. At least the sight of other people going about their daily rituals on Nantucket's downtown streets helped to ease her disquiet.

When she reached the corner of Orange Street, she crossed the cobbled width of Main Street and walked a short distance down to Arno's for breakfast. The restaurant, which had managed to avoid touristy pretentions, was already crowded with locals getting their morning meal and trading tidbits of island news. She took a seat on one of the stools at the counter, smiled to the young waitress and ordered coffee and an English muffin. Absently she listened to the hum of conversation around her, but her thoughts were elsewhere. What was she to do? Forget the whole incident? Could her visitors have been more ghostly than alive? She shook her head forcibly. Nonsense. She didn't believe in ghosts—at least she believed in nothing for which there was no tangible proof, and she, for one, had never seen a ghost; nor did she know anyone else who'd encountered one. Then, what *had* she seen? It must have been a dream—it *had* to have been!

As soon as possible she was going to search for the old deeds and at least get some clue to the previous owners of the house. The only occupant she remembered hearing about was the old recluse, Obadiah Jordon. Her grandparents had told her what a state the house had been in when they'd bought it from him. He'd been a hermit of sorts and a pack rat, too, and in his last years had rarely left the house. He'd certainly made no effort to clean it, and the Sternwoods practically had to shovel the debris out after him.

A copy of the local *Inquirer and Mirror* was lying on the counter. A previous reader had folded back several pages, leaving the paper open to the classifieds. Catherine's eyes skimmed distractedly down one of the columns, then stopped. "Wanted: Good home for year-old golden retriever. Gentle, friendly, good watchdog. Moving and must leave Barney behind. Call 228–9997." She didn't have to think twice. Jotting down the number, she finished her breakfast and went to the pay phone at the back of the restaurant. A friendly female voice answered and within a few minutes, Catherine had gotten directions and made an appointment to see the dog at eleven o'clock.

Feeling strangely reassured, she left Arno's and set off down the elm-shaded sidewalk. She wasn't ready to go back to the house yet, and as long as she was in town, there were errands she could run. She opened an account at the Pacific National Bank and visited her grandparents' lawyers to sign some papers for the estate settlement. By the time Catherine again climbed the gradual slope of Orange Street, past the old Unitarian church with its square, wood-framed clock tower, the intruder in her house seemed more and more a dream. She'd been doing too much in the past few days. Her overworked mind had rebelled.

Catherine went straight to her car and climbed in behind the wheel. Quickly checking the paper with the directions she'd scribbled, she started the Porsche's engine and let it warm up. The low-slung car had been one of her first indulgences when Classics had started booming. Carefully she backed out of the narrow drive and headed up the street, away from the center of town. The address she was seeking was in one of the newer developments halfway across the island. She found the gray-shingled cape set among a stand of stunted island pines without any trouble.

Forty-five minutes later Catherine left the little house with a large, golden-haired, happily panting passenger in the seat beside her. She and the dog had been friends at first sight, and there'd been no doubt in his previous owners' minds that they'd found the right new mistress for Barney. Even as she swung the car out onto the main road, Barney leaned over and swabbed her arm from elbow to wrist with his pink tongue.

"Hey, not while I'm driving!" Catherine reached over and rubbed his shaggy head. "We're going to be good friends, aren't we?"

Catherine made a quick stop at the supermarket and stocked up for both of them. When she got to the house on Orange Street, she clipped a new leash to Barney's collar before letting him out of the car. He was wiggling in excitement over his new surroundings, practically dragging Catherine across the back yard as he stuck his nose to the ground and began to explore. She let him satisfy his curiosity before pulling him to the back porch stairs and tying his leash to the railing. She then collected her purse and her groceries from the car and unlocked the back door—a task made difficult by the fact that Barney wound his leash about her legs in an effort to get through the door before her.

"No, stay!" she commanded him, stepping out of the way of the leash and nearly overturning the bag of groceries. She squeezed through the door in front of him and paused in the entrance to the kitchen. Despite the sunlight streaming through the windows, she was struck almost immediately by a feeling of uneasiness at being back in the house. It was ridiculous. She hadn't been uncomfortable the day before when she'd been cleaning and straightening. Only since last night . . .

She deposited her package on the kitchen table and went back for Barney, who'd already begun to whine. Once she'd untied him, he bounded into the kitchen, nose to the ground once more. He glanced over his shoulder to where she stood unloading the bag of groceries, then set off through the other rooms of the house. She could hear the clicking of his nails on the wood floors, the thumps of his feet as he climbed the stairs. A few minutes later the thumps resumed as he came back down, and with tail wagging and tongue hanging, made his appearance in the kitchen, obviously satisfied with his new quarters.

Unconsciously Catherine sighed in relief. Animals were supposed to be sensitive to strange presences, and Barney was behaving as if all were perfectly normal. She filled a dish of water for him and set it on the floor. After slurping, Barney circled the kitchen, then laid down with a sigh beside the table, from which position he could watch everything Catherine was doing.

In the ensuing days, as the island greenery blossomed in the late April sunshine, Catherine added personal touches to the house. She hung a few cherished paintings she'd brought from California; she arranged vases of fresh flowers and placed potted ferns and hanging ivy in the kitchen and sunny windows of the house. She put out her favorite scented soap in the bath, spread magazines neatly on the coffee table. She'd fully stocked the kitchen, and had climbed up to the widow's walk on the roof and been exhilarated by the view.

Yet, for the third night in a row Catherine woke suddenly from her sleep and sat upright in bed. The dream had been the same as other nights. Her skin felt clammy as she stared about the bedroom feeling she wasn't alone. Her mind was still filled with her dream— of images of the sea and old square-rigged sailing boats; of a man standing on deck who looked so like the apparition she'd seen entering her front door. In her dream she'd seen him standing beside her bed, looking down at her as she slept. It had seemed so real! Yet as she gazed around in panic, she saw no one. She heard Barney snoring peacefully on the rug, and in the dim light of her bedside lamp, the room looked exactly as it should. Still she shivered as she slid down under the covers and tried to fall back to sleep. There was a lingering scent in the room—spicy, masculine—like a man's after-shave. She willed it to be her imagination or an odor breezing in through the partially opened windows. But it was three o'clock in the morning. Pulling the covers entirely over her head, she squeezed her eyes shut.

She didn't rise until close to ten. She showered and dressed feeling a strange oppression, a heaviness to her mood that had grown more noticeable with each day she spent in the house. The sleepless nights were dragging her down. She felt listless, sapped. These dreams—so strange, repeating themselves since the first night she'd been in the house—what did they mean?

She filled the kettle at the kitchen sink and was walking toward the stove when the screen door banged open behind her. In her half-awake state, she presumed it was Marjorie.

Her eyes widened when she turned and saw who was standing in the doorway.

"Treasa!"

Her sister strode in, a wide grin on her face, as relaxed and unconcerned as if she'd seen Catherine the day before. "Hey, Sis! How're you doing? Did I surprise you?" Treasa dropped a zippered canvas carry bag on the table. The bag was inscribed with scrolled blue letters, *Cherise*, no doubt the name of the yacht her sister was currently crewing on.

"Surprised isn't the word. What are you doing on the island? Last you wrote, you were in France."

Catherine went forward to give Treasa a welcoming kiss on the cheek. Treasa frowned down at Barney and pushed his friendly snout away before hoisting another canvas bag off her shoulder and onto the table. "We were heading north after Antigua race week and stopping in Nantucket for a couple of days. I didn't know if you'd be here or out on the Coast, but I thought I'd check it out." She glanced around the kitchen, then to her sister. Her smiling face narrowed, particularly her large brown eyes. "So you inherited it all? I'll tell you I was burned when I got those legal papers. I could have gotten off boats if they'd split it down the middle."

All Catherine's hopes that Treasa had changed vanished with those words. "You got a trust fund."

"That little bit?" Treasa scoffed. "I went through the year's income in a couple of months."

"But you get free room and board on the boat, plus your salary. What are you spending it on?"

Treasa shrugged her shoulders, not the least perturbed. "Good times."

"You're crazy."

Treasa shrugged again. "It's *my* life." Her large, doe-like eyes studied her older sister. Her lips twitched in a smile that was at the same time both cynically tired and innocently childlike and lost. "Why didn't you write and tell me you were moving out from the Coast? I only took a chance walking up here."

"Your letters haven't exactly been frequent either—and I did write, to the last address you gave me. I've only come out here for a year, to try it out."

"What about your business in Santa Barbara?"

"Marcie's keeping an eye on it."

Treasa, her arms unburdened, pushed her long blond hair from her face. Catherine was only a year and a half older than her sister, and there was a remarkable resemblance between them. Catherine's hair was shorter, only shoulder length, while Treasa's hung past her shoulder blades like a white gold mane. It suited her, and Treasa knew what looked good on her—more particularly, what appealed to men. The sisters' eyes, features and builds were what made them look so similar. Catherine's profile was a bit more classic. Treasa was a bit taller, but they'd been mistaken for each other many times.

Catherine cast a look over the bags her sister had dropped, trying to unravel her surprised and confused thoughts. It wasn't unusual for Treasa to drop in on a whim without warning. What was surprising was that she'd sought Catherine out in the Nantucket home. Or was it, considering Catherine had just inherited the house that Treasa felt entitled to half of? Caution was in order. "You came prepared, if you didn't know I'd be here."

Treasa laughed. "Is this the best kind of greeting you can give me after not seeing me for nearly a year?" Impulsively she threw her arms around Catherine.

Catherine returned the hug. She did love her sister, despite Treasa's instability. "I'm just surprised. It's good to see you."

"That's better." Light-hearted again, Treasa turned toward her bags. "Where should I put these? The front room, or are you using that?"

"I thought you lived on the boat?"

"Oh, God, Cath, you don't know what it's like. I'm so glad to get off of that boat for a while. All I do is break my butt all day on charters, and Tom—the captain—is getting to be a pain. I only went on the boat because of him. Now he tells me I'm getting too laid back, not working hard enough. After waiting on people and serving drinks and dinner and wiping up their slops when they get sick, taking a watch when the boat's short crewed, I've had it! We'll pick up another bunch of charterers in Newport and from there go up to Maine, where the owners are getting on for a month. 'Yes, sir, this . . . yes, ma'am, that.' Yuk!"

"You used to like it."

"Things change."

"Don't you have work to do even if you're docked?"

"Tom doesn't know I'm gone. He went ashore to run some errands. Besides, seeing you is more important than his crumby job and his attitude. He can stuff them both. All last year it was just me and him; that was before he hired on a cute little New Zealand cook in Antigua. Althea—bitch! I hate her!"

"Sounds like a few stories I've heard from you before." Catherine couldn't help the twinge of sarcasm in her voice.

Treasa shrugged. Treasa was, and always had been, out for herself alone, but her soft, pleading smile and the weak, victimized "everyone's-always-been-against me" expression in her eyes inevitably touched a forgiving chord in Catherine. As far as Treasa was concerned, it had always been someone else's fault. Treasa gave her sister a bewitching smile. "Why are we talking like this? We should be having a reunion."

When Catherine didn't immediately respond, Treasa's tone grew pleading. "Come on, Cath. It's not my fault I can't get my act together like you can. I love you. Don't be so hard on me."

"Oh, Trea, I'm not being hard. It just seems that the only time you think of me is when you want something."

"You've always misunderstood me. All I've ever asked for is your help. How do you think I feel when you act as if you don't even want to see me?"

"I *do* want to see you. In fact, I wish I saw you more often, but let's have our reunion tonight. Get back to the boat before your captain finds out, and you lose your job."

"I don't care if he finds out," Treasa pouted. "I'm getting off the damn boat anyway. Serve him right."

"Getting off here?"

"Sure, why not? As long as you're here—"

"What are you planning to do? This is an island, remember, dependent on the tourist business."

"I'll find a job or wait for another boat. Meanwhile, I'll live here, of course."

Slowly Catherine shook her head. "You can't live here."

"What do you mean? We're family. You got this GD big house for nothing. What kind of sister are you?"

"Are you willing to split the expenses with me if you live here?"

"Split them? Why should I? It's *your* house."

"So you'd end up mooching a free ride off me until you got it in your head to take off again. Don't forget, Trea, I know you real well from past experience."

Treasa's eyes flashed as the thrust hit home, then suddenly she sighed helplessly. "Yeah, you're right. I've been a pain, haven't I? Look, we're only going to be here three days. We don't have any charterers, so they don't need me at night. Can't I at least stay here two nights?"

Treasa was gazing at her like a lost puppy.

"Well, sure, you're welcome to stay a few nights. You should know that—as long as you don't jeopardize your job."

"No problem."

Treasa took her sister's hand. "I guess I can put up with Tom's shit a little longer, 'til we get to Newport or something."

"I'll give you a ride back down to the boat. You can leave your gear here for now. I'll put it away. You can use Grandma and Grandpop's old bedroom."

"You want me to go back now? Come on, Cath. I just got here."

"Trea, you've got a job. And I'll see you at dinner."

Treasa threw up her hands. "All right."

Catherine grabbed her purse off the counter. "Come on."

Reluctantly Treasa followed with a pout on her pretty lips, but her pout disappeared and her eyes narrowed slyly as she walked around Catherine's gray Porsche and got in the passenger seat. "You must be doing *real* well, sis, to have wheels like these—brand new, too."

"It was my first luxury in six years."

"Some of us really have it made."

"If you'd saved the money you made on boats, you'd have something, too."

"Cut the moralizing," Treasa said tiredly. "I've heard it before."

They traveled the short distance through town to the wharves in silence.

"Come on," Treasa said, as Catherine parked the car. "Walk down and I'll show you the boat."

Catherine agreed, surprised at Treasa's unexpected change of mood.

They headed down the Straight Wharf. *Cherise* was docked way at the end. By the time they reached the boat, Catherine estimated they'd walked by several million dollars' worth of sleek watercraft —and it wasn't even high season yet.

"Here she is." Treasa paused beside a gleaming, sixty-five-foot single-master. "Not bad, eh?"

Catherine's knowledge of boats was negligible, but she nodded appreciatively.

"She's a Swan 65-1-S," Treasa explained. "Come on below. Take off your shoes first." Treasa stepped across the short ramp to the deck and Catherine followed. There were more lines and pulleys than Catherine could keep track of, but the deck itself was sleek and devoid of unnecessary decoration. Below decks the wood-paneled interior glowed softly under many painstakingly applied coats of varnish. Everything was absolutely immaculate. Treasa showed Catherine through the galley, the salon, aft to the owners' cabin, then forward to the crew's quarters.

As they strode up the companionway, Treasa stopped in midstride as a pretty, curly-haired brunette popped her head around the door of one of the forward cabins.

"Oh, Althea." The coolness was clear in Treasa's tone. "Meet my sister, Catherine. Catherine, Althea. I'm giving Cath a tour of the boat. She lives here on the island in my grandparents' old place."

"How nice to meet you," Althea smiled, her voice musical with a British intonation. "I was just straightening up a bit, but come on through if you like."

"Where's Tom?" Treasa asked curtly.

"Still in town, I think."

"And Mickey?"

"He was on deck, last I saw."

"He must have gone off down the wharf. Anyway," Treasa continued, "these are the crew's quarters, such as they are." She motioned to a narrow-bunked cabin and a compact head as she led Catherine forward. She then pushed open the door to the fo'c'sle. There were four up-and-down bunks fitted into the triangular area of the bow.

"There's no privacy at all," Catherine exclaimed.

Her sister and Althea both laughed. "We manage, and when there aren't any charterers on board, we spread out over the rest of the boat." The tour finished, Treasa turned back to the galley area.

"Have you lived on the island long?" Althea asked Catherine with interest. "How do you like it? Isn't it isolating?"

"It could be, I guess, in winter, but I haven't been here long enough to know." She felt comfortable with the other girl's easy friendliness and continued. "I only moved here two weeks ago, although when we were kids we used to spend a lot of time on the island. Treasa said you're from New Zealand. How did you get on boats?"

"It was about the only way I could get away from New Zealand. I *did* find life there isolating."

"You're making yachting your career?"

"No. I'm seeing the world, and it will do for now. My dream is to get into the States, but it's almost impossible to get working papers."

"But there're hundreds of itinerants crossing our borders every day."

"Illegally, I would imagine."

"They manage to stay here somehow."

Althea only lifted her brows. "I could stay illegally, of course, once my visa expired, but what good would that do if I wasn't able to earn a living?"

"Oh, come on," Treasa interrupted brusquely. "I get so sick of hearing this Green Card talk. It seems like all that foreign yachties talk about when they get together is new angles for getting into the States, getting working papers! What's wrong with boats?"

"You've talked of quitting," Catherine reminded her sister.

"For different reasons," Treasa frowned, glaring at Althea's back.

"Well, I better get going—"

A male voice shouted from above. "Treasa, Althea, give me a hand."

The girls turned.

"Tom," Althea said quickly, hurrying toward the salon.

"Look at her, will you?" Treasa muttered. "Kissing ass again."

"Oh, cut it out, Treasa. She works here. She's just doing her job."

"Bull."

Catherine headed down the passage, entering the main salon as a lean but muscular, sandy-haired man came down the stairs from deck. He handed the waiting Althea a large, square package and was still holding another in one arm, when he glanced across and saw Catherine.

His eyes widened for an instant. "You cut—wait a minute. You're not Treasa."

Catherine tried to smile, feeling a little uncomfortable. "No, I'm her sister, Catherine."

"Catherine, eh? Tom Wilson." He continued the rest of the way down the steps, dropped his package on his navigation desk, and extended his hand. "Nice to meet you. What brings you on board?"

"I'm living here in Nantucket. Treasa asked me down to show me the boat."

"Oh, yeah?" He looked past Catherine to Treasa as she came into the salon. "Hey, Treasa, I didn't know your sister lived here. I thought she lived out on the West Coast."

"She did until a couple of weeks ago. She moved into my grand-parents' place."

"That's right. I remember you talking about it." He studied Treasa as if the incident he was remembering hadn't been altogether pleasant. He looked back to Catherine. "Well, how do you like her—the boat?"

"Great, though I don't know much about sailboats—any kind of boat, for that matter."

"Too bad we're not going to be in port longer. I'd take you out for a sail. We're leaving for Newport in a couple of days, picking up an early charter."

"So Treasa said." Catherine tried to make a quick assessment of Tom. He wasn't what she'd pictured from her sister's cryptic comments. She'd expected more of a playboy. He seemed professional in his manner, but one never knew.

"Speaking of which," he looked to Althea, "did Mickey get back with the parts for the radar?"

"I haven't seen him."

"If you girls have finished the inventory of the galley, I need one of you to run up to town with an order. You know we won't have time to stock up in Newport."

"I just finished up," Althea answered.

Tom flashed her a warm smile.

Treasa's expression was black.

Catherine felt distinctly that she was interrupting the business of the boat and spoke quickly. "I'd better get going. I was just on my way out."

"Don't run off." Tom's voice sounded distracted—merely polite. "If Treasa's finished cleaning up the aft cabins—"

"I haven't."

He swung around toward Treasa. "You've had three hours."

"Gimme a break." Her tone was curt, almost rude. "I've had other things to do, and I haven't seen my sister in months."

He frowned, gave Treasa a hard look.

Catherine rushed into the break. "Really, thanks anyway, but I've got an appointment, and you've got work to do here."

Tom nodded, his gaze still riveted on Treasa, whose eyes were smoldering.

Quickly Catherine started toward the stairs, smiling to Althea and Tom. "Nice meeting you both. Thanks for letting me see the boat."

"Good meeting you, too, Catherine," Althea answered with a smile, though her attention, too, was concentrated on Treasa and Tom. "Hope to see you again before we sail."

Tom merely gave a wave.

Chapter 3

Back at the house, Catherine placed several follow-up calls to realtors she'd talked to about a storefront for her business. Unfortunately, no one was available to take her out until the following afternoon. She felt disturbed and restless. She couldn't get her dreams of the last few nights totally out of her mind. They weren't the kind that were quickly forgotten upon rising.

And now Treasa. Her arrival usually meant trouble. It wasn't as if she didn't deeply care about Treasa. She loved her to the point that it caused her gut-wrenching agony to watch her sister head further and further down a self-destructive path. And it seemed there was nothing Catherine could do but watch. No outpouring of love and support seemed to help; talking to Treasa and encouraging her to make use of her potential didn't help; condemning her life-style didn't help. Each time Treasa got scared and promised reform, Catherine's hopes rose. And each time those hopes had been smashed on the rocks when Treasa quickly slid back into her old habits, or worse. Catherine quite frankly didn't know what to do, yet she felt responsible for her sister. Had *she* done something to twist Treasa's nature in the years since their parents' deaths?

Unable to shake off her restlessness, Catherine decided to go up and look through the attic. It was the only place she hadn't touched in her cleaning. Not that it was a job she relished, but at least it would keep her mind occupied. In the process she might come across the old deeds to the house, which she hadn't found among any of her grandparents' belongings.

Dressed in old clothes, with a scarf tying back her pale blond hair, she started up the narrow stairs to the attic. Tongue lolling and tail wagging, Barney scrambled up behind her. As Catherine looked around, the dog immediately headed off in exploration, his big paws leaving prints on the dusty floor. The peaked roof was high enough so that Catherine could easily stand in the center. Behind her was another narrower staircase leading up the widow's walk. In front of her was a profusion of stacked boxes, old magazines, pieces of broken furniture, cordless lamps, empty picture frames, and cartons of old clothing. From the extent of dust and cobwebs, it was obvious her grandparents hadn't come up here in recent years. Sighing, she started toward the collection of odd pieces of furniture. Perhaps she could salvage something for use and sale in her shop.

She ran her hand over an old ladder-back chair, turned it over to examine the base and rungs. Except for needing a new rush seat, it was intact and solid. She set it aside to take downstairs. After examining a few other broken chairs, she spied some odd Victorian pieces behind. They wouldn't have appealed to her grandparents' taste, but she could certainly use them in her decorating assignments. There was a decent mirrored hall hat rack, several globed gas lamps with crystal pendants, a small, velvet-tufted upholstered footstool, a heavily carved walnut side table, and a matching pair of bronze statuettes. One by one, she pulled the items out. With a little cleaning and polishing, they wouldn't be half bad.

She was reaching in to dislodge a gilded picture frame when there was a sudden crash behind her. Barney let out a yelp. Catherine jumped up and spun around just as Barney leaped out of the way of a falling metal floor lamp. The frightened dog lunged sideways, hurtling all of his seventy-five pounds of weight against a precariously balanced pile of bundled magazines.

Catherine ran forward, but was too late. The five-foot-high stack teetered, then tumbled forward into the center of the attic floor, raising a huge and choking cloud of dust and sending Catherine into a fit of sneezing. Terrified, the dog darted toward his mistress and quivered against her legs as Catherine blindly patted his head and tried to reassure him in between her sneezes.

"Just some old magazines . . . okay, Barney . . . relax."

When the dust finally cleared, and the dog had quieted, she leaned over to push the bundles out of the center of the floor. "Why did Grandma ever save all these magazines?" she muttered to herself as she shoved at the old paper. Then she noticed dates on some of them. All were from the 1920s. Perhaps it wasn't so bad after all. Collectors had begun coveting the old magazine ads, particularly of

automobiles, and the color covers made nice prints, once framed.
She quickly glanced over the other bundles that had been at the base
of the fallen stack. These were even older, going back to the turn of
the century. She was about to settle herself cross-legged on the floor
to examine them more closely when she noticed a board and batten
door in the wall that had been hidden by the stack of magazines.
Strange. Why would her grandparents have piled so many magazines
in front of what was obviously a door to a storage closet?

Curiosity getting the better of her, she cleared a path to the doorway and turned the primitive wooden latch. As she pulled the door
outward, the bare bulb hanging from the attic ceiling illuminated a
rectangular enclosure with a sloping roof that dipped toward the
eaves. A coating of dust much thicker than in the rest of the attic
covered the floorboards. Bending double, she stepped inside. The
closet was empty except for what looked like an old trunk pushed
against the far wall and a blanket-wrapped object about the size and
shape of a picture frame or mirror leaning against the wall beside it.

Careful not to bang her head on the low beams, she went first to
the flat-topped trunk. She had to rub off a thick layer of grime before
she was able to determine that the trunk was actually constructed of a
fine-grained wood, perhaps cherry or mahogany. It was beautifully
crafted, too, with raised, beveled trim extending all around. From
her knowledge of antiques, she judged it not to be a trunk at all, but a
portable chest—perhaps a seaman's chest, and a high-ranking seaman's at that. She reached for the latch that, though green with tar-
nish, was obviously solid brass and of an early date. Thankfully the
chest wasn't locked, and as she began lifting the lid, she saw a brass
plaque screwed to the front just above the latch. She ran her fingers
over it to wipe away the film of grit. Despite its tarnished condition,
she could easily decipher three engraved initials: L.A.B.

She frowned. The initials meant nothing to her. They certainly
weren't those of anyone in her family. Her grandmother's maiden
name had been Clark. Lifting the lid the rest of the way, she peered
inside to see a sliding, compartmented wooden tray that had been
used for small personal and toilet articles. She pushed the tray to the
side, and sighed in disappointment to see that the main compartment
of the chest was empty. Still, it was a beautiful piece and a real find,
and she could imagine how it would look once it was cleaned and
polished.

Yet she was puzzled. Why would her grandparents have left a
valuable piece of furniture like this in a storage closet? It was just the

sort of thing that would have appealed to them. She wondered again
about the stacks of magazines in front of the door. The dates on the
magazines were all prior to the time her grandparents had lived in the
house. Was it possible they hadn't known about the storage closet?
Or had they left the magazines there for some reason?

Reaching around the end of the chest, she sought for a handle.
Her feeling that it had been a seaman's chest was confirmed when her
fingers touched the carved wooden bracket and tightly woven rope
becket, two distinguishing features of old sea chests. Gripping the
becket, she dragged the chest out onto the main attic floor. As she
studied it in the brighter light, she saw that all the joints were dove-
tailed, and that only six wide boards had been used in the chest's
construction—a sure sign of age. Though the outside of the wood
was too finely finished to detect any plane marks, the inside of the
boards felt hand planed. The chest would be a rare prize when polished up.

She then ducked back into the closet for the remaining object.

Barney whined from outside the doorway.

"I'll be out in a second, Barney." He subsided, and she heard the
click of his toe nails as he paced the floor.

Kneeling before the object, she studied it more carefully. It was
about three feet high and two feet wide. The blanket covering had
been carefully tied in place with thick twine, which, despite its obvious age, was still sturdy. She'd need scissors to cut it away. Praying
she wouldn't disturb a mouse nest in the process, she lifted the bundle and, crouching, carried it out of the closet. It wasn't terribly
heavy, which made her think that it was, indeed, a painting or framed
print.

Edging down the narrow attic staircase with Barney at her heels,
she carried the bundle across the second floor hall and into her grandfather's study. She leaned it against a chair, then went to the desk for
a pair of scissors. Her hands and shirt front were covered by a brown
grit, but she barely noticed as she clipped away at the old twine,
pulling the cut pieces away. Barney was right there beside her, his
wet nose edging under her hand.

"How can I get this open with you hanging all over me? Sit!"

The dog obeyed.

Finally she began unfolding the dusty blanket. Only when it lay in
a heap on the carpet did she stand back to get a view of what was
beneath. She'd been right: it was a painting—a portrait of a man,
and an extremely well-executed one, too, in a burnished wood frame.

But as she examined the subject more closely, a finger of ice ran
down her spine. The face was frighteningly familiar. The features
and bone structure above the clipped, dark beard were strong. The
firm mouth was turned in a half smile; the eyes, blue and dark-
lashed, were gazing off into the distance and bore tiny crinkles at
their corners caused by laughter or squinting into the sun. Soft waves
of dark hair framed the tanned face. The man appeared to be in his
thirties. He wore a white, high-collared shirt under a dark, broad-
lapeled jacket with a loose white tie at his neck. All that was missing
was the top hat.

It couldn't be the same man. Rapidly she walked to the open
windows of the study and took several deep breaths. It had been
dark. She'd seen his features only by the light of the moon and the
carriage lamp. It was only a coincidence that she saw any resemblance at all. She'd succeeded to some degree in the last days in
putting the whole incident into a far corner of her thoughts. She
didn't want to be reminded of it now.

Gradually she relaxed, convinced that she was being ridiculous.
The portrait was of some unknown man, and it had no more connection to her than any old portrait she might come across while antiquing. That was all there was to it.

Swallowing, she turned and slowly walked back to view the portrait again—this time with complete objectivity. The artist had been
good. He'd breathed life into his subject; the man's features seemed
alive and of flesh, not paint. She stepped closer and bent down to
look for a signature. There was a barely distinguishable scrawl in the
lower right hand corner. "Remley" or "Fenley." It wasn't quite clear.
She could check the registry books to see if an artist was listed under
either name. There were no other identifying marks on the portrait;
no name plate on the frame, the rear of which was protected by an
old but fully intact heavy brown paper backing. Catherine wondered
a bit about that. The backs of oils were generally left uncovered, but
perhaps a previous owner had been overfastidious about dust.

Because of its blanket wrapping, the painting itself was relatively
dust free. Catherine lifted it and looked around for a safe, temporary
storage place until she could decide what to do with the portrait. As
she glanced about the room, her eyes were drawn to the empty paneled area above the fireplace mantel. Oddly enough, there was even
an old hook nailed into the wood in precisely the right spot. Perhaps
her grandfather had once had something hanging there. Following an
impulse she didn't fully understand, she pulled a chair over to the

fireplace, stood on it, and lifted the portrait, carefully hanging it and straightening it to line up with the bookcases to either side.

Stepping down, she walked across the room to survey her work. The portrait was perfect where it was hung, seeming of an age with the room and the furnishings. Sunlight from the rear windows danced over the male likeness. The gentleman's blue eyes seemed to flash and twinkle as they gazed out toward the windows and the view beyond. The dark brown hair glimmered with reddish highlights. The firm mouth seemed ready to break into a smile.

For a moment Catherine started; then quickly assured herself that the life in the portrait was only the effect of the sunlight. She reached down to pick up the old blanket and remnants of twine, then calling for Barney, who was curled up in the corner, she hurriedly left the room.

With far less assuredness than she'd felt a few moments before, she climbed the attic stairs to retrieve the chest and the rest of the things that needed cleaning. After several trips she got them all down to the kitchen, where it would be easier to work. Beginning with the chest first, she gently scrubbed away the layers of grime, and polished and buffed until the old finish was once again glowing softly and richly. She then polished its brass plate and latch to a golden gleam. The engraved initials seemed to jump out in front of her eyes. Who had this L.A.B. been? *Did* he have any connection to the portrait?

The chest was in better condition than she'd imagined—a real work of art. For the time she pushed it into the corner of the kitchen. It wasn't a piece she had any intention of selling. She'd find a place in the house for it—perhaps at the foot of her bed.

The balance of the afternoon went quickly as she washed and polished. Piling her "finds" in the corner of the kitchen, she put dinner on the stove. Catherine was just climbing out of a much-needed bath when she heard her sister call from downstairs.

"Hey, Cath! Where are you?"

"In the bathroom. I'll be right down."

When she entered the kitchen a few minutes later in clean pants and top, Treasa was at the counter uncorking a champagne bottle.

"We're going to celebrate!" Treasa announced cheerfully, working away at the cork.

Catherine saw that three other bottles of wine were standing on the kitchen table. A glance at the labels told her they were of an excellent and expensive vintage, but before she had a chance to ask

Treasa where she'd gotten them, the cork popped free, and Treasa was pouring out a glass of the bubbly liquid and handing it to her sister. She quickly filled a glass for herself and set the bottle down.

"To our reunion," Treasa grinned, lifting her glass. "Come on, drink up!"

Catherine wondered if Treasa had already been drinking, but she took a sip from her glass.

Barney, tail wagging, went over to Treasa, panted up at her.

"Go away, dog. You can't have any of my champagne."

"Come here, Barney." Catherine patted her leg, and the dog immediately obeyed, sliding down on the floor at her feet.

"I've always loved good champagne," Treasa said expansively. "And I need it now. What a day! What a totally rotten day. Too bad you left the boat when you did." She took another sip from her glass, reached in her bag for her cigarettes, withdrew one from the pack, lit it, and inhaled deeply. "If you'd stayed around, you could have listened to Tom lace into me."

"Oh?"

"For not getting the aft cabins done. Of course, I couldn't have, since I was up here."

"Treasa, don't you think you're a little belligerent. He's your boss."

"No! He pushes us around like we're slaves. Althea butters him up, but I'm not about to. Mickey agrees with me, too. He's thinking of getting off in Newport."

"Is he?"

"Yeah. What's cooking? Smells pretty good—not that I'm ready to eat yet. I need to relax first."

"Chicken. Nothing fancy. I was up in the attic all day."

"The attic?" Treasa looked amazed. "What for? On a day like this, you should have been outside."

"I wanted to look around up there."

"And what did you find—a few skeletons?"

"Yes, and one had a sign hanging from it: 'I'm going to haunt Treasa until she straightens up her act.'"

For the barest instant Treasa's face paled.

Catherine laughed. "You don't think I'm serious, do you?"

"No, really, don't kid around with that haunting stuff. I messed around with a little of the occult in Europe. I don't want to have anything to do with it."

"For goodness sake, Treasa, do you really think there're skeletons in the attic? There's nothing but piles of old magazines, boxes, and furniture." Something stopped Catherine from mentioning the portrait and the chest.

"Yeah, yeah, I know." Treasa smiled a little nervously, then tried to brush it off. "I'm being dumb. But, listen, don't *ever* get involved in that stuff."

"I don't plan on it." If I can help it, Catherine added silently as she put down her glass of champagne and went to the cupboard to collect two plates and silverware. She carried everything into the dining room and started setting the gleaming oblong table. That done, she returned to the kitchen and checked the dinner. Treasa had finished one glass of champagne and was pouring herself another.

The chicken was done. Catherine checked the rice, then poured dressing over the salad and tossed it. She began putting the food into serving dishes, as Treasa, off in her own world, leaned her hip against the counter and continued ranting about conditions on the *Cherise*.

"I know you think I'm crying poor, but Tom's always getting on my case. Yeah, maybe today I deserved it since I came up here instead of cleaning, but shit, the way he looks at Althea, always smiling, this mushy look in his eyes. It makes me sick!"

"For one thing, after seeing the way you acted today, I think you start it. You were nasty and sarcastic. You're working for him, and I wouldn't blame him if he got angry. For another, you're imagining things about Althea. If Tom was nice to her, smiled at her, it was because she did her job. You didn't."

"Yeah, I heard her sweetening you up today, and you fell for it, hook, line, and sinker. You'd rather take her side than mine."

"I'm not taking anybody's side. As far as I'm concerned, once *Cherise* sails, I'll probably never see any of them again. I'm just telling you how it looks to me."

"Tough."

"All right, tough. It's your job." Catherine started carrying the serving dishes into the dining room. Treasa followed carrying the rest of the champagne and her glass, but not the other serving dish. Catherine went back for it.

Treasa set down the bottle and her glass and returned to the kitchen for her sister's, setting it in front of Catherine's plate. "You're wasting good champagne—1979."

Only after Catherine had pushed each of the serving dishes in front of Treasa, did Treasa help herself to a little from each. Catherine was hungry. She hadn't eaten lunch. She filled her plate and started eating. Treasa took a forkful of rice, toyed with cutting up her chicken.

"When I left the boat tonight, Althea and Tom were up in the cockpit with a couple of beers, talking." Treasa finished off her champagne.

"So, what does that mean?"

"Tom and I never sat in the cockpit with a couple of beers. She's a conniving little wimp. She's probably sneaking into his cabin every night after the rest of us have gone to bed."

"Treasa, what's the matter with you?"

"Nothing. I know her type real well." Treasa got up, went to the kitchen, and brought back one of the bottles of wine uncorked. She filled her empty glass, then Catherine's.

"That's the way it is in boating, sister. Make hay while the sun shines. They expect you to put out, but that doesn't mean they won't drop you for the next cute piece that comes on board."

"Treasa, let's change the subject."

"Why? I want to talk about it. I've got to get all this stuff off my chest. You've never lived. All you do is work."

"I work because I have to support myself. And I've certainly lived."

"How?"

It was so ridiculous. Catherine felt like she was being put on the defensive with Treasa's brown eyes staring at her. "I started a business. I put years into it, and it's making me big money now. And I've traveled."

"Yeah, on two-week trips, orchestrated through a travel agent. That doesn't mean diddly-pip. You haven't really seen anything. I don't call that living."

"Better than traveling in fantasy land all the time."

"Drink some of your wine, Cath. You need it. You're so uptight. You have any men in your life?"

"I just moved here."

"What about out on the Coast?"

"Yes, there were men."

"You can't kid me. I'll bet all you could think about was that business of yours. I've been all around the world."

"There's a difference. You've been bumming and sleeping your way around on boats. I've been working for what I've got—and I've got it. And you've had too much to drink."

"I've only had a couple of glasses of wine."

"And what did you have before you got here?"

"A couple of scotches. God, you're a pain!" But Treasa put down her glass and made a pretense of eating.

Catherine's stomach was slowly tightening into a ball of apprehension. She couldn't help it. She didn't react this way about alcohol when she was with other people. She enjoyed letting her hair down and having a good time as much as the next person, and occasionally got totally smashed herself. But as soon as she saw Treasa reaching for the bottle, a whole different reaction set in. All she could think of was a lot of bad experiences. Treasa didn't know when to stop—ever.

Treasa spoke up a moment later in a suspiciously contrite voice. "I'll eat. That's what you want, isn't it? Don't worry about it. I haven't had that much to drink. I'm only mildly sloshed. One on the boat; one in town before I came up here." She chewed a forkful of chicken. "You know you're self-righteous, sis—a real prig."

"Listen, Treasa," Catherine said angrily, "just because I don't happen to sleep around with every Tom, Dick, and Harry doesn't make me a prig—nor does the fact I'm not a total hedonist like you! You only see me that way because I don't want to go out and destroy myself, and I won't condone you doing it either!"

"Miss Goody Two-Shoes. Everybody loves Catherine because she's such a blah, cookie-cutter piece. You did what everyone wanted you to do. That's why you got this place, and I didn't. You always got everything, even when we were kids. Catherine got straight A's, Catherine was a cheerleader, Catherine got a scholarship. The sun never set on Catherine."

"Not everything was wonderful for me, damn it! I was so uptight worrying about what Mom and Dad would think, I closed myself into a little shell. They expected me to be perfect—nothing was ever good enough. I only could have certain friends; I only could do certain things. You did whatever you wanted, and they never yelled at you. They never complained about your report cards, your friends; you stayed out later than I did, and I was older."

"You think they didn't give me a hard time, too? The problem for you was that you bought it, Cath, and I didn't." Treasa stared at Catherine with drunk, yet focused eyes. "I did what I wanted. Funny thing, when you won't do what someone else wants and you don't get scared off by their threats, they let you do what you want. You never learned that."

"So you blow your whole life being a degenerate. You've made absolutely nothing of yourself—and you've got a lot to offer."

"Maybe." Treasa laughed, took a long slug from her wine. "I don't particularly give a damn."

"It's time you started giving a damn."

"Sure, so I can be kicked in the ass again like I was in Grandma and Grandpop's will. Cut out, just like that—"

"You weren't cut out."

"It's the same," she sneered. "You'd never know I was a member of this family, the way I've been treated."

"How many times did Grandma and Grandpop help you out with a loan? How many times have all of us tried to bail you out of trouble?"

"If I had the money, I'd pay you back."

Against all her resolutions, Catherine was losing her temper. "You've been on what—ten boats in the last five years?"

"Maybe a dozen. So what? That's the way it is in yachting, moving around."

"Not that much. And who do you come to when you're down and out—when you've quit over some stupid thing and can't find another job?"

Treasa leaned forward. "You see! You don't care about me. Nobody cares about me. I'm just the forgotten orphan in this family. Why do you think I drink? Why shouldn't I when everybody hates me."

"You're getting maudlin."

"You're so good, aren't you? Can't understand when everyone else doesn't get their act together like you do."

"Oh, shut up, Treasa. Whenever you have too much to drink, you go on like a broken record, and you don't make any sense either. I'm going to bed."

"Of course. This talk is too heavy and honest for you. You don't want your cookie-cutter world upset. You don't even know how to relax and have fun!"

"You've already polished off a bottle of champagne and half a bottle of wine by yourself. Is that what you need to have fun?"

"If you'd drunk more, I wouldn't have had to. Besides, life is a bitch, then you die. Why not get drunk?"

Catherine got up from the table. "Good night."

"Yeah, good night."

Only after Catherine had washed and changed into her nightgown, did she allow herself to think about her anger. She was furious; she felt like a corked bottle ready to explode. Why had she even sat and listened to Treasa's mumbo jumbo? She couldn't possibly be as uptight as Treasa would have her believe. She simply had standards and principles. If only Treasa would cut down on her drinking —and drug use, too, Catherine suspected. Drugs were so easily accessible in Treasa's ports of call—she might have a different perspective on things, too. Catherine knew, frustratingly, that there was little she personally could do to bring about that change. How many professional counselors had told her the same thing? As much as a family member loved and wanted to help an alcohol or drug abuser, it was up to the abuser to solve the problem. Until he or she realized the problem and made a personal effort to resolve it, outside help was to little avail, and in some cases only promoted the dependency syndrome. She'd been told point-blank to let go and let Treasa fall flat on her face, even if it was in the gutter. Catherine's own problem was that she hadn't yet been able to do so.

It was only for two days, she reminded herself—one more night.

Feeling nowhere near ready for sleep, she unlocked the study door, calling for Barney to follow her as she stepped inside. Tonight the room looked homey, cozy, warm, reminiscent of her grandfather. For a change she felt no uneasiness or fear, even when she deliberately stared up at the portrait over the fireplace. It was just a painting—that and no more.

As she walked across the old oriental carpet, Barney went to his usual place in the corner and curled up. One window was slightly open, and the drapes were pulled back. The view of the harbor was magnificent—a myriad display of twinkling bits of brightness in the distance. Lifting the old brass telescope from the table, she focused it on the mast lights of the big yachts, the flashing beacon at Brant Point, the red and green glow of the navigational buoys. Lowering the telescope, she looked out to the familiar lights of the town nearer by.

A sea-scented breeze gently fluttered the curtains. The lamp behind gave off just enough illumination to brighten the room, but not enough to hinder Catherine's view. She sighed, feeling some of her frustration with her sister flow away. Distant sounds drifted up from the wharves and harbor: the slow ding of a bell buoy at the harbor's opening; the musical clanking of halyards against metal masts.

Drawing a deep breath of air into her lungs, she turned slowly.

A man was seated at her desk with his back toward her. He appeared to be writing busily in a ledger, his work lit by a shaded glass oil lamp on the desk top by his arm. Dark curls of hair lay against his white collar.

He lifted his head as though he'd heard a noise, then sighed and laid down his pen. His profile was revealed as he turned: a straight, only slightly bridged nose; a strong, beard-covered jaw and chin; firm, sculpted mouth; dark brows over deep blue eyes. A few locks of thick, brown hair fell over his brow. He was a living duplication of the portrait over the fireplace.

He flexed his shoulders, threw back his head as though to relieve the tension of the muscles in his neck, placed his long-fingered hands on the arms of the desk chair, and rose.

For a few seconds he stood beside the chair, only twelve feet from Catherine. His height was emphasized by the low ceiling of the room. His legs were long, and his upper body showed to advantage the fitted, hip-length brown jacket he wore.

He walked toward the clock on the wall beside the desk, opened its glass-doored front, lifted a key from inside, and turned the winding mechanism. When the clock was fully wound, he returned the key and slowly closed the glass front.

Turning toward the windows, he faced Catherine. He seemed preoccupied. He was looking in her direction but appeared not to see her, as if she were a bit of air he gazed through to focus on the view beyond. He walked slowly toward the windows where she stood, stopping not two feet away.

Catherine could have reached out her hand to touch him, but she felt frozen. Instead, she just stared at him, a very solid and tangible apparition gazing out toward the harbor as she had done moments before. He lifted his hand and drew the curtain further to the side, pressed his palm against the window frame, and leaned slightly forward.

Catherine saw the tiny lines at the edges of his eyes, the individual, curling hairs of his thick, carefully trimmed beard. His mouth tightened, and for an instant he narrowed his eyes; then he expelled a long, sad-sounding breath.

Before Catherine could catch her own breath, he had turned from the window and was walking across the carpet toward the desk. He reached for the oil lamp, turned down the wick so that it gave out only a dim glow. Carrying it in his hand, he moved toward the door to the adjoining bedroom—her bedroom.

The latch clicked as he turned the knob. The door opened. He stepped through and closed the door behind him.

Stumbling after him, she grabbed for the doorknob, flung the door wide. The lights of Orange Street filtered into the room. Her eyes swept about, searching for some sign of him. He was leaving the bedroom by the door to the hall.

Catherine quickly followed. She was not going to let him slip away. She intended to solve this mystery! She was close on his heels as he left the room, crossed the hall, and started up the attic stairs. His booted feet echoed on the wide boards of the attic floor as he headed toward the steep stair beside the chimney that led to the widow's walk on the roof. Hardly believing what she was doing, she started up the narrow treads herself, remaining a safe distance behind. He flung back the hatch door at the top of the stairs and stepped out onto the flat, railed walk that circled the chimney.

Peeking her head through the opening, she saw the white railings shining in the moonlight—a full moon; she should have guessed. He'd gone to the rail facing the harbor and stood with palms braced down against it.

Not knowing where she got the courage, she eased herself up off the stairs, and slowly stood.

A wind had come up during the last hour; not a harsh wind, but cool. She shivered in her light clothing, but quickly forgot her discomfort as she looked over to him.

Raw, potent emotion emanated from his person as he stared out to the harbor and beyond to the sea. There was no weakness evident as he lifted his head to take a deep breath of air.

Catherine didn't dare move as she watched him—a man unto himself, fully engrossed in his own thoughts, fully in communication with the sea he watched.

He neither spoke nor moved, and that gave her the courage to inch closer, until she was within a foot of reaching out and touching him. She lifted her arm; her fingers touched the fabric of his jacket, felt the substance beneath. He was solid flesh!

Suddenly he turned and looked directly down at her face. His eyes acknowledged her presence. He saw her there, and his expression was one of shock. Even in the moonlight she saw the color drain from his cheeks and his eyes widen until she could clearly see the whites.

He stared. She stared, too terrified to think of her next action.

His lips moved, silently at first; then he forced out a harsh cry. "Gwen, my God! How is it possible?"

In his eyes was a look Catherine had never seen in any man's eyes. He brought his hands from the railing and reached for her, gripping her shoulders. She felt the strong pressure of his fingers burning right through her nightgown, digging into her flesh. He gazed at her with an intensity that was mind-boggling—and very, very human.

"When I saw you before," he uttered hoarsely, "I thought you were an illusion, but you are real . . . alive!"

Catherine gasped. He'd seen her before, too!

His brows knit together as he scrutinized her features. "But you're not Gwen! Who *are* you?"

Catherine wrenched away, twisting free of his hands and turning for the stairs; nearly falling down them in her haste to get away.

"Wait! Don't go. We must talk!"

She tore across the attic floor. What had she expected when she'd followed him to the roof? A vaporous ghost? Would that have been less terrifying than what she was feeling now? His footsteps echoed behind her, coming fast as she fled down the stairs to the second floor. She gripped the banister of the attic stairs with both hands to keep her rapidly moving feet from slipping on the treads. Breathless, she ran across the upstairs hall to her bedroom door.

This was all absurd! As she reached her door, she looked back over her shoulder. He was rushing out of the attic door. Their eyes met. He motioned with his hand as if to tell her to wait. In panic she slammed the bedroom door, locked it; ran to the study door and locked it as well. She wasn't even sure why she'd run—why she was reacting in such terror. She should discover more about him, not hide away, but she *was* terrified.

Within seconds the handle of the hall door turned, then rattled, and his fist pounded upon the wood. "How dare you lock my own door against me! And why do you run? We must talk. If you are not Gwen, then tell me who you are!"

She dared not move; she simply stood, shaking. Again his fist banged on the door as if he'd break it down. Catherine cringed.

"Let me in! For God's sake I'm not going to hurt you. I merely want an explana—" His voice ceased abruptly in mid-word. There was dead silence—not a creak, not a whisper. If her fear had been great before, it was shattering now.

Slowly she made her way to the door. His silence could be a ruse to get her to open up. With shaking hand, she turned the key, eased the door open. She was prepared to slam it again quickly if he was on the other side. He wasn't. The hall beyond was empty. Cautiously she stepped out of the room, swept her eyes over every inch of the hall and stairs. No one. He might have gone into one of the other rooms, but the floorboards were old and creaked under the lightest of footfalls. She would have heard him. She stared at the spot where he'd stood seconds before. She'd touched him—she'd *felt* his warm, living body. And he'd simply . . . vanished!

She heard footsteps coming quickly up the stairs. She pressed herself back against the doorframe, sure that he was reappearing. But it was only her sister.

Treasa topped the stairs, looking totally at ease, if slightly drunk, and glanced over to Catherine. "I thought you'd gone to bed," she said lightly, as if their conversation at the dinner table had never taken place.

"I—I was just getting ready." Catherine tried to steady her voice.

"Well, I'm too wound up to sleep."

Catherine's knees began to tremble in delayed reaction. She forced herself to breathe more slowly. "You . . . didn't see anything . . . unusual downstairs, did you?" She felt like a fool once the words were out of her mouth, particularly when she saw Treasa's quizzical, then amused expression.

"What do you mean—unusual?"

"Oh, I don't know. I thought I heard something . . . like someone was in the house."

"Yeah—me." Treasa grinned outright, then sobered slightly as she studied Catherine's face. "You look washed-out, white as a sheet. You feeling all right?"

If only she could confide in Treasa, but she'd feel like a total idiot doing so. "No, I'm fine . . . just tired, I guess."

"Hmph. Well, I'll see you in the morning. Don't let the boogie man get you." With a toss of her head, Treasa turned and walked to the bathroom.

God, Catherine thought, if Treasa only knew! Catherine waited just inside her bedroom door as Treasa walked past the attic stairway, right through the spot where *he* had stood shortly before, and went on into the bathroom. From the bath she went to her own room, returned with a magazine in her hand, and headed back downstairs. Catherine listened as Treasa's footsteps retreated down the hall toward the dining room. She heard no screeches or yells of alarm. In a moment

Treasa came back up the hall and went into the living room. Seconds later, the radio went on and Treasa began humming along.

Only then did Catherine close the bedroom door. Going back into the study, she found Barney asleep on the carpet. And what had that marvelous watchdog been doing but snoozing while the intruder roamed about the house at will!

The poor dog didn't know what was happening as Catherine grabbed his collar and pulled his protesting body up. He woke, shook himself stiffly, and with her hand on his collar, followed her sleepily from the room. Catherine locked the study door behind her, then locked the door to the hall as well, but she doubted she'd get any sleep that night.

Who *was* he? What was he doing in her house? She certainly hadn't been dreaming tonight! Who was this Gwen he'd mistaken her for? Was his intent simply to terrify her? But he hadn't seemed evil. She'd felt no physical danger in his presence, except from her own fears. She was almost certain now that whomever she was seeing had lived in the house some time in the past. His was the face in the portrait, and he was totally familiar with his surroundings, but—and her eyes suddenly widened—when he'd been in the study, that room had not been exactly the same as she knew it. There'd been subtle changes—oil lamps instead of the electric ones; different upholstery on the chair; different things on the bookshelves. She was seeing the man among his own belongings, as if she were the intruding apparition, not he!

She pressed her hands to her face and stifled a cry. All she had to do was walk out her front door and travel the distance to Main Street to see and hear the life and bustle of the twentieth century all around her. Why, when she was in her own house, the cherished home of her grandparents, was she made to feel as though she'd slipped into another dimension altogether?

Chapter 4

Catherine woke in the morning curled up in a ball, fetus-like, not wanting to pull the covers from over her head although the alarm was buzzing. Barney's cold nose prodding her under the covers finally prompted her to get up.

Feeling exhausted and shaky, she went downstairs to find pretty much what she'd expected—a mess. The dirty dishes were still on the dining room table, as was the empty wine bottle. Treasa had obviously stayed up long enough to finish what was left. The ashtray beside Treasa's plate was overflowing with cigarette butts. In the living room Catherine found another dirty ashtray and a soiled glass. The house otherwise seemed perfectly normal. What had Catherine expected to see—evidence of her ghostly visitor?

She decided to leave the mess where it was until she'd had her coffee and had gotten Treasa up. As she went to kitchen to put on the kettle, the sun was shining through the kitchen windows. It was a beautiful day, though Catherine was in no state of mind to appreciate it. She let Barney out, then marched back upstairs and knocked loudly on Treasa's closed door. When there was no answer, Catherine pushed open the door to find Treasa huddled under the covers.

"Treasa, it's time to get up."

"Mmmm." But Treasa didn't move.

Catherine went to the bed and unceremoniously pulled the covers off the sleeping girl.

"Hey," Treasa growled, reaching for the covers that were no longer there. "Leave me 'lone . . . go away."

"It's seven-thirty. You've got to go to work."

Treasa rolled over, buried her face in the pillow. "Give me another hour. I'm tired."

"You should have gone to bed earlier. Come on, Treasa, get up."

"No"

"Yes!"

Realizing Catherine would give her no peace, Treasa slowly hoisted herself up on one elbow, made a face, and rubbed her eyes. "Oh, God. I feel awful."

"A cold shower should help, and there's some aspirin in the medicine cabinet. I'll have a cup of coffee ready when you come down."

Catherine waited until her sister had actually climbed from bed and started toward the bathroom before going downstairs herself. The kettle was boiling, and she made coffee. When she heard the shower running, she went to the back door and let Barney in. She then readied a cup of coffee for her sister. In a moment she heard Treasa's footsteps coming down the stairs.

Although she was dressed in clean clothes and her hair was freshly washed, Treasa's face showed the results of her night's drinking. Her eyes were puffy and her skin was pale. Catherine immediately handed her a cup of coffee. "Do you want some breakfast?"

Treasa mutely shook her head, took a drink from her cup. "Never eat breakfast."

"I'll drive you down to the dock when you're finished with your coffee then." Catherine went to stand by the windows to stare outside, deep in her private worries, while Treasa finished off one cup and made herself another. She quickly drank that down.

"Okay, let's go," she said sourly, grabbing her woven African handbag off the floor.

Without a word, Catherine picked up her own purse and extracted the car keys, walked out to the Porsche, and climbed in. As they drove down toward the head of the Straight Wharf, neither sister spoke. Only when Catherine stopped the car and Treasa climbed out, did Treasa say shortly, "See you tonight." She slammed the car door behind her and sauntered down the wharf, her bag slung over her shoulder.

Catherine was sorely tempted not to go back to the house—to just keep driving and driving. Of course, life wasn't that easy; she couldn't simply run away, particularly on an island. But what was she going to do? How was she going to deal with the ghost? Merely thinking about it made her face pale as she wondered if she actually was losing her sanity. Once back at the house, she resigned herself to cleaning up the previous night's dishes. Collecting the dirty plates, she remembered she had an appointment with a realtor that afternoon. How was she going to continue on with the business of her life as if everything were normal? Would she even be able to concentrate? Her head felt fuzzy as though it was stuffed with cotton wool.

There was a knock on the kitchen door, which Barney answered with a series of barks.

"Catherine, are you there? It's Marjorie."

"Come on in, Marjorie. I was just finishing the dishes." She dried her hands on a dish towel as her gray-haired neighbor came through the door.

"I don't want to interrupt," Marjorie said quickly, "but I found these old books on the history of the island and thought you might be interested. This house is mentioned."

"Really!" Catherine's hand shook beneath the dish towel. "Would you like a cup of coffee? I was just going to have one."

"As long as I'm not holding you up." The older woman sat down at the table as Catherine made the coffee. As usual, Marjorie was dressed casually and somewhat haphazardly, though today her blouse was at least tucked into her slacks.

Marjorie was studying Catherine's face. "Is everything all right? You look upset."

"No . . . well, yes, I am upset. I've got a lot on my mind, and my sister showed up unexpectedly yesterday."

Marjorie waited.

Catherine debated over what to tell the older woman, but she needed someone to talk to. "I don't know how much my grandparents told you about her."

"It bothered them that your sister never kept in touch . . . and, frankly, they were concerned about her life-style. They wanted to help, but her problems weren't something they knew how to deal with." Marjorie ran her fingers through her short hair. "Is she here for a visit?"

"She came through the door yesterday morning looking like she was ready to move in. The boat she's crewing on had come into Nantucket for a couple of days." Catherine paused, brought the coffee to the table and sat down.

Marjorie shook her head. "It wasn't a good reunion, I take it."

Catherine briefly described to her neighbor what had gone on since her sister's arrival.

"What a pity. Is she bitter about the fact that you got the house?"

"She mentioned it, but I'm sure more is coming."

"You know why your grandparents split things up as they did—they didn't feel your sister was responsible enough."

"Yes, I know."

"At least she's only here for a few days," Marjorie added consolingly.

"The way she's behaving on the boat, she's just as likely to get fired."

There was a moment's silence as Catherine stared into her coffee cup.

"Well, maybe looking through these books will help take your mind off your problems for a while. They contain some very accurate information about life on the island during the whaling days. This house is mentioned, and ours is, too."

"What does it say about the house? Catherine asked quickly. "Does it mention any of the previous owners?" Her voice was strained.

Marjorie didn't seem to notice. She flipped open one of the books. "Let's see. A Captain William Winford is mentioned as having made a large donation to the Unitarian Church. He was a highly successful whaling captain and resided in this house in the 1830s."

Catherine was frowning. "Do they mention any other owners?"

Marjorie was still reading. In a moment, she shook her head and looked up. "There's a passing reference to the Coffins—of course, this book is basically concerned with the whaling industry." Marjorie paused. "Have you looked for the old deeds at all?"

"Yes, but I didn't find them."

"I can think of a few places where your grandmother might have stashed them. Did you look through the secretary in her bedroom?"

Catherine nodded. "I went through all the drawers in the bedroom. I didn't find anything but some old letters in the desk."

Suddenly Marjorie put down her cup. "I'm not doing anything for the rest of the morning. Why don't I help you look for them."

"Would you mind?"

"It would be the best diversion I could have. Your grandmother had a great desire to preserve anything that might be of historical interest, particularly anything to do with this house. She would have been sure to put the deeds in a safe place where they wouldn't inadvertently be thrown out in the spring cleaning. Now, what would she have considered a safe place? If not in any of the desks—did they have a safety deposit box?"

"Yes. I've gone through it. No deeds, except theirs for the property and some stock certificates and old bank books."

"I have an idea!" Marjorie rose quickly. "Your grandmother used to use the small front parlor as her personal library. All of the old books she collected were in there. I wonder if she might not have wrapped up the deeds and put them on the shelves as well. Let's have a look."

Catherine followed on Marjorie's heels as she strode briskly toward the front parlor and stopped in front of the floor-to-ceiling bookcases on the outside wall. She stood there with hands on hips as her eyes surveyed the shelves.

"Do you really think my grandmother would have hidden deeds in a bookcase?"

"Not hidden so much as stored them with the rest of her historical books and documents. All the books she collected are on these shelves. They rarely got moved, except to dust around the edges."

Conversation dwindled as Marjorie began at one end of the bookcase and Catherine at the other. There were so many volumes, some with fragile bindings that had to be handled carefully.

"I hope I'm not leading you on a wild goose chase," Marjorie spoke almost to herself, as she extracted a volume, leafed through it and put it back. "Too bad these aren't in alphabetical order. Look inside the books, too."

Catherine extracted a book. *"A Modern History of Massachusetts,"* she read, and flipped open the cover. "Published in 1870. Nice etchings." She replaced the book, reached for another and another, shoving the volumes slightly aside to see if anything was wedged in between.

Finally Catherine let out a cry. She'd been drawing out a tall leather volume when a thick envelope slipped from between the pages and fell to the floor. Catherine was immediately on her hands and knees. She turned the envelope over in her hand, examining the writing. There, written in faded ink, were the words, "Old Deeds."

"Marjorie, I've found them! You must have ESP."

"Hardly," the older woman chuckled. "Bring them over to the windows here. The light is better."

Marjorie sat in the chair, while Catherine perched on the footstool, opened the envelope, and carefully extracted the old, brittle documents. The first that she unfolded was dated 1888. Handwritten in a spidery yet official scrawl, it conveyed the land and building on

Orange Street from the estate of the deceased Thomas Nathaniel Jordan to Obadiah Jordan.

"Here's the deed to old Obadiah." Catherine smiled, handing it to Marjorie and lifting up the next. That deed was dated 1880, conveying the property from Rufus Coffin to Thomas Nathaniel Jordan for the sum of one thousand dollars. "Hard to believe that a hundred years ago this house sold for a thousand dollars."

"Pretourist time," Marjorie quipped.

The next deed was far more fragile, although the writing was clear and legible. It was dated 1846, and for the sum of eight hundred dollars, it conveyed the property to Rufus Coffin from the estate of Lucien Alexander Blythe, Esquire. Catherine could feel the blood suddenly pounding against her eardrums. L.A.B.

She tried to keep her hands from shaking as she handed Marjorie the deed. Catherine unfolded the next in the pile. The deed was dated September 28, 1839, and conveyed the property with buildings thereon standing from Captain William George Winford of Nantucket to Captain Lucien Alexander Blythe, late of England, currently residing in Nantucket, for the cash sum of seven hundred and fifty dollars.

Catherine barely suppressed a cry. She swallowed and gave Marjorie the document. She noticed Marjorie frown as she read.

Only two deeds were left, but Catherine could barely concentrate as she read them. The first, dated 1830, conveyed the land and buildings from Jonas M. Stilton of Nantucket to Captain William G. Winford, also of Nantucket. The last, very fragile document was dated 1801 and conveyed the property from Jedrah Abel Jones to Jonas M. Stilton.

Catherine waited silently for Marjorie to continue reading. "The house goes back prior to 1801," the older woman mused. "Either this Jedrah Jones built it, or the earlier deeds were lost. Hmmm," she muttered to herself, then looked up. "I'm remembering an old story that was told to me—in fact, I'd forgotten all about it until I saw these deeds." Marjorie pulled two deeds from the pile and clutched them absently in her fingers, her brow furrowed. "I heard the story from an old woman who lived in the house on the corner of Plumb Lane and Orange when Evan and I first moved here twenty-five years ago. I hadn't even met your grandparents then, and actually I kind of wrote off a good part of the tale as nonsense. Mrs. Wills must have been ninety then, but her mind was sharp as a tack. She knew all the island history and could talk for hours. When she heard we'd bought the Lacy house, she began telling me its history. Then one afternoon she said to me—and I can still picture her sitting in her old rocker by the front window: 'Now that house next to yours that used to be old Obadiah's, it has some history to it . . . some strange happenings, too.'"

Marjorie shook her head. "Funny that I've forgotten all this until now. In any case she told me that in the heyday of whaling in the 1830s the house had belonged to a wealthy whaling captain and his family—William Winford, obviously. When he retired, he sold the house to a young man, a captain, too, although he didn't make his living in whaling but had his own small merchant fleet. This young captain was English and apparently handsome enough to turn the heads of the strictest young Quaker girls in town, yet he seemed to have no interest in forming any attachments. He socialized when invited and was accepted into the affluent circles of the Macys, Coffins and Starbucks, but an air of mystery hung about him. Although he was obviously a man of means and background, he never discussed his past. No one knew anything about his life before he arrived in Nantucket except that he was well traveled. On a regular schedule his merchantmen pulled into Nantucket for trade, and he was always down at the docks when his ships were in. Although he'd captained the largest vessel himself, once he arrived in Nantucket, he never sailed.

"Obviously, gossip about him began to spread. His crew, though they held him in high esteem, occasionally talked in town. They spoke of a tragedy in his past, of a sudden change in him during his last trip to England. He'd gone off the boat a happy man and came back a shell of himself.

"The gossip about him was fueled by the fact that each evening his neighbors would see him up on the widow's walk at sunset, pacing, gazing out to sea, returning inside only when the last lingering light was gone. And sometimes late on a clear, moonlit night they would see his shadow again up on the walk, standing in lonely vigil.

"The young captain lived in the house five or six years. Then one day he disappeared. Even the manservant who lived in the house with him was mystified by the disappearance. One of his merchantmen had sailed with the tide the night before, so it was presumed he'd sailed with his ship. Several of his ships put into Nantucket, but there was no sign of the captain. His manservant finally closed up the house and left on one of the vessels. A while later a letter was received from an attorney in London, ordering the house to be sold to the highest bidder and the proceeds forwarded to London.

"The mystery probably would have been forgotten if not for the strange things that began happening at the house. When Mrs. Wills was a girl, there was talk of a man's silhouette being seen up on the widow's walk late at night, and the young couple living in the house began to talk of strange feelings. The wife, expecting her first child, said that when she was home alone, she felt as though there were someone else in the house with her—not menacing, but unsettling. She could never spend more than a few minutes in one of the upstairs rooms without feeling as though she were intruding. Her husband agreed that he felt much the same in that room. Of course, his wife was pregnant, and he may have been humoring her. They also talked of a portrait they'd found hidden in the attic, which they'd soon put back in its hiding place because of the frightening sensation it gave them."

Marjorie was staring at the carpet and was unaware that Catherine's face had gone chalk white. She continued speaking thoughtfully. "There were rumors later on of the man seen up on the widow's walk, but old Obadiah apparently lived in the house for years in eccentric but obvious contentment, and your grandparents certainly never mentioned anything to me about ghosts or strange feelings." Marjorie frowned. "Then again, your grandmother didn't like to go up in the attic. I was here one day years ago when she was still spry, and she offered me some things for my church's rummage sale. Your grandfather was out in the barn fixing some furniture, but she called him to go up in the attic and get the things."

Marjorie finally looked up at Catherine's face and gave a visible start. "Good heavens! What *is* it?"

Catherine could barely speak. Shakily but with purpose, she rose. "Come with me," she motioned to Marjorie. "I have something to show you."

"I didn't mean to frighten you," Marjorie said with concern. "That tale of a ghost is pure nonsense."

"Just come. You'll see."

Catherine walked quickly from the room and up the stairs.

"Really, Catherine, are you sure you're all right?"

"Wait," was all Catherine would say as she led Marjorie into the study, directly to the fireplace, then pointed to the portrait hanging above it.

The older woman's eyes followed Catherine's motioning hand. "Where did you get it?"

"In the attic."

"This attic?"

"Yes. Wrapped up and in the back of a storage closet under the eaves that hadn't been opened in years. The only other thing in the closet was an old sea chest . . . with the initials L.A.B."

It took Marjorie a moment to respond. "Lucien Alexander Blythe."

"That's what I'm thinking."

"Oh, my Lord. No wonder you turned white." Marjorie looked back to the painting. "You think, then, that this is his portrait."

"It would seem." Catherine was afraid to add that she'd seen the same man in the flesh in that very room only the night before.

"Incredible," Marjorie mused. "But I don't understand. I doubt there was an inch of this house your grandparents left untouched. Why was the portrait left in the attic? It's far too excellent a work for them to have disregarded."

"I know. I thought of that when I found the closet. But remember what Mrs. Wills told you about the young couple and the portrait they found? Actually I only saw the closet because Barney knocked over a huge stack of bundled magazines that was blocking the door. The dates on the magazines went back to the turn of the century. I thought maybe my grandparents hadn't known the closet was there. The painting, the chest, and the closet itself were covered with years of dust."

"I don't know what to make of it. Is there any kind of identification on the portrait?"

"None, except for the signature of the artist—Fenley, or something like that. And the initials on the chest I found in the closet."

"Do you mind if I have a look?" Marjorie was already striding toward the portrait. Lifting it from its hook and resting it on the carpet, she studied the canvas, the frame. "I see the signature." She turned the portrait around and pressed her fingers over the paper backing. "Have you lifted this to look underneath?"

"No. The portrait's exactly as I found it."

"Would you mind terribly if I cut it away? There's probably nothing underneath, but we might as well look."

"Go ahead." Catherine was already going to the desk for a pair of scissors.

Carefully Marjorie cut away the old paper. "I'll pay to have this replaced."

"Don't be silly. I'm as curious as you—more so. An oil doesn't need a backing anyway."

In a moment Marjorie drew away the old paper and both women strained their eyes toward the back of the canvas. A square of parchment was braced in the right hand corner of the frame. With trembling fingers Catherine removed it and licked her suddenly dry lips. Her voice was nearly a whisper as she read:

"To Captain Lucien Alexander Blythe of the *Goddess*, who saved me in Calcutta from sure tragedy and on whose ship I have found great pleasure and friendship. May this likeness of you relay a small measure of my eternal thanks. Colin Renley."

Chapter 5

Portsmouth, England
1839

Lucien Blythe stood at the rails of his merchantman, oblivious to the activity around him on deck and on the nearby wharfs—to the shouts and cries of the dockhands, the scents of pitch and spices, of salt and unwashed bodies, of manure from the huge horses drawing dray wagons in a steady stream to and from the Portsmouth docks.

His vessel edged out of Portsmouth harbor, nosing past the white Needles of the Isle of Wight, then on into the English Channel. The seas were rough from the brisk winds, yet the sky was a sharp blue. The scene before him was etched in clear detail out beyond the farthest whitecap. A lone gull circled over the spreading white of the main and topsails, extended in their glory to catch the full measure of the westward wind carrying them into the Atlantic.

At that moment he felt none of the pride he should in watching the *Goddess* slice through the waves as if she were their supreme mistress. She was his vessel—his pride and joy after so many years of diligent work, designed by his own hand. He had built up quite a business—he, the younger son of an earl, a young man who should never have had to taint his hands with trade. He'd done it out of a need to prove to himself that he *could* do it, and out of an equally demanding need to quench his thirst for adventure. From the time he was a small boy hearing tales of fellow Englishmen making their fortunes in the Far East and India, his greatest longing had been to escape the confines of convention and the boundaries of Great Britain. But those days of dreaming were past. He was now thirty, and he'd done what he'd set out to do. He'd sailed many of the oceans of the world, traded in exotic ports. He'd taken on cargoes of ivory, spices, silks, mahogany, teak, jute, whale oil, machinery, cloth, cotton, rum, and furs. He'd amassed enough in his bank accounts in the last ten years to tide him over for the rest of his life.

His knuckles showed white where he clenched the varnished rail. What did any of it matter anymore?

The crew of the *Goddess* had not expected Captain Blythe to come aboard ship that morning. In fact, they hadn't expected to see Captain Blythe at all. When they'd docked in Portsmouth eight days before, he'd left his vessel an exuberantly happy man—one who was looking forward to the future. He'd announced long before they'd docked that when the *Goddess* sailed again, she would have a new captain on the bridge—Perry Chisholm, his former first mate. But something tragic had occurred in the interim. Lucien Blythe's strong features seemed to have aged five years in the course of a week.

"Captain?"

Lucien turned numbly at the voice behind his shoulder. His own voice was hoarse. "Yes, Perry?"

"I don't wish to pry, but I'm concerned. Are you quite all right?"

"Yes . . . my problem is a personal one. It is not something I wish to talk about at the moment."

"Is there nothing I can do?"

"No. As I said, I'm coming along for the journey only. The vessel is now in your command. I simply need time alone."

"Would you join me in my cabin in an hour for a port?"

"Thank you, Perry, but another time."

Captain Perry Chisholm studied Blythe, who was only a few years his senior and who had taught him so much in the years they had sailed together. At last he nodded and walked quietly away.

Lucien remained at the rail until long after the sun had set, responding not even to his manservant Gladstone's pleadings to come below for a light meal.

"Later, Gladstone. My appetite is not what it should be."

"But, Cap'n—"

"I will not fade away for lack of food."

Unhappily, the servant, a former crew member, left. The ship had settled in for the night when the Captain finally went below himself to the small, paneled cabin just forward of the captain's cabin, reserved for the very occasional guest on board. Gladstone had left a brass wall lamp burning dimly. It was enough to light Lucien's way as he closed the cabin door and stripped off his jacket, trousers and white shirt. The single-berth accommodations were cramped in comparison to his former quarters, which were by right now Perry's, but

Lucien cared not. Turning out the oil lamp, he threw himself down on his back on the narrow, short bunk to stare blindly into the darkness. He found no peace there either.

The *Goddess* rolled over the waves, her timbers creaking gently in accompaniment. He moaned, and tears ran unheeded from the corners of his eyes.

The days blurred one into the next and the next. Four weeks after their departure from Portsmouth, a call echoed out from the crow's nest. "Land ho, fine on the port bow!" Stepping forward over the spotless, teak deck planks, Lucien squinted across the green, white-capped waves toward the low patch of land ahead. Nantucket.

During the four-week passage he'd hoped his pain would dull and his raw emotional wounds would begin to heal. Yet he felt little better now than he had upon leaving England. No, that wasn't quite true. The day he'd left England he'd been impervious to everything but his grief and guilt. Death would have been welcome. Now, he felt again the life in his veins, enough to realize that his guilt and suffering were to be his constant companions, and there would be no easy escape.

They docked early that afternoon, coming in with the tide over the bar into Nantucket Harbor. The town rose up the low hillside behind the docks, its neat houses shingled gray. With their cargo of English tea, bales of woven cloth, and machinery parts, they were a welcome arrival. Several brokers were waiting along the dockside as he and Perry left the ship. Although the captain of the vessel had responsibility for the disbursement and sale of cargo, as owner of the *Goddess,* Lucien would have offended no one by conducting the negotiations himself. He felt in no state of mind, however, and after speaking briefly with the brokers, who knew him from previous visits, he introduced Perry as the new captain.

"Captain Chisholm will begin discussions with you, gentlemen, and we can conclude any unfinished business in your offices tomorrow morning." Lucien tipped his hat and walked quickly away. He had no particular direction in mind. He knew only that he needed to get off ship and walk.

He left the wharves and started up Main Street, remembering days spent on the prosperous island in the past. He'd always felt a special comfort and affinity for the place, with its Quaker homes climbing the low hills; the activity along the wharves, where the rollicking sailor's taverns were in such contradiction to the refined and quiet

respectability of Nantucket's residential streets; the open skies of the
moor-like landscape beyond the town; the sweeping views of the
ocean. Bonneted and demure Quaker ladies swished past him in
plain, full skirts with shopping baskets on their arms. Dozens of dray
and farm wagons were tied at either side of the street, horses stomping or dozing in front of the many storefronts in the two- and three-
story wood-framed and occasionally brick buildings. Awnings were
stretched over the sidewalk in front of several. In the space of two
blocks he passed Thomas Coleman's Sail Loft, Garner's Hardware,
Easton & Sanford Watchmakers & Jewelers, Winslow Whittemore
Furs, Cromwell Bernard Tailor, Adams' & Parker's Grocery, E.T.
Wilson's Furnishing Warehouse, Cobb's Dry Goods, and the neo-
classical brick structure of the Nantucket Pacific Bank at the corner
of Centre Street. Several shade trees poked up through the sidewalks,
but otherwise the landscape was rather treeless, much of the wood
having been cut for practical purposes and not many hardwoods
adapted to the windy island climate and sandy soil.

A seaman or two passed, running errands for his ship or exploring
town. Occasionally a fine carriage rolled over the cobblestones,
coming from or going to one of the whaling ship owners' mansions
farther up Main Street. As he walked, he left the noise and bustle of
the harborside behind. The gulls continued to screech overhead, but
now he could hear the chirping of smaller birds. The scent of pitch
wasn't so strong and the pungence of the crude whale oil and by-
products being off-loaded from the whalers no longer seared his nos-
trils.

Wandering with no real direction, he crossed Main Street near the
Nantucket Pacific Bank and started up Orange Street. The scent of
the sea now mingled with the scent of the wild roses that flourished
on the island, brightening the moors and climbing over picket fences.
Passing the tall, white clapboard front of the Unitarian Church,
whose square bell tower could be seen from beyond the bar, he
looked ahead to a view of immaculate homes, some with dormer
windows poking from their roofs and widow's walks standing atop;
all nearly flush with the sidewalk, with narrow side gardens filled
with late summer blooms. The gardens reminded him of home, of
Oak Park. But Oak Park wasn't home any longer. He had no desire
to return to England.

His everpresent pain was his companion, yet there was something
about the tranquility of the scene before him and around him that
eased the constriction around his heart. It seemed as if the island was

telling him that here he might find a small bit of peace; and it was peace that he sought, above and beyond all else.

He continued on, pausing under one of the few trees along the sidewalk—a maple—and glanced across the cobbled street. He was facing a two-story house with black shutters at each of its windows. It was older than many of the other homes on the street. Its brick basement walls didn't lift it so high off the ground as its neighbors. Its front door could be reached via two stone steps instead of the usual set of five or six wooden ones heading down on either side of the doorway in Quaker style. The twelve over twelve windows twinkled in the sunlight. Two chimneys thrust through the roof, a railed widow's walk surrounding them. There was nothing in particular to set the house apart from others on the street, except for the boxes filled with bright flowers beneath each of the four lower-story windows. Yet something about the house drew him. He sensed a murmuring voice, offering peace and respite from his misery.

Without fully understanding why, he crossed the street. The front door of the house was painted a bright blue. It was surmounted by a semicircular glassed transom. The brass knocker on the door in the shape of a ship's figurehead was newly polished. He read the polished brass nameplate on the door. "Winford." On impulse, he lifted the knocker and rapped loudly, not sure of what he would say when the door was opened. One did not walk up to a stranger's door, knock, and tell the owner how much you were drawn to his property.

His dilemma was resolved when there was no answer to his knock. He continued up the street, glancing up the narrow, shelled drive at the end of the house to a small but adequate barn, a back garden. At the next winding lane, he turned down the hill toward Union Street, but strangely the house on Orange Street remained in his thoughts throughout the evening. He'd come to Nantucket with no plans of settling there—with no plans in any direction. His future had seemed a blank void, but now the idea teased at him. Something drew him. Perhaps here, on an island thirty miles to sea, alive yet away from the maddening world, with no real ties to his past, he might find a small bit of the solace and forgetfulness he needed.

He rose early the next morning, and after a brief talk with Perry about the previous day's business proceedings, he left the ship. Forcing his mind to the business he must conduct, he went to the offices of the various brokers where he contracted sales for his cargo higher than anticipated. Then, on a whim, as he passed the office of Obed Starbuck, Insurance & Real Estate Broker, on Federal Street, he stopped. He did not know Obed Starbuck, but he knew the family to be one of the wealthiest and most influential on the island and among the island's earliest settlers.

A portly, balding man sat at the desk opposite the door. He looked up as Lucien entered.

"May I be of help, sir?" the gentleman asked, his eyes quickly assessing Lucien's impeccable attire.

"You might." Lucien hesitated, then went toward the desk. "I am Lucien Blythe, owner of the *Goddess*, presently docked in your harbor."

The other gentleman rose, extending his hand. "How do you do? Obed Starbuck." His steady and intelligent brown eyes again studied the captain. "And how may I help you?"

"I am making inquiries about residential properties that might be for sale on the island."

"Of course. Have a seat. What exactly did you have in mind?"

"A comfortably sized house within convenient distance to town."

"Well," Starbuck considered, "there are several. Can you be more specific about what you had in mind?"

"I saw a house yesterday that is very similar to what I am looking for. It was on Orange Street. The name on the door was Winford—"

Starbuck's brows went up. He sat a bit straighter in his chair. "An amazing coincidence that you should mention that house. It has only just come up for sale."

"It has?"

"Yes. I've not even had time to put a sign on the door. Captain Winford is retiring and moving closer to his daughter on the mainland."

"Remarkable."

"The house would not be available for another month, however."

"That would present no problem," Lucien mused. "My vessel will be sailing in a few days for New Bedford and New York, then returning here in about a month's time." Lucien drummed his fingers on the arm of his chair and considered the strange quirk of fate. Incredible that the house he'd been drawn to was actually up for sale.

"Would you care to see the property?"

Lucien looked up. He felt disoriented. "Yes, I suppose I would."

"If you have a few moments to spare now, we could walk over. I have the keys."

Lucien made up his mind and rose quickly. "Very well."

Starbuck lifted a set of keys off the pegs behind his desk and stepped around it. "You are planning on settling on the island?" he asked.

"It is a thought, although I have made no decisions."

"Well, I believe you will find this house very suitable—the home of another man of the sea, but then most of us on Nantucket have our connections to the sea in one way or another." He motioned to the clerk who was sitting in a partitioned cubicle at the far side of the room and whom Lucien hadn't noticed at all upon entering the office. "I shall return in an hour or so."

"Yes, sir."

"English, are you?" Starbuck continued conversationally as they stepped out onto the street.

"Yes."

"Your family will be joining you?"

"I am not married."

"Ah ha," Starbuck chuckled. "Then prepare yourself to be besieged by invitations from the local matrons with eligible daughters."

Lucien tried to force a smile, but his throat suddenly felt tight with renewed pain.

As if sensing Lucien's reaction, Starbuck let the subject drop. "You say you are the owner of the *Goddess*, is it?"

"Yes, and several other vessels trading frequently in these waters."

"You will be sailing with one of your vessels?"

"No. I am contemplating overseeing my fleet from ashore."

"I see."

They were approaching the house. It appeared as welcoming to Lucien as it had the day before. As Starbuck fitted the key in the lock of the front door, Lucien felt an anticipation to see the rooms within. He was not disappointed. The interior was well maintained and reflected the loving care of its owner. From the square front hall, they stepped right into the main parlor. Lucien nodded in satisfaction at the room's proportions and the traditional furnishings much to his own taste. They crossed the hall to a small parlor, which Lucien thought would be more practical to him as a sitting room/library. Through a connecting doorway they entered the spacious dining room, and from there proceeded to the large rear kitchen, with its huge fireplace and iron cookstove and adjoining pantries. Starbuck next led him down the center hallway to the stairs. "Full cellar below. Would you care to see it?"

"Not at the moment."

They continued on to the staircase, then through each of the four chambers on the second floor. Again, Lucien nodded to himself. One of the chambers could be Gladstone's. He fancied the two rooms to the left of the staircase himself. They were connecting, and he envisioned the rear chamber, with its sweeping view of the harbor, as a study. He would have bookcases built to hold his treasured library as well as the mementoes he'd collected from around the world.

He strode to the windows and stared out. A small garden was laid out behind the house, then the land dropped off steeply toward Union Street. Over the rooftops of the houses on that lower street, he had a clear view of the harbor and the forest of masts at the dockside. His keen eyes picked out those of the *Goddess*. Beyond that were the humps of Coatue and the blue sweep of Nantucket Bay.

"The house also has a full attic and roof walk," Starbuck explained, as he directed Lucien to a door off the hall and up another set of stairs. "This area could easily be converted into additional rooms, should you find the need. Perhaps you would like to see the prospect from the roof walk?"

"I would indeed."

They followed a narrower set of stairs through a hatchway to the roof. Lucien stepped across the walk and paused, struck by the sweeping scene before him. He might have been standing in the crow's nest of his ship. He leaned his hand against the rail, then turned suddenly to Starbuck, speaking words he was barely aware of forming in his mind. "I will take it."

"You've not even asked the price!"

"It will make no difference. This house is exactly what I want."

Starbuck recovered from his surprise. Rarely did a sale proceed so quickly. "I am delighted, of course, and Captain Winford will be as well. The price, by the by, is seven hundred and fifty dollars."

"A fair one."

"Captain Winford has agreed to hold a mortgage himself if that would be more convenient."

"I shall pay in cash."

"Indeed." Starbuck seemed bemused at the rapidity of the transaction.

Lucien had turned again to the view and gazed out to the sea. Starbuck could not see Lucien's blue eyes focusing on something far beyond the horizon; nor could he see the flash of agony in his eyes. By the time Lucien turned back to the broker, his features were composed.

"We shall be sailing in two days. You said the house will not be available for a month."

"Correct, but if you will leave a deposit, I shall draw up the necessary papers while you are away, ready for signature on your return."

"Excellent." Despite his lack of definitive plans when he'd entered Starbuck's office, Lucien knew he'd done the right thing. It was an intuitive feeling. "I shall bring the deposit to your office this afternoon." He extended his hand. "A pleasure to do business with you Mr. Starbuck."

"Likewise, I am sure!"

The *Goddess* sailed on schedule on a clear-skied morning, the changing tide easing her out of the harbor and over the bar into Nantucket Sound, then northwestward toward New Bedford. Though his soul was still far from peaceful, Lucien was well pleased with the business completed on Nantucket. Having made some sort of decision about his future helped ease the conflict within.

Late that afternoon he stood on the quarter-deck beside Perry, conversing quietly with his former first mate, who seemed to enjoy the company. The sunset spread out in a molten orange-gold on the waters ahead.

"This will be my last voyage with you for a while," Lucien said unexpectedly.

Perry glanced over with surprise, though he waited for Lucien to continue.

In a moment he did. "I have purchased a house on Nantucket."

Perry's brows arched sharply. "So soon? Last we spoke, you had no plans—"

Lucien sighed. "Yes, I know. Though I do not believe in whimsy, something drew me. Difficult to explain, Perry. I find it impossible to speak of what happened in England. I need time to think and put my world back in order, and there is a certain peace offered on that island. I found a house that will suit me admirably, and from a business standpoint, Nantucket is just as central to our shipping as England. Yes, New York would have been better still, but I couldn't exist happily in such a crowded, teeming environment. I need space about me."

"I can understand that." Perry paused, studied his former captain's face. "I imagine you have carefully considered."

"As carefully as I am capable of at the moment . . . and no decision is irrevocable . . . except death."

The breeze off the water suddenly became chill with the setting sun. Lucien pulled the collar of his sea coat up around his ears. "I wanted you to know. I shall send a message through to Portsmouth to my other captains when we dock in New York." With that Lucien strode away, up the deck, to the bow of the ship, where he stood at the rail staring out into the darkening seas.

A storm was brewing on the eastern horizon as the *Goddess* approached Nantucket three weeks later after discharging and taking on cargo in both New Bedford and New York. A portion of the cargo taken on in New York was Captain Blythe's, though he would speak to no one about the contents.

With the rising winds all but the topsails had been furled. Her hold full of cargo, the *Goddess* battered through the rising chop. The gleam of the beacon at Brant's Point was a welcome sight.

The last of the lines had been secured to the Long Wharf pilings when the freak autumn storm hit full force. Slashes of lightning streaked across the sky, followed by the rumbling boom of thunder. The black clouds overhead released a sudden downpour that lashed across the deck. The men still in the rigging furling sails hurried at their task, knowing what likely targets they were.

Though he was no longer in command of the vessel, Lucien stood on the deck in the beating rain beside Perry until the last man was down, the last hatch battened and the ship safe against the storm. Perry started toward the companionway stairs, then turned when he realized Lucien wasn't following.

"Come below!" he called over the wind and rain. "A drink in my cabin."

"In a moment!" Lucien called back, motioning for Perry to continue.

He didn't wait for Perry to respond, but pulled the hood of his oilskins from his head and turned to face the full force of the storm. The rain beat against his cheeks like pellets, coursing off his beard and hair, down his neck. He welcomed the chill, the raw power of the elements. He walked forward and stared out over the rain and the storm-whipped waters of the harbor. He lifted his face, eyes closed. The howling wind and explosive bangs of thunder hid his cries. "Gwen . . . forgive me!"

Chapter 6

At exactly two Catherine pulled the Porsche into the parking lot of the realtor's office just outside of town. She had to wait only a minute before one of the salesmen stepped out of the side office and came toward her with hand extended. He was attractive, neatly dressed, and about thirty. His eyes momentarily widened as he saw Catherine.

"Hi, I'm Ryan Gorham."

"Catherine Sternwood. Nice to meet you."

"Same. I've got a couple of places lined up for you to look at. Retail rentals are kind of tight right now, beginning of the season and all, but there are two possibilities right in town, several farther out."

"I'd like to be in town, if possible."

"Just let me get my papers, and we can go." He went to the secretary's desk and took a manila folder off the top, flipped it open and returned to Catherine.

"You said you're looking for a place to run a decorating/antique business. You just starting out?"

"No. This will be a branch, actually. I already have the business established on the West Coast. I have someone managing it while I set up here."

"I see." He held the door for her. "You're planning on staying on the island?"

"For the time. I haven't quite decided."

He motioned her across the gravel lot toward a late model imported sedan parked just beyond her Porsche. As they passed the Porsche, he gave it an appreciative look. "Nice car."

"Thanks. It handles well."

Catherine sensed rather than saw his startled reaction and tried to hide her smile. He said nothing more as he opened the passenger door for her.

"I think you'd probably like a place that's available on Centre Street. Good location, lots of traffic, and even a couple of private parking spaces in the rear. The rent's pretty well up there, though."

Catherine nodded and said nothing more until he'd parked behind a two-story, Quaker-style wood frame building with shop space in the front. They entered through the front door.

"As you can see," he continued glibly, "the fixtures are great— lots of shelving, a couple of built-in display cabinets, good traffic pattern. Back here is a nice-sized storage room, a half bath, rear door for deliveries."

"What's the rent?"

He quoted a figure.

"Including utilities?"

"Heat, not electric."

Catherine continued walking around the front area, mentally calculating how she could use the space. She'd need several areas where she could set up mini room displays and additional space for any antique furnishings she brought in for sale. She needed only a quarter of the shelving along the walls. Most of it would have to come down. She supposed she could make use of one of the display cabinets, but not both. She checked the lighting system and the outlets.

"How long is the lease?"

"Two years with a first option on renewal."

Catherine nodded. She could see that he was becoming more self-assured with each of her questions.

"If you're interested, I wouldn't wait too long," he added, causing Catherine to smile. "I've got several other clients seriously looking at the property."

Catherine paused just an instant. "Let's take a look at a couple of others before I make up my mind."

"You're not going to find another location like this."

"Maybe. I still want to look."

He seemed somewhat disgruntled, but hid it well. "Where're you from on the Coast?"

"Santa Barbara."

"Nice. I was out there a couple of years ago."

"Were you?"

"You look Californian."

"Why? Because of my blond hair?"

He laughed. "You've heard that before, I guess. I spent quite a bit of time in California. Mostly in the San Diego/La Jolla area. I was selling real estate out there, but I missed the East Coast."

"You live on the island all year?"

"God, no. I'd die out here in the winter—business-wise anyway. I spend the winters in the Boston area, working for another firm up there."

He showed her three more spaces in the next hour, none of which impressed Catherine as much as the first, but it was also obvious the rent for the first was too high.

"So, what do you think?" Ryan asked as they headed back toward his car.

"How long has the Centre Street space been listed?"

"Ah." He stumbled, gazing at the listing sheet. "They've forgotten to put the date on here."

"I'd say that it's been listed for a while. The price is too high. That's why no one's taken it."

"You may not be aware of it, but rentals in town have just about gone through the roof."

"Not that far. I'll consider it if the owner's willing to come down in price." She quoted him a figure.

"That's three hundred a month less!"

"Right. I don't think it's worth more than that, particularly considering the seasonal nature of business here."

"Well . . . I'll phone them and get back to you this afternoon or tomorrow."

They'd reached the real estate office. Catherine smiled and extended her hand across the car. "Thanks." She climbed out and headed for the Porsche.

The rest of the afternoon was uneventful, although Catherine was more uneasy than ever after her and Marjorie's discovery of the deeds and of the identity of the subject of the portrait. She didn't look forward to Treasa's arrival home either. She prayed there wouldn't be a repeat of the previous night's scene.

As it turned out, Treasa totally surprised her. She arrived home sober and made no mention of opening a bottle of wine for dinner. Throughout the meal itself, she was pleasant, complimenting Catherine about the food, reminiscing about their early childhood, asking Catherine about her decorating business. Treasa had never shown the remotest interest in the business before that. She helped Catherine clear the table and offered to wash up since Catherine had done all the cooking.

Catherine was both surprised and suspicious. What did Treasa have up her sleeve? Or was it actually possible that something she'd said to Treasa about her life-style had gotten through? Had Treasa been doing some thinking?

With thoughts of her ghost in mind, Catherine had taken Marjorie's books into the living room and was perusing them when Treasa came in after finishing the dishes and strolled restlessly around the room.

"It hasn't changed much since we were kids, has it? At least Grandma and Grandpop never had frumpy taste." She strode across to the baby grand. "You ever play the piano?"

At the mention of the piano, Catherine involuntarily shivered, but quickly pushed the feeling away. "I never played."

"You used to take lessons."

"A year's worth. I didn't have any talent. You were the one who was musical."

"Yeah. I still like it." Treasa went to lift the keyboard covering.

"The key's in the bench," Catherine called.

"Why do you lock it?"

"Grandma always did for some reason. I've never bothered to open it."

Treasa lifted the bench top, found the key, unlocked the piano and settled down on the bench. She ran her fingers quickly over the keys. "One of my friends in the Med. had an electric keyboard. I fooled around with it a little."

To Catherine's amazement Treasa launched into an upbeat rock song, banging out the chords easily from memory. She played for several minutes and when she was done gave out a laugh.

"Ha! I haven't forgotten."

"That was really good, Trea!"

"Not bad since I haven't touched it in eight months." She rose, closing the piano.

"Why don't you play some more?"

"I don't feel like it tonight. I think I'll watch the tube for a while." She walked over to the console cabinet at the far end of the room and opened the cabinet doors, turned on the set, and settled herself in the chair facing it. Catherine tried to get back into her reading but the talk from the television disturbed her. Her ear kept picking up on the dialogue of the adventure movie Treasa was watching. She didn't want to go into another room where she'd be alone and possibly see the ghost again. Finally, she put her book aside and went over to the other chair facing the set.

"I haven't seen this one before," Treasa muttered, eyes glued to the screen. "Pretty good."

The sisters watched in silence until the end of the movie, Treasa occasionally smoking but making no effort to get a drink. When it ended, she rose and stretched. "Well, I'm going to bed."

"Do you want me to get you up in the morning?"

"If I'm not up already."

"When are you sailing?"

"Late in the afternoon. I'll be back to get my gear."

"Okay. Good night."

"Night."

Catherine was totally bemused by Treasa's behavior. Why the change in attitude? What was up?

Calling Barney, she turned off the lights in the living room and went upstairs. She looked nervously around the bedroom before climbing under the sheets, but after her lack of sleep the previous evening, she dropped off instantly.

That night she had the same recurring dream. She jolted awake, her heart pounding, feeling as if someone had gently touched her. She'd sensed his presence—somewhere nearby—in the bedroom. She was sure of it, though her searching eyes found no trace of him. Only a lingering scent of Bay Rum cologne remained.

She slept later than usual, and Treasa was gone by the time she got up. She'd made up the bed, too, which gave Catherine a jolt. Perhaps she should give her the benefit of the doubt.

After straightening up the house a little, she went upstairs to her bedroom and pulled out the paperwork she'd brought with her from California. She generally worked at the desk in the study, but she no longer felt comfortable in there. She didn't want to be reminded of him—to have him intrude in every moment of her day. She took her work down to the kitchen table instead. If she was getting close to finding a rental, she should start the other wheels turning—ordering some additional inventory and basic supplies. She was having fabric samples and swatches shipped out from the West Coast, together with some basic prints and accessories, but only enough for setup. Before sorting through the catalogs from various suppliers, she picked up the phone and dialed her Santa Barbara shop. She'd had two calls from

Marcie since she'd arrived in Nantucket, and everything seemed to be running smoothly.

The phone in California was picked up after two rings. "Classics. May we help you?"

"Yes, this is Lucrezia Borgia. I'm in the most dire straits. I need all of my house redone by this weekend—party, you know."

"Catherine, is that you?"

"Sure is. How're you doing, Marcie?"

"Great, just great. It's good to hear from you."

"Good to talk to you, too! I just called to check in. How's the weather out there?"

"Gorgeous as usual."

"I'm homesick."

"When are you coming out?"

"As soon as I have the new shop settled, I'll be out for a visit. I miss Santa Barbara and all you guys. Anything new?"

"In fact, there is! We got two contracts this week—one for the Winthrope estate, and one for—listen to this—an Arab multimillionaire who's just finished building this incredible house on the water. Palace is more like it. The Bartoks recommended him to us."

"Wonderful. But can you do it yourself?"

"Most. I'm getting together a package for you with all the room descriptions and dimensions and whatever they've told me about their preferences. Actually, they've pretty much given us free rein. I'm sending some photos of the house, too, so if you could come up with some ideas . . ."

"No problem. I'll start working on them as soon as I get them. How's the new girl working out?"

"Great, so far. Listen, I was going to call you later and ask. Do you think you could ship any antique pieces out here—earlyish American and collectibles. Not the real expensive stuff. I've had quite a few people coming in looking for that sort of thing. They don't want the California look."

"What size things? Furniture?"

"Small pieces, but mostly accessory items—old kitchenware, prints, oils, old tools, anything in wicker."

"Shipping large pieces, unless I get a trailerload, would be exhorbitant, but smaller items—sure I could ship a couple of cases out, I should think, once I find some. Retail there is probably twice what it is here. Let me look around. I'll take a trip over to the mainland. I think I've found a rental out here, and I'll be needing some things shipped myself. What do we have in inventory..."

Catherine talked for another five minutes. When she hung up, she was smiling but feeling nostalgic, too. She picked up several catalogs off the floor. The front door knocker rapped loudly. Barney immediately jumped up from his place on the floor and, with a loud series of barks, bounded out of the room and down the hall.

Who would be coming to the front door at this time of day? She called to Barney to be quiet, pulled back the bolt, and opened the door a few inches.

She couldn't have been more amazed to see Treasa's boss, Tom Wilson, standing on the other side.

"Hi," he said quickly. "Sorry to bother you. I'd like to speak to your sister."

"She's not here—"

"Where *is* she?"

"Well, she went down to the boat this morning. I thought she was still there."

"I haven't seen her since four yesterday afternoon."

"You haven't? I don't understand. She had dinner here last night, never went anywhere, and was gone this morning before I got up."

"She didn't tell me she was spending last night off the boat."

"Sorry, I thought you knew. She said that since you didn't have any charterers, it was all right."

"She was supposed to take watch last night! Althea and I went into town at four. She was in the aft cabins laying in the fresh linen. Mickey thought she was still there when he left a half hour later. He even called out and told her he was leaving. What time did she get here?"

"Five or so."

"The whole boat was left wide open half the night for anyone to come on board and help themselves. She *knew* she was supposed to stay on watch. If she was going to get off, she should have told me, and we could have locked the boat up."

"But didn't she show up this morning?"

"She sure didn't. Like I said, I haven't seen her. I only found my way here because Althea remembered the address from something Treasa had told her."

"Oh, no—"

"Oh, yeah." From the color and expression on Tom's face, Catherine knew he was barely controlling his temper. "Well, this is the last time she's pulling this kind of stunt. I've been a soft touch up until now, but I'm responsible for that boat, and *I* could have lost my job. When and if she gets back here, tell her she's out of a job!"

"What's she going to do?"

"That's her problem!" He saw the dismay on Catherine's face and softened his tone. "Sorry, I don't mean to dump this in your lap. It's not your problem."

"It will be if she doesn't sail."

"Look, I have a pretty good idea how you feel, but I'm running a boat. I can't keep being a babysitter when she gets herself into messes. I made excuses for her too many times in the Med.—thought she was just a mixed up kid. Well, she is—mixed up, that is, with *no* sense of responsibility. My goodwill stretches only so far!"

"I think part of Treasa's problem right now," Catherine said almost desperately, "is that she's jealous of you . . . and Althea—" When Catherine saw Tom's expression, she wished she'd never opened her mouth.

"Look, your sister and I managed to stay friends, but we've *never* had anything going. When she first came on the boat, well . . ." he paused, seemed embarrassed. "People get lonely, and I'm human. She's attractive, and she can be nice when she wants to. But that was it. I think I made it pretty clear from the start."

"You don't have to explain." Catherine closed her eyes. "I know Treasa's history. I should have guessed."

"She's not all bad, but I sure didn't lead her down the garden path either."

"I know . . . I know."

Tom rubbed his hand over his face, obviously uncomfortable. "I wouldn't have come up here and hit you with all of this if we weren't sailing in an hour."

"An hour? Treasa said you were sailing late this afternoon. Did you change your plans?"

"No, I planned to sail by noon today all along. I told her that yesterday."

Catherine groaned. "That's that, then, isn't it?"

He cast her a sympathetic look. "Sorry. I almost wish I hadn't come up here to tell you. I've got to get back. I've already lost a half an hour." He started to turn from the door.

Catherine tried to pull herself together. Unexpectedly he reached across the space between them and lightly squeezed Catherine's arm. "I'm really sorry about this. I didn't mean to ruin your day, too."

Then he strode off quickly, almost at a jog trot down Orange Street, anxious to get back to his boat.

Catherine closed the door, threw the bolt, and then turned and climbed the stairs, continued on up the stairs to the attic, then up the last set, to the roof and widow's walk. After her last experience, she wondered at the wisdom of going up there, but now she felt a need. She stood with her hands on the low railing, looking out to the harbor until she saw what she thought was the *Cherise* leaving the Straight Wharf and heading out of the harbor.

Chapter 7

Treasa walked into the house at four, her features carefully arranged in a picture of perfect dismay. "Cath, the most terrible thing's happened. You won't believe—"

"Oh, I bet I would. The *Cherise* sailed without you."

"How did you know? I couldn't believe it myself! Tom and I had this terrible fight. I went into town to get something, and when I got back he'd already sailed."

What an actress. "Never mind the lies. Tom was here, looking for you. I know exactly what happened."

"When was he here?"

"Late this morning. He said he hadn't seen you since yesterday afternoon—that you skipped out on your watch last night, and the boat was left wide open. He came to tell you he'd had enough and that you were fired."

"Cath, you didn't believe him, did you?"

"Yes, I did."

Treasa stared at her sister's unforgiving face. "Don't you see? He was just trying to make himself look good!"

"Why waste his time? He was never going to see me again."

"He was trying to get even with me. He and Althea planned the whole thing to get me off the boat."

"Cut the bull, Trea. Tom didn't come all the way up here to feed me a pack of lies. *You're* the one who planned this. You just never figured in your plans that Tom would talk to me and blow your story."

"That's not true! Cath, listen to me—"

"You wanted to get off the boat, and you concocted this little scheme to get yourself fired. Is that why you were so sweet last night—to soften me up? You knew you were supposed to be down on the boat on watch."

"All right, believe him! See if I care. I'm only your sister, but that doesn't mean anything to you!"

"Treasa, you know perfectly well that I've tried to help you for years. The problem is that you won't help yourself."

"You haven't had the problems I've had. You haven't had all kinds of stuff thrown at you. You're sitting here in a house that I should have inherited half of, safe and secure."

"That again . . ." Catherine's voice was quiet.

"Well, it's true, isn't it? You've got everything. I haven't got a thing! You'd rather see me out on the street, starving."

"I wouldn't!"

"That's easy for you to say, but you don't want to try to help me. What am I going to do? Where am I going to go?"

"Down to the dock to look for work on another boat."

"There aren't any big boats in."

"What do you mean? The harbor's full of them."

"Not the kind that are hiring permanent crew—it's not that easy to get a job, you know."

"You should have thought of that before you got fired."

"God, Cath, have a heart!"

Catherine let out a loud, frustrated sigh, turned and banged her fist down on the kitchen counter. "All right! You can stay here for a while. I don't have any choice, do I? But, damn it, you're going to go out and get a job. I don't care if you have to wash floors."

Her eyes moist and sad, Treasa stepped forward, put her arm around Catherine's shoulder. "Don't be mad at me, Cath. Please. I can't stand it. I can't help the way I am. I'll try harder. I'll get a job—I promise."

The next morning after breakfast Catherine plopped the classified section of the newspaper down in front of Treasa and told her to start looking.

Treasa perused the want ads. "But there's nothing here I'm qualified for."

"You can wait tables. That's pretty much what you've been doing on boats."

"It's not the same. I don't like carrying trays around and kowtowing to customers."

"If it's the difference between eating and not eating, you can put up with a lot of things. There're two waitress ads right here—one at the Swan and one at Tuesday's. That should be easy. They're only looking for help for one shift."

Treasa made a face.

"Look, you haven't got any money. I'm not supporting you while you sit around here being picky and choosy. Think of the tips, if nothing else motivates you."

"Okay!" Treasa roughly pushed back her chair. "I'll go down and apply."

"You never know, you may like it."

"Yeah, yeah." With a disgruntled frown, Treasa grabbed the paper, shoved it in her bag, and headed for the door. "I'll see you later."

"Good luck."

When Treasa was gone, Catherine went out into the garden. Her head felt ready to explode. Pulling a lawn chair into the center of the back yard, she sat down, leaned back her head, and let the warm rays of May sunshine sink into her body.

She glanced around the sorely neglected lawn and garden. She could vaguely remember what the yard looked like when she was a child. The apple tree had been pruned, and the bench beneath it had been painted a fresh white. The hedge at the back of the property had been clipped to an even height. There'd been a narrow bed of flowers along the back of the house, and a wider, perennial border along the fence to the Schmidts'. As Catherine stared at the old border, she had a sudden inspiration. She'd transform that part of the yard into an English-style garden. The climate was temperate enough for a variety of flowers to survive the winter and the gardening would probably be therapeutic for her, too.

A few hardy plants had been tough enough to survive the weeds. She'd save them and fill in with new plants. Briefly closing her eyes, she visualized a summer garden in full bloom. Tall hollyhocks to the rear along the fence, then phlox and larkspurs, perhaps some dahlias, and daisies, of course, in the center. The height of the flowers should be graduated until they ended with some low border plants along the edge of the lawn. Perhaps she could fit in some rose bushes, too. She loved roses.

When she opened her eyes, she was no longer staring at a weed-choked jungle, but at a perfect English garden in spring bloom! Though not yet in flower, hollyhocks lifted their stems along the fence. In front of them were the bright blossoms of spring phlox and various shades of iris. Why hadn't she thought of iris? There were daisies and cosmos and lupin—some plants in flower, some preparing themselves for the hot summer months. A brief gust of wind swayed the stems of the hollyhocks, rustled the leaves of the other plants, sent the heads of the phlox dipping downward. The lawn was a bright green and neatly clipped. The apple tree was pruned and a mass of white blossoms. A birdbath gleamed from the center of the garden. As she watched, a sparrow dropped down to splash within it. Incredible!

A male voice called suddenly from the upstairs of the house. "Jeremy!" She nearly jumped out of her skin. A British voice, and one she'd heard before.

She swung toward the house, staring upward. The study window was open. A shadow moved beyond the glass, leaned toward the opening, and peered out. She saw his face clearly. He was staring at her—his blue eyes wide.

A large gray cat, meowing loudly, emerged from the underbrush at the far side of the yard. Catherine gaped as the cat trotted across the lawn, directly in front of her feet, then up the back steps of the house and through the partially opened kitchen door. But she'd closed the kitchen door!

Turning swiftly in her chair, she searched for Barney, who'd been dozing in the sunlight behind her. He wasn't there. Instead she saw an empty space of lawn, then the gravel and crushed shell surface of the drive, where a black carriage and horse droppings were clearly evident.

Eyes popping, she turned once more to the house. The breeze lifted the curtains of the study windows, but there was no shadow. She looked to the back door just as Lucien Blythe stepped through!

He came quickly down the steps, straight toward her. Her fingers gripped the arms of her chair as she watched him approach. The rest of her body seemed paralyzed.

When he was directly beside her chair, he dropped a hand on her shoulder. His expression was both annoyed and determined, and there was no mistaking the fact that he was a flesh and blood man. The sun reflected brightly off his white shirt, the sleeves of which were rolled to his elbows. Dark hairs curled on his tanned forearms. He squinted slightly against the sun's glare, but his eyes were snapping.

"I think it is time we got to know each other. I am Lucien Blythe—"

She nodded, then stuttered, "I know..."

"Then you have the advantage. *Who* are you? And *what* is going on here? What were you doing on my roof walk several nights past? Why did you lock yourself in my bedroom? I had to break down the door—only to find you gone! Where did you vanish to? What are you doing right now in my garden?"

"I—I live here."

"Interesting. To my knowledge only my manservant and myself are occupying this house at the moment." He glanced at the bare legs below her shorts. "You make a habit of sitting in stranger's gardens in your underclothing?"

"I'm not in my underclothes! And you're rude!"

"Our definitions obviously vary. Who are you?"

"Catherine Sternwood."

"Good, we are making progress. Now, tell me what you think you're doing by flittering in and out of my house."

"I'm not!"

"I've seen you on numerous occasions, to the point I'm beginning to wonder at my sanity. You cannot deny you were on my roof walk, since I both touched and spoke to you. Unfortunately you so startled me, my thoughts were not very clear at the time. You closely resemble someone I used to know."

"Gwen."

"Yes. You haven't answered my question. Why are you trespassing on my property?"

"This is my property! I live here. You're . . . no more than a ghost!" She rushed out the last words.

His teeth flashed as he smiled. "A ghost, am I? My dear, I believe you are somewhat confused. Perhaps you've suffered some upset recently and your mind is in a state of agitation—" He glanced down meaningfully at her skimpy clothing.

"I'm not crazy, if that's what you're inferring. But I'm going to be. Go back to wherever it is ghosts belong—"

"Come now! Look around you. That is my carriage sitting in the drive. I designed this garden myself after one at my childhood home in England."

Yes, Catherine had to admit she saw the carriage, the garden. She shuddered.

He lifted his hand from her shoulder and looked down at her with bemusement. "What can I do to—"

He was gone; just as he'd vanished in the upstairs hallway. Cath-

erine jumped out of her chair as if she'd been given an electric shock.
Her eyes swept the garden. The beautiful bed of flowers, the birdbath—all gone. In their place was the former weed-choked jungle
and unpruned apple tree. She nearly tripped over Barney, who was
now sprawled out again, sunning himself directly behind her. Her
Porsche gleamed in the drive.

Forcing back a scream, she ran for the house. The kitchen door
was firmly shut. Racing through the kitchen and hall, she climbed
the stairs to the study. What was she expecting to find—a bearded
man standing before the windows? A gray cat curled up in the chair?

Not pausing to think of her fear, she pushed open the study
door. Sunlight streamed in through the windows, brushing gilded
fingers over the bookcases, the fine old furniture, the oriental carpet. Otherwise, the room was empty. Everything was in its place,
precisely as she'd left it, with the wood dusted and glowing, the
metals shining.

Almost against her will her eyes went to the portrait over the
fireplace. She shivered to see the same masculine features there that
she'd so recently viewed in the garden.

"All right, I've had enough!" she cried. "You've succeeded in
scaring the daylights out of me. What is it you want? Do you want
me to leave? I'll have you know that this is *my* house, too!" She
glared at the portrait, not caring how absurd she looked, yelling at a
painted piece of canvas as if it were a living human being. "I'll tell
you one thing I'm going to do—and *that* is to take your portrait out
of here! Hiding it in the attic doesn't seem to work, but maybe the
guest room will do. No one ever goes in there—and I suspect you
never did either when you lived in this house!"

Pushing a chair in front of the fireplace, she climbed up and
removed the portrait, refusing to look at the male face and the lips
that seemed to be twitching in amusement. The movement of his lips
was *purely* her imagination, yet she held the painted side of the
portrait away from her as she stormed out of the study, across the
landing to the guest bedroom door at the front of the house. She was
totally unconscious of the charm of the rose-wallpapered room with
its pine furnishings and hand sewn quilts on the twin beds. She carried the portrait directly to the far side of the room, and into the small
closet, propping it face forward against the wall in the corner. She
rearranged the hangers holding laundered sets of extra drapes so that
they totally hid the portrait from view.

"There! A nice cozy spot for you. Now stay out of my life!"

Banging the closet door shut, she locked it, took the key, quickly crossed the room, stepped out into the hall, and closed and locked the bedroom door behind her. If she'd been thinking with less anger, she would have realized that locks and keys make no difference to a ghost, but her act of defiance was sufficient for the moment.

Running back downstairs, she rushed through the kitchen, grabbed her bag, then flew out the back door. Opening the gate across the driveway, she headed for her Porsche, and called to Barney, who bounded toward the car, glad for the chance for a ride. The dog leaped into the passenger seat, and Catherine backed so quickly out of the drive, the gravel spun beneath her tires.

Her thoughts churning, she wove her way randomly along the roads leading out of town. Five minutes later she realized that she was headed toward 'Sconset and had already passed the turnoff for the airport. Perhaps the peace of that quiet one-time fishing village with its quaint, ancient cottages would restore her.

Was it peace she was seeking, though? It was people she needed; people whose presence might help her forget what was going on— for the moment anyway.

She spun the car around and headed back toward town, taking a left at the road leading to Surfside. The white-frothed surf would be pounding. The Atlantic wind would ripple over the grass-frosted dunes behind the beach, gulls would be crying. In the summer the tourists would be congregated on those yellow gold sands, soaking up whatever rays of sun they could.

Barney ran with her down the path to the beginning of the beach. Walking was difficult in the sand that swirled up to her ankles with each step. She made her way to the hard, wet sand at the water's edge. Over the wet sand, she and Barney trotted. Catherine let the wave edges play about her ankles and suck the sand from beneath her toes as they receded. Barney jumped on all fours chasing after each wave, offended when the white froth covered his face. Behind them their footprints marked the wave-washed beach; some soon obliterated by the incoming surf; others left in shadowed perfection in the sunlight. A many-tailed kite flew above, twirling, dipping, swaying, drawn by a sudden updraft high into the skies, then shot down again swiftly, to recover at the last moment and shoot high again. As Catherine paused to watch, Barney snuffed his nose to the sand and started digging, coming up in a moment with an old quahog shell in his mouth. Proudly he held it in his jaws as Catherine studied the couple flying the kite. They looked so happy, but she was sure they had their own insecurities and doubts, much like those that were overpowering her at the moment. Did she appear happy to them? There was nothing in her demeanor as she stood with the wind whipping her white gold hair from her face to describe the worry in her mind, hint at the battles she was fighting against.

Catherine should have been looking forward to setting up her business in Nantucket, happily anticipating the challenge of starting a new chapter in her life. Instead she was trying to deal with a ghost. The worst was that, despite her fears, she felt incredibly drawn to him. She'd always had a special feeling about the house—its history, the furnishings, colors, and smells that reminded her of happy childhood hours—and Lucien Blythe seemed the embodiment of those feelings. History come to life. She remembered the sensations she'd had in the study, as if something was to happen there. Had he something to do with it? Had she unconsciously been waiting for this meeting? Had her thoughts of the past drawn him?

By the time she and Barney headed home at four, it was growing cool. She left the beach with the resolution that she was not going to think any further of him. She'd simply pretend he wasn't there. Whether she felt a dizzying attraction or not, she couldn't allow him to throw her life into turmoil.

Fifteen minutes later Catherine braked the Porsche to a stop in the gravel drive on Orange Street. Before she let Barney out of the car, she went back and carefully closed the gates across the drive, then she let the dog free and started to the back door, Barney running ahead of her. Halfway to the door she stopped as she saw her sister sprawled out, sunning herself in the middle of the lawn. Three empty beer cans were strewn on the grass beside her. Treasa lifted herself on her elbow.

"Oh, hi, you're home."

Catherine stared at her sister. She felt disoriented, preoccupied, and able to concentrate only on trivia. "That's my bathing suit."

Treasa glanced down at the slim bikini covering her shapely frame. "Yeah. Looks good, doesn't it?"

"Where did you get it?"

"In your dresser. Well, don't look so upset. Mine was shot and faded to hell, so I checked your room."

"What right did you have to go in my room?"

"Why not? God, we're sisters aren't we? And you never use the thing, I'll bet."

"You could have *asked* first, Treasa."

"How could I when you weren't here?"

Catherine swallowed, trying to still the bubble of anger that welled up inside her. "How did the job interviews go?"

"I've got a job—cocktail waitress."

"Wonderful!" The news snapped Catherine out of the doldrums. "When do you start?"

"Tomorrow."

"Congratulations."

"Thanks." Treasa lazily lifted the can of beer and drained it. "Oh, yeah. You got a phone call. Some realtor. He sounded real cute . . . and anxious to talk to you. Watcha got going? Business or pleasure?"

"Business. Did he leave a message?"

"Said he'd stop by here later this afternoon."

Catherine wondered how Ryan Gorham had gotten the address. "I could use a beer. I'm thirsty."

"Oh, sorry, Cath," Treasa spoke without apology. "That was the last one."

Catherine pressed her fingers to her forehead and started toward the house.

"You don't have to worry about supper," Treasa called. "I started it. Just stick it in the oven."

Catherine looked over her shoulder, amazed, but Treasa was already walking past her, swinging around the doorway of the kitchen and up the hall.

Catherine went into the living room, found an opened bottle of red wine in the back of the liquor cabinet, and pouring herself a glass, slowly paced the room. What was she going to *do?* She needed to talk to someone—but who? Not Treasa certainly.

Barney, who'd followed her into the room, suddenly gave a bark, then hurtled up off the carpet and raced toward the front door. An instant later the doorknocker sounded.

Catherine set down her glass of wine and went toward the front hall. It took her a moment to remember that Treasa had said Ryan Gorham would be stopping by. She managed to pull herself together as she threw the bolt and opened the door, shooing Barney back as she did so. Ryan Gorham's smiling, attractive face greeted her. As she saw him standing on the brick steps, she realized he was taller than she'd thought he was.

"Hi," he said pleasantly. "I left a message with your sister. Hope you don't mind my stopping by the house."

"No, fine. How'd you find it?"

"You said Orange Street. I just checked with information for the street number. I thought you'd want to hear what the owners had to say about the Centre Street property."

Catherine realized she was being rude by leaving the standing on the doorstep. "Yes, of course. Come in." She motioned him into the hall, closed the door, then walked on into the living room.

She paused in the middle of the room. Ryan was busy tending to Barney, who, now that his mistress had approved the visitor, was leaning up against Ryan's leg for pats.

Ryan looked up. "They accepted your offer. They quibbled, but I convinced them that they were crazy to refuse. You have the place if you want it."

"Great." Catherine tried to concentrate on the business at hand, but she kept seeing flashes of the garden and Lucien Blythe. "Have a seat."

He went to the couch. Catherine sat down in the wing chair opposite. "I've brought the binder papers along with me. We'll draw up a lease, of course—" He began reaching into his jacket pocket.

He handed the papers to her. She read them through. "They look all right to me. Do you have a pen?" Satisfied, she scrawled her signature. "You'll want a check. Let me get my bag." She rose and went to the kitchen, and returned in a moment with checkbook in hand. She started writing out the amount of the deposit.

"Just curious," Ryan asked mildly, "but aside from opening a new store, what are you doing here? The island jumps in summer, but off-season? You're married?"

"No."

"Not a year-round place for singles."

"I know."

"Cold winters, isolation, all of that."

"I inherited this house from my grandparents. I've spent a lot of time on Nantucket before now. It's a special place."

"So it is. That's why I keep coming back, I guess. There's something about the island—either you love it so much that it gets into your soul, or you hate it."

Catherine lifted her eyes. He was expressing so clearly what she often felt. She nodded.

"I even put up with all the tourists here in the summer—and it gets worse every year—to come back for a few months." He laughed, ran his fingers through his hair. "What am I telling you this for? You're a client. I'm supposed to be praising the wonders of the island."

"You don't have to. I'm here because I know both sides, though I've never spent a whole winter here, so I'll see about that."

"You're okay, even if you come off pretty stiff up front."

"Do I?" Catherine grinned and handed the signed papers over to him. "I'm a businesswoman."

"How'd you like to go out to dinner sometime?"

Catherine's rule of thumb was not to mix business with pleasure, but she and Ryan Gorham had just finished their business together. Why not have a social evening? She needed it, heaven knew, and he was certainly appealing.

She pushed her thick blond hair off her cheek and behind her ear as she considered. "I suppose we could . . . sure." She smiled.

"Saturday night? Or do you have other plans?" He folded the papers she'd just signed and shoved them in his pocket.

She hesitated.

"You have other plans. How about Sunday?"

"I don't have other plans. Saturday would be fine."

"I'll pick you up here at seven? Where would you like to eat?"

"Wherever you'd like."

"There are a couple of good new restaurants in town. Do you like French food?"

"Love it."

"Music?"

She nodded. "Particularly piano." She shuddered inwardly at what she'd said. Did she really want to hear piano music?

Ryan started to rise. "I'll let it be a surprise."

"Great." Yes, it would be good to get out of the house—wonderful, in fact!

As they reached the hall, Treasa came strolling up from the kitchen. Her hair was gleaming, swinging down her back, and her trim figure was shown to advantage in a Greek fisherman's shirt over silk pants that could have been bought only in Paris. She took one look at Ryan through her long-lashed eyes and smiled.

"Ryan, my sister, Treasa. Treasa, Ryan Gorham."

Treasa beamed and took Ryan's hand. "Hi. I talked to you on the phone today, didn't I? Did you guys get your business straightened out?"

"Sure did," Ryan answered, "to everyone's satisfaction."

"Good. Cath needs something to cheer her up."

"Oh?" Ryan looked both puzzled and intrigued.

"Yeah," Treasa winked. "She takes everything so serious. I keep telling her to lighten up and have some fun."

Ryan studied the girl. "What brings you to Nantucket? Are you in the design and antique business, too?"

"No. Actually I sailed in a couple of days ago. I'm what is often referred to as a yachtie. I've crewed on the big sailing yachts here and in the Caribbean and Med. for the last five years."

"Interesting."

Treasa fastened her brown eyes on Ryan. "I've got to go. See you again, I hope." Her voice was soft, welcoming.

Ryan nodded, seemingly not sure what to make of it all, yet he watched Treasa as she sauntered back toward the kitchen, before he turned again to Catherine.

"You and your sister look a lot alike."

"I know."

Quickly he studied her face, but said nothing. He reached for the door handle. "I'm looking forward to this weekend."

"So am I."

He winked, and after a brief second, he turned toward the door, pulled it open, and stepped through. "See you then."

Catherine felt strangely empty when he was gone. He'd brought life and sanity into her house. She thought about their date as she put dinner into the oven. Since Treasa had already gone out, she ate alone at the kitchen table. When she finished cleaning up, she realized how tired she was. In fact, she was exhausted, yet she put off going to bed and sat at the kitchen table for a while with her head in her hands, hoping Treasa would return home before she went up. She felt ridiculous. She couldn't stay up half the night, and the ghost didn't seem to have any qualms about showing himself whether Treasa was in the house or not. Besides, she'd promised herself she wasn't going to let him bother her anymore.

Finally she rose and, leaving the back door and kitchen lights burning for Treasa, she went through the rest of the downstairs and darkened each room. Lastly, she checked the bolt on the front door and, with Barney at her heels, climbed the stairs. With superstitious precaution, she locked both the connecting and hall doors to the study and pocketed the key, then got ready for bed. Barney, as usual, curled up on the carpet at the side of her poster bed. Still, she left a small bedroom light burning against the shadows.

Once she was beneath the covers, sleep came quickly—a deep,

dreamless sleep of exhaustion that left her in peace until the late hours of the night, when she was jarred awake by the sound of piano music. The chords and melody of a Beethoven sonata rang louder and louder in her ears. The music was rendered with expression and perfection. She jerked up into a sitting position. She wasn't dreaming—the music was real. Had Treasa come home and started playing? The comforting thought vanished as quickly as it had come. It wasn't Treasa at the piano. She didn't have to investigate to know that. Treasa didn't play classical.

"God damn it!" she thought, as she covered her ears.

Chapter 8

Catherine didn't see her sister until close to noon. She'd already been to town to run some errands, and she'd only come in the back door when Treasa stumbled into the kitchen, still in her bathrobe.

"You must have gotten in late last night."

"Yeah." Treasa went to the cupboard for a cup. "*Dark Sprite* was in. I ran into some of the crew in town, and they bought me a couple of drinks."

"You didn't play the piano when you got home, did you?" Catherine tried to make her voice seem carelessly unconcerned.

Treasa looked at her strangely. "At *that* hour? Are you crazy? Why?"

"Oh, no reason. Just wondering."

"Funny thing to wonder about. That's the second time you've thought you heard something. You starting to see things that go 'bump' in the night?" Treasa laughed.

"Of course not," Catherine said tightly.

The next few days passed free of any ghostly visitations. Catherine's hours were full as she continued preparing for her shop opening. She hit all the island antique and consignment shops, checked the paper for tag and garage sales, and investigated every one. She found a few bargains, but on the whole, everything was overpriced. In the end she'd made a daytrip to the mainland, and in some of the quieter, out-of-the-way spots—not that there were many of them left on Cape Cod—found a few affordable things. These she stored in the barn with the rest of the merchandise that would eventually go to her shop.

On Saturday morning, she left the house early to make an appear-

ance at the weekend garage sales before the "deals" were gone. She
had lunch at a small restaurant in 'Sconset, then returned to town to
do her weekly grocery shopping and get ready for that evening's
date. It was late afternoon when she finally pulled into the driveway
and carried parcels into the kitchen. Treasa was at home, rummaging
through the refrigerator. She took one of the grocery bags from Catherine's hands and helped her unpack, but when Catherine had put the
last of the food away and started out of the kitchen, Treasa stopped
her.

"You're not making anything for dinner?"

"I have a date. Help yourself to whatever you want."

"A date? Who with?"

"Ryan."

Treasa's eyes grew calculating. "Keeping secrets from me, eh?"

"I just forgot to tell you."

"Forgot to tell me? Ha. Leave it to you to snatch up the cute
ones."

"It's only a date."

"Hmph."

"How's work going?"

"Oh, great—just fine," Treasa said easily. "I have to leave in a
few minutes." She pulled open the refrigerator door and grabbed a
beer out of the six-pack Catherine had just bought. "When's your
date?"

"Not until seven. I'm going to go take a bath."

Turning away, Catherine hurried up to the bathroom, feeling incredibly pleased at the turn-about in Treasa—no grumbling, no com-
plaints about the job. As she passed the study door, she cast one
surreptitious glance in that direction, but refused to let any uneasiness about Captain Blythe sneak into her mind.

When she'd finished bathing, she put on her makeup and went
into her bedroom to dress. She selected a white skirt and blousey
turquoise top from her well-stocked wardrobe, circled her waist with
a heavy turquoise-inlaid silver belt, and slid on matching dangling
earrings. Stepping into a pair of white sandals, she inspected herself
in the tall wood-framed mirror. Satisfied, she took the brush from the
dresser top and ran it through her hair. Before leaving the bedroom,
she touched on a bit of her favorite, expensive perfume, then quickly
went downstairs.

At five of seven, Catherine went to the kitchen to wait for Ryan's knock. Treasa had already left the house. To the chorus of Barney's barking, she went up the hall to let Ryan in.

"Hey, there, fella," he laughed, as Barney wiggled in front of his mistress for first greeting. "He knows me already."

"He has a good memory. Come on in." Catherine's voice was warm though she felt a bit nervous as she motioned Ryan into the hall and shut the door behind him. He looked handsome in a light sports jacket and tie—less conservative than in his working hours.

He lifted his brows appreciatively as he saw her. "You look very nice."

"Thanks." Catherine smiled, feeling more relaxed with Ryan's friendly aura in the house. "We'll go out by the back door. This door only has a bolt lock."

"Sure. You're lucky to have a place like this. Historic houses in Nantucket, if you can find them, go for a small fortune now."

"I'm not about to give it up in a hurry. We can go out here. Be good, Barney." The dog wagged his tail and curled up on the old quilt she'd laid down in the corner of the kitchen, resigned to be left at home alone.

They headed down Orange Street under a moonlit sky. The center of town was crowded with weekend visitors, but Catherine was listening to Ryan's conversation and paid little attention. Ryan led her down Centre Street, past her new shop window.

"A couple of days," he motioned to the empty storefront, "and you'll be there."

"I've been thinking about that. I still have a lot to do. Quite frankly, I didn't think I'd get a shop so soon."

"That puts you in a bind?"

"Not at all. My West Coast office is already sending out some things. They can have fabric, wall paper, and paint samples here to me within days. All I need are a few good antiques and period furnishings to use in the room displays I'll be doing. I've been out antiquing and tag-saling."

"You've got a whole houseful up there on Orange Street."

"That furniture's not for sale, although I did find some pieces in the attic I wouldn't mind retailing. I'll need more though, and some good sources of supply."

"If it helps, I know an old couple selling a house mid-Island, out toward 'Sconset. They've been there for years. Off the beaten track.

I'm not an expert on antiques, but I liked what they had inside, and they want to sell everything."

"There are probably fifty dealers after them already."

"No, I don't think so. They haven't sold a thing yet. They want someone who isn't looking for a fast buck to come in, appreciate their stuff, and give them a fair price."

"I'll give them a fair price. I always do. In the decorating business, I can usually sell a piece for its top value. I don't have to take advantage of the seller to get a profit."

"I'll give them a call. I'm sure they'd talk to you on my recommendation. I listed the property."

She gave him a sidelong look and a teasing smile. "You think that's reason for them to trust you?"

For an instant he seemed offended, then laughed. "Okay, I know, realtors have a reputation for enhancing the facts, but I try not to misrepresent. Besides, my parents knew them. We're old friends."

"Okay, then, and thanks."

"Any time. By the way, I finished drawing up the lease and brought it along for you to look at tonight, though don't feel you have to. As I said, this is strictly a social evening."

"I'll look at it. It'll only take a few minutes."

Catherine could hardly believe when two hours had passed. The restaurant on Broad Street that Ryan had chosen was cozy; their meal had been delicious, and their conversation stimulating. Catherine hadn't laughed so much since she'd arrived on the island. She felt like herself again, rather than a confused person on the verge of a nervous breakdown. When they'd finished their coffee, Ryan suggested a place near the waterfront for after dinner drinks. She agreed, and they walked down under the stars. The town had quieted down somewhat, but not a great deal since it was only ten o'clock. They found a place on Straight Wharf, overlooking the harbor, that wasn't overly crowded. As they sipped their drinks, Ryan reached over and took her hand.

"This has been fun."

"It has."

"I'd like to do it agian."

"So would I." An hour later, he paid the check and they started walking back to Orange Street. Catherine thought about how good it was to be out in a man's company—a man who was real.

When they reached her house, Ryan walked her around to the back door.

"Would you like to come in for a coffee . . . a brandy?"

He considered. "No. Thanks. I'll give you a call. Maybe we can do something one night during the week."

"Sure. I'd love to." She studied his face under the back porch light.

He touched his fingers to her cheek, then he suddenly glanced up to the back of the house, in the direction of the study window. He frowned briefly then looked back to her, smiled and dropped a kiss on her lips—a warm and pleasant kiss that he ended almost reluctantly. Yet as he lifted his head and stepped back, Catherine sensed a distancing in him. He glanced up at the house again with a momentarily furrowed brow. Subtly he shook his head, then reached down and tweaked her chin. "I'll call you soon. We'll set a date for during the week."

"Yes. Thanks again, Ryan," she called as he let himself out the gate. She waited until he was out of sight before she went into the house, feeling suddenly confused. The evening had been great. What had happened at that last moment? It wasn't anything tangible, but she'd sensed his withdrawal as they'd been standing by the door. He'd looked up twice to the back of the house, in the vicinity of the study window. She had a horrifying thought. Did the ghost have anything to do with it? Had Ryan sensed Lucien Blythe's presence? Was the Captain capable of doing such a thing? It was more than she wanted to contemplate.

Barney rushed over with licking tongue and wagging tail.

"Oh, yes, I'm glad to see you, too," she bent down and hugged him. "You baby. Have you protected us?"

His ultralavish licks seemed to tell her he had.

"Well, I guess we ought to go up to bed." But Catherine was too wound up for sleep. She wanted to think over the evening a bit. She went into the living room instead, turning on the wall switch, then crossed over to the liquor cabinet. Kneeling down, she extracted the brandy bottle, amazed to discover that the bottle, which had been nearly full five days earlier, was just about empty. She checked the other bottles in stock, and found likewise. Treasa? But why would she be sneaking Catherine's liquor. She had a job now. Then again, she'd asked Catherine for a couple of weeks' grace in paying her board—something about buying uniforms. There was enough in the bottle for one nightcap, and Catherine found a glass and filled it. She didn't want to think about Treasa either at that moment.

Brandy in hand, she sat down on the couch and stared thought-

fully at the white birch logs in the semidarkened fireplace. She
hadn't realized just how much she'd missed her social life since
she'd come to Nantucket, and she liked Ryan. He could be a bit too
cocky and glib-tongued at times, but that was what made him a good
salesman, and right now Catherine needed to be around a gregarious,
outgoing person. She wondered if he *would* call, then chastised herself for her negativity.

She was startled by the sound of voices in the hall. Treasa must
have come home and brought company with her. Catherine turned
toward the living room door, then froze.

"Lovely evening, isn't it, Cap'n?"

"Lovely indeed."

"Something in the feel of the breeze reminds me of nights in the
West Indies, sneaking past Saint Bart's and that wasp's nest of pir-
ates—giving them the wink of our eye, so to speak."

The Captain chuckled. "Aye, though it wasn't quite so balmy
when that one devil snuck up on our stern and tried to make a cheese
of us."

"But you handled it well, Cap'n, turning to windward and letting
the *Goddess* fly when their old tub couldn't make two knots into the
wind. Surely took them about when we fired *our* cannon right into
their mainsail!"

"The good days, eh, Gladstone."

"Aye, Cap'n, and what can I get you?"

"Thank you, Gladstone, but that will be all for this evening."

"You're sure, Cap'n? I'd be glad to put together a light meal for
you. You've had a long day down there on the docks."

"Yes, but I had a late luncheon at the pub with one of the brokers.
I'm not terribly hungry. I can find something for myself in the galley
should I change my mind."

"Very good, sir. I'll go on up, then. Good night."

"Good night, Gladstone. And do make sure I am up early tomorrow. I have the rest of the cargo to oversee before the *Goddess* sails."

"Aye, sir, I shall."

Firm, steady footsteps continued toward the living room. Catherine stared toward the door.

The Captain entered the room. He wore a dark suit. Reaching one
hand to the white tie at his neck, he pulled it loose as he strode past
Catherine, totally oblivious to her presence. His determined stride
carried him across the room in the direction of a small sideboard
opposite the fireplace. The sideboard stood in the same place as her

grandparents' liquor cabinet, and on its gleaming top reposed a crystal brandy decanter and several glasses. The Captain unstopped the bottle, poured himself a liberal drink, and lifted it to his lips, swallowing quickly. Catherine could hear him sigh as he ran his fingers through his hair.

He stood for a moment in silent contemplation, then he walked over to the table where an oil lamp was now burning, picked up a long, thin paper, pushed it down the lamp chimney, and ignited its end. Protecting the flame with his hand, he went to the piano and lit each of the candles in the branched candelabra on its top. He blew out the taper and sat down on the piano bench. Throwing back his head, he flexed his shoulders for a moment, then he began to play.

The melody, soft, yet tearingly poignant, was one Catherine had never heard before. His brows dropped over his eyes in concentration, yet he looked not at the keyboard but into space, his lips subtly moving, a muscle tightening slightly under his cheekbone. The candlelight glimmered on his hair and brought out deep red highlights. His shoulders stretched and flexed with the movement of his hands and arms over the keyboard, and the cloth of his tailored jacket pulled across them, reflecting different shades in the flickering light. The music grew passionate, intense. She saw the emotion written on his features and felt the same emotion in the slow tingle coursing through her limbs.

Suddenly his hands crashed down upon the keys. The discordant sound rang off the walls of the room. "No, damn it—no!" he cried. "Why must I think of it?"

Catherine shot up from the couch, dropping her glass. His eyes swung in her direction. He froze and stared at her with the same disbelief and dread that marked her own features. In a fluid motion he pushed back the piano bench and stood, his eyes all the while glued to her. He came forward with sure movements and no trace of hesitation. In an instant he was beside her, reaching out and grasping her arm as if afraid she'd flee.

"Enough! Once and for all tell me what is going on!" He faced her squarely. His expression was uncompromising, yet deep with question. "How did you disappear from the garden as you did— leaving me feeling the madman for talking to thin air? Why are you here now intruding on my privacy? Have I stepped into a dream world where illusion exists hand in hand with reality? And do not tell me again that I am a ghost!"

Her mouth had unconsciously fallen open. She snapped it shut.

He seemed so real. She stared down at his hand, which was very definitely pressing into her flesh. "I don't *know* what's happening," she cried.

He frowned, shaking his head. "You stand here in front of me, where no one was a few minutes ago, yet, if I am not very much mistaken, within a minute or two, you will vanish without a trace. How are you accomplishing that feat?"

"I'm not the one who's vanishing." Her voice felt caught somewhere halfway up her throat.

"Oh?"

"You are."

"Since we are standing in my drawing room, amid my furniture and possessions, perhaps you would care to explain that groundless supposition?"

She tried to pull her jangled thoughts together as she would a pile of laundry off the bedroom floor. "You can't be alive," she choked out. "It's impossible! I have a deed proving you sold this house in 1846—nearly one hundred and fifty years ago!"

"You're talking total and utter nonsense. The year is 1844, as I am sure you are well aware. It should also be quite obvious to you that I am very much alive!" As if in evidence, his fingers tightened on her arm. "You shall have to come up with something better than that."

"Look, it's the truth. I live in this house. I inherited it from my grandparents, who bought it fifty years ago—almost one hundred years *after* you left. It seemed a very normal house, and I was a normal person until I moved in a month ago—"

"A month ago? Yes, it was about then that I first noticed you wandering about one of the rooms. Before I could get to you, you scooted off and slipped out of the house."

"I didn't slip out of the house."

"But you all but admit that you were trespassing on my property, and you have yet to explain to me how you are appearing and vanishing in front of my eyes."

"Stop and listen to me!" Catherine wasn't sure from where she was getting her courage, but she had to get through to him somehow. "I live here all the time. You only occasionally see me, as I only occasionally see you, when for some reason or other you decide to materialize, together with all your furnishings—just like a ghost would!"

He had the audacity to chuckle, then quickly sobered. "Not a laughing matter, is it?"

"I thought that taking your portrait out of the study would be enough to still you. How naive."

"You moved it? Why? I had the devil of a time finding it and putting it back where it belonged. I blamed Gladstone, who looked at me as if I'd gone mad. I *have* gone mad. No, what am I saying? *You* are mad!"

"You haven't listened to a word I've said."

"Oh, I've listened."

"But you don't believe me."

"Of course, I don't. If I did, I *would* be mad."

"You are Lucien Alexander Blythe, in the flesh. Correct?"

"Yes, my dear." He spoke with resigned patience, as one might to a dense pupil.

"Did you possess a sea chest with your initials on the front?"

"Handcrafted before my first voyage. A fine piece. It sits in my study, but I fail to understand the purpose of your questions."

She prodded on. "Did you store both that chest and your portrait in an attic cupboard?"

"Definitely not. They are both too valuable to me."

"But that's where I found them, covered with years of dust. Someone put them in that closet. If not you, then someone who lived in this house after you."

He glared, but she'd given him a jolt. "Do not add further insult by endeavoring to foretell my future. I will admit something uncommon is going on—"

"It certainly is. Either you're incredibly long-lived, or you're a ghost."

"When I first saw you, I thought *you* were a ghost—Gwen's ghost."

Catherine felt a strange tremor about her knees as he lifted a hand and ran his fingertips along the curve of her chin. His expression had abruptly changed, softened. "You are so like Gwen in appearance, it amazes me . . . your eyes, your hair, the shape of your face."

She didn't know what to say, but doubted she could have gotten the words past her lips in any case.

"At least I can be consoled by the fact that Gwen is not haunting me."

"Neither am I."

"So you claim to come from the future—rather farfetched."

"It's the truth."

"I suppose there is evidence along those lines—your clothing, or frequent lack of it, for instance, and your lazy manner of speech. It is just so incredible—so absurd! I credit myself with having an open mind, but this stretches it a bit."

"Don't you think I feel the same way, being terrorized?"

"Am I terrorizing you?" His eyes danced with amusement. "To my knowledge, I've not had the pleasure of terrorizing anyone before. You've given me several shaky moments as well, you realize."

She nodded. Actually, she hadn't considered his reactions at all. She hadn't thought about ghosts feeling fear.

His expression had taken on a more serious cast. His brows dipped together as he studied her. That intent, concentrated stare chilled her, because it was so human. "Perhaps I believe you. Is it possible that we are both living in this house in different periods of time?" he asked.

Part of her mind wanted to believe that. The sane side of her mind told her it couldn't be. "No. It's impossible! You *have* to be a ghost —or this is a very vivid dream."

"Despite my earlier allusion to that possibility, this is not a dream. I certainly am very much awake at the moment, *and* alive. You would appear to be as well." He glanced down at his hand on her arm, then back to her face. "I am not a ghost, my dear lady, any more than you are. What can I do to prove that to you."

Unexpectedly he reached behind her and plucked something off the side table near the chair. "I don't know why Gladstone insists on putting this out. His sentimentality is obviously greater than mine. But in the event you caper off again—which no doubt you shall— here is a little gift." He pressed a small oval frame into her palm. "A miniature of myself as a child. You appear to dislike my portrait. Perhaps you will like this better."

Catherine stared down at a tiny painted face of a young boy in a frock coat.

"Adorable, wasn't I?" The Captain grinned.

She lifted her eyes to his. Her voice was hushed. "This can't be happening. We live a hundred and fifty years apart from each other!"

The laughter went out of his eyes, though they remained riveted on her face. His voice grew softer, more intimate. "You make me think of other ways of proving my mortality." Then he was leaning over her, drawing her close and kissing her firmly on the mouth.

Had she had time to react, she probably would have fainted in shock, but he spun away.

"My apologies. That was rash of me . . . and foolish." He turned back to look at her, but even as he spoke, Catherine knew the illusion was slipping away once again. So did he. Dismay, and a touch of anger showed in his face. Then Catherine was staring at an empty room—her own living room. Unconsciously she raised her hand to her lips. The heat of his kiss still burned. The imprint of his fingers showed markedly on her arm. She opened her palm and saw the young face of Lucien Blythe gazing up at her.

She stumbled from the room and up the stairs. She had no idea where she was going. Never before in her life had she felt such a reaction to a man's kiss . . . but he *was* a remnant from the past, wasn't he? She pushed open the study door and turned on the light. His portrait was back over the mantel, just as he'd said. She stared at it. How good a likeness of him it was.

Numbly she walked on into her bedroom. She gripped the bedpost and leaned her forehead against the carved wood. Barney started barking downstairs. It took a moment for the sound to register in Catherine's mind. She heard Treasa's voice below, singing the words of some popular song.

What was she going to do about a ghost who had suddenly become a living, breathing person?

Chapter 9

A small fire was burning on the fireplace grate to take the chill out of the spring air. Lucien Blythe walked first to the windows, but the sun had set an hour before. He could see little but the twinkling lights of the town below. He lit one of the oil lamps and settled down in the leather armchair that he'd positioned at a comfortable angle to the fireplace. Leaning back, he sighed. The day had been full, and he'd spent too much of it thinking about the incident of the previous evening. The whole thing left him shaken. He'd worn himself out with his puzzling. After a light meal, which he knew Gladstone was in the process of preparing, he'd go to an early bed. In the interim he sipped his brandy and absently looked about the familiar belongings in his study, channeling his thoughts to something other than the mysterious woman in his house.

The bookcases to either side of the fireplace were filled, not only with books, but with the treasures he'd collected from around the world: the Chinese jars and jade carvings, scrimshaw and ivory, exotic shells. On the walls hung his two Indian tapestries and the African headress that had been a gift from a chief with whom he'd enjoyed a strange camaraderie—the two of them speaking in hand signals but communicating with remarkable rapport. The sea chest that he had had specially made before his first voyage on the *Goddess*, and which had traveled around the world with him, stood beside the desk. His brass telescope rested on the table between the windows for easy access, as did his brass sextant, though he had no practical use for that tool any longer.

And the portrait over the fireplace that seemed somehow involved with all that was happening. He remembered the day the young artist had presented him with the portrait six years before. He'd picked up Colin Renley in Calcutta, where the young man had come running to him across the docks. The day had been unbearably hot and humid, the sun hanging overhead in the sky like a burning, orange globe. Lucien's shirt had stuck to him in damp patches as he'd seen to the loading of the last cargo of hemp.

"Please, sir," the young man had cried. "You have a ship sailing, I understand. You *are* Captain Blythe?"

"I am."

"Colin Renley, sir, at your service. I am in dire straits, and I understand you are an Englishman, sailing for British ports."

"That is so, but I am a cargo merchant."

"Might I ask, sir, under extraordinary circumstances, that you allow me passage on your vessel? I will gladly work for my portage, but I must leave Calcutta!"

Lucien's brows rose. "Oh?"

"Nothing outside the law, please understand, but my funds have run out. With the monsoon season approaching, you are the last vessel to sail, and I cannot hold out here any longer."

"I am not in the habit of taking on passengers."

"Would you not make this one exception—I am *truly* desperate, Captain!"

"Just what, may I ask, brought you to Calcutta in the first place?" Though Lucien was sympathetic to the entreaty in the wide blue eyes, he knew the young man needed a lesson well taught.

"The art, sir, and the scenery and culture and ruins so different from that of the Western world. You see, I am a painter—"

"A painter?"

"And quite good, if saying so does not make me seem a braggart. I came here to paint and study. I have canvases to prove it, if you wish to see." Colin motioned down the dockside to where a young Indian boy was standing beside a pile of bags. "A friend of mine was leaving to join the East India Company, and I shared his cabin. We traveled together until Delhi, where he got an assignment. We could no longer share board together, and I had so little money left. Paintings do not sell well here. I worked my way back to Calcutta, but I have no funds left at all."

"What's your destination?"

"Any port in England. I shall walk back to Yorkshire if necessary."

"Can you climb the rigging, swab a deck?"

"Well, I have never tried, but I am sure I can learn. I was used to doing physical things on my father's farm. I was a disappointment to him when I left to become an artist."

Lucien seemed to consider for a moment. "All right. But you shall work. Make no mistake about it. I have no room for a lazy passenger."

"Anything you say, Captain!"

"Get your bags."

Colin scampered back along the dock. Lucien followed. He saw Colin digging in his pockets and doubted the lad had enough to pay the child watching his bags. Lucien dipped into his own pocket and handed over a few coins, then grabbed up two of the bags. "You take the trunk, my new shipmate. A lesson in the labors that are to come."

The voyage went pleasantly. Lucien and Colin got on well, and the lad certainly earned his passage. He was tanned and healthy when, a few days out from England, he came knocking on Lucien's cabin door, carrying a long object under one arm.

"This is a surprise." Lucien swung his legs off his bunk. "I'd have thought you'd be in your bunk by now."

"I have something for you, Captain."

"Oh?"

"Yes, Captain. It is the only way I have of thanking you."

"No thanks were ever needed. You've worked for your passage."

"Just the same, I wanted to do this for you." Self-consciously Colin unwrapped the bundle under his arm and leaned it against the cabin wall.

Lucien stared across to a portrait in oils of himself. The overhanging oil lamp lit the painting so that it seemed to come to life. He might have been looking in a mirror—the eyes, the planes of his face, the beard, and the lips turning in a grin. "Heavens, it is excellent!"

"Thank you, sir."

"Where did you ever find the time?"

"Have you not seen me with my pad on deck?"

"Aye," Lucien laughed, "and thought you were sketching the gulls. Well, I shall certainly treasure this, Colin. It shall have a special place among my belongings. I foresee a successful future for you."

Had all of that been six years ago?

There was a knock on the door. Lucien started up from his musings. "Come in."

"Your dinner, Cap'n." Gladstone entered with a tray. "Not very fancy, I'm afraid."

"I require nothing fancy this evening. Thank you. Just set it on the table there. Have you eaten?"

"No, sir, not yet."

"Then bring your dinner up here and join me. I could do with some company."

"Very kind of you, Cap'n. I will."

When Gladstone returned a few minutes later with his own tray, he and Lucien pulled straight chairs over to the table. Lucien poured them each a glass of wine.

"So, Gladstone, how did your day go?"

"Fair to middlin'. I've started sorting out the cellar. Some of the stocks were running low, so I went into town to order in new . . . spent a few minutes jawing with the chaps down at the docks."

"Have you ever missed living aboard ship?" Lucien cocked a brow in the servant's direction.

"Aye, a bit, Cap'n. But it was time for a change. Setting up here was a good idea." Gladstone paused, then added decisively, "A good move for you, sir, after England."

"Mmm, I suppose you are right. I thought tomorrow I would take a ride across the island. With the *Goddess* gone, I need a change of scene."

Gladstone studied him perceptively. "Something troubling you, Cap'n?"

Lucien briskly shook his head. "No . . . nothing I wish to speak about in any case."

Jeremy came across the room to rub his head against Lucien's boot, then jumped up into his lap.

Gladstone made a disapproving noise. "Don't know how you can put up with that animal climbing all over you."

"Why, Gladstone, he's a charming gentleman, and you like him well enough yourself, though you won't admit it."

"Aye, I suppose I do. Remember the first day we were here, and he came beggaring? He knew a good thing when he saw it."

Lucien leaned back in his chair, patted Jeremy's head, and chuckled. He remembered well. He'd been in the galley with Gladstone, warming his hands by the woodstove that Gladstone, after much cursing, had managed to light.

"What we need is a cat, Gladstone," he'd said, "to curl up in front of this stove. I never kept a pet on board."

"Funny you mentioning it, Cap'n, but a skinny-looking stray kept coming up to the back door this afternoon while I was setting up the galley. Persistent bugger. I finally had to give him my boot."

"You don't say. Perhaps when he saw the activity around the house, he thought he would move in as well. I wonder if he's still about."

"Now I don't know about that animal, sir. Had the looks of a scrabbling Tom to me."

"Precisely what we need, my friend—another gentleman resident." Lucien had gone to the rear door with lamp in hand, opened it and looked out to the stoop. His action was met by a loud "Meowr."

"Ah, ha. Your boot doesn't seem to have worked, Gladstone. Yes, come in, my fine man." He'd held the door as a boney, yet arrogant, steel gray Tom strode into the kitchen, head and tail high, and brushed the side of his head against Lucien's trouser leg in thanks. He'd then proceeded immediately to the stove, where he paced back and forth, luxuriating in the warmth.

Gladstone had stood frowning, not ready to give approval, but Lucien was grinning. "I believe I quite like this chap. Let's have a bit of milk for him and the scraps from our dinner."

"Are you sure, sir? Feed these strays once and you're never rid of 'em."

"I don't know that I want to be rid of him, aside from which, I rather like being adopted."

Obviously against his better judgment, Gladstone had gone to the larder and poured some milk into a saucer. Lucien was already piling the dinner scraps into another, which he set down beside the cat. A loud and immediate purr issued from the gray animal as he attacked the food as though he hadn't eaten in a week.

Lucien had risen and watched the cat with satisfaction. "We shall have you fit as a fiddle in no time. The poor fellow was half-starved, Gladstone."

"Aye, Cap'n," the servant grumbled.

"And think of all the rats and mice you won't be needing to poison. What shall we call you, chap?" he spoke to the cat, considering a moment.

"M'sister had a Tom just the color of him," Gladstone put in. "Used to call him Jeremy, though I always thought it a high-sounding name for an animal."

"Jeremy. Yes, I like that. Jeremy it shall be. Well, eat up fellow."

Lucien patted the cat again and smiled at the memory. "And he didn't destroy the furniture either, as you feared."

"No, Cap'n. I suppose he's behaved himself."

The two men chatted a while longer, then Lucien went down with Gladstone, carrying his own tray and collecting a bucket of hot water to take upstairs for washing.

Yet before going to bed, Lucien was unable to ignore the impulse to go up to the roof. He climbed the steep staircase and stepped out on the walk, breathing deeply of the clean night air. He went to the rail and stared out to sea. Only a few stars spattered the sky.

Though his sense of grief and loss had never left, it had subsided since he'd come to Nantucket. He was no longer caught unawares, looking across a room at a party or through a crowd on the street, by features, or bright blond hair, or smiling lips reminding him of Gwen. He'd grown accustomed to the truth that she was gone and he would never see her again. Just as he'd ceased torturing himself with futile daydreams of what it would have been like to have Gwen beside him in the house, as his wife.

His life was as full as he could expect it to be. His merchant fleet was thriving, his captains were honest, his cargoes remunerative. The hours of his days were busy, as they had been for the past four years since he'd come to Nantucket.

Why now—four years after the fact—was he seeing this strange woman in his house? Why did he have this feeling of her being near him, living under the self-same roof as him even when she wasn't visible? Gladstone had seen nothing unusual, and after his first questions to the servant, Lucien had been too embarrassed to ask again.

He'd been happy in the house—he *was* happy in the house—as close to a state of happiness as he ever expected to be. It was home to him now. He'd found a small nitch of contented space that was his own and which he guarded jealously. Several times he'd been tempted to sail again; head out across the sea that would always be in his blood, but he knew such a trip would bring him into English ports, and he hadn't been ready to face that. He'd received regular letters from his brother and sister-in-law and his niece and nephew, who begged him to come home. They missed him, the children especially. He missed them all, too, yet he couldn't go back. Maybe someday, but not yet. His life on Nantucket was fulfilling enough.

Or *had* been until she started appearing.

He must put it from his mind, if possible; bury himself in his work—or, on the contrary, perhaps get out more. With determination he left the widow's walk and went down to bed.

In the morning he dressed for riding. But he didn't feel altogether alert as he pulled on his riding boots. Those damned dreams again. She or them would be his undoing. He stomped downstairs and, after a quick breakfast, went out to the barn. Lovely Sarter, whom he'd purchased through a dealer on the island, had proved his worth. He easily shifted between saddle and harness, and that day Lucien intended to ride.

Pierce was polishing the carriage as Lucien entered the barn, and Lucien motioned for him to continue what he was doing. "I will tack up myself, Pierce." He lifted the saddle and bridle off the rack and went to Sarter's box, tacked up the horse within minutes, and led him outside.

Quickly mounting the prancing beast, he trotted Sarter down the short drive, then out of town. The horse moved eagerly beneath him, glad for the exercise, but Lucien kept his speed in check until he was off the more heavily trafficked Nantucket lanes. He heeled Sarter into a canter, and they continued steadily at the pace, down the winding tracks across the moors, skirting farmers' fields and sheep pastures, past copses of stunted island pine and uncultivated hummocks dressed in wild rose. Lucien had no direction in mind, and the horse certainly couldn't have cared as long as he was running.

At the ocean near Quidnet, Lucien urged Sarter down onto the wide sandy beach. With the Atlantic breakers on the left, they galloped across the wet, packed sand above the water's edge. He tried to clear his thoughts of all but the feeling of release, of the surging muscles and smooth rhythm of the horse between his legs, of the steady muffled drum of the horse's hooves drowning out his doubts and fears. His solitary escape must finally be unsettling his mind— why else did this woman, when she was with him, seem as alive as himself? Was she alive? Were they actually crossing times? He could find no other logical explanation for what was happening. How could she possibly think *him* a ghost? And her mention of having deeds to this house! What an imagination she had. He could not understand his own motivation in kissing her on their last meeting. Such a crass and foolish thing to do. He'd spun away from her feeling as though he had indeed held Gwen in his arms once more.

Sarter's pace slowed only when they reached the beach below 'Sconset. Lucien glanced up the sandy cliffs to the tiny village of fishermen's cottages and reined Sarter across the deeper, dry sand

and up the track leading to the village. They came out near the small
village square, the quaint cottages hunched like tiny brown wooden
gnomes all around it and the neighboring lanes. Without pause he
headed Sarter back to town at a mile-eating canter. They followed the
'Sconset Road, passing four of its milestones, before Lucien pulled
Sarter back into a trot; and, as they entered the streets outside of
town, into a walk to cool the animal off.

The ride had helped ease his frustration immeasurably. Lucien put
his visions from his mind, and for several days they stayed away.
The *Auriel* was in, and his time was occupied down at the docks and
in various brokers' offices. The evening before the *Auriel* sailed, he
returned to the house very late, entering by the back door. Gladstone
was seated at the galley table with a checkerboard in front of him.
Jeremy was seated atop the table on the opposite side of the board.

The Captain paused and looked back and forth between them.
"Checkers with a cat, Gladstone?"

The servant shrugged sleepishly. "Well, actually, Cap'n, I play
both sides. Just gives me a feeling of having a partner with Jeremy
sitting there. He watches every move, you know . . . sometimes puts
out his paw and moves the pieces himself."

"The cat has more talents than I had imagined." Lucien chuckled
and started out of the kitchen. He went on into the parlor, where one
oil lamp was burning. He strode directly across the room toward the
piano and took a seat on the bench. He was glad he'd purchased the
instrument on impulse four years before in New York. He played
often now, his old skill having returned after not too many torturous
sessions. He wasn't about to be put off by the fact that the last time
he had sat on the bench, his female visitor had suddenly appeared
before his eyes.

Resting his fingers on the keys, he considered, then began playing. The music was soothing to him, but it brought memories, too.
Memories of nights when he had played for Gwen at Oak Park. His
parents had still been alive, and they would sit to the far side of the
music room, while Gwen stood beside him at the piano, gazing down
with love in her eyes. The melody he was playing had been one of
their songs.

It was too much. He stopped and quickly rose from the piano. He
took the lamp in hand and hurried upstairs. He went to his study,
pulled a well-known book from the shelf, opened it before him on the
desk, and began reading. It was a love sonnet. Gwen's favorite.
Tears came to his eyes. Was he mad to be reading the sonnet—delib-

erately torturing himself? He flipped the book over on the desk and left the room for his bedroom.

What had possessed him that his fingers had strayed to the melody that was his and Gwen's; that he'd pulled out the book of sonnets? He breathed deeply, trying to salve the old wounds that he'd just opened afresh. Lighting a candle on the mantel, he began to undress, hanging his jacket in the wardrobe and dropping his other garments over the arm of the chair. He reached up for the candle and began to turn toward the bed. He halted.

Her head rested on his pillow; her pale golden hair spread out like a halo surrounding it. Her eyes were closed, and one arm rested above the bedcovers. He blinked his eyes, but the vision remained. Slowly he walked toward the bed. She didn't move. Her breaths were soft and regular. A golden dog snored on the bedside rug. Lucien carefully stepped around him, staring down at the woman in his bed. He wasn't dreaming. She was there. He reached down and lightly touched her bare shoulder. She stirred slightly in her sleep. He knew at that moment that he could crawl under the bedcovers beside her. The temptation to do so was undeniable. He was remembering her lips and how they had felt beneath his own. How would the soft curves of her body feel within his arms? Like Gwen's? It had been too long since he'd slept close beside a woman.

He spun away with such rapidity he nearly extinguished the candle in his hand. He went to the window and sought for control. "Damn her," he muttered under his breath. "Damn this mad apparition for destroying my peace!"

Chapter 10

Physically spent, Catherine put away her painting materials at close to eight and locked the shop door. She hadn't eaten, but she felt no appetite. Neither did she want to go back to the house alone. She doubted Treasa would be home; she'd be working. Catherine started walking. She felt unsettled. She considered going to Marjorie's. She wanted to talk to someone about what was happening to her, yet how did one sanely go about describing a living ghost?

After wandering for an hour, she found herself at the open-air wharf-side bar where she and Ryan had had a drink. He'd never called her back, and that had disappointed her, and confused her as well. She paused in the entrance to the crowded bar, debating whether to have a drink on an empty stomach. Maybe a cup of coffee. What else was she going to do with her evening?

She started in, looking for an empty table. Turning toward the semicircular bar beyond the tables, she stopped in her tracks. At a table at the end of the bar, she saw her sister . . . and Ryan. They were too engrossed in their conversation to have noticed her, or anyone else in the bar. Treasa was laughing, tilting her blond head toward Ryan, whose eyes never left her face. Their hands were clasped over the tabletop. Treasa whispered something in Ryan's ear. He leaned closer and they kissed.

Her face paling, Catherine fled before either of them could see her. She headed up the wharf. When had Treasa and Ryan gotten together? Treasa was capable of anything, but she'd expected more of Ryan. Had he tried to call her and had Treasa intercepted the call? Had he come by the house to deliver the keys and lease for the shop?

She'd reached the far end of Union Street before her steps

slowed. She collapsed against the trunk of an old tree whose roots were lifting the brick sidewalk. Couldn't he have called her, like a gentleman, and explained? Couldn't Treasa have warned her?

She heard voices. A group of people were coming up the sidewalk toward her. Hastily she stepped from under the tree and hurried away, into the next narrow lane leading up to Orange Street.

Barney was overjoyed as she unlocked the door and entered the kitchen. The poor dog. She'd left him alone all day. He hadn't been fed yet either. She filled his dish with dry dog food from the sack in the pantry, and as he gobbled it down, glancing over his shoulder every few bites to make sure she didn't leave again, she sat down at the table and propped her chin on her clasped hands.

She'd had only one date with Ryan. She wasn't in love with him certainly. It was the principle.

Eventually she went upstairs, bathed, and changed into her nightgown. She was walking toward the bed when the room suddenly went dark. The overhead bulb must have blown. Disoriented, she stopped in her tracks and waited for her eyes to adjust to the darkness. As she did, she noticed a slant of light coming from the partially opened study door, but she knew for certain she'd turned the light off in that room. Perhaps Treasa was back, searching for another stash of booze. Catherine was about to investigate, when the light in the study was extinguished. The door from the study to the hall opened and closed. Footsteps sounded firmly in the uncarpeted hallway, then descended the stairs.

Groping her way to the nightstand, she reached out for the bedside lamp. The lamp wasn't there. Her hand connected instead with a candlestick and a box of matches. Fumbling in the dark, she struck a match, lit the candle. The Captain's furnishings surrounded her. His white shirt and a jacket were flung over a chair arm. A pair of riding boots stood on the floor by a tall wardrobe. On the dresser top were a bowl and pitcher, a man's brush set, cuff links, and a handful of strange-looking coins. The bedcovers were a deep green.

As she stared about in amazement, she heard his footsteps coming back up the stairs. He was coming toward the bedroom door. The door was opening. He stepped into the room, candle in hand. He saw her and his jaw fell. His gaze swept over her from head to foot, lingering on her sheer nightgown.

He smiled, slowly. "My, what a pleasant surprise."

She could feel her heart pounding. "I . . . I—"

There was a barely perceptible flash as he vanished, and Catherine was left standing in the center of her room, the overhead light now burning brightly. It took her several moments to collect herself. She realized she was shaking. Numbly she turned, walked to the bed, and climbed between the sheets, afraid to acknowledge even to herself that she wished he'd stayed longer.

Not surprisingly, she didn't sleep well and woke feeling irritable and cross. When she discovered Treasa had never come home the previous evening, her mood quickly progressed to anger. She saw Marjorie over the fence as she left the house and went over for a cup of coffee.

"You look terrible," the older woman worried as she let Catherine into her homey kitchen. "What's wrong?"

"I didn't sleep very well last night."

"You've been doing too much, with your shop opening and all."

Catherine nodded, feeling her physical and emotional exhaustion. "Between my sister and this ghost, I'm ready to scream or have a nervous breakdown—or both!"

"Ghost?" Marjorie's eyes widened.

"Forget I said that! It's just my nerves getting to me. Last night I saw my sister out with a guy I'd been dating. I'm not sleeping soundly—too much on my mind." Catherine let out a sigh. "I didn't mean to come over and dump on you."

Marjorie pushed her glasses up her nose and quickly sat down beside Catherine. "That's perfectly all right. I don't mind in the least. Sit back and relax. The state you're in, every problem will seem blown out of proportion. Better?"

Catherine nodded.

"If your sister is creating such havoc in your life, you should really throw her out."

"She's actually been behaving herself. She got a job. It's just last night. Not that Ryan and I were serious . . . I was just so shocked to walk in to Harborside and see them together."

"Mmmm," Marjorie frowned. "Perhaps that says something about this young man's character. You're better off without him."

"Oh, yes. I'll recover."

Marjorie rested her arms on the kitchen table. "Now what's this about a ghost?"

"Nothing!" Catherine swallowed hard and cursed herself for the slip. "I've just been having some strange dreams." If only she dared confess the truth to Marjorie, but she didn't.

"Just dreams?" Marjorie quizzed.

"Yes." Catherine endeavored to keep her voice calm.

"I was just wondering about that story I told you. Perhaps it's been bothering you more than you think . . . putting ideas in your mind?"

"No, Marjorie. Really, I'm sure I'll be fine once the shop opens."

Before going to town, Catherine went back to the house to collect a box of fabric samples from her bedroom. As she crossed the upstairs hall, she noticed that Treasa's bedroom door was closed, meaning Treasa was within. Without hesitation, Catherine walked over, knocked lightly, and pushed open the door. Treasa turned lazily as Catherine entered. She held a glass of scotch in her hand. The opened bottle sat on the dresser.

"Well, hi, Cath. Thought you'd gone to your shop."

"Treasa, what are you doing drinking at this hour? It's not even eleven o'clock!"

"Just a drink."

"And where'd you get that bottle—not out of my stock by chance?"

"I'm short of cash. You can spare it."

"How can you be that short? You've got a job now."

Treasa flicked a careless hand.

Catherine went over and took the scotch bottle. "You've had enough."

"Get off my case. What I do in my own room is my business."

"What you do in my house is *my* business."

"Oh, *your* house, is it?"

"Yes, and I don't want you sneaking my liquor!"

"I've been talking to some people—" Treasa smiled. "Your realtor friend for one."

"Yeah, I saw the two of you last night. Thanks for warning me. Don't you even have that much decency?"

Lazily Treasa stepped forward. "They think I can contest the will and get what's due me—my half of this house, in other words. I'm sure a lawyer would agree."

Catherine felt her frazzled nerves stretch to the breaking point. "Is *that* what you and Ryan were planning and giggling about last night? You got your fair share! Your trust fund was equal to the value of this house when the estate was settled."

"And what good is that when I can't touch anything but the income?"

"You can when you're thirty-five, and it's nobody's fault but your own. You've got a job now. Between that and the trust income, you can live—" Things suddenly started falling in place in Catherine's mind—her dwindling liquor supply, no board paid yet, Treasa out with Ryan at an hour when she should have been working. A hot shock of anger coursed through her. She swung to her sister.

"You haven't been working, have you? You don't have a job. You never did. That's why you're so anxious to get half of this house. You've been lying to me all this time!"

Treasa gazed back, not the least dismayed. "Nobody wanted to hire me. Could I help it? I had to get you off my back somehow."

"Bull! You're nothing but a cheat, and a drunk!"

"I'm sick of hearing it. I'm sick of people standing in judgment of my life. It's mine, and I'll do what I want."

Catherine stepped over, wrenched the glass of scotch out of Treasa's hand, and threw the contents in her face. "You little bitch!"

Treasa gasped and wiped the scotch from her eyes. "What the hell's the matter with you?"

"I've had it—that's what's the matter! I'm sick of you lying to me, and I'm sick of you taking advantage of me! From now on there are some new rules in the house. You're coming down to the shop with me to work!"

"Like heck I am. I'm taking a nap. I can hardly keep my eyes open."

"Work with them closed, but you're coming! And you'll be working with me every day."

Treasa stared at her sister with narrowed eyes. "So, you find out I've been dating Ryan, and now you want a little revenge? Could he help it that you were never around when he called, and I was?"

"You never told me he called!"

Treasa gave an elegant shrug. "Would you have cared? You didn't seem very impressed after your date with him."

"Let me decide what messages I care about getting!"

"Too late now anyway. You know what they say—all's fair in love and war."

Catherine clenched her teeth. "Get your bag. Let's go."

Treasa only smiled.

"You can threaten me with contesting the will, Treasa, but as far as the law is concerned, *I* own this house, and *I* will decide who stays in it and who does not. You come down to the shop and work, or I'm throwing you out!"

"You wouldn't throw me out out. I'm your sister, and I haven't got any other place to go." Treasa's voice was still airy, but her confidence was deflating.

"That argument may have worked in the past, kiddo, but it won't work now. I *would* throw you out. In fact, I'd love to! And if you step out of line *once* or treat me with anything less than respect— you're out! Your bags will be on the street, and *nothing* will persuade me to let you stay! Clear? Now, get going!"

Angrily, knowing she'd been outmaneuvered, Treasa grabbed her bag off the bed and flung from the room. Scotch bottle in hand, Catherine stormed after her.

Chapter 11

At lunchtime Catherine paid a visit to her grandparents' attorney. She was lucky to catch John Fletcher in; luckier still that he had a few free minutes to talk to her.

He shook her hand pleasantly as he let her into his office. "How's everything going up at the house?"

"That's what I came to talk to you about, John. I need your advice." She took a seat in the chair beside his desk. "My sister's turned up on the island." Quickly she explained all that had occurred since Treasa's arrival. "She's not happy with the way the estate was settled. She wants half the house and warned me that she's going to contest the will."

The lawyer rubbed a hand over his mouth. "Not good. Has she seen an attorney?"

"I'm not sure. She said something about my hearing from her lawyer, but she didn't say who it was. I just want to know where I stand legally."

"She can contest the will if she likes, but my feeling is that the best she could get is an equal fifty–fifty split of everything—meaning you'd get half of her trust fund. I don't see that she would have anything to gain, and any reputable counsel she gets would give her the same advice. It wouldn't be worth the expense." He paused. "It's not as though your grandparents left her out. She got what at the time was an equal share of their assets. Of course, real estate is escalating rapidly, but the trust monies are well invested."

"She can't touch the capital until she's thirty-five. I think that's the way she's looking at it right now. If she got half the house instead, she could force me to buy her out or sell the house altogether, giving her the cold cash."

He clasped his hands on the desk top. "Frankly, I don't think you should worry about it, Catherine. Very possibly she's throwing out this threat simply to test you. If she *should* initiate any action, refer her attorney to me. And don't discuss this with her at all. If she brings the subject up, tell her to see me as well."

"What should I do about her staying in the house? Until today when she started working at my shop with me, she hasn't been paying her way. Could I make her leave?"

"It's your house. You can do as you like."

Catherine sighed, but she was relieved, too. "Thanks a lot, John."

"Anytime."

Treasa said nothing further in the next few days about contesting the will, and Catherine received no communication from any attorney. She began to think John was right, and Treasa had only been testing the waters. Neither had Catherine seen anything of Captain Blythe. The fact that she was actually feeling a pang of disappointment both amazed and frightened her. She should be putting their strange encounters as far from her thoughts as possible. Yet every time her gaze fell on the young face in the miniature he'd given her, she remembered his kiss, and the mere memory of it brought a flush of color to her cheeks. It couldn't have been a dream or hallucination, regardless of the fact that she could find no logical explanation. Moreover, she couldn't deny that her curiosity about Lucien Blythe, the man, was growing.

As they finished getting the shop ready, Treasa actually showed a small trace of enthusiasm—enthusiasm she no doubt would have hidden had she been aware of it. They set up the displays in each of the windows, using the antiques and collectibles Catherine had purchased on the island, as well as new and unusual pieces she'd had shipped out from the West Coast. They filled the shelves with eye-catching accessory items, and rolled two low racks of upholstery and drapery swatches into a well-lighted back corner of the room so that customers could browse through them at their leisure. On the walls they hung a variety of paintings and prints.

As Catherine was about to hang a largish abstract oil on the wall along the back of the shop, Treasa called over to her. "That's not the best place for that painting. You should put it with the display in the left window."

Catherine hesitated, considered the muted pastels of the painting. "I don't know. The colors in the window are all bright."

"Yeah. That's what I mean. It's a good contrast. It's not like they clash or anything. Antiques mixed with modern. Isn't that what you're trying to do?"

In a moment Catherine nodded. "You're right, I think." She hoisted the painting, carried it to the window. "Give me a hand. Hold it here while I go outside and look." In a moment she came back, nodding her head. "Great. It's just what the window needs. It really catches your eye now. We'll need to string a wire from the ceiling." She glanced over to Treasa. "Good idea. You've got a lot of good ideas. Why don't you set up that corner display I was having trouble with?"

Treasa cocked her head and flicked her shoulders. "Sure." But she was obviously pleased with Catherine's compliment.

On the fifteenth of June Classics II opened, just in time for the season. Catherine had flooded the weekly newspaper that went out to the tourists, as well as placing a classy but eye-drawing ad in the *Inquirer and Mirror*. Street traffic alone would bring people into the shop. Her location was prime. Of course, every time she thought of the location, she was reminded of Ryan and felt a small ball of disgust in her stomach. Then again, the idea of contesting the will probably had nothing to do with him initially. She wondered if he and Treasa were still seeing each other.

On opening day, she served wine and elegant canapes she'd had a local caterer make up. She was well pleased at the crowd that came and went from the shop, several making purchases, many asking questions about her personal interior design work. Even Treasa was smiling, enjoying herself and being courteous to the customers at the same time.

"Hey, this isn't bad, sis," she said during a break in the traffic.

"Work can be interesting if you're doing what you like."

"Hmph," Treasa said noncommittally as several more customers came through the door, distracting them both.

Treasa as usual left for the high life in town after the shop closed. She never asked Catherine to join her, and Catherine wasn't about to ask. She walked the short distance back to Orange Street alone, not looking forward to a solitary evening. She should be out celebrating with someone who could share her small moment of success.

Perhaps her subconscious yearning for company conveyed itself, because Lucien Blythe appeared that evening when she least expected him, walking up behind her as she took a TV dinner from the freezer.

"What have you got there?" She felt his light touch on her shoulder. His warm, mellowly accented voice made pleasant music in the kitchen.

She nearly dropped the cardboard-wrapped package on the floor. She quickly collected herself, though her hands trembled.

"It's my dinner, and why must you come up behind me, scaring me to death?" Catherine spoke in pure reaction. She spun around and was momentarily jolted to be looking into his blue eyes once again. He was smiling, too, and his white teeth gleamed in sharp contrast to his dark beard.

"I have been here for a number of minutes, brewing myself some tea. I saw you let the dog out, throw your purse on the table, pour yourself a glass of wine, let the dog in, go to this box—an ice box, is it?"

"You're seeing it *my* way!" she burst out. "The room, I mean. You're seeing it with my things in it!"

"I was just realizing that." He glanced around. He didn't look entirely pleased. "What is that strange apparatus over there that the kettle's sitting on? What happened to my good wood stove? And what are those abominable frills doing on my windows?" He pointed to the country curtains that framed each of the double windows over the sink.

Feeling strangely lighthearted, Catherine chuckled. "The strange apparatus is a stove—a gas stove—and I happen to like those curtains. My grandmother made them herself."

He'd followed her to the counter and watched her—she could feel his eyes staring over her shoulder—as she drew the foil away from the dinner. "You don't mean to say you eat that," he said.

"It's not cooked yet. It's quite edible." Catherine was barely aware of what her fingers were doing.

"It would not pass my lips."

"I've haven't offered you any. Ghosts aren't supposed to eat in any case."

He ignored her last statement. "I believe I shall have a glass of that wine." He reached around her for a glass, gripped it in a strong, well-shaped hand, and poured from the bottle on the counter. He lifted the glass to his lips. "More than bearable," he said in a moment. "You are celebrating something?"

"I should. I opened my shop today." How cheerful her voice sounded now, even in her own ears.

"Your shop? Indeed. What kind of shop? I've noticed that with their husbands so often away, the women on this island are independent."

"As you've no doubt noticed, I don't have a husband, and I doubt you would recognize my shop if I told you. I'm an interior designer."

"You sell furnishings." He chuckled. "I saw some pamphlets on your dresser top."

She swung around to face him. "Then you have seen me in this house, in *my* environment!"

"I've only had a glimpse in the past few days. Speaking of which, I have been reflecting on matters since our last conversation. First," he spoke quietly, "I wish to apologize again for my rash behavior that night. I shouldn't have kissed you . . . though I quite enjoyed it. Our meeting since then was quite a pleasurable surprise, too, though of not nearly long enough duration. Delightfully interesting, however."

A pounding started somewhere in the region of her heart. She saw the hint of a dimple in his cheek and knew he was deliberately teasing her. She turned quickly toward the stove. He followed right behind as she turned the oven on and stuck her TV dinner in. Barney was curled up in his usual corner of the kitchen and, aside from lifting his head in quick inspection, accepted the Captain.

"The more I consider our situation," the Captain continued, wagging his finger, "the more I am convinced we are coming in and out of each other's lives in entirely other than a ghostly manner. Both you and I are far from vaporous beings, and we appear to be living out our own lives on separate planes—a century and a half apart—except during these chance meetings. I certainly have no explanations of how this might be possible, but it's rather undeniable that it *is* happening." He paused, went off on a different tack. "I notice that you do not seem entirely happy—that something is troubling you."

She gave a laugh. "Of course something has been troubling me! You! What sane, logical person wouldn't be upset when they start seeing a ghost who lives, breathes, talks, and touches?"

He chuckled. "You've affected me similarly. But it is more than that. You are much too serious. You rarely laugh. I wonder if we meet because we share this mutual bond. I came to this house, this island, to escape the pains of life as well."

"There's one flaw in your deductions. I *didn't* come to this house to escape anything. I came because my grandparents left me the house, and I knew they would have wanted me to come and live here. I was very satisfied with my life." But his comments disturbed her. They sounded too much like things Treasa had said in the past.

"Was? Aren't you now?"

"You know what I mean."

"I know what you'd like to think you mean." Again he paced behind her as she crossed the kitchen to get her glass of wine. She could almost feel his body heat. Certainly she was aware of his scent —that very masculine soap or cologne she'd smelled before in her bedroom.

"You look lovely this evening," he added. "Despite the fact your skirt is rather short, it does show off your legs to advantage. And I rather like a woman in that mannish sort of attire, jacket and shirt front and all."

"It's a blouse, and I'm dressed perfectly in style. This suit cost me two hundred dollars in California."

"Women have always been known to keep their dressmakers in top notch. You've been to California?"

"I lived there before I came to Nantucket."

"Indeed. What is it like? Rather uncivilized, I would imagine."

She frowned, then grinned. She supposed he would find certain things about the modern California life-style uncivilized. But he was thinking of California in terms of the 1840s. Heavens, the gold rush hadn't even begun in 1844!

"By the time I lived in California, it was quite civilized," she answered, "as civilized as this island, for instance."

"I've often contemplated sailing around the Horn. It's one of the few voyages I've not attempted."

"There are easier ways to get to California than by sailing around the Horn."

"You don't mean traveling overland."

"Or by air."

He didn't seem startled so much, as amused.

"I'm serious," she added quickly, when she saw his expression. "Man has mastered flight—oh, not by attaching wings to the arms..." She hesitated, trying to think of an easy description. "They've built machines that fly and can carry hundreds of passengers."

"Come now!"

"Believe me, it's true. If you read a current newspaper or magazine, you'd see. In fact—" She spied a pile of the same that she'd left on the floor to be taken out with the trash. She went over and picked up the bundle and dropped it on the kitchen table. "Here. Look through them."

With a skeptical expression he sat down at the table and lifted a copy of *Time* magazine. His skepticism became amazement as he leafed through the pages, studying the photographs in particular. "Quite unbelievable. I'm acquainted with daguerreotypes, but these are excellent."

The last thought in Catherine's mind at the moment was eating, but she set her dinner on the table and sat down, glad to take the weight off her increasingly jelly-like knees. His eyes skimmed the column of print under a NASA photo of a shuttle launch. "Incredible." He flipped through a few more pages, then looked up. "If only I could read through these at my leisure."

"Take them."

"I shall, if that is at all possible." He gazed across the table at her. "The more I talk to you, the more befuddled I feel." He laid his hand lightly on hers. "You truly are what you say you are. Almost too much to comprehend."

"I feel the same way."

"I find myself thinking about what is happening too much for my own peace. Do you?"

"Yes."

"Why don't you have a man with you in this house? You are widowed?"

"I've never been married."

"Being alone is not always pleasant."

"I didn't say I want to spend the rest of my life alone. There've been men, of course . . . several . . . but I've had my business to get started—that took priority."

"Ah, yes, I know too well. I'll tell you that such motivation is not always the wisest course. I lost a great deal by single-mindedly pursuing my shipping enterprise above and beyond all else. I woke up too late, as you might as well."

"What did you lose?"

"The thing of greatest importance to me, though it's not a subject I discuss in detail." His sadness and regret were evident. She felt she was touching on something too close.

"Well, you shouldn't make any generalizations about me. We barely know each other."

He smiled. "Extraordinary that we should know each other at all!

However, since we seem tied to living in the same house, I cannot help but notice certain things. I must say I admire your self-sufficiency and independence, but you should be finding some pleasure in life—before it's too late."

"I do find pleasure. Really, Captain—"

"Lucien. It's what my friends call me."

"We're friends?"

"In our circumstances, it's far wiser a relationship than being enemies, wouldn't you say?"

She smiled. "Yes, I would say."

"So tell me more about you." His hand still covered hers. It felt entirely warm and human.

"Such as?"

"Anything you'd care to say."

She hesitated, feeling awkward. "Well, I'm twenty-seven. As you know, I've never been married. I was born in Massachusetts and have lived in California for the last fifteen or so years. My parents were killed in an automobile accident when I was twenty. I've been on my own since...started my business..." she lifted her shoulders. "I don't know—what else is there to say?"

"What do you like to do, aside from work?"

"I've always liked history and antiques...and art. I was an art major."

He cast her a questioning look.

"I studied art and design in college," she clarified.

"You attended university?" He seemed amazed.

"Women didn't in your day, I realize. It's common now."

"Interesting."

"We also vote."

"You don't say!"

"Don't you approve?"

"I must give it a little thought. I cannot imagine certain women of my acquaintance being knowledgeable enough about political and social issues to choose wisely."

"We are educated now, remember—not confined to the drawing room with our needlework and tea parties."

He had the good grace to laugh. "Is that the way you see it? I'd never given the matter much thought—women have their place in life, and men another. I have always respected the woman's role."

"But would you want it?"

He considered. "I see your point. But why should women want to be anything other than they are? There are two sexes for a reason."

"We still *are* women," she teased. "I believe you made some comment on my femininity earlier. We are also equal individuals with equal intelligence and talent. We were never allowed in a male-oriented society to step off our pedestals and make use of our abilities—which was also a very convenient way for men to retain their power."

"So you hold men in contempt?"

"Not at all. At least, *I* certainly don't. It's not only men, but history and the mores of society that created the situation. There was a time when women allowed themselves to be imprisoned in gilded cages."

He pursed his lips and looked down. "Gilded cages? Is that what she felt? I wonder..."

"Who felt?"

He quickly shook his head, brushing away whatever he was remembering, and looked back at her. "I wonder how long these strange meetings of ours shall continue? A rhetorical question, of course, since you can have no better idea than I. I have always been of the belief that there is a reason for everything in life, good and bad. Perhaps we both have a lesson to learn from all of this."

She glanced down, wondering. He removed his hand from hers and lifted his wine glass. She felt the loss and raised her eyes. He was gone. The stack of magazines had vanished with him.

A half ton of bricks might have been dropped on her with the same effect. How could he be gone when they'd just begun to talk! She'd *enjoyed* his company and conversation. She needed someone like him—needed it very much. She'd felt different while he was with her—alive, stimulated. Here was a man who truly intrigued her.

In the same breath, she saw the absurdity of what she was thinking and feeling and pressed her fingers to her temples. Lucien Blythe had technically been dead for a century or more—he was a man who came and went at the blink of an eye.

Chapter 12

She couldn't stop thinking about him or stem her growing curiosity about this man who was a cohabitant in her house. In the following days, Catherine read through every Nantucket historical text she could find, seeking some mention of Lucien or confirmation of Marjorie's story. She drew a blank. Except for a passing reference to one of his vessels calling in port, Lucien Blythe appeared to have left no imprint on the written history of the island. Of course, she had the deeds which were positive proof of his having resided there. She reread them and studied his signature—bold and strong—that of a man who knew what he wanted. Yet she was left thirsting for more facts.

Their situation was impossible. If only she could bury her thoughts of him and immerse herself in the other aspects of her life. Treasa, at least, seemed to be behaving herself after their confrontation. She'd paid Catherine a week's board, and she managed to pull herself out of bed every morning and get to work on time. Catherine's life would have been running fairly smoothly if not for Lucien Blythe and her anticipation that he might drop in at any moment.

She was thinking of him a few days later as she went into the study to get some paper out of the desk. She stopped in her tracks in the doorway, her heart suddenly pounding.

He was sitting in the armchair, the stack of periodicals she'd given him piled on the floor at his side. He glanced up from the one he was perusing. A smile lit his face and flashed in his eyes.

"So we meet again! Come, sit down."

She did so with only an instant's hesitation, perching herself on the stool near his feet, since it was the most convenient seating. She was only too aware of her reaction as he carefully studied her face.

His eyes were still smiling, but his voice was serious. "I was exceedingly disappointed at our abrupt parting in the galley—in the midst of such an interesting conversation, too. What do you think precipitates it?"

"I don't know. I was just as surprised to look up and see you were gone."

"Hmmm." His fine mouth twisted thoughtfully. "I've been trying to piece it all out. I'd just lifted my hand from yours and was taking a sip of wine. I thought perhaps the break in contact."

"But you weren't touching me all the time before that."

"True. However, during our previous meetings, there was some physical contact."

"Not always."

"I only noticed you on the roof when you touched me. And in the garden, when I lifted my hand from your shoulder, you vanished. Likewise, the night when I'd been playing the piano."

"We're talking to each other right now and not touching," she reminded him.

"Yes, and perhaps we should insure ourselves against sudden disruption."

She was sitting less than an arm's length away, and he leaned forward in his chair and took her hand. As usual, she felt an unexpected jolt when he touched her—certainly not unpleasant.

"It's rather comforting holding your hand," he said. There was no innuendo in his voice. "So small. I've not held many female hands in these last years."

"I should think you'd have plenty of opportunity."

The laughter came from deep in his throat. "Indeed, should I so choose."

"According to the story about you, you always remained aloof to the local ladies' charms."

His smile vanished. "What story?"

"It's not derogatory—just a tale passed down word-of-mouth over the years. My neighbor told me when we found the old deeds to the house. She'd heard it from an old woman who'd lived up the street. The story started, I guess, because you kept to yourself so much. People have a tendency to speculate when they can't discover the facts to gossip about, particularly on a small island. You do keep to yourself pretty much, I gather, and you do present a glamorous, mysterious figure."

He snorted.

"Anyway, your gossip-worthiness was apparently enhanced when you left the island without warning and never returned."

"So your suppositions about my leaving this house were based purely on this story."

"No. As I told you, I have a deed dated 1846. You or your estate sold the house through a firm of attorneys in London."

"You have this deed in your possession?"

"Yes, and it seems authentic."

His eyes darkened. "Much could happen over the next two years, but it's rather chilling to be told what one's actions will be."

"It's not necessarily bad, you know."

"You are not the one who will be affected. Hmph! I wish you hadn't told me."

Catherine hadn't thought ahead to his reaction. In his place, she didn't suppose she would have enjoyed such news. "You're right. I'm sorry."

"Why should this tale about me have lasted so long? I'm only one of many owners of this house."

"Well, there's a reason. But I don't think you want to hear about it."

"You might as well tell me the rest."

She dropped her gaze, then looked up, first to the portrait, then to the very alive, matching blue eyes staring at her from the chair. How could she ever have thought him a ghost? The masculinity fairly vibrated from him as he waited for her answer. "A young couple who lived in this house after you started having strange feelings in certain rooms. According to the story, they found a portrait, which they hid away in the attic because of their reactions to it. Your portrait, I gather, since I found it hidden there in a cupboard no one had touched in years."

She paused, not particularly liking the expression on his face. But he seemed to be waiting, and in a second she plunged on. "Later, people saw a solitary male figure up on the widow's walk. It was not anyone who lived in the house. Since, according to the story, you'd spent a great deal of time on the walk, the figure was presumed to be your ghost."

"Not this again. I am not a ghost!"

"I'm just repeating the story."

"And quite frankly, I think it's nonsense. The product of unoccupied, overimaginative minds."

"No doubt. I told you that you wouldn't like it."

"And I shouldn't be raising my voice to you." He threw back his head and sighed. "If only we could find some answers here. There must be some tie, but it's all far beyond anything I've ever contemplated. It is as if the present and future exist at the same time, and you and I merely cross between the two."

He drifted into silence. Catherine sought for something to lighten the mood. "What do you think of what you've read?"

"Read? Oh, your modern newspapers. Fascinating, though I've barely made a dent. I've been busy with my fleet the last few days. It's quite shocking some of this. I'd hesitate to believe it if it weren't in front of my eyes. I wonder how you can exist comfortably in such a mad world. Travel across the Atlantic in hours instead of weeks— and into space! Weapons that can wipe out half a continent. And this—" Without thinking he released her hand to leaf through the magazine on his lap. "I was astounded . . ."

He hadn't finished the sentence when he vanished, and Catherine fell to the floor with a thump. There was no footstool in her study.

Her disappointment was equal to what it had been at his last sudden departure—or her sudden departure, depending on whose eyes viewed the scene. What she felt more than anything else, as she sat on the floor viewing the empty wing chair, was frustration . . . in grand proportions. Some convolution of nature had brought them together against all physical odds, had allowed them their marvelous conversations, yet would separate them on a whim, with the swiftness and surety of a sharp knife.

Then she remembered what he'd said about physical contact. He'd dropped her hand just before disappearing. Perhaps that was the clue. Rising, she tried to remember what she'd been doing prior to their meeting. She'd come into the study for paper. Paper for what? To sketch room designs, of course. She shook her head, got the paper, but procrastinated about leaving the room. Finally she did, but for the rest of the night, she got little accomplished.

The following days were the same. Thoughts of him would pop into her mind at the least opportune moments, interfering with her concentration. In the shop Treasa would have to call her several times to rouse her, as Catherine mentally replayed every word of their last conversation. She visualized each nuance of his expression, the way he moved his hands or smiled, the way his eyes lit with laughter when he teased, the aura of self-confidence he projected— capable, strong, and able manager of his business—and his sensitivity, too, with his music and his ability to acknowledge past hurts and listen to her with open ear and mind.

They met several times, in several places, and each meeting left her increasingly shaken, yet filled with an undeniable yearning.

At times it seemed he wasn't someone newly met, but someone she'd known well before. That rare quality existed between them— instantaneous rapport—a special chemistry. She found herself wishing to spend more time with him, despite the absurdities. She felt more and more comfortable in his presence; more and more convinced that there was a purpose behind their coming together. She was at ease in his world, relishing and never ceasing to be amazed at the first-hand contact with the history she'd always loved. And her fantasies carried it further. At night she'd dream of being held in his arms, of feeling his body against hers, of knowing him physically. Her pulse would start racing; she'd waken sometimes in a cold sweat, thinking he was actually there. What would it be like to fall in love with a man such as him and have that love returned? Had she actually ceased thinking of him as a man from another dimension? Was she seeing him instead as a man who was as much a part of the present, living world as she was? But he *was* alive. And her reasons for drawing back and holding away from their relationship grew weaker by the day.

Yet, in her own world, she could afford no time for dreaming. The room layouts, photos, and specifications for the design job for the Arab multimillionaire had arrived from Santa Barbara. All her thought processes had to be in perfect order if she was to get the finished layouts and her suggestions back to Marcie with any timeliness. The shop was busy, too. While Treasa manned the floor and register, Catherine concentrated on prospective design clients, and neither of them had much spare time.

In the end Catherine brought the California work home with her at night and on the weekend, spreading it out on the dining room table as she plotted room layouts on graph paper. Of course, the knowledge that Lucien might appear at any moment left her looking up at the slightest noise.

For over an hour on a beautiful Sunday when she should have been outside or at the beach, she carefully pulled swatches, making a list of which wall, window, or piece of furniture was to be covered with each. She sighed with satisfaction when she'd finished, finally feeling as though she'd accomplished something. Then she read through the original request of the owner and, to her horror, found she'd been decorating the room with the wrong color scheme altogether. The colors she'd been working with were for the dining room, not the living room.

She slammed her hands down on the table top. This had to stop! Her business would be a shambles if she didn't put him out of her mind and start dealing with reality.

Stomping upstairs, she went into the study, picked up her grandfather's telescope and trained it out the window.

"And what are you gazing at with such concentration?"

Catherine abruptly lowered the telescope and swung around. "How long have you been here?" The sharp tone of her voice belied the rush of excitement she felt.

"What a rude greeting," he chuckled. "In fact, I just arrived— more to the point, *you* just arrived, since I see my vessels out there in the harbor." He took a step forward so that he was standing directly beside her. "A whaler is being brought in over the bar on the camel. "Do you see it?" He pointed in the direction of the harbor mouth.

She did see it. She forgot everything else as her eyes widened to a view of Nantucket Harbor of 1844. The docks at the foot of Main Street were surrounded by a forest of masts and rigging. Huge wooden hulls lined the wharves, their bowsprits nearly touching each other across the wharf's width. Barrels and hogsheads containing precious whale oil were stacked in every available inch of space, side by side with bales and crates of other cargo. Dockhands scurried like ants between the cargo and ships. Other vessels were anchored further out the harbor, awaiting a space at the docks. The land surrounding the harbor appeared almost treeless. The finger of low land leading to Brant Point Light was no more than a series of dunes and beach grass, completely undeveloped. She lifted the telescope to her eye for a better view. The Captain's hand covered hers as he directed the glass toward one of the wharves. Involuntarily her hand trembled.

"Look down to the end of the Long Wharf. Do you see the two vessels to the end? Those are my merchantmen, the *Goddess* and *Sophia*. The *Goddess* was my first vessel. With her I made my fortune and saw the world. Three years later I purchased the *Sophia* and refitted her. She was then called *Pursuit,* but I wanted a more noble name—the *Goddess* had served me so well. Have you been to the

Hagia Sophia in Constantinople? No, probably not. It's a wild and sometimes dangerous city."

"Istanbul."

"I'm speaking of Constantinople."

"It's called Istanbul now, and yes, I've been to the Hagia Sophia."

"Ah, then you know the temple's beauties and that it was purported by legend to have been built in honor of a great mother goddess, Sophia, who was in favor before and about the time Christianity took hold. Legend has it that she was worshipped as an equal to Christ. Of course, the present church would disallow that the temple was built in a goddess's honor, but the building left an impression on my mind, and I named my second vessel after her."

"You have two merchant ships?"

"No, four."

"You're as wealthy then as the stories said."

"I suppose that would be a correct assumption, though it no longer matters. Once it did, to the point where I lost much. I can't feel that way again."

"Why? You said something before about losing a great deal."

"It's not a subject I feel comfortable discussing."

"Then why do you continue to run your fleet, if you feel nothing for it?"

"My business is something to keep my hours occupied. What else would I do?"

"I don't know. Do you ever sail?"

"I captained the *Goddess* for many years. Now I sail only on rare occasions."

"Why did you give up the sea?"

"Please, Catherine, I would prefer to drop this conversation."

"Why?"

"Why, why, why!"

"Very well! Don't talk about it, but there must be some reason why you're haunting this house."

"That point has already been settled. I am not haunting it!"

"All right, crossing times."

"At the moment, you are the one who is doing so. I was standing here at these windows, enjoying the view and the prospect of the sunset, and I look over to see you standing in my study."

"True, but—" She lowered the telescope and turned so that she was facing him, at too close proximity. She'd not realized he'd moved to stand directly behind her. Their eyes met. She took a step back in reaction but collided with the end of the table.

His whole demeanor was alluring, right down to his suddenly twinkling eyes. "I'm enjoying this. Aren't you as well?"

At something in his expression Catherine gripped the edge of the table.

"Aren't you?" he repeated.

"Yes . . . yes."

His smile deepened. "You think about me as much as I find myself thinking of you, waiting for our next meeting."

"How would you know?" Her voice was a whisper.

"I can sense it, and your lack of denial is a sufficient answer."

"Do you realize what you're doing to me? To my business?" Her voice was hoarse, hushed. "I can't concentrate, expecting you to appear at any moment. I'm getting behind on an important project—"

"But think of what you're gaining from our meetings. How many people of your century have seen Nantucket as you're seeing it now?" His tone was quietly reasonable. "And think of what I am gaining. I read through all of your newspapers and magazines. As I told you, were I not quite sure that they contained factual accounts, I'd disbelieve most of what I read. Travel into space, energy created through the splitting of an atom that cannot even be seen, machines that can think like the human mind? Exhausting to try to comprehend it all. Several things I didn't understand. The words were used frequently with no explanation. One was the phone. Is that the object I saw you speaking into on one occasion? Oh, you didn't see me."

"Yes. That's the telephone. Your voice travels through wires."

"Interesting and practical. One contraption of the future world I wouldn't mind having. The other was the television—TV?—which I presumed might be that box you have in the parlor that shows pictures as if one were watching a stage drama."

"You have an interesting way of describing our modern conveniences. Didn't you find yourself so entranced that you could hardly pull your eyes away?" she teased.

"I might have if whatever it is that makes our worlds cross hadn't seen fit to take *me* away. To think what I could do with all of this knowledge."

"But you *can't* do anything with it!" Catherine burst out. "You might change the course of history."

"Yes, I realize. And quite frankly, I'm content with things as I know them. Such a mad pace of life wouldn't suit me. It's no wonder you're so tense and serious. How else would you survive?"

"You won't allow me to pry into your life, but you feel free to pry into mine."

"Am I prying? I thought I was merely observing. I've noticed another young woman strolling about the house. She looks very much like you."

"My sister. You saw her?"

"I did. I thought at first it was you and was ready to question you about your behavior next time I saw you."

"What was she doing?"

"Pouring herself a rather stiff whiskey from the stock in the parlor. She then lit a small cigar. She turned on the music box—if one would call what she was listening to music—and began dancing about the room, moving her body in various suggestive ways. I was reminded of certain primitive, ceremonial dances I'd seen in my travels about the world."

"Damn it."

"Pardon?"

"I'm talking about my sister and the fact that she was drinking in the middle of the afternoon."

He was silent for a moment. "I thought it odd myself. Why is she living here?"

"The boat she crews on came into Nantucket for a few days. She came up to see if I was at the house, then got herself fired from the job."

"A *woman* as crew?" He was astonished.

"Things are different now."

"Obviously! You said she is out of a job deliberately?"

"Yes. You see, she seems to think she should have inherited half this house. She got a trust fund instead." Briefly Catherine described the situation and everything leading up to it.

"You shouldn't have to put up with such abuse in your own house—nor do I wish to put up with it in *my* house."

"You've seen her in the house in your time?"

"No—no. But it's all the same."

"She's been working in the shop. I told her she had to, or I'd throw her out."

"Sound reasoning."

"Why are you smiling like that?"

"Did you enjoy the song I played the other evening?"

He startled her with his sudden change of subject. "How did you know I heard you? You woke me from a sound sleep."

"For that I apologize. I presumed you heard at least part, because I found myself seated at the piano in your drawing room, and it wasn't that late in the evening. I'd just come home after a chat with one of the captains of my vessels."

"I didn't recognize the song you played, but it was beautiful." She smiled remembering; remembering, too, how long she'd lain awake.

"It was my own composition."

"You're very talented."

"You haven't asked me what my inspiration was."

"Gwen?" As she said it, she prayed it wasn't so.

"No. Someone who looks very much like her."

Catherine understood what he was inferring, but she could only gape at him.

"Someone I find myself thinking about all the time, who is becoming more and more a part of my life. I saw you asleep in bed and felt so tempted . . ." The color of his blue eyes deepened. "I thought at first that this fascination I felt for you stemmed from your resemblance to Gwen. The attraction was so all encompassing, it took me by surprise. But soon I realized it had nothing to do with Gwen. It was *you* who intrigued me—your independence, your strength, your own uniqueness. When we talked I felt our minds were working together—as equals, shall I say? I've never experienced that before with a woman. Not that the other women of my acquaintance are unintelligent, but they shy away from men's talk and subjects of controversy." He paused. The expression on his face made her shiver. "But that wasn't all. There is the physical, too. There seems to be some undefinable attraction between us. Do you agree?"

"Yes, I've felt it," she whispered against her better judgment.

No more than six inches separated them. She felt a strange compulsion to run, yet what was happening was what she'd daydreamed *might* happen. A furry gray blur hurtled up toward the table behind her. The blur landed with a thump, connecting with the telescope, which rolled with a bang into the lamp. She heard an outraged *rowwr!* and jumped forward right into Lucien Blythe.

"Only Jeremy, my cat."

She nodded as she realized.

For an instant they stood chest to chest, then his arms slowly came around her. She had no power to resist—even while her mind was racing, silently shouting out all the reasons why their imminent action was foolish . . . mad . . . taking them into a territory where neither should tread.

When his lips covered hers, they were only a man and a woman, and they came together like the explosive meeting of two souls fated to eventually join. He drew her closer—his body was hard, strong, enticing. The current that raced between them swept everything out of its path. Yet as his mouth moved on hers, it was unexpectedly soft, sweet. Her hands went around his neck, her fingers tangling in the thick hair at his collar. When he drew her closer, pressing his hips to hers, her knees acquired the consistency of butter.

"My God, what have I started?" he said.

A nagging, delicious ache settled in her loins. She'd never felt so drawn to anyone. With her lips against his, she whispered his name, again and again.

"I know . . . it's been building toward this, hasn't it? You and I . . . almost inevitable." His kisses deepened; his breathing grew ragged. He seemed to have no more desire or ability to put a stop to what was happening than she.

He shifted his arms and lifted her, carried her from the study, into the bedroom. Gently he laid her on the bed and slid down beside her. Beneath his jacket she felt the hard muscles of his back. In her dazed mind she was amazed that she should be holding him like this, feeling his body so intimately pressed against hers—a man from another century! It didn't matter. He was real. There was nothing ghostly about his caresses or her reaction to them.

"Do you know how often I've dreamed of this?" he whispered. "Those times I've seen you asleep in bed and fought with all my will not to join you?"

"I've dreamed, too. I've felt you there."

"But now it's not a dream."

"No."

They didn't speak again for a long time, aware of little else but the physical desire that raged between them, as it had raged between man and woman since time immemorial. Unable to get enough of each other, unable to dam the unexpected floodtide, they clung together, hungrily kissing, limbs entwined, forgetting all else but their urgent need. Their hands sought beneath each other's clothing to touch soft, hot skin. His hand slid up her thigh, under her skirt. She murmured her pleasure as he pushed the cloth upward and let his fingers gently roam over her flesh. With trembling hand, she sought the fastening of his trousers. He helped her, freeing himself into her hand, moaning as her fingertips made contact. He moved over her.

Yet on the brink of discovery, Lucien froze.

As if suddenly awakened from a trance, he stared down at her, his eyes widening. In the next instant, he was lifting himself, bracing his hands against the mattress to either side of her head.

"What am I doing?" His tone was horrified.

Catherine stared at him uncomprehendingly.

"To take you like this?"

She lifted her hand toward him, touching his bare shoulder, but he sat up with a jerk and stared down at her, his eyes not clearly focused. "Forgive me . . ."

"For what?" she breathed raggedly.

"You deserve more! I respect you too much to compromise you like this."

She tried to clear her brain and focus her thoughts on what he was saying. But, of course! He was a man of the nineteenth century. Free love was not something he understood. "You're not compromising me."

"Am I not?" He stared down at the bedcovers, at their state of undress, and a slow shudder rippled up the muscles of his back—an internal shudder, reflecting the thoughts going through his mind. "I haven't considered you. I've given absolutely no thought to the consequences of my actions!"

She gasped. "Why do you say that?"

He shook his head, rubbed his hand over his face. "Yes, I want you—more than I have wanted any woman for a very long time, but what can come of it but pain? The two of us are not of the same world. Why haven't I seen until now that it defies all sanity for us to become intimate? There can't be a future for us. All I can offer you is an interlude—neither my name, nor security!"

"Lucien, in my world that doesn't matter."

"It matters greatly to me. I've begun to think that you and I have been thrown together because of a lesson I never learned before."

"It's not so."

"Oh, Catherine, it is. There are things you don't know. History can repeat itself." He looked at her, his face drained of all color. "I should have realized—seen what was coming. I should have had more self-control, right from the start. But I've allowed my desire for you to blind me to reality. I'm sorry—"

"I'm *not* sorry. You shouldn't be either. I'm responsible for my own actions. Perhaps we should never have met, but we have!"

He reached over and took her hand. His fingers pressed hot against her skin, reminding her of all that her body had been feeling moments before. "And perhaps the only sanity would be for us not to meet again—end it before we bring each other real pain."

"No!"

"I know myself and my own limits," His voice was deep, echoing from the pits of his soul. "I cannot keep seeing you, talking with you, interacting with you, without wanting to see what exists between us follow its natural course. But there is no natural course for us! We are not a normal man and woman. Our lives are being lived out in different centuries!"

"Why can't we enjoy it for what it is—for what we *do* have?"

His eyes locked on hers. "Would that be enough? Wouldn't we always be hoping, grasping for more, so that when the inevitable comes, we'd be truly devastated?"

"What inevitable?"

"Our meetings could end at any time, Catherine. I didn't realize until now how much of a possibility that is—or how much of a loss it would be. And there's more—something else. I can't allow myself to do to you what I've done to another." His voice sounded hollow, despairing.

"For God's sake, what did you do? Tell me about it."

"I can't! I am not shutting you out, just understand."

"Don't be a martyr. Talk about it."

"No!" He thrust the word out through gritted teeth and seemed to pull further within himself.

"Please, Lucien, listen to me." Her head was spinning. He couldn't possibly mean what he was saying!

He squeezed her hand. His eyes locked on hers. "I don't make this decision easily. In the short time we've known each other—in our brief encounters—I have become very close to you. I don't want it to end . . . but I think it *must*. Perhaps it would have been better if we'd never met."

"You're wrong, Lucien."

But he'd already released her hand. He rose from the bed. He backed farther away, his expression wretched but determined.

She sat up, reached for him. Her eyes stared imploringly.

"Let us not forget each other and what we might have had." As the last word left his mouth, he vanished, like a shadow erased by a cloud covering the sun.

"Don't go!" This time she did scream. She wrapped her arms about herself convulsively, then scrambled off the bed. She spun around and stared into every corner of the room, as if he might still be standing there. She saw only his discarded jacket and shirt on top of the bedspread. Grabbing them up, she buried her face in them and sobbed. His scent clung to the material, and she breathed it in. He couldn't have meant it. He couldn't be ending it!

Chapter 13

But seemingly he was. She spent the first twenty-four hours doing little else but staring out the window, hoping he'd relent in his decision and make an appearance. She thought over his words, feeling blinding frustration and loss, then anger and pain. How could he do this to her? How could he take it upon himself to make a decision that affected both of them so drastically? What had happened in his past to leave him so scarred and afraid?

She felt fear for herself, too, that she'd become so deeply involved in such an unnatural, impossible situation and was allowing it to totally disturb her life. It wasn't rational. He was right. They were mad to consider the possibilities of a relationship or a future. Their only course was to stop it now before they were both in over their heads and drowning. But she couldn't turn off her feelings for him —her memories of him—like water from a faucet. It wasn't that easy!

Days passed. He didn't show his face. Her pain became depression, then gradually resolution. It was obvious he had meant what he said and was making every effort to sever their relationship. She had no choice but to try to forget him as well—start afresh as if she'd never met him. Her sanity depended on it. She could not continue on in her present state. If only she didn't miss him so much!

She went to the shop the next morning with a new determination, working right through to lunch and only once allowing her thoughts to stray to Lucien Blythe. Treasa took her lunch break first, and Catherine got together the materials she needed for a prospective client she was meeting in 'Sconset at two. Her work was interrupted several times by walk-in customers, and she was beginning to feel a little frazzled by one o'clock, anxious for Treasa to get back.

Five after one; ten after one; and no Treasa. When another twenty minutes passed, and Treasa still hadn't returned, Catherine's irritation had grown to anger. If she didn't leave in another few minutes, she'd be late.

Finally, at twenty to two, she had no options but to lock the shop doors, get in the Porsche, and head for 'Sconset. She couldn't risk putting off her client by changing their appointment. Unfortunately, the meeting didn't go well. After the prospective client had taken Catherine through each room of the house, and Catherine had made suggestions about what could be done and sketched out possible room plans, the woman decided she couldn't really afford to redecorate and would put it all off until the following summer.

Catherine returned to town to find the shop doors still locked. Treasa had a key, so she'd obviously never come back from lunch at all. Catherine reopened for the remaining hour of the day, but accomplished nothing worthwhile. Only a few customers came in, and she made no sales.

Her head was banging miserably by the time she pulled into the driveway on Orange Street. Her first stop after she let herself in the back door was the medicine cabinet, where she grabbed a couple of aspirin. Though she'd had no lunch, she'd gotten past the point of being hungry and had no enthusiasm for cooking supper. She went down to the kitchen anyway, and was just entering the room when the screen door swung open. In strolled Treasa, grinning, with three men in tow. Never before had Catherine felt more like cheerfully wringing her sister's neck—an act which was made impossible with three strangers standing in the kitchen.

"Cath," Treasa called easily, "meet my friends, Jan, Peter, Ted. My sister, Catherine. Just call her Cath." Treasa's eyes were shining as she turned back to Catherine. "I couldn't believe it when I went down to the dock at lunch and saw the *Escapade* was in. We haven't seen each other since Antigua. God, what a great time!"

Catherine nodded to each of the men. She tried to speak quietly. "Treasa, I had to close the shop this afternoon when you didn't come back from lunch."

"Did you? Oh, sorry, sis, but I just had to catch up with these guys. We had so much to talk about."

"You can't just go off when the spirit moves you. You've got a job."

Treasa laughed. From the sound of her laughter and slightly slurred speech, her afternoon had obviously been spent at the dockside pub. "Want a drink, guys?" She headed toward the refrigerator. "What have we got? A couple of beers. Any more scotch, Cath?"

"You drank it all."

"Did I? Oh, well. But I know where there's a bottle of rum! Be right back. Make yourselves at home, guys." She slipped out of the kitchen and up the hall.

Catherine was left with the three men, all in their late twenties or early thirties and dressed in shorts, T-shirts, and boat shoes.

The tallest, a handsome, tanned blond with an Australian accent, interrupted the momentary silence. "Sorry. Looks like we've come at a bad time. Treasa wanted to show us the house."

"Did she?" Catherine tried to focus her thoughts. She couldn't hold these three men responsible for Treasa's behavior. "I'm afraid I didn't get your names straight."

"Peter," the blond answered. "Ted and Jan." He motioned to the other two, who extended their hands.

"Nice to meet you all."

"Look," Peter continued. "Treasa's being a bloody scatterbrain bringing the lot of us up here, crashing in on you. We'll take her back to town and get her some dinner...make sure she gets back here right and tight."

The three visitors were obviously as uncomfortable as she was. "Sorry, I don't mean to be rude. If I sound short, it's because I just got home from work and have a roaring headache."

"That's what I meant about crashing in."

"It's okay." She smiled and tried to forget her irritation with Treasa. "Where are you all from—aside from the boat?" She noticed three distinctly different accents.

"I'm from Australia," Peter answered. "And Jan's English."

Catherine looked toward the dark-haired man. He wore the healthy, weathered look of a serious professional. "Where are you from in England?"

"Cornwall," he answered shortly.

She swung her eyes to the last in the group, Ted, who was sandy haired, green-eyed, and wore a handlebar mustache. "And where are you from?"

He smiled. "A long way off—Falmouth, on the Cape."

"Really? Treasa and I were born in Falmouth."

"Yeah, she told me."

"I'm surprised we never met in such a small town."

"Maybe we did. We've all changed a little since then."

"What's your last name?"

"McCormick."

Catherine thought back over nearly twenty years. Then her head shot up. "Teddie McCormick! Of course, I remember you. You hit me in the head with a baseball. Fifth grade, was it? No, you're older than me. You were in sixth."

"Miss Drum's class. Sure, I remember now. Cathy with the braids. Nearly knocked you out, didn't I?" His eyes twinkled mischievously as he looked her up and down. "Things *have* changed!"

"They don't call me Cathy anymore."

"They sure as heck don't call me Teddie either."

Treasa came quickly around the corner form the hall and entered the kitchen, rum bottle in hand, effectively cutting off all previous conversation. She set the bottle on the table. "We're in business. Almost a full quart." Treasa grabbed four glasses out of the cupboard, went over to Jan, and linked her arm through his. "Come on guys. On to the living room." She started from the room, and as she sidestepped Catherine, added. "Oh, join us if you want, Cath. I forgot to get you a glass."

It was a shame that Treasa was too pleasantly hazy to notice the cool glint in Catherine's eyes. Catherine debated joining the others —but why not? The company might cheer her up . . . at least take her mind off herself and the Captain. And she'd deal with Treasa later.

As she started up the hall, she saw that the Australian, Peter, had paused outside the living room. He waited for her as she approached.

"Nice house."

"Thank you."

"You said you just got home from work. What do you do for a living?" His voice was pleasant, curious.

"I have an interior design business out on the Coast—California —and just opened a branch here." Her headache was finally beginning to go away.

"I was an art and design major in Australia before I started sailing."

"Were you?" Catherine asked with interest. "Did you do anything with it?"

"I puttered," he grinned, "but I wanted to see the world, so when a friend of mine offered me a job crewing on a boat sailing for Europe, I took it."

"You're not sorry."

"I've done well enough. I'm captain now, and the money's good, though I don't know that I want to stay on boats the rest of my life."

"What would you do?"

"Go back to my artwork." He maintained eye contact as he spoke —a sign of a person who had nothing to hide, Catherine thought. "How long have you lived on Nantucket?"

"A few months."

"Do you like it?"

"Yes . . . basically. I haven't had enough time to make any decisions."

He laughed. "I know the feeling of not having enough time in any one place."

"Will the boat be staying here long?"

"A week or two . . . maybe more. The owners haven't quite made up their minds yet."

"Peter!" Treasa called sharply from the front room. "Come in here and have a drink. And you can answer a question for me."

Shrugging goodnaturedly, Peter motioned Catherine ahead of him. A heated discussion was going on between the other three. Treasa looked up.

"Peter, who was the first at the rock in the Fastnet race last year? Wasn't it a French boat?"

"Not on your life, dear. It was the Aussies."

"Just 'cause you guys won the America's Cup last time doesn't mean you have to get cocky. Besides, I don't believe you. I'm sure it was the French."

Peter shook his head and laughed. "Have it your way."

"You're not drinking." Treasa splashed some rum in a glass and handed it to him. He took it, though he simply held it in his hand as the others went back to their discussion, with Treasa dominating the conversation and talking a mile a minute.

"Hey, Treasa," Ted interrupted. "Just hold it. Your mouth goes off through your ears sometimes. I've been trying to tell you that your sister and I remember each other from Falmouth. Did you know that Cathy and I used to play baseball? She was a real slugger, except that she was on the *other* team." Quickly, amusingly, he described a game in the school yard when he'd been pitching for one team, and Catherine had come up to bat for the other. It was the last inning, with the score tie. Catherine had hit a homer last time she was up. Ted was a nervous wreck as he wound up to pitch, so nervous that the ball had slipped out of his sweating hand, to fly in a whizzing curve and hit Catherine right in the eye. "Of course, I didn't mean it," he explained. "I was as upset as the next guy that she'd been hurt. The long and the short of it was that she walked. The next guy up to bat was a loser, and I knew it. Cathy had been the team's only hope to get the winning run. I struck him out, and you should have *seen* the look I got from your sister—swollen black eye and all!" He gave an irrepressible chuckle. "She walked around with a shiner for a whole week—"

"Just a second, Ted," Catherine laughed. "If you'll remember, after the game I caught up with you on the way home and beat the heck out of you because I thought you'd done it on purpose. *You* walked around with a shiner, too!"

"Oh, geez, who wants to remember those minor details. I told the guys I'd walked into a door."

Treasa was glaring at him. "What's all this with my sister. *I* grew up in Falmouth, too, you know!"

"Kid, you were probably still in diapers when all this was going on." When he grinned, his curled mustache pointed up like that of the evil banker tying the girl to the railroad tracks. He returned his attention to Catherine. "Remember old Miss Crowley? We used to call her Miss Crotchety. Thought she'd drop from a stroke just walking down the hall."

Catherine laughed at the memory, but Treasa huffed and siddled closer to Jan on the couch. "Who's interested in all this ancient history? You're showing your ages. And stop looking at her like that!" she added to Jan in chilled tones.

"Why?" Jan gave his first real smile. "Your sister's nice to look at."

Treasa cast him a deprecating look. "We were talking about Antigua Race Week . . . before I was so rudely interrupted."

"Best part of the whole week was the wet T-shirt contest."

"You would say that, Ted," Treasa quipped.

"I liked the 'drag' race better," Peter added. "God, you guys looked funny in high heels and miniskirts. Such beautiful, hairy legs."

"You looked pretty cute yourself, Peter, filling out Janey's bikini top with coconuts."

The sailing stories continued, Catherine thoroughly enjoying them and the new insight she was getting into the yachting world, which was really a small community. She listened and laughed, her earlier irritation totally disappearing; feeling more relaxed than she had in ages. Every one of the guys had a story, although Ted was the comedian.

A few minutes later, Peter spoke quietly to Catherine. "You must think we're all crazy."

"Not at all. It's great."

"Just the same—for me at least—it would be nice to talk about something other than boats once in a while. Is there a quieter place?"

Catherine nodded and led him across the hall into the small sitting room. The stories and loud voices had gone on long enough—she was ready for a break, too. Peter glanced around the room, nodded. "I like old homes." He walked immediately to the bookshelves, examined the titles. "Wonderful collection. Yours?"

"My grandmother's. You like to read?"

"Immensely. Unfortunately, there's no place to store a library on a boat." He turned from the bookshelves. "I left most of my things in Perth."

"That's where you're from in Australia?"

He nodded.

"How long have you been captain of the *Escapade?*"

He considered. "Nearly three years. I've been sailing for about ten."

"I envy you for all the traveling you've done."

He chuckled. "Sounds glamorous, does it?"

"Obviously."

"Your life sounds just as exciting to me. Why did you move here from California?"

Briefly Catherine told him something of her life, California, her business. She felt comfortable talking to him. There was no phoniness or pretention about him.

His eyes never left her face as they talked. He was thirty-one, only a few years older than she. He felt he was reaching a crossroad in his life, though where that crossroad would take him, he wasn't sure.

"I've missed out on a lot of opportunities by staying on boats. You've got a business established. If I move ashore, I'll pretty much have to start from scratch."

"But look at what you've done instead. There's always a trade-off. You can't have everything."

Treasa suddenly stuck her head around the door. "What's this? A private party?" She looked from Peter to Catherine. "We're going back into town, Peter. You ready?"

"Yes. I have to check on the boat. Be there in a minute."

She studied them a moment longer, then turned and left.

Peter didn't rise immediately. "I've enjoyed talking to you," he said quietly.

"Likewise."

"Will you have dinner with me tomorrow night?"

The invitation surprised her, but her answer came more quickly than she would have imagined. "Yes. I'd like that."

"Good." His eyes crinkled at the corners as he smiled. "Shall I meet you here . . . about six-thirty?"

"That would be fine."

Before they left the room, he took her hand. A look passed between them. Then they joined the others in the kitchen. Treasa was hanging on Jan's arm. She immediately tried to link her other arm through Peter's as they started toward the back door. Catherine didn't miss the subtle sidestep he made, avoiding Treasa. He glanced back over his shoulder to Catherine and winked.

Not in a million years had she imagined the afternoon would turn out as it had. Her immediate acceptance of Peter's invitation still startled her. She felt a twinge of guilt. Then she thought of the last days of agonizing and the futility of her longing for Lucien Blythe. It could never work. Lucien had said it, and she knew it to be a fact now, too. Nothing would ever put them in the same world together. She had to face it.

Chapter 14

Their dinner date at an intimate waterside restaurant was a success. Peter was charming, and they chatted like old friends. She felt she'd known him for much longer than twenty-four hours. He seemed to feel likewise, and to her amazement, her thoughts hadn't turned to Lucien Blythe more than twice all evening. He still hadn't shown himself, even in her dreams, and she was daily becoming more resigned to the fact that it *was* over. Not that she didn't ache terribly missing him, but here was a normal man in the shape of Peter, who might help her recover . . . and forget her living ghost. They'd walked back to the house under a star-filled sky, and as Peter said good-bye at the door, he asked her to spend all of Sunday with him, picnicking at Great Point.

He picked her up at nine in the morning in a rented Jeep, and they set out for the northeastern end of the island. The sun beat down from a clear, cloudless sky as Peter steered the jeep over the sand roads to Great Point. To their left lay the calm waters of the Head of the Harbor; to their right, beyond the high grass-covered dunes, was the Atlantic. The deflated sand tires of the Jeep dug into the soft surface of the road, which was carefully marked to prevent vehicles from straying over the ecologically sensitive beach grass and scrub.

Catherine reached for the roll bar as the Jeep bounced around a corner in the narrow track. "I'm glad you're behind the wheel."

"You're driving back, mate." He grinned. "Can't let me have all the fun."

When they reached the end of the point, they parked on the harder gravel and shell-strewn sand and walked along the beach with Barney bounding in excited circles around them. They had a sweeping view out to where the waters of the Atlantic met those of Nantucket Bay. The race caused by the meeting currents was clearly visible, rippling in the sunlight as it reached out from the shore.

Peter motioned out to the rip. "Quite a few boats have gone down out there."

"It's always amazed me how anyone could navigate through waters like that. You can't even see the dangers below."

"If you know what you're doing, it's not so difficult. There're charts and most rough spots are marked by buoys. The unexpected storm is what can do one in."

They continued walking shoulder to shoulder, although Peter's was several inches above her own. Catherine relished the warm sun on her face and shoulders, the cooling wind that wipped her hair back from her brow and Peter's pleasant companionship. A few people were around, surf fishing, wandering over the dunes, as Peter and Catherine were. Barney brought bits of driftwood, which Peter heaved out over the sand for the dog to fetch. They found the remains of the Great Point Light—no more than some brick foundations—which had fallen only a few years before in a storm after sending out its signal for more than a century. The constant onslaught of the sea and the wind had pulled the sands from beneath its foundations, and it had tumbled forward into the Atlantic.

Gathering the picnic basket and cooler from the Jeep, they chose a spot that was protected from the winds yet gave them a clear view of the ocean. Peter spread the blanket, and they settled cross-legged in the sun, nibbling on the chicken Catherine had brought and the pâté and cheese Peter had contributed from the boat stock. He uncorked a bottle of Pouilly Fumé and poured a bit into two long-stemmed wine glasses.

"How elegant!" Catherine lifted her glass to him. "Crystal?"

"Only the best." The rims of their glasses tinkled together. "Actually, we do a lot of these lavish picnics for charterers, right down to the china. I never could understand someone wanting to have all that stuff carted ashore for a picnic."

"It's romantic." She sighed, lazing back on her elbows. "Just like this is."

"Especially with a lovely lady like you." His eyes reflected the blue of the nearby water. "You're easy to talk to," he continued. "No games . . . do you know what I mean?"

"I think I do."

"I've met a lot of women, but it seems that all too often after you get past the preliminaries, there's nothing to talk about."

"I've met men like that, too."

She rolled to her side so that she was facing him. "You said you'd like to get back to your art. In what way?"

"Painting. It was one of the things my ex-wife and I used to fight about."

"I didn't know you'd been married."

"I was young—nineteen. She got pregnant. We were married for two years, then it fell to pieces. I should have known it would happen. She wanted all the traditional things—a proper husband with a proper, upward-moving job, a proper house in the right part of Perth, two children, friends who thought just like her. I couldn't have dealt with it."

"So you sailed instead."

"Only after our divorce, which was hellish. She remarried a year later, and the bloke she married had some strange ideas—one of those jealous sorts. He didn't want me around Mary Jane." He fingered his wine glass. "And he didn't want me to see our daughter. Mary Jane listened to him. I think she's always been afraid of him. When I showed up to see Samantha, I could count on a huge row developing. Of course, since I was sailing, that was only every six months or so. I started worrying about what it would do to Sam to see her parents fighting over her. I decided she was better off if I stopped showing my face. I sent money, of course."

"But it hurts."

"I wonder if she'll grow up forgetting who I am. She's eleven now and hasn't seen me since my last trip home two years ago."

"I'm sorry."

"C'est la vie. And why am I talking about such depressing things? I want to show you a good time today."

"You are." She reached over and touched his arm. He smiled. "Do you ever paint anymore?"

"I can't mess about with canvas and oils on the boat—particularly since it's not mine." He glanced down as he drew patterns in the sand with his finger. "I sketch sometimes, but I've been feeling frustrated and angry with myself, particularly on this last passage from the Caribbean. I don't know if I can deal with another season. It's time I made a move. What, where, when, and how are the questions. I've got a bit of money saved."

"Could you get off boats for a while, stay in one place long enough to do some painting? There are dozens of galleries that will take artwork on consignment. I could probably handle some of your work myself."

Laughing, he reached over and took her hand. "You haven't even seen my work. It might be no more than a pile of rubbish."

Catherine remained serious. "Somehow, I don't think it would be."

"I'll show you some of my sketches if you like."

"Yes."

A quiet look passed between them, then Barney came bounding over with a stick and dropped it on the blanket. The current was too strong for swimming, but they splashed around in the rollers at the edge of the beach. Catherine found her gaze lingering on Peter, noticing the supple trimness of his body, tanned a deep all-over bronze to contrast with the sun-bleached blond of his hair. He ran with Barney up the beach, paused to cast a stick far up onto the sand. His movements were lithe and natural.

As the sun sank lower in the sky, they walked up to the top of the nearest dune arm-in-arm and looked to the west and the rose- and orange-tinted clouds on the horizon. Peter drew her closer. With his fingertips he brushed some grains of sand from her nose.

"I don't want this day to end," he said quietly.

She tightened her arm around his waist. "Neither do I."

"Then let's not end it. I could get a room at the inn in Wauwinet, if you like. A change of scene for you, and more privacy."

She hesitated, glanced away. She didn't want to go back to the house and have the spell of happy forgetfulness broken. The house was Lucien's domain, and hurtful thoughts and reminders of him would intrude even though he'd chosen to remove himself from her life. Yet she felt a pang of uncertainty. Things were moving so fast. Experience had shown her that sometimes it was all right if they did. And this was one of those times. It was the Captain that stood in her way. What if he relented, came back? No, damn it! No, she was not going to allow him to stand between her and any future happiness she might have. She'd suffered enough! Whether he came back or not, there'd be no future for them. They could never live together in the same world. He would always remain a man out of history—a fantastical illusion!

"Catherine?" Peter gently nudged her.

Her eyes cleared. She nodded quickly as much to herself as him.

"Yes, let's. A little adventure. But what about Barney? Will they take him?"

"I'll make sure they do. I know someone who works there." Running his fingers through her hair, he leaned over and kissed first her forehead, then the tip of her nose, then her mouth. His lips tasted of salt; his skin smelled of the sun; and his arms held her with the same heat.

In a few minutes they packed up their picnic gear and reloaded the Jeep. True to his word, Peter put her in the driver's seat. After her initial nervousness, Catherine got the hang of steering through the drifts of sand, with the heavy-duty suspension of the Jeep bouncing them into and out of each rut and depression. When she wasn't using the gear shift, their hands met in the space between the two bucket seats.

She parked in the grassy lot opposite the inn and glanced down at her bikini-clad body. "I forgot—I don't have a change of clothes with me."

"I kind of like you the way you're dressed right now, and you've got that T-shirty bit you had on when I picked you up."

"So much for designer clothing." She ruffled his hair.

"It won't matter here. I'll go get the room."

Catherine climbed out and rummaged in her straw beach bag, which also contained their sandy, damp towels. Thankfully, the dress had escaped the effects of the sand and salt. She shook it out, and Peter returned, looking marvelously satisfied with himself. He held up a key in front of her. "We've got one of the small, cozy rooms overlooking the water. Pays to have friends." When he stopped beside her, he added more quietly. "Actually, it's very small and not let out unless there's a full house, but he promised me there's a fantastic view."

"Sounds fine to me." Catherine felt lighthearted—free, untrammeled by any responsibilities or the rules she normally subconsciously imposed on herself. Who cared if she didn't go home that night? It was her life after all!

Peter had leaned over the seat of the jeep and was extracting the few things he needed—the white shorts and jersey top he'd worn to pick her up and his Docksiders. Catherine clipped the leash to Barney's collar.

"There's a line at the back of the building where we can tie Barney for now," Peter explained. "One of the owners has a dog. He can stay in the room with us if we take him up the back stairs tonight."

"You've arranged everything."

"Where there's a will, there's a way—to quote a famous adage, the author of whom escapes me." He dropped his arm over her shoulder, and they walked across the sandy road toward the long, two-story, gray-shingled inn.

Peter brought Barney around back as Catherine went up to the room and unlocked the door. It was small, tucked under the eaves, but it was charming, with an eyelet-covered bed, side chair, bureau, and window giving a view of the Head of the Harbor. She dropped her bag and Peter's things on the bed and opened the window to the sea breezes. In a few minutes Peter entered the room. He came toward her where she stood in the window dormer, ducking his head under the sloping ceiling to either side.

"Will it do?" he said in her ear.

She nodded, turning toward him. The rays of the sinking sun splashed through the window, circling them.

They took turns showering and washing away the sand, then went down and had a drink on the lawns, watching the sun set over the water. He looked very respectable in his white shorts and shirt with "Escapade" emblazoned over the left pocket. She'd found a scarf in her bag and had sashed it around the waist of her T-shirt dress, which made the whole look very chic. Later they had dinner in the country-style dining room. There were a number of other diners but they paid little heed. Peter asked for a table in the corner. They held hands across it, stared at each other in the candlelight, oblivious to any looks they received. The waitress had to call quietly to them twice before they noticed her standing by the table awaiting the dinner order.

When they went back up to their room after a luscious meal and a bottle of champagne, Peter took her in his arms and spoke with his lips in her hair. "I don't know how to describe what I'm feeling right now. It seems so fast and sudden . . . but it's not, is it? I want to make love to you . . . I have all day."

His words didn't surprise her. She'd known where things had been leading. Their relationship already contained that special ingredient, and she'd been waiting for a man like Peter for a long time. If it hadn't been for Lucien Blythe—but that could never be! She knew it in her heart.

When Peter saw the shy look in her face, he asked quietly, "Am I wrong? You want it, too, or aren't you ready?"

She did want it, but a persistent worry remained. Was she wrong in following her impulse and jumping in with both feet? Unlike her sister, she was more cautious about becoming involved. She didn't hop from bed to bed, but this night with Peter seemed to be exactly what she needed. She made a decision. "I want it, too."

He took her hand. A quiet urgency rose in him. Their arms circled. With the cooling air blowing into the room from the open windows, the contact of their bodies felt even more warmly welcoming as they lay down together upon the bed.

He came to her hungry, and as she lay tight in his embrace, she remembered how she'd felt with the Captain . . . to be one in the best and loving sense of the word. The thought slipped in and out as fast as it came. It startled her, frightened her, that he should be so vividly in her thoughts even then. She gripped Peter more tightly.

He was gentle, he was everything he should be. His every action told her this was more than sex, but caring, too.

The cool wind from the sea felt good now as they lay in each other's arms, their bodies heated by their physical actions and the love they'd given each other.

He rolled off her slowly, not wanting to press his weight on her smaller frame. But he continued to hold her. He kissed her ear, the side of her brow.

A few moments passed. She felt soft and mellow and warm. She wouldn't think of Lucien Blythe. She wouldn't let him ruin this new beginning. The wind ruffled the window curtains so they made a gentle flapping sound against the sills. Quite waves washed on the beach below.

"Would you leave here?" Peter murmured.

"Here?" Her own voice was still foggy.

"Nantucket."

Quietly she considered. "A month ago I would have said I'd stay out the year. Now . . . nothing's been the same since I came here."

He ran his hand down her arm. "I'll be leaving soon."

"Soon!" Her throat tightened.

"From what the owners said when they called me last night, sooner than I thought. We'll be pulling out in about two weeks. We have twelve days left. I've been counting them with dread all day."

She felt a hand clutching at her heart. Over already? She licked her lips. "Where will you be going?"

"Marblehead. Then Maine. It's not so far. Catherine, I want to keep seeing you."

"I want to keep seeing you!"

Peter sighed and shook his head against the mattress. "This makes my life on boats seem so much more intolerable. I have to decide soon. I have to find a way off—and I don't know if I can go back to Australia."

She burrowed deeper into his arms, wishing for peace, steadiness, *sanity*. He could be the answer.

They left the inn at eight the next morning, reluctantly, but Peter had to get back to the boat, and Catherine had to open the shop. As they drove the few miles to town, Catherine felt as if she were seeing the familiar landscape with new eyes. Each moor seemed more brightly decorated, the sky a more brilliant blue; she breathed in the scents of the sea and the wild roses and pine as if they were exotic perfume. She glanced over to Peter, and he seemed equally affected by what had taken root between them in the past twenty-four hours. He held her hand as if he didn't want to let go.

When they stopped in front of the house on Orange Street, Peter pulled her close for a kiss. "I'll see you tonight. I'll come by as soon as I can get away from the boat."

"I'll be waiting."

She went inside feeling as if her feet had suddenly sprung wings. In a sweet daze, she climbed the stairs. This must be love—the most wonderful kind of love—without anxiety and constant fear! She pushed open her bedroom door, and let out a scream.

Her room was a shambles. Books had been wrenched from the bookcase and scattered on the floor. The bedcovers were bunched up and dragged off the mattress. Clothes had been pulled from the closet and bureau drawers.

Had Treasa done this? She'd kill her! Catherine stepped around the fallen books. Atop some clothes taken from the bureau lay the Captain's miniature. She picked it up. It was undamaged, but she felt a strange chill. Had he done this? No, he wasn't malicious. She forced the thought and its implications away. It had to have been Treasa, but why would she have been so destructive? Catherine went on into the study, but found that room neat and pristine.

Treasa wasn't in the house, and Catherine could only surmise she'd gotten up early. She spent a good thirty minutes straightening her room, and then went through every other room—nothing else was disturbed.

Catherine rushed through her shower and dressing, and arrived at the shop with only minutes to spare until opening time. Treasa came in a few minutes later with her carry bag over her shoulder. "Oh, hi," she called to Catherine. "I tried to call you last night, but you were out. I spent the night with Jan."

"You weren't home?"

"No, Jan and I were out late. We spent the night on the boat." She leaned against the cash register counter, smiling. "I didn't see any sign of Peter all night."

"He was with me. You're *sure* you weren't home. My room was a total mess!"

"Listen," Treasa said with annoyance, "I told you I've been staying out of your room. I haven't been near your stuff." She cocked her head to the side. "You're serious—your room was really torn apart?"

"Clothes all over, books all over."

"A burglar! Was anything missing? Did they go in my room?"

"Nothing was missing, and none of the other rooms was touched."

"Then who did it?"

"I haven't the vaguest . . ." Catherine's thoughts had turned inward. She stared at the wall and spoke under her breath. "Unless it was our ghost."

Treasa had heard her. "What ghost!" She straightened with a jerk. "I don't want to hear anything about ghosts. I told you!"

Catherine was actually alarmed by Treasa's reaction. "Relax, Trea. Why are you so upset?"

"After what happened in the Med. . . ." It was Treasa's turn to stare blindly at the wall, her eyes wide.

"What happened in the Med.?"

"Oh, a bunch of us used to play with the Ouija Board. We met this fortune teller, Monique, in one of the small towns on the coast of France. She didn't look weird or anything, and a lot of the yachties used to go to her. I went a couple of times. She liked to play around with séances and used to get a group together. Then one night she brought out the Ouija board. Nothing happened at first, but when she and I were on the board together, it worked. I thought it was a lot of laughs when it started spelling out stuff. We contacted somebody—I won't even repeat the name." She shivered. "He said he'd been a criminal five hundred years ago. He'd been burned at the stake for raping and murdering five young girls. But he wanted to repent, he said. His soul had been in limbo. He wanted to do something good to make up for his sins.

"I was spooked, but I thought it was all a joke. I thought Monique had rigged the board so that little indicator thing moved around, even if I wasn't putting any pressure on it. I figured she was trying to put a scare into us all for the fun of it. The next time the guys went up, every one wanted to do the Ouija Board, and I went along. I don't know if you've ever played around with that thing, but you're supposed to ask silly questions and get silly answers. Forget the silly questions. He was there as soon as we put our fingers down. Monique asked what day he was born and where—other stuff about his life. I thought it was my imagination, but the further the questions went, the more I felt this incredible evil feeling. I can't describe it. It was like something awful was sitting behind me. I stopped. I picked my hands right off the board. The other guys thought I was being stupid. I don't think Monique did. That bitch knew.

"I wanted to quit right then and there. We didn't go to Monique's for a couple of weeks, and when we did, I told someone else to take the board. Marissa volunteered. The board had never worked for her before. That night it did. He was back. Their hands started moving so fast, it was hard to follow the pointer. I don't think anyone was able to keep track except Bill, who was sitting next to them, writing each letter down. I started feeling like there was someone behind me again. I wasn't the only one who was uncomfortable. Everyone seemed to shift closer and closer together. Even Monique was looking nervous. She was answering this guy back through the board. I don't know what she was saying. Then the God-damned board just levitated right off the table and went flipping around the room. It was like a lethal object, just missing some of our heads. Monique went for the lights, turned them up full. We'd been sitting in candlelight. She yelled some kind of foreign curse at the board. She grabbed it from out of the air—and for that I give her credit. She flipped it in half. There was a fire burning in the fireplace. She pushed the board in between two logs and stood right there watching with a fire poker in hand until the whole thing finally caught. When it was ashes, she turned back to the rest of us.

"'That was evil. We were foolish to continue contacting that spirit. It's never happened to me before, but that spirit took control.' Monique looked around at all of us. I was so damned scared. So was everyone else. She said, 'I have broken the connection, destroyed the board, but I warn all of you to never touch the Ouija again. He could come back to you he's known . . .'" Treasa shuddered and rubbed her arms.

"I see," Catherine said quietly. No wonder Treasa was terrified at the mention of a ghost. "Listen, Trea, it's all right. I'm sure your spirit hasn't come back." That wasn't a lie. "There's nothing evil in the house."

Treasa seemed somewhat reassured, but she wagged her head. "I wish you'd never brought up the subject."

"So do I," Catherine answered.

Catherine refused to contemplate the cause of her disordered room. If the Captain *had* done it, why? Such destruction was out of character for him. It was still possible Treasa had been lying and used the mention of the ghost to sidetrack Catherine. In any case, she was going out with Peter that night and could procrastinate about drawing any conclusions.

They went to the movies, then he took her back to the *Escapade*. They were alone on board. The others had gone into town. He showed her around the boat, which was larger than the *Cherise* and of a different design, but just as immaculate and gorgeous below. She understood how he would find it difficult, if not impossible, to paint. His own cabin was not particularly large, and the main compartments had to be kept pristine for the owners.

Sharing a huge can of Foster's, they sat up on deck and looked out to the night lights of the harbor. His arm was around her waist, and she leaned her head on his shoulder, feeling as if she was in a safe haven. They sat in comfortable silence, simply enjoying being close. Then Peter cleared his throat.

"I've had some bad news. I've put off telling you all night. The owners called today. I have to sail sooner than I thought."

"No!"

"That's just what I said to myself. I don't have to tell you, Catherine, that I don't want to go."

She'd turned to face him.

"The owners will meet the boat in Marblehead, then we'll go off sailing for a week."

"You won't be able to come down here then."

He shook his head. "Not until they've left."

She felt growing panic. "I know it's only a week or so, but it just seems . . ."

"Like we're being cheated," he finished for her. "But it's not the end."

"I know . . ."

He drew her close. "We'll make the next days really count. And

I'm going to be doing some thinking—some serious thinking about getting out of this business and coming ashore."

With the boat empty, they could sit on deck in privacy. The knowledge that he would soon be leaving lent an urgency to their conversation. It had all happened so fast, but that didn't matter. The love growing between them seemed more like a bond that had been nutured for months. And for Catherine it was an essential means of forgetting Lucien Blythe.

Catherine spent the night on the boat, rising at dawn, and reluctantly kissing Peter good-bye.

"I'll see you at lunch," he whispered sleepily. "In fact, I'd like to have a look at that shop of yours."

Chapter 15

"I don't know what I had pictured," Peter said as she showed him around the shop at lunchtime, "but this is quite the place." He put his arm around her shoulder. "Good work."

"Speaking of which, what's that under your arm? Your sketches?"

"I dug them out for you to have a look. I'm a little nervous about showing them to you."

"Why?"

"Maybe because your opinion's so important to me—especially since I've seen your shop." He laid the cardboard portfolio on her desk. "Have a look."

Catherine quickly did. There were perhaps a dozen in all, of varying subject matter, though a good number were of the sea, for obvious reasons. She held up a sketch of a rugged landscape. "Where's this?"

"Australia."

"I thought so." There was a mildly impressionistic character to his work, but it was fresh—his own. "You've got to start painting, Peter! These are terrific. If you could get this feeling in oils—"

"I did, once. My oils are all back home."

"You've got talent. You could make it."

"You think so, eh?" He was obviously pleased. "All the more for me to think about while we're sailing next week. Maybe I'll have a go at some painting when I get back down here . . . if you could spare me a corner to let the canvases dry."

"Of course. In fact, the upper floor of the barn is empty. You could use it as a studio."

"You're a love. What time are you closing up tonight?"

"Five-thirty."

"I'll meet you here." He dropped a kiss on her cheek. "See you then."

Treasa had come back from lunch while they'd been talking. She smiled coyly to Peter as she passed, and when he was gone, she came to stand by Catherine's desk. "So what's going on? You two got hot and heavy pretty quick. You surprise me."

"Why?"

"I didn't have you figured for falling in love—with Peter, especially. He's always been pretty independent."

"We just hit it off."

"What are you going to do after he leaves?"

"We'll keep seeing each other. He's going to come down from Marblehead after the owners leave."

"Don't count on it."

"What do you mean?"

"He's a yachtie, Cath! Here today, gone tomorrow. I've seen Peter with plenty of women. He never hangs in there long. He'll have half forgotten about you by the time they get back from sailing . . . unless the boat happens to come back to Nantucket."

"He'll be back. He wants to get off boats and paint."

"So, he wants to stay in the States, eh? Needs an American wife to make him legal. Haven't you figured out the game plan yet, Cath?"

"It's nothing like that at all."

Treasa sniffed. "Kid yourself. It's not my problem."

"And what about Jan?"

"What about him?"

"You've been going hot and heavy, too."

"Yeah, but only while he's here. We're not kidding ourselves. You really should have seen Peter in the Med." She smirked and strode away.

Two customers came into the shop, preventing Catherine from continuing the conversation, but she knew Treasa's game.

The next days passed with frightening speed. On Peter's last night, Catherine invited him to her house for dinner. She showed him the barn loft.

"It's perfect," he exclaimed as he paced the room. "Good northern light. I'm surprised you never thought of using this yourself. What was it? Looks like the walls were plastered at one time."

"Old servants' quarters, I think. With all the space in the house, I haven't needed it except for storage."

"You're sure you don't mind?"

"Of course, I don't. I'll just be happy to see you painting again."

"Likewise, my love."

They barbecued in the backyard, sipping drinks afterward in the deepening twilight. Crickets chirped from the garden, and a Brahms symphony played softly from the cassette player Catherine had placed on the window sill. They sat with their chairs side by side, holding hands.

"Tomorrow at this time," Peter mused, "I'll be at the Cape Cod Canal. I'll probably anchor in Buzzards Bay for the night. If I can get to a phone, I'll call you. Otherwise, I'll call you from Marblehead."

"It's gone so fast."

He squeezed her hand. He seemed lost in thought, then he turned to her. "I was talking to Jan this afternoon. He passed on something your sister had said. I gather she'd as soon see the two of us split up, and she was going to talk to you."

"She already has."

"It's not true, you know. This is no fling."

"I don't believe everything Treasa tells me—not half of it."

"The last few days I haven't been able to think straight. My whole world's gone upside down. I love you, Catherine."

Their eyes met and held. It took her a moment to digest what he'd said.

"I wanted you to know before I left . . . if you hadn't guessed already."

The Brahms tape clicked off. Everything in the garden suddenly seemed very still, except for the crickets. For a brief instant a shadow appeared in the middle of the lawn. A fleeting image that flickered into focus for a fraction of a second. Lucien Blythe. She blinked her eyes. Peter seemed to have noticed nothing. When she looked again, the image was gone. The Brahms resumed. Catherine was amazed at the wrenching reaction she felt at seeing Lucien for the first time since their near lovemaking. She shuddered and buried her face against Peter's chest. "I love you, too," she whispered.

An hour before Peter was to sail, Catherine asked Treasa to watch the shop.

"I'm not staying here alone while you go off partying."

"All right, close the shop then, but I'm going to spend some time with Peter before he leaves."

"So it hurts all the more when he doesn't come back?"

She ignored Treasa and walked down to where the *Escapade* was docked. Peter waved to her from the deck. Jan and Ted were both scurrying around, checking lines, bringing cartons below.

He called to them. "Get the rest of the supplies stowed. I'll be back in an hour." He joined Catherine on the dock, put his arm around her shoulder and hugged her. "Let's walk. I always get wound up before we sail, and I'll be spending enough time on the boat the next couple of weeks."

They ambled with no direction in mind, but both were quiet, knowing they had only an hour left. "Is the boat all set?"

He nodded. "It's not a long trip, and there's a decent wind so we can sail instead of motor. I'm just bloody hating the whole thought of it. I'll talk to the owners when they come on board."

"You're going to tell them you're leaving?"

"I want to see what their plans are for the boat for the rest of the summer. They talked of hauling it out in a marina in Maine for repairs and to get the hull scraped and painted. I think I'll try to convince them of the need. If the boat's hauled, that will leave me with lots of free time." He gave her a sidelong glance. "You know I meant what I said last night."

"Why would I suddenly think you didn't?"

"Sailing jitters. I'm not much good at good-byes."

"It's not good-bye."

"Righto, mate."

Returning to the dock an hour later, she went on board with Peter as he made a last inspection. Treasa was on board, too, talking to Jan.

"So you closed the shop." At that point Catherine couldn't have cared.

"You told me I could." In a moment Treasa and Jan walked up the deck toward the dock. As Catherine watched Treasa go ashore and disappear in the direction of the pub, Ted came over with a cheery grin.

"Looks like we're off again. Onward and upward."

"Have a safe trip."

"Yeah, Peter always manages, and with me on board, how can he help it." He winked broadly. "Seriously, it's been good seeing you again."

"Likewise. Hope to see you again before summer's over."

"Hope so, too. Hang in there." He laid a light hand on her

shoulder, then strode forward and started unfastening the sail covers. Catherine wondered if she ever would see him again—probably not in Nantucket.

"Guess we're set," Peter said when he returned to her side. "I'll walk you back to the dock."

There was no privacy, but still he took her in his arms for a long kiss on the dockside. "I'll call soon."

She nodded. Her throat suddenly felt choked up. He pressed her fingers, and as if he could find no words, spun around and went back on board.

Catherine stayed long enough to see the lines cast off, Jan and Ted hauling them on the foredeck as Peter stood at the wheel, maneuvering the boat from the slip. It was too painful to watch the slow progress of departure. With a final wave to Peter, she hurried back to Orange Street and up to the widow's walk. She arrived in time to see the *Escapade* leaving the mouth of the harbor. Catherine's hands gripped the railing as she watched the crew raise the mainsail. The white canvas fluttered for a moment, then the sail caught and was set.

At the sight of the sail, Peter's departure seemed all the more real. She swallowed against the growing constriction in her throat. Perhaps Treasa had been *right*. Perhaps, once away from Nantucket, the special thing they'd shared would no longer seem so special to him. It would fade amid other comfortable, pleasant memories. She lifted her hand to her cheek to discover it was wet. Only a few days, and he was gone, too . . .

"What's the reason for your tears?" The sharp voice at her elbow made her jump. "The gentleman with whom you've seen fit to spend so many nights away from the house?"

"You scared me!" She swung her head to stare up at Lucien.

He was in shirtsleeves, rolled to his elbows as if he'd been working. There was a film of perspiration on his forehead, and his dark curls clung damply to it. He looked tired.

"No doubt I startled you," he said. "Your thoughts have obviously been elsewhere."

They still were at that moment, though with the Captain's sudden appearance, they were unfocused, stunned. She strained her eyes toward the harbor, but the scene was the Captain's, not her own. "Do you see what you've done?"

"*I've* done? I merely came up here for a breath of air. You are the one who's been behaving erratically!"

His presence was too magnetic to be ignored. She found herself staring helplessly at his bearded face—a face that still turned her knees to water. She hadn't forgotten the emotions he roused in her. She'd been deceiving herself to think she could forget. "Me? Didn't you tell me it would be better if we never met again?" Something seemed to have gone wrong with her voice. It felt choked.

He ignored her in his own urgency to make a point. "You've been out of the house for nights on end with your new paramour—"

"It *was* you who went through my bedroom and left it a shambles!"

"Not your room—mine. And I did nothing but vent a bit of anger in my own domain. I'd just seen you there and was frustrated that you'd disappeared again. I flung a few things around."

"A few things?"

"Perhaps I became carried away. I intended to rectify matters, but I slipped back to my frame."

"You hadn't just seen me disappear. I wasn't even in the house. You deliberately disrupted my belongings!"

He ignored her again. "Who is this man you are seeing?"

"After what you've done to me, it's none of your business." She peered up at his tight expression and suddenly had a niggling suspicion. "You wouldn't be jealous, would you?"

"I am neither jealous, nor particularly interested. Only curious." He squinted out toward the harbor. "I happened to be standing in the upstairs hall when he arrived at the door to collect you. I noticed he was rather disreputably attired—short pants, no jacket. Even in Calcutta, men have the courtesy to wear a suitable jacket in the evenings."

"This is not Calcutta, nor is it 1844. He was dressed perfectly well."

"Not in my opinion."

"You're not dating him."

Lucien balled his fist on the rail. "I also saw you briefly in the garden—touching scene that! If he is such a gentleman, why have his actions brought you to tears?"

"I wasn't crying over anything he'd done to me. His ship just sailed."

He swung his head around and regarded her closely. "He is a seaman?"

"A captain of a sailboat—about a seventy-footer."

"One of those frivolous pleasure craft I've seen in your harbor," he scoffed.

"I didn't notice anything frivolous about it. It's a beautiful boat."

"You've been aboard?"

"Yes, several times."

"Hmph!" He glared at some point in the landscape. "I should take you aboard one of my vessels and show you a *real* ship."

"You can't. And I thought women were considered bad luck aboard a working vessel."

"Not necessarily. I would make an exception. You've certainly wasted no time in finding other diversions since our last meeting."

She flinched. "You said it defied all sanity for us to be together— that it was a mistake. We were from different worlds. I found a man in my own world."

"Must you have taken me quite so literally?" he said roughly.

"How else should I have taken your words?"

"You did not have to go out and immediately pluck up a substitute."

"You haven't shown your face in weeks! Do you realize how *I* felt? What was I supposed to do? I had to forget you. You left me no choice!" Just talking of it brought back all the torment she'd experienced.

He expelled a heavy breath. "Unfortunately, I did not foresee or give enough thought to my own reactions. When you were away from the house so much, I became concerned . . . oh, damn it, I missed you!" He said the last as if he might as well get it off his chest. "I've found since our last meeting that I've been slipping more and more often into your world—of course, you were never here to appreciate that fact. I've wanted to talk to you as well, resolve what's to come to pass between us . . . to tell you I'm sorry."

Catherine was suddenly finding it difficult to remain resolute. "You didn't stay away deliberately?"

"No, not after the first several days."

Something inside wavered. She tried to think of Peter. All she saw was the grave expression on Lucien's face. "Nothing can come to pass for us," she whispered.

"Are you completely convinced? I've begun to question that belief myself. Why else have we been brought together?"

"Don't do this to me!" she cried. "Don't confuse me! It took me too long to sort it all out and find some kind of peace."

"Ah, you'd prefer I suffer with my own confusion, silently."

"You didn't seem terribly confused when you told me it would have been better if we'd never met!"

"I was wrong. I was also being influenced by what had happened in my life in the past."

"Captain, I can't take another round of that kind of emotional upheaval. I don't want to. I've been thinking, too, and you were right. Intimacy between us won't work. Let's just go on the way it was in the beginning. We know we'll see each other from time to time. We'll accept it at that—but no more." Did she mean it? With Peter gone, how would she feel seeing Lucien and being confronted with her own reactions to him?

"We will remain ships passing in the night at regular intervals—is that what you are saying?"

"Yes." That would be safe, wouldn't it?

She glanced up and caught him watching her. His look sent a shiver down her spine.

"You will continue seeing this man, or has he sailed off for good?"

"He'll be back, and yes, I'll see him."

"You seem to have a penchant for men of the sea. I suppose I should console myself with that. You have feelings for him obviously."

"I love him."

"So suddenly!" His lips tightened into a grim line.

"It was one of those things."

"Yes, I'm familiar with those 'things,' as you say. I found myself very recently nearly involved in one."

"Captain, you're deliberately trying to upset me."

He gave a rueful chuckle. "Am I so obvious? Come below. I want to experiment with something." He took her hand.

She was thrown by his sudden change of mood, but curious, too. What was he up to now?

"Don't release my hand," he told her as he led her toward the stairs from the roof.

"Why?"

"Patience. You shall soon see. I have been wondering about this for several days now." He descended the narrow staircase first, stepping sideways down the treads. He led her across the attic, all the way down to the ground floor, then down the hall, through the kitchen, and out the back door. Catherine had never seen all of the house with his decor. She would have liked to explore all the rooms, but she sensed his urgency and said nothing.

Once they were outside, he began walking with her around the small backyard, strolling the boundaries from one end to the other.

"I've always loved your garden," she said, more to herself than him. "I was going to plant mine to look just like it, but never got around to it."

"You shall have to spend more time in my garden then, won't you?"

The pressure of his hand around her was firm and warm, but his touch was putting unwanted thoughts in her mind. Caution told her to break the physical contact before she got herself in trouble. "What *are* we doing?"

"I thought that was obvious. We are walking about my garden."

"But why?"

"So I might test my theories." With that he led her toward the barn and stepped in through the open doorway. Catherine was fascinated to see the old building in its original state. It smelled of hay and leather. A horse nickered from somewhere in the dimness.

"You've yet to meet Sarter," Lucien said. "Let me introduce you." He proceeded to the box stall in the corner, leading her past the black carriage parked in the center of the barn. As they approached, the horse stuck his head over the stall door.

The animal was as elegant on close inspection as he'd seemed when she'd viewed him pulling the carriage her first night in the house. Lucien rubbed a hand over the horse's neck, then scratched behind one pricked ear.

"You like that, don't you, my friend? This charming lady is Catherine, who perhaps you may be seeing again on a future occasion." As if he understood, the horse pushed his muzzle forward and nudged Catherine's shoulder.

She grinned. "You've trained him well."

"Actually, he's rather intelligent as horseflesh goes. But come, we're not finished yet." He drew her along, out of the barn and up the crushed shell drive, then out onto the bricked sidewalk. Catherine gaped as she looked up and down the street, seeing familiar buildings in an 1840s setting. There were few trees and several of the buildings of her era had yet to be constructed. Still, she was amazed at how little Orange Street had changed with the march of time.

"What do you think?" Lucien asked.

She could only wag her head in bemusement. Farther up the street, a delivery wagon was stopped in front of one of the doorways. A woman in a long, full-skirted gray dress with a white apron tied about her waist stepped out onto the stoop and spoke to the driver of the wagon, although her voice didn't carry to where they were standing.

Lucien started walking down the sidewalk, away from the delivery wagon, urging her along. Catherine forgot all else in her stupefaction. To be walking down Orange Street in 1844 Nantucket was beyond belief. Her eyes swung from one side of the street to the other, noticing little things—the hitching posts in front of doorways, the horse droppings on the street, the shutters framing every window.

"I can't take you very far in that short skirt you're wearing." The Captain paused as he noticed some pedestrians approaching. He steered them around and started back toward the house. "But I think my point is proven."

"What point?" Catherine asked, dazed.

"That physical contact has something to do with our remaining together—not always, but since we've been holding hands, we've not parted. And we've left the immediate vicinity of the house. We are not tied to it. You see, I could take you down to one of my ships, properly attired, of course."

"And how would you explain me? As a friend who's making a brief visit from the twentieth century?"

"That might pose a problem, mightn't it? Particularly here, where everyone knows everyone else's business. I shall have to give the matter some thought." He led her back into the grounds, into the center of the garden.

"Next we shall have to try it when I am visiting your century. I'm immensely curious to see the results of progress. Now, for the next part of the experiment." His eyes captured hers. "As much as I dislike bringing this meeting to an end, I'm going to release your hand. If I'm not mistaken, we'll soon part."

Before he did so, he leaned over and planted a gentle kiss on her forehead. "Until we meet again, my dear. Now that your sailor's gone, try to spend more time in the house." His voice was persuasively soft. He stepped back. Within seconds he was gone.

Catherine felt dizzy as she gazed around her own garden. The Captain's experiment had left her drained. Too many thoughts were coming at her from too many different angles. How would their situation change if they acquired the ability to remain in the same plane whenever they chose? Would it work all the time? She felt so vulnerable whenever she was with him; all common sense fled with the wind. And she'd only just begun to feel she'd acquired some rationality about their relationship. Why did Peter have to sail now? With him at her side, she wouldn't be so susceptible, so confused.

Chapter 16

The phone rang about ten. Catherine had been trying to read in bed and getting nowhere. She couldn't concentrate. She quickly reached for the receiver on the nightstand.

"This is the marine operator speaking. I have a call for you from the yacht *Escapade*."

"Yes . . . go ahead."

"Hi, it's Peter."

"Hi! Where are you?"

"Buzzards Bay. We got in late this afternoon. I'm calling on the VHF. Do you know how it operates?"

"No."

"Well, from your end, it's no problem, but if you talk while I'm speaking, I won't be able to hear you. I've got to release the button at this end first. A nuisance sometimes, but it also prevents a too-chatty person from interrupting in mid-sentence. So how are you?"

"Fine. I'm glad you called." Her voice relayed her relief. Sanity again. "How was the trip?"

"No problems. Not much of a trip in this weather . . ."

"How long are you staying in Buzzards Bay?"

"Say again. I missed that. You started talking too soon."

She repeated her question.

"Just until morning. We should get to Marblehead tomorrow afternoon. I'll call you again from there. After that we'll be sailing, and I don't know when I'll get the chance."

They talked for ten minutes, only twice finding themselves both speaking at the same time. "I'll be thinking of you," he said as he cleared off. "Can't wait to see you."

Catherine laid the receiver in its cradle. No sooner had she done so than she heard a crash in the kitchen. She went running down to find Treasa ineffectually cleaning up the remnants of a broken wine bottle. Its contents were splashed all over the floor and lower cupboards.

Treasa looked up and squinted. "I dropped it. Just slid right out of my hands."

"Here, I'll help you." Catherine grabbed the broom to sweep up the glass. "I don't suppose you ate dinner tonight."

"Dinner?" Treasa swayed slightly, grabbed the countertop. "Oh, yeah I did. I had some fries . . . and a hamburger, I think."

"Where have you been? The Harborside?"

"Yeah." Treasa grinned and leaned back against the cupboards. "Couldn't hang around here and be bored—'specially since the *Escapade*'s gone."

"I thought you didn't care." Catherine kept her voice mild as she finished cleaning up the mess.

Her body swaying slightly, Treasa squinted at her again as if trying to pull her thoughts together. "I didn't say I didn't care. S'not worth caring. I'm meeting some new friends. Better'n vegetating in this place like you're going to do now that Peter's gone." Her lips formed a crooked grin. "Bet you haven't heard from him either."

"He called tonight."

"Hah. Isn't that a surprise. Really trying to get in there with you, isn't he?"

Catherine came to Treasa's side. "How about a cup of coffee?"

"Never drink coffee after twelve. Upsets my stomach."

"Then come on up to bed."

"I'm fine. Leave me alone." Treasa started on a wobbly course toward the refrigerator. "Another beer and I'll be okay."

"Why are you drinking like this?"

"'Cause I'm bored. What else is there to do?"

"There's no more beer or wine."

"Fine—got some in my room." Treasa stumbled out of the kitchen, up the hall. Catherine followed. She knew the futility of trying to talk any sense into Treasa in her present state. She just wanted to be sure she arrived in her bedroom in one piece.

Treasa gripped the banister, taking one unsteady step after another. "You my watchdog?" Treasa called over her shoulder.

"I'm going to bed, too. I'm just walking behind you."

Catherine waited at the top of the stairs until Treasa had navigated to her bedroom, sat down on her bed, then gradually curled up on top of the covers and passed out. Catherine found a blanket and spread it over her sister's sleeping form, turned out the light, and went to her own room.

She climbed back into bed, worried. Treasa was obviously far more upset about Jan's leaving than she'd let on. She'd been good, but now that the boat had sailed, immediate regression. Yet what was gained by Catherine's own worrying? She couldn't talk to Treasa, or give her any comfort that night.

Treasa was too hungover to get out of bed the next morning, and figuring she'd be useless in the shop anyway, Catherine left her there. As she crossed the backyard, Marjorie called to her from over the fence.

"I haven't seen you in an age. How are you?"

Catherine walked over to the fence. How comforting Marjorie's face seemed. "I'm pretty good. I've just been busy now the shop's open."

"I've been meaning to come down and have a look. In fact, I'll try to stop in today. You look much better than the last time I saw you. Would it have something to do with that handsome blond fellow I noticed barbecuing the other day?"

Catherine felt the flush rising in her cheeks. "Yes. Peter and I have been seeing a lot of each other."

"I'm pleased for you. You're much more relaxed." Marjorie looked off into the distance as if she were having a private debate within herself, then she pushed her glasses up her nose. "There's something else I wanted to ask you."

Catherine waited.

Marjorie ran her fingers through her hair. "You'll probably think me an old fool . . . but do you remember when we talked, and you mentioned a ghost? Well, I don't think you were dreaming. I've seen someone up on your widow's walk . . . and in your backyard. A man, with a beard, distinctly resembling Captain Blythe of your portrait. Not very often—"

"You have!" Catherine stood dumbstruck.

"Heavens, I didn't mean to scare you. Actually, I don't think it's anything to be scared of—he didn't seem ominous. Just an image." She glanced at Catherine's face. "Then again, maybe it was no more than my imagination, remembering what you'd said and those old stories—"

Marjorie's phone started ringing. She looked distractedly over her shoulder. "Oh, dear! I have to go. I'm expecting a call, and Evan's not home." She grabbed Catherine's hand. "Forget I even mentioned it! I'll talk to you later."

Catherine wasn't able to forget what Marjorie had mentioned. It presented new problems. Marjorie's probing curiosity and open mind wouldn't let such an event as seeing Catherine's ghost go unexamined. She'd want to talk about it, and perhaps experiment, and Catherine wasn't quite sure how she could put her off—but put her off she must.

Not long after, Treasa came home with two strange characters in tow. If not precisely "punkers," they were one step away. Rita and her boyfriend, Arty, were both in their mid-twenties, with spiked, bleached hairdos and a style of dress that looked like they'd raided the Salvation Army bin. A variety of outrageous earrings pierced the lobes of their ears, and Rita sported a small gold ring through her right nostril. They couldn't have been less typical of the average Nantucket inhabitant. When Treasa made lazy introductions, the two merely nodded toward Catherine, otherwise ignoring her and following Treasa into the living room.

Catherine tried to put aside her uneasiness. You couldn't judge a book by its cover, she reminded herself. They were probably decent people, despite their outrageous attire, and Treasa was lonely. She hadn't gone on another drinking binge, but she seemed restless and unhappy with Jan gone.

The next evening as Catherine quickly dusted the house, she noticed a blank space in the arrangement of her grandmother's Oriental ginger jars on the dining room sideboard. They were all priceless pieces. She counted them. There were only five, where there'd been six before. She questioned Treasa about it, who only shrugged. "That old junk."

"Look, if you accidentally broke one, just tell me. I'm not going to get mad."

"I never go in the dining room. You probably put one of them in the wrong place yourself."

For a few days Treasa's new friends didn't put in any appearances at the house, and aside from the mystery of the missing jar, Catherine began to relax. Then Catherine noticed that not one, but several, pieces of scrimshaw in the study were gone. She'd always appreciated the beauty of the hand-carved ivory and knew every piece.

Could the Captain be up to his games? No. She had a different suspicion altogether.

She went downstairs immediately and found Treasa. Her new friends had come visiting, and all three were lounging on the back lawn. Each had a beer can in hand. Rita and Arty looked up lazily as Catherine called to Treasa from the back door.

"Come here a minute. I want to talk to you."

"What now?"

"Just come here."

Treasa did. Catherine wasted no words. "Some of the scrimshaw's gone."

"So. What do you want me to do about it?"

"I want to know what happened to it."

"How should I know?" Treasa's expression was a combination of bafflement and worry. Catherine couldn't tell which was the stronger emotion.

"Do you ever bring your new friends up here during the day?"

"If I do, it's my business."

"I don't want them here. In fact, I don't want *anyone* in this house except you when I'm not home."

"Don't worry about it." Treasa shrugged, turned and left.

From the kitchen window Catherine saw Treasa join her friends. The three of them immediately exchanged rapid comments. What was going on? Between Peter and her dilemma with the Captain, Catherine had been allowing the situation with Treasa to slip. It was no one's fault but her own, but the time had come to put a stop to it. She was more and more convinced that her suspicions were correct. The two punkers weren't just weird, they were possibly thieves. She went for the telephone, but her finger stopped in mid-dial. What was she going to tell the police? She had no proof, only a wild suspicion. She could have them kicked off the property, but she hadn't a doubt that they'd be back when Catherine wasn't around to stop them, perhaps with revenge in mind.

She started toward the kitchen door prepared to walk out and confront them, not stopping to think that she was obviously outnumbered. Halfway across the kitchen, she walked full force into the suddenly materializing form of the Captain.

He started to laugh, but his good humor vanished when he saw her face. "Something's troubling you. I sensed it when you called—"

"When I called?"

His expression grew mystified. "It seemed that. I was in the midst of computing a sailing schedule when I felt this compulsion to come to the galley."

Catherine's hands grew cold.

He sensed her reaction and took her arm. "We'll think about that later. Tell me what's wrong."

Catherine glanced toward the kitchen windows. Treasa and her guests were still on the lawn, sitting closely together and talking secretively. Lucien followed her gaze.

"My God! Who—or what—is that?"

"New friends of my sister's. Charming, aren't they."

"Repulsive." His lips curled. "What are they doing here?"

"No good, I'm sure. I have a feeling they've conned Treasa. Some valuable things have started disappearing from the house—scrimshaw, Chinese porcelain. I think they're responsible, but I don't have any proof. I was just on my way out to kick them off the property."

"Why would your sister wish to steal things from the house?"

"For cash. Out of revenge that I inherited it, and she didn't. She tried to contest the will and apparently found out she didn't have a leg to stand on."

"Then do call the authorities."

"I was going to, but what can the police can do? I don't have any real evidence except that some valuables are missing."

"They can begin a search for the missing items. If these two reprobates are in need of cash, they would surely try to pawn them."

"I don't think they'd try to sell them on the Island, and what will they do if they find out I've put the police on to them? Lucien, I'm scared. I wouldn't be surprised if they dealt in drugs, too. Treasa's really unstable—susceptible . . ."

He took her cold hand in his. His voice was hard. "In which case, you shouldn't be going out there alone confronting them. I see it is time I put a hand in this myself."

"What can you do?"

He chuckled mirthlessly. "A number of things."

"Treasa's terrified of ghosts! She told me about a scary experience she had."

"Interesting. Of course, I am not a ghost, but she won't know that, and as long as I am here so conveniently at the moment . . ."

"What are you planning?"

Quickly, with a slight twinkle of glee in his eyes, he explained.

She nodded mutely. The three were still sprawled on the grass.

The Captain walked to the back door, his hand locked around Catherine's behind his back as insurance against his departing before his task was done. He pushed open the screen. As Catherine pressed against the doorframe, out of sight, he stepped onto the porch.

"Treasa," he called. "Treasa!"

She spun around, eyes wide. The other two were facing away from the door, and seemed too disinterested to react. Treasa stood up.

Lucien released Catherine's hand and went quickly down the stairs. He grabbed Rita's and Arty's shirt collars from behind, lifted them bodily off the grass, and pushed them toward the gate.

"What the hell!" Arty growled, reaching up to wrench off Lucien's hand. Rita's expletive was more screeching. "Get your f'n hands off me! What's going on here?"

"You are being requested to leave," Lucien spoke with the heavy authority he must often have used with his crew. "And do not return! *That* is an order. Should you decide to do so, you shall deeply regret it!"

He shoved them against the gate, but the physical connection that worked between Catherine and him failed to keep him in the same dimension with the others. Just as he pushed them forward, his image simply flashed out—was gone.

Catherine saw it happen, swallowed hard, and watched through the back window as the punkers grabbed at the fence and spun around to face their attacker. Their looks of confusion and bewilderment brought a grim smile to her lips.

"Who the hell was that?" Arty peered around, blinking his eyes.

Treasa was standing in the same spot, her mouth hanging open.

Rita brusquely pulled her shirt into place and glared at Arty. "You must have gotten some bad stuff—either that, or I'm going crazy."

Treasa bolted toward the back door and came pounding into the kitchen.

"Who was that?"

Catherine's face was blandly puzzled. "Who was who?"

"That man?"

"I didn't see anybody."

"Hell, you didn't! He walked right out of the kitchen door."

"This kitchen door?"

"He had a beard. He called to me and he picked Rita and Arty right off the ground. Then all of a sudden, he wasn't there anymore.

Oh, God! The ghost!" She brought her hands up to her face. "No! Nathan! He's come back!"

Arty pushed in through the back door. "What kind of weirdos you got roaming around here? Or was that supposed to be some kind of joke? Damn it, get me a beer, Treasa. I need it."

"It wasn't any joke," Treasa stuttered.

He crossed his arms over his chest, ignoring Catherine. "Then what the hell's going on, Treasa?"

"Nothing! Just get out of here. Go! I'll talk to you tomorrow."

He didn't seem inclined to move.

Catherine stepped forward, feeling a strange new confidence. Barney came to her side and, very unlike his usually docile, friendly self, growled menacingly in his throat. His lips lifted to bare shiny and sharp white fangs. "You heard my sister. Leave—both you and your girlfriend. And don't set foot near this property again, or I'll call the cops."

He snorted. His eyes glinted maliciously at Catherine. But in a moment he turned and banged out the door. Treasa closed the inside door behind him and locked it. Her hands were shaking like leaves in a wind storm. Her face was drained of all color. She went immediately to the refrigerator, withdrew a wine bottle, poured a glass, and swallowed it in almost one gulp. "I saw him, Cath—I did! He scared me out of my mind."

"I'd be scared, too, if I was hanging around with those two creeps."

"They don't have anything to do with my being scared."

"Oh? I'd have a better look at them if I were you. I don't want them in this house. I think they've been stealing from me, and if they show their faces around here, or you do one more thing to upset me, you *are* going—and you know damn well I'll do it, too!" Heartless as it seemed, Catherine wheeled around and left the kitchen. "I've got work to do."

As she walked up the hall, she sent out a silent message of thanks to the Captain.

She got a call the next morning at work from Peter. He sounded rushed. "The trip's been extended," he said after their greeting. "We're cruising up to Nova Scotia. We'll be gone at least another week, and we'll be sailing the whole time. I may not get another chance to phone. But there's good news. I've talked them into putting the boat up in the yard in Camden, Maine, for repairs. I figure there's at least a month's work, maybe more."

"That's wonderful! You can paint."

"And we can see each other. I'm missing you."

"Missing you, too."

Treasa was spaced out all day, nervous, dropping things, jumping at the slightest noise. She didn't mention the ghost again, and Catherine had decided the best course was to let her sister stew in her private worries. Treasa said she was going to run some errands after work. Some gut feeling motivated Catherine to check the house carefully when she got home. At first everything looked fine, then she checked her jewelry box. Her diamond stud earrings were gone. Her first thought was that she'd put them away in the wrong place. She tended to be haphazard about her jewelry. When had she worn them last? One night when she was out with Peter. She thought back over the evening. Had she dropped them on the boat? No, she remembered taking them out the next morning at the house and putting them . . . where?

She'd promised Marjorie she'd go to a historical society meeting with her that night, and she had only a few minutes to eat and get washed up. She considered canceling, but Marjorie would be disappointed, and she wasn't sure the earrings were missing.

Carefully locking the house doors, she went next door to Marjorie's and together they walked to the Atheneum, where that evening's meeting was to be held.

Catherine was enormously thankful that the subject of the man Marjorie had seen on the widow's walk didn't arise during the evening—not until they were walking back home, when Marjorie spoke somewhat hesitantly.

"I hope I didn't upset you with what I said the other day."

"No." Catherine waited nervously for what was coming next—prayed Marjorie would let it rest at that. She wasn't so lucky.

"I've been thinking about it. I have several friends," Marjorie continued in a rushed, explanatory tone, "who don't consider ghosts a bunch of nonsense. These are very reputable people—certainly not fanatics—who tend to have open minds on the subject. You might say they have psychic abilities. I spoke to one of them about what I'd seen. She'd be willing to come around to your house to see if she can pick up any . . . vibrations . . . whatever."

Catherine panicked. "No!" She tried to temper her tone and decided blunt, partial honesty was the best solution in sidetracking

Marjorie. "I mean, there's no need. It is Lucien Blythe. I've seen his image here and there in the house, and he's not menacing." At least not menacing to anything but her emotions, Catherine added silently.

"You've seen him? Where? Very often?"

"In various rooms, in the garden and on the widow's walk. I thought I was losing my mind at first, too."

"Goodness! I wonder what it is that keeps him in and about the house?"

She had to prevent Marjorie from becoming any more curious. "Maybe it has something to do with the story you told me," she said finally, "and whatever he came to Nantucket to escape. But I'm sure it's only a temporary thing—maybe because I found his portrait, and you and I were thinking of him." How lame that sounded in Catherine's ears, but Marjorie seemed to accept it.

"Yes. My, my, this is quite exciting! Well, perhaps it isn't for you—having a ghost living with you and all. Now I understand why you looked so frazzled a few weeks back. You should have told me then."

"And risk losing the only friend I had on the Island? Besides, I'm fine now. I got used to him—like having a pet around the house." Oh, what a good liar she was becoming!

Marjorie chuckled. "A pet. What an interesting way of thinking of it. How I'd love to see him myself, aside from these glimpses. You don't suppose he'd show himself while I was in the house with you—"

"No, I don't think so. I mean—no one's ever seen him in the house but me." Lies, lies, when he'd presented himself to Treasa only the night before.

Marjorie's brow creased with disappointment under her gray curls. "I suppose you're right. Best not to rock the boat. It's obviously been rocked sufficiently. I wonder if it did have something to do with your finding the portrait?"

"I haven't a clue."

"True. Well, now you know that anytime you want to talk you can come over and see this crazy old lady," Marjorie said as they parted. "And do let me know about anything that happens!"

Catherine let out a much needed sigh of relief as she walked the rest of the way home. She felt like a wretch for lying to Marjorie, but the *last* thing she wanted was an outsider, a psychic one in particular, poking around in the house. For reasons not fully clear to herself, she was feeling protective of Lucien—very protective.

As Catherine turned the back doorknob, she was surprised to find it locked. Nearly every light in the house was burning, indicating Treasa must be at home. She dug out her keys, unlocked the door. As she stepped into the kitchen, she was further surprised that Barney didn't even raise his head from his rug. Treasa was huddled at the kitchen table. Her face was devoid of color. From the red-rimmed eyes, it was evident she'd been crying. She rose and rushed over to Catherine.

"What's wrong?" Catherine exclaimed.

"The ghost . . . he came back . . ." Treasa was trembling so badly she could barely speak.

"Came back where?"

"In the living room. I . . . I was pouring a drink. All of a sudden he was there. He came over to me and took the glass right out of my hand. He grabbed the bottle, too. I . . . I was so scared . . . I didn't stop him. He stared at me . . . the look in his eyes! He told me I'd better not be hiding another bottle, or he'd be back to get it. He said he didn't want to see my two friends anywhere near the house again either. He'd be watching me, he said. Then . . . then he disappeared . . . right in front of my eyes! Cath! What am I going to do?"

"Do what he told you to do for starters."

"But he's a ghost! This can't be real! Oh, my God!" she sobbed. "You believe me, Cath, don't you?"

"Unless you were hallucinating."

"No! I'd had two drinks. That's all! What if he comes back?"

"I don't think you have anything to worry about tonight."

Treasa was barely listening. She was shaking her head and dragging in sobbing breaths.

"Were your friends robbing this house, Treasa?"

The other girl shuddered.

"My diamond earrings are missing. Did they have anything to do with that? Treasa, answer me!"

Treasa nearly collapsed into the chair at the table. "I . . . I didn't mean for it to get so bad. I didn't, Cath! There was all this old junk in the house. Part of it should have been mine anyway." Tears poured from her eyes. She tried ineffectually to wipe them away with the back of her hand. "They said they'd give me a good price and throw in some grass in the bargain. They said nobody would miss the stuff they took anyway—just a few things. But they kept wanting more. I didn't know they took your earrings! They made me give them the key to the house . . . said they'd squeal to the cops and frame me if I didn't. They must have come up here today . . ."

"Shit! So they have a key and can come in here anytime they want. I'm calling the police."

"No—please—don't!" Treasa practically got on her hands and knees. "They'll implicate me!"

"Maybe you deserve it! I'm not going to let them get away with this, Treasa!"

"Change the locks. They won't come in the house while you're here."

"How did they get past Barney, by the way?"

"They said something about tranquilizers in a piece of meat."

"What! How could you let them do that to Barney?" Catherine immediately went over to the dog and knelt down beside him. She ran her hands over his gleaming, golden coat. "You poor baby!" Barney lifted his head and licked her hand, seemingly telling her that he appreciated her concern, but he was fine—if tired.

"Oh, please, Cath. I didn't know until afterwards. I'll try to get your stuff back—or at least pay you for it."

Reassured that Barney would soon recover, Catherine rose and paced the kitchen. She went to the back door and as a precaution threw the old bolt lock that was never used. "All right, I'll decide what to do tomorrow, but I'm calling the police."

"No!"

"I'm going to tell them I think I've seen a prowler—ask them to keep an eye on the house tonight."

She went to the phone, dialed and briefly left the message with the police dispatcher. Then she turned back to Treasa.

"You'd better go to bed."

"I'm not going in my room tonight."

"You can't stay up all night."

"I'll sleep on the couch. Can . . . can I keep the dog down here with me?"

"I thought you didn't like Barney."

"I'd feel safer."

"Okay. I was going to leave him down here anyway in case your friends decided to come around. Oh, Treasa, how could you get yourself in such a mess?"

"I didn't bring that ghost around! You don't believe I saw him, do you?"

Catherine only studied her sister's haggard face. She wasn't going to tell her just how completely she *did* believe.

"Start looking for another place, Treasa. You have five days to get out."

Chapter 17

Something wakened Catherine in the middle of the night—a sense, a feeling. Slowly she pulled herself up from the depths of slumber, rolled to her side, and opened her eyes. Lucien was sitting on the edge of the bed looking down at her.

She sat bolt upright.

"I was just preparing to get into bed," he said, "and saw you. Catherine, I promise not to do anything you don't wish. I need to talk."

Staring at him, she tried to pull herself fully awake. The room was lit only by two candles on the mantel. In the reflection she saw the softness in his expression and some painful rippling, too. She felt herself relax, believing him. He was too much a gentleman to deliberately deceive her.

He laid one hand over hers above the coverlet. The other rested on his thigh, and he flexed his fingers restlessly as he spoke. "All too often lately I can't find sleep. I sit in that chair across the room and think . . . wondering where I shall go from here . . . wondering what the inevitable conclusion to all of this is. I should be getting on with my life in my own world. Instead, I think of you." Silence reigned for a moment; a single set of hoofbeats echoed on the cobblestones outside the open window. "Tonight, for instance, I went to dinner at the Macys'. I was aware of why I'd been invited. They have a lovely and charming daughter, Lucinda, who's taken quite a fancy to me. If I had any wits about me, I'd appreciate her interest, not only for her own merits, but for the eligibility of the connection."

Catherine was thrown off balance by an unexpected twinge of jealousy.

"Usually I am not so rude," he continued quietly, "but tonight I found myself nearly falling asleep as we conversed. I could not wait to return here."

His fingers tightened on her hand. "Before meeting you I shied away from romantic relationships with a fervor because of what I'd suffered with Gwen. I'd decided never to seriously involve myself with another woman."

"What *did* happen, Lucien? Tell me."

"You know I don't wish to speak about it."

"You can't bury old pain. It doesn't go away. It just festers."

"I don't wish to talk of it."

"You must! Tell me. Was it so terrible that you can't go on living again?"

For a long moment he was silent. His free hand had closed into a fist on his thigh. "Very well. If it is so important for you to know, go into the study tomorrow. I will try somehow to leave my journal on the desk. If I am not successful, next time we meet, ask me to give it to you."

"Get it now."

"No. I am not yet ready to break this connection."

Catherine was beginning to wonder if she was ready to break the connection either. Against all common sense, she was soothed by conversing with him, even if it was the middle of the night. "I want to thank you for your intervention with Treasa tonight."

"Ah. So it did some good."

"She was nearly hysterical when I came home—so shaken up that she admitted conspiring with her new friends to take things from the house."

"You remind me," he interrupted quickly. "I have something for you, although they are not with me at the moment. A pair of diamond earrings and a gold necklace."

"*You* took them?"

"I retrieved them. I happened to come across those two unsavory characters in the house today. Unfortunately, I was in the midst of dressing, and had just pulled on my trousers. I was reaching for my shirt when I looked up and saw them at your bureau. They turned and saw me suddenly appear out of nothing, a half-naked phantom. I'd have wished for more dignity, but it was rather amusing to see the expressions on their faces. Their appearance was perversely amusing to me as well—court jesters was the term that came to mind. They both let out high-pitched yelps. I put on my most threatening face—

it's always worked exceedingly well with surly new crew members. I reached out my arm and told them to hand it over. They did, with alacrity. I added that they were nothing but a couple of swine and if I ever saw them within a mile of the house again, I would stew them over a low fire. I wanted all other articles they'd removed from the house returned *tout de suite*, intimating that I knew and saw everything they did, even when *I* wasn't visible. Weak-livered specimens, both of them. They were literally shaking in their shoes. It was quite enjoyable, actually. I only wished I could have seen their faces when I vanished and was once again in my own quarters, with your jewelry in my hand. I do not think you will have trouble with them again."

Catherine chuckled merrily, picturing the scene he described in all its vividness. "How perfect! You couldn't have planned it better if you'd tried. Treasa told me she'd given them the key to the house. I was afraid they'd come back. They drugged Barney today, you know."

"Barney—that lovable, large rag of fur you own. Disgraceful! He recovered?"

"Yes. He's fine."

"You show an immoderate amount of affection for that dog. A pity you find it so difficult to show the same amount of affection for your fellow humans."

"Meaning?" Her voice had gone low.

"Ah, me, I suppose."

"Captain, if you remember, I was willing to show you a great deal of affection."

"Yes, but that changed—my fault! Lightning strike me dead for my foolishness!"

"You were being sensible. I wasn't."

"And since then you have held me at arm's length. Do you treat your seaman similarly?"

"There is a reason for my holding you away."

"I've not noticed him about at all. His doing, or yours?"

"He'll be back."

"At twenty-seven one borders on becoming a permanent spinster."

"Don't be silly. Single women aren't called spinsters anymore . . . and I was starting a business."

"Hmm, the difference between your world and mine—that a woman should put a business concern over a secure marital connection. However, I maintain that there is more to it than that."

Her brows arched suspiciously. "Such as?"

"Your intense seriousness about life—which I've mentioned before. You hide behind it as if burying some inner unhappiness."

Catherine was growing annoyed. "Now listen, Captain. I've been alone since college. Whatever I have, I've had to get by myself. Before that, when I was growing up, I was expected to get straight A's, make the cheering squad, date the right type of boy, who had a career ahead of him. I had to be the best at everything to win my parents' praise. Of course, that wasn't so, but they did start taking it for granted I'd succeed at everything. It seemed like all their attention was on Treasa, who was such a problem kid." She threw up her hands. "I have good reason for taking life seriously! And why am I telling you this? I don't want to talk about it. I'm not perfect. Nobody is!"

"Then why must you try so hard to be perfect?" he asked gently.

"I don't—it's not—you've no right to pry into my personal life and draw unfair conclusions!"

"I believe you just chastised me for the same reluctance to talk. Ah, Catherine, I'm sorry ... don't cry. No, *do* cry. I believe you need it."

His arms folded around her, and he cuddled her, bringing his lips to the top of her head and nestling them there.

She was hardly aware of what he was doing. All the old, bad feelings had bubbled up. All the anxiety—all the times when she'd stayed up past midnight studying, the ball of nerves in her stomach every reporting time. What if she didn't get Honors? What if she didn't make the squad? What if she didn't get that award in art design? What if she didn't bring some wonderful achievement or plaudit home to win praise and appreciation? She would be cast into a desert where no one wanted to touch her. She'd fail!

Lucien's arms tightened. She buried her head against his neck and her tears made his skin wet. His hand played comfortingly over her back. But as her tears subsided, she felt a growing tension in him.

"You feel better now?"

"Yes. I'm sorry ... I didn't mean ..."

"No apologies are necessary. I am in full sympathy with your tears. You've suffered under a burden, and now you have that of your sister as well."

"I'm not a weakling!"

"No, of course, you're not—only a human being." He leaned away, releasing his hold on her. "And I must leave," he whispered, "before I lose control."

She understood the wisdom of his words. yet this time she was reluctant to see him go. He smiled to her; gently touched his fingers to her cheek, then rose and walked through to the study, closing the door behind him. No doubt he would remain there until nature saw fit to separate them from each other once again.

She felt an unexpected temptation to go to the study and talk to him some more. Only a strong will controlled that urge.

In the morning, as she lifted herself on her elbows and began to rise, her hand connected with something hard, half hidden beneath her pillow. Twisting around she saw a red leather-bound book. Lucien's journal?

Drawing it from beneath the pillow, she set it on her lap and opened the cover. In flowing penmanship was written, "Lucien Alexander Blythe. Journal."

She flipped the gilt-edged page and began reading.

Chapter 18

14 August 1839

It is time I consigned all of this to paper. Perhaps in doing so I can exorcise a small degree of my guilt and pain. As I write I am leaving England behind. It will be many years, if ever, before I return. Gwen is dead, and I wonder if I should not be as well, so empty is my soul.

I first met Lady Gwenivere Malcolm when she was six years old, a baby to my manly fourteen. Her parents and mine were great friends. The Malcolms and their only child often visited at Oak Park. Since I was the youngest son and closest to her own age, it became my duty to take charge of the brat and entertain her. How I despised chasing after her when I could have been off with my brother and his friends, racing our horses over the pastures and putting them to fences, shooting wild grouse. Instead I was consigned to the lowly task of nursemaid. However, soon I went off again to Eton, and I saw little of Gwen during those next years while I was away at school. I was as often as not off visiting friends when her family paid their visits. Not until shortly after I had come down from Oxford did I renew my acquaintance with her.

I was spending a few months at home before embarking on my career at sea and was in the process of building the *Goddess*. My father was understandably uneasy about my decision to build up a merchant fleet. It smelled too closely of "trade" and was not the career for an Earl's son. However, he supported me in my venture with a good deal more understanding than I might have given in his position.

Lord and Lady Malcolm had been called north on urgent family business. Since they felt the seriousness of the business might depress the spirits of their young daughter, they asked my parents if Gwen might spend the time at Oak Park.

She arrived in due course. I was twenty-one at the time, and she was just a budding ingenue of thirteen. I looked upon her as a child, while she made an idol of me, following on my heels wherever I went about the house and grounds. I found her an annoying pup, always underfoot. Yet I always recall being struck by her natural grace, the promise of beauty in her maturing features and body, her honesty and straightforward delight at being permitted to do anything at all in my company. When she pleaded with me to show her how to take her pony over the fences as cleanly as I did my own mount, I relented and became her teacher. When she begged to come along when I set off for an afternoon's fishing, I found her a pole. I would sneak off with my gun for a bit of shooting in the east woods, only to look back over my shoulder halfway there and find the imp shadowing my footsteps a few yards back along the path.

"All right, Gwen," I'd sigh, "come along if you must. I've not the time to walk you back and start out all over again. But do stay close and not run off in the woods where I might mistake you for a partridge."

A delighted smile would light her face. "Oh, yes, Lucien. Anything you say."

That was the day I taught her to shoot, showing her how to hold the gun, allowing her to use my handkerchief tied to a nearby branch as a target. Monogrammed, expensive, and full of buckshot when I retrieved it.

A message arrived from Lord and Lady Malcolm, advising that they would be detained in the north. Their business was not going as smoothly as expected. Gwen remained. The days became weeks, but it was langorous summer, and no one was in much of a hurry. My plans were going well, but my vessel would not be ready until early autumn. I had two months to while away, enjoying myself. I made frequent visits to London and the shipyard where my vessel was being constructed, but during my days at Oak Park, I became accustomed to Gwen's familiar form, her rosy cheeks, and the twinkle of mischief in her eyes. I was invited to join some friends in Scotland. I surprised myself at the time, putting it off from one weekend to the next. Gwen celebrated her fourteenth birthday, but it never occurred to me to see her any differently than I always had. She was still the capricious colt, scampering at my feet, devouring my every word and looking to me as perfection personified. That adulation made me uneasy. It was not part of my nature to welcome such worshipfulness, but I shrugged it off. Gwen was an adolescent going through that stage we all must go through as we make the transition from childhood to adulthood. One moment she was crawling madly through the bushes after the dog with her skirt up about her knees; the next she was the perfect young lady, meticulously conscious of her attire. She would soon grow out of her overblown admiration of me, and in a few months, I would be off to sea.

My parents, busy with their own projects and responsibilities, seemed to take it as an assumed, yet unacknowledged, fact that I had taken Gwen under my wing. I drifted from one day to the next. In August Lord and Lady Malcolm wrote to say they hoped to be back by the end of the month. I rode out alone one afternoon. I'd received some distressing news. The completion of the *Goddess* had been delayed by serveral weeks, and I was having problems with some of the London merchants who had made cargo agreements with me. Suddenly they were dragging their heels, and it seemed I would have to go to London again. I rode for a while. Of course, Gwen soon came pounding up behind me. She must have noticed my scowling brow, since, for a change, she said little as we rode. I saw the marker at the end of the estate lands before I was aware of how far we'd ridden. The day was hot, and the horses lathered. I decided to rest them at a nearby stream in the wood.

I sat down on the grassy bank beside the stream, paying little attention to Gwen, who, after she'd tied up her horse, plopped down beside me.

"My, but it's warm," she exclaimed. She lifted her thick golden hair off her shoulders and fanned her face with her hand. "I think I shall go wading. You don't mind, do you, Lucien?"

"Do as you like, child," I answered, "only don't get drenched."

She quickly removed her shoes and stockings and, her skirts held high, waded out into the middle of the stream. I watched her from the corner of my eye, but my thoughts were elsewhere. "Ah, this feels good," she giggled. "Come in wading, Lucien."

"If I was your age, I would," I spoke with the superiority of my years.

"Is that what happens when you grow older?" she teased. "You become a stick in the mud? Dread the thought!"

"You're only fourteen, Gwen. You have a few years left before finding out."

She splashed out of the stream and once again plopped down

beside me, her skirts above her knees. She was totally unselfconscious, but her face had grown serious. "Will you wait for me, Lucien?"

"Wait? Wait for what?"

"For me to grow up."

She caught me off-guard, but I fluffed her off. "By then, Gwen, you will have other things in mind to do. I will be gone sailing. You won't be presentable to society for another five years and have a lot to learn in that time."

"Pooh! More of that sop my governess pushes on me. I am learning all I wish to learn from you."

"That's not so!" I frowned.

"But it is!" She leaned back on her elbows and laughed. "This summer has been the most wonderful in my life."

I made the mistake of looking over at her. Her eyes weren't those of a child. I suddenly saw the woman in their depths and felt myself being drawn, noticing the changes I'd been blind to before. Her breasts now swelled within the bodice of her gown. Her waist seemed so slim I could have cupped my hands about it. Her skirt was still flounced up about her knees, and the soft skin of her bare calves and trim ankles glowed in the sunlight.

She reached out her hand and took mine and leaned back on the grass, facing me, her face alight with youthful happiness. "I want this summer to go on and on . . . never end."

"All things must come to an end . . . good and bad."

She smiled softly. "But it is nice to dream."

I couldn't seem to take my eyes from her face. My gaze moved over her warm mouth, the lips slightly parted in a dreamy smile, the eyes so radiant.

"Lucien, what is it like to be kissed? Is it pleasant?" She leaned slightly closer.

"It can be at times. It would depend upon whom you are kissing."

"Will you kiss me, Lucien?"

"Gwen, you're still a child!"

"No, I'm a woman now. I've had my menses. Kiss me."

"You're being ridiculous!"

"Then I will kiss you." Before I could stop her, she'd reached her arm around my neck and had pressed her mouth to mine. It was the kiss of an innocent, but I think I knew then that I was lost. A fire sparked in my blood. With total lack of guilt or guile, she urged her body up against mine, and it was a woman's body. I felt my own body reacting, felt the sudden hardness and heat in my loins. Her kisses continued, and before I knew it, I was kissing her back. Her hand slipped beneath my jacket, and my arms went about her as well.

In the back of my mind something cried no! I lifted my head. "Gwen, we must stop. I am a man. Don't press me further."

"But I want to feel this closeness."

I found my hand on the silky skin of her thigh. Did she know what she was bringing about, this child—witch? My mind cried out to see reason, but with every pressure of her hips, the fire within me blazed stronger. She was like velvet, sweet velvet in my arms. Perhaps in her innocence, she didn't realize what she was doing, but her hand slid over my hip to the front of my breeches.

Whatever control I had left, went with that touch, so gentle, yet so insistent. I made love to her completely on that streamside. I cannot hold her responsible for that act. I was not a will-less being. I should have regained control of myself. However, I didn't, and when it was over and she lie smiling and sweetly satisfied in my arms, I realized the depth to which I'd sunk. Not only had I taken her virginity—but she was fourteen years old!

I felt sickened by remorse and disgust with myself. She lay there so innocently beneath me, unaware of how I had just ruined her and her future. I moaned in my grief, and she reached up and rubbed her hand against my cheek.

"It's all right, Lucien. I wanted you to make me a woman. Who else but you."

"Gwen, you don't understand." I rolled away from her. "You are a child of fourteen. You should not have been violated by a grown man as I have done to you today. You are young—far too young! It's wrong!"

"You are the only man I shall ever want. How can it be wrong? Someday we shall be married."

"Gwen, listen to me. What you desire at fourteen is not necessarily what you will desire when you are of marriageable age."

"Marry me now."

"Unthinkable. Your parents would never allow such a thing. You would be socially ostracized—we both would."

"I care not. I will wait, Lucien."

It was impossible to convince her that what we had done was wrong. She was as devoted to me as ever, though I felt my own guilt must be written all over my face for the world to see. Particularly when it occurred to me that she might have conceived. I went about as a man tormented. Should she discover she was with child, I would, of course, have married her, but even so, the scandal that would arise would be appalling. Not the most lenient in society would condone the marriage of a fourteen-year-old girl. Already in my mind's eye I could see the looks of condemnation that would be cast in my direction; my parents' shocked disbelief and disillusionment; her parents' contempt and horror.

Then, too, there were my dreams for my own future: my merchantman nearly ready to sail, the exotic foreign ports of the world beckoning me to come gather their riches and fill my eyes and being with new sights and sounds. It would all be impossible if Gwen was pregnant. My sleepless nights must have shown in the gray pallor of my face. Even Gwen's warm smiles could not lighten the despondency of my mood. Just the sight of her was enough to prick my already bleeding conscience into an open sore. I fought the impulse to avoid her, knowing the worst thing I could do to her—as if I hadn't done enough already—would be to show her rejection. She remained my constant companion, though I avoided any physical contact. Gwen didn't broach the subject of the streambank herself, but there was a new intensity to her affection, and I had to admit I felt a deep stirring in my heart for this spontaneous, openhearted creature who so willingly gave herself into my hands and protection. I knew what I was feeling was a form of love, though it did not have the intensity of mature passion.

I made my trip to London. Upon my return Gwen came to me in the stable where I was grooming my horse. She stood nearby for several minutes, silent and watchful. My nerves were stretched to the breaking point. If Gwen's calculations had been correct, she should be expecting her menses at any time. The waiting had become an agony for me. She stepped closer, reached out, and took my hand. I know I stiffened.

"Lucien, what is wrong? You are so cold lately. Don't you like me anymore?"

"Of course, I do. You should never doubt that."

"But you don't laugh or smile. Since that day in the woods, you won't touch me."

"Gwen . . ."

"Was it so bad?"

"No . . . yes . . ." How could I explain the seriousness of the situation without transferring my guilt to her shoulders, particularly when she'd seen no sin in what we'd done?

"I've made you unhappy."

The sadness in her eyes made my heart turn over. "Come, let's walk out into the orchard. We need to talk." When we were well out of earshot, I motioned her to a garden bench under one of the apple trees. "Gwen, I know that a sheltered girl of your age cannot have been told much of the facts of life, but surely you understand that what went on between us that day should not have happened. You are far too young. And what is troubling me is that I have put you in this untenable position. You are too young to be married, too young to bear a child, and I should not have allowed it to happen."

"But I love you, Lucien. It doesn't matter to me that I'm so young."

"It matters to me."

"You think me a child!"

"I do at times, but at other times the feelings I have are not those of a man for a child."

"Then wait for me until I am old enough."

"That may not be possible. If you're with child—"

"I am not. My bleeding came this morning."

My relief was so extraordinary, had I not already been seated, my knees would have collapsed beneath me.

"Now you can smile again," she cried. "You needn't walk about in a blue study any longer." With that she flung herself into my arms. The scent of her hair was intoxicating, as was the feel of her warm soft body. "Kiss me, Lucien . . . please!"

Her lips were so close, so tempting. It took all of my strength to push her away. I didn't realize until that moment how much I'd secretly been hungering for the taste of her, the feel of her. Yet I was not about to repeat my mistakes.

Her eyes were filled with hurt and dismay. "You don't love me at all, do you, Lucien."

"Oh, yes, sweet girl," I said hoarsely. "Yes, I love you."

"Then everything is all right." Her eyes were bright with happiness. Suddenly they clouded. "But when my parents arrive in a week's time, I shall have to go away from you."

"We will see each other, though we cannot let anyone know what's happened between us. That is very important, Gwen. You must not let your parents guess that we are more than friends. When you are closer to marriageable age, I shall let them know my intentions to marry you."

"That's years away!"

"We have no other choice. I am a man of honor. I will marry you, Gwen."

"You shall be away at sea!"

"I will be home for visits, and in that time, you shall grow up into the beautiful woman you promise to be. You will have a chance to discover yourself and decide if I really am the man you want for the rest of your life."

"Of course, you are!"

I felt better for our talk and the knowledge she had not conceived, but I was still torn by the circumstances. Lord and Lady Malcolm arrived a few days later. As their carriage pulled up at the door, Gwen ran down the front steps to greet them, still child enough to enjoy their reunion.

"My word, Gwen," her mother exclaimed. "How you've grown. I can scarce believe it! William, look at her, will you? A young lady! Oh, my, but it's wonderful to see you again, daughter." She kissed Gwen's cheek, drew her close as Lord Malcolm came around the carriage.

"Well, princess, you are a lovely sight to see. Your mother is right. You've grown into a young woman."

I stood with my parents near the front door, watching the reunion, feeling a pang in my chest, reminded of what I had done to change this girl into a woman. And soon she would no longer be around to tag my footsteps. I would no longer be able to look over and see her laughing eyes and rosy cheeks, hear her tinkling laughter. I suddenly knew I was going to miss her terribly.

Tears rose in my eyes as I watched their carriage depart the following day. My mother noticed my reaction. She gave me a studied look. "The child is growing, isn't she?"

I only nodded.

A moment later she continued. "Lovely girl, Gwen."

"Yes, very sweet."

"And she seems quite attracted to you—puppy worship. Though in a few years . . . have you given any thought to marriage yet, Lucien? You are reaching that age."

I nearly choked. "Yes, I have given the matter some consideration."

"In five years you shall be twenty-seven. Not so very old, and you have this shipping nonsense to occupy you until then."

"My shipping venture is not nonsense, Mother."

"No, of course not. Just a slip of the tongue." She smiled, satisfied, and let the matter drop. If she only knew the truth, I thought to myself.

A month and a half later I sailed. If my parents found the steady stream of letters I received from Gwen in the interim strange, they said nothing. I replied to her, though my letters lacked the intensity of hers. My mind was consumed by my approaching voyage. I was an experienced sailor. My father kept a small yacht on the coast near Lymington, so I felt self-assured as I took command of the *Goddess* and acquainted myself with my crew—seasoned men, most of them, drawn away from other vessels by the higher wage I was paying.

Of course, I suffered from the overconfidence of youth, and soon had some of the wind knocked from my sails. It was during that first voyage that Gladstone and I forged our friendship, as he stood by my stead when I blundered and passed on his own extensive knowledge of the sea.

I learned much in those first years. I saw the exotic lands that had always tantalized, sailing into ports in the Far East, Africa, and the Mediterranean, crossing the Atlantic to the United States and the Caribbean. My success was greater than my wildest imagination. My hold was always full of cargo, reaping good returns. My reputation was growing. At the end of two years I had seen clear to purchasing my second merchantman, the *Sophia,* while I remained in command of the *Goddess.*

I reveled in the adventure and excitement. I loved the sea in all its moods. Yet each time we sailed into Portsmouth, I rushed north, to Gwen. At seventeen she had reached her full height, the curves of her figure ripening. In her eyes was the glow of a woman who had learned to know herself. I could never look at her beauty without being filled with joy. Over those years she'd remained faithful to the promise she'd made on the streambank. Though our times together since had been few and had sped too quickly, each time we greeted each other again, it was as if I had never left. My sense of duty had spoken as well when I'd promised to marry her years before, but now, my feelings had matured. I loved her with all my heart. Each time I looked into her eyes, I was consumed with desire, but I was older and wiser and had better control over my emotions. When next I took Gwen, she would be my wife.

She pressed me for that wedding, subtly. She saw no need to wait until her eighteenth birthday for our betrothal to be announced. Both our families were privy to the fact we were in love. Yet I procrastinated. I did not feel my fortunes were yet secure. I wanted the best of everything for Gwen. I wanted to set her up in a lovely house in the country with sufficient funds in the bank to keep her in style. I was the second son. My brother, John, would inherit the title and estates on our father's death. I had no expectations aside from those gained by my own resourcefulness and energy. Gwen told me she didn't care for any of that. She only wanted to be with me.

Stubbornly, I held to my views. "My love, I don't want you scrimping and pinching pennies, growing old before your time. I want to see you dressed in the height of fashion, your beauty shown to advantage. I want to bring you into London each season, to the country each summer. I want to see our children grow up without worry, without care."

"I am not so caught up in worldly possessions," she argued.

"You are accustomed to them. You've known no other life. And once we are married, Gwen, I want to come ashore for most of the time, be by your side. The funds I've set aside in the Bank of England would soon be eaten away by the purchase and maintenance of the home I have in mind for us, and at this point I cannot afford to put both my vessels in the captaincy of another man."

"Then take me with you!"

"Shipboard is no place for a woman. Rough seas, few comforts, a company of rugged seamen. I don't want you to endure that, Gwen."

"Let me decide what I shall endure. Lucien, I don't need to be coddled and protected."

"No, Gwen." I was adamant to all her pleas. I thought I was doing what was best.

"Each time you sail, Lucien, I'm so afraid you shan't return; that you shall be shipwrecked in a storm."

I drew her into my arms. "Do not look at the dark side. Ships have an amazing record of carrying their crews safely from port to port. The chances of my breaking my neck on the hunt course are greater than the risk of my drowning at sea. Just two more years, Gwen. Can you not wait that much longer?"

Shortly after her next birthday we were officially engaged. I gave her a dazzling emerald, a treasure found on one of my trips to India. The dazzle of happiness in her eyes equalled that of the stone. We threw a huge ball in celebration. All our local neighbors and friends were invited. There was dancing, feasting, and partying into the wee hours of the morning. We set our wedding date for the following year. I contacted estate agents and began my search for our future home. Once again I sailed, but tragedy intervened during that year. My mother passed away after a severe bout with influenza. My father, pining and grief stricken, just withered away and followed her several months thereafter.

I was in Marseilles when the news reached me. I sailed directly home, but it was obvious, in the grieving atmosphere of Oak Park, that Gwen's and my wedding must be postponed, for just a little while.

We spent every spare moment together at either Oak Park or her parents' estate. We visited country homes and chose the one where we wished to raise our children. I paid the purchase price in cash and when I looked at my bank account had a sudden rush of panic. I had added two vessels to my fleet that year. The investment had been a good one, but it had sorely depleted my cash assets. Perhaps it was self-serving greed rather than common sense and sound business logic, but I knew I must make one more voyage before our marriage. As I look back, I tend to see my motivation as greed. Gwen and I would have survived nicely—perhaps not in total wealth and elegance—but we would have been happy. We had sufficient to live in comfort, and the return from the two new vessels would gradually have refilled the coffers. Of course, all of this is hindsight. None of it can be redone. I must have known instinctively then that I was wrong because I hesitated telling her of my decision.

My brother had taken up residence at Oak Park with his wife, Abigail, and their two children. My brother and I were close, and the family group was a loving one. They welcomed me with open arms and made no mention of my finding my own quarters. They welcomed Gwen as well, as the sister she would soon be.

Those days before I made my intended last voyage were the happiest in my life. Gwen and I walked and rode over the estate together, reminiscing of the days when I'd thought her no more than a tiresome brat.

She laughed up at me. "I thought you were a god, Lucien. I'd no experience with other boys. You were everything to me. You still are."

"And you are everything to me."

She stopped and stepped around to face me. "Are you sure, Lucien? Are you certain your vessels don't mean even more?"

"Don't be silly, Gwen. How could they mean more to me than you?"

Her eyes had gone a deeper brown. "You're sailing again, aren't you?"

I closed my eyes and swallowed. "Yes."

"Why? Why must you do this to me?" She wrapped her arms around me. Her head fell against my chest. I could hear her quiet sobs.

I frankly did not know what to say to rationalize my actions. Why was I leaving again—money? Holding her in my arms, I sought for words of comfort. "It will be a short trip, my love. Only a few months, and as soon as I return, we will be wed. No need for a lavish ceremony or preparations. We will post the bans and have the vicar join us at Oak Park."

Her head shot up. "If you wish no more than a simple ceremony, marry me before you go. I will stay with my parents until you return from sea and we move to our new home."

"I cannot," I flinched. "I am sailing tomorrow."

"And you didn't tell me! How could you!"

"I didn't know how to break the news." What a poor excuse I made. I did not blame her for storming off. Of course, we could never stay angry with each other. At dinner I took her aside and apologized. She was close to tears but told me she would abide by my decision. She would come with me to the docks in the morning and see me off.

I was mentally exhausted as I climbed the stairs to my bed that night after sharing several brandies and conversation with my brother. I sent my manservant to his own bed and quickly began undressing. My thoughts were on Gwen and the wisdom of my decision. I felt so torn. I felt a sudden yearning to hold her in my arms. As if my thoughts had been read, the bedroom door opened, and Gwen slipped through.

"Gwen, what are you doing here?"

"I came to see you." She stepped purposefully across the room.

"You should not be here alone at this hour. Go back to your room before someone discovers you."

"No, Lucien. I am not leaving." There was a strength in her voice I'd never heard before.

"You must. Think of what will be said if you're found here."

"Why? I didn't think of it eight years ago when it was so much worse. Should I be afraid of a little censure now?"

"You were a child then. You didn't understand."

Her luminous eyes looked up into mine. "I understand enough that I never felt guilt, as you did. I wanted you then as much as I want you now. I knew in my childish way what might happen when I asked you to kiss me, but I loved you."

I stared at her, unable to speak as she stepped closer. The silken cloth of her nightgown hid nothing, particularly in the dancing flames of the fire.

"Eight years is a long time to wait, Lucien. I don't want to wait any longer. I don't want you to sail again without feeling your love . . . without the two of us being one."

My mind whirled. For so long I'd fought the very desire she was expressing. Of course, I wanted her. Of course, I wanted to feel her in my arms and make love to her. I'd held on to my self-control by only the slimmest of threads, and it was weakened to the breaking point as she moved up against me and put her arms about my neck.

"Make love to me, Lucien," she whispered.

"Gwen, you know why we must not," I groaned. "Please don't tempt me. I am only trying to do what is right and honorable and wait until we are married."

"I don't care about right and honorable any longer. It has always been right and honorable for us. What does a piece of paper mean. I love you."

"And I love you."

At the feel of her curving body beneath the silk, sanity fled. My arms closed around her, and my need rose demandingly. My desire for her, repressed for so long, could not be stopped.

Within moments we were both standing naked in the firelight, touching as we had longed to do for so long. Then we were on the bed together, and I was making love to her without reserve, totally, completely, and she gave herself to me with the same openness. The sensations were so incredible, my climax so intense, that I only realized after that I'd not withdrawn before spilling my seed within her.

We remained together most of the night, too contentedly happy to rush the parting. When we said our farewells at the ship the next day, I felt a reluctance to leave her like nothing I'd felt before.

"Just three months," I whispered as I kissed her at dockside. "I love you, Gwen, so very much."

"I love you, too, Lucien. When you come back, it will be for-ever."

"I promise—with all my heart."

* * *

Finally, in July of 1839, I was coming home for good. As I stood at the bridge looking out over the chopped seas, Portsmouth was in sight. I remember smiling as my thoughts went to Gwen. How I anticipated her joyous smile of greeting, the light in her eyes, the soft sweetness of her lips when they once again touched mine.

What a trip it had been. Our reunion had been delayed months beyond my promised three, but we would be together for good now. I'd had much time to think during the voyage, and I'd realized just how great and deep my love for her was. I'd missed her with a yearning ache, which had been made acute by all the mishaps and delays of the voyage.

The cargo had not been ready when we'd docked in Calcutta, and it had been too lucrative a one to pass by. I waited seven days, chaffing at the bit in the blistering heat. Finally it was loaded, and we sailed for Singapore. We left that port still behind schedule, and because of our delays in Calcutta, we were beset by the doldrums as we crossed the Indian Ocean. Days on end with not even the slightest breeze. I fretted. We still had Colombo to put into, then Cape Town. From there it would be straight sailing until we reached England. Shortly after we put out from Colombo, we ran into heavy seas, then heavy storm. The *Goddess* rode it well, like the queen she was, but sustained damage to her mainmast. We were off the east coast of Africa and limped into the nearest port, a tiny out-of-the-way spot in Mozambique. Materials for repairs were not readily available. There'd been more weeks of waiting. I'd sent a message to Gwen in Colombo via a vessel sailing several days before us for Liverpool, but I had no means of sending further word of our delay. At long last we were ready to sail again, but we were months behind schedule. I sent another message from Cape Town, but my own arrival in England would probably coincide with the missive's receipt.

That passage from Cape Town to Portsmouth was the speediest I'd ever made. The crew cheered as we came into Portsmouth two days ahead of any record we'd previously logged. I sent them all out to the pub with an extra portion to celebrate. And celebrate we all could. I'd more than made up for the delays and aggravation of the voyage with the profits on my cargo.

Leaving my first mate, Perry, who was soon to be the *Goddess*'s new captain, in charge, Gladstone and I loaded my personal belongings on a carriage—all my varied treasures from around the world that would soon grace Gwen's and my new home. I took the reins myself and set the horses at a merry pace toward Waltham, five miles from which stood Oak Park.

So great was my own anticipation and joy, I expected all of the family and Gwen would be awaiting my arrival on the steps. Of course, they had no way of knowing I was arriving that day. I bounded up the sweep of steps into the front hall, leaving Gladstone to take care of the baggage. I was met by one of the footmen, whose face showed momentary delight at seeing me. He suddenly sobered. "My lord and lady are in the morning room. Shall I announce you, sir?"

"Certainly not, Tremley, I'll surprise them."

I ignored the concerned look in Tremley's eyes and hurried across the hall. I found not only my brother and his wife, but my niece and nephew as well, gathered in the sunny room.

John and Abigail rose quickly, startled. The two youngsters were much quicker. They rushed across to me, wrapping their arms around my legs. "Uncle Lucien! You are home. What have you brought for us this trip?" They danced about my legs, looking like tiny little imps. "Do you have some stories," my nephew cried.

"Indeed I do—a storm at sea, no less," I laughed, ruffling their heads as my brother and sister-in-law came forward, both giving me hugs of welcome.

"Children," Abigail cried, "do calm down. Give your Uncle Lucien a bit of room to breathe." She glanced to my brother. "Perhaps I should take them to the nursery for a few minutes?"

It was then I noticed the tension behind my brother's smile. He nodded to his wife.

"Come, children. You will have plenty of time to see Uncle Lucien. Let your father and uncle talk a moment." With a hand on each of their shoulders, she nudged them out of the room.

I turned to my brother. Our eyes caught. "Something is wrong, John."

"Let us go into the library, Lucien."

I wanted to grab John's shoulder, have the news then and there, but as John turned, I saw the strain on his features and followed.

Closing the library door behind us, John went immediately to the side table and lifted a decanter. "Brandy?" he asked.

I nodded, suddenly, chillingly feeling that I'd be needing it.

Neither of us said a word as John poured two glasses, handed me one. My brother and I are of the same height, although he is the fairer of the two. As we stood facing each other, I again noticed the look in his eyes.

He sighed, took a sip from his glass, began to walk about the carpet. "I do not know quite how to tell you what I have to say." He came over to me, laid his hand on my arm.

"Gwen?"

"Yes."

"She is ill—hurt!"

"No." He swallowed. "She is dead."

I recoiled as if I'd been shot. "No! Don't tell me such nonsense!"

"I am telling you the truth, Lucien. She is dead." His face was filled with such sympathy. I sank back against the wall, my legs barely holding me.

"No . . . no . . . I cannot believe it!" I peered down blindly at my shaking hands. "How?"

He came to stand beside me, laid his hand on my shoulder. "In childbirth."

"What! Oh, my God!"

"She said it was yours. You'd made love during your last days home. She seemed delighted, Lucien—"

"I didn't know! I would have returned!"

"She received your message. She understood. She knew you were coming back. When . . ." he cleared his throat nervously, ". . . she went into premature labor last month, she sent a message for me to come to her. I think she knew. Before she died, she gave me this." He reached in his pocket and withdrew her betrothal ring. "She wanted me to give it to you as a sign of her everlasting love."

I could only stare in total agony—an agony beyond belief. "The babe?"

"Your son died with her."

Like a man deranged I screamed out my pain. I cried until there was nothing left inside me. I only wished for the mercy of death where I might join Gwen.

But life is not so merciful. I sail from England now with this relentless burden on my soul . . . a grief from which I shall never escape. I care not what happens. I shall never forgive myself.

Chapter 19

For several moments Catherine stared at the page in front of her, suddenly understanding so much. She rose from the bed and walked into the study to stand beneath his portrait. She gazed up at the now familiar features and felt an overwhelming sympathy and compassion. No wonder he had come to Nantucket and shunned the sea. No wonder he had talked of history repeating itself. The facts in the journal seemed to cast a new light on their meeting and the guilt he suffered as well. But he shouldn't continue to blame himself. In all likelihood he couldn't have saved Gwen even if he'd been constantly at her side. He must learn to forgive himself. She empathized with his pain, and only wished there was something she could do to help him.

As if her thoughts had called him, he suddenly appeared at her side.

"You've read the journal?" he asked quietly.

"Yes . . . I'm so sorry. What a terrible thing!"

"Terrible, yes," he sighed, "but nothing I didn't bring upon myself."

She took his hand. "Lucien, you've got to stop blaming yourself. You couldn't have saved Gwen."

"I could have been at her side when she needed me the most."

"You didn't know. And she forgave you. Can't you begin to forgive yourself and put it all behind?"

"I have begun to recently," he said quietly.

"You have?"

"Yes . . . because of you. You've helped me heal, Catherine, and for that I'm very grateful."

* * *

Peter called her that afternoon at the shop.

He sounded exuberant. "I've got good news for you. We're in Maine."

"Wonderful! How was the sailing trip?"

"Bearable. We had a few days of bad weather and fog, but overall it was okay. Glad it's done. I can't leave here until we put the boat up in the yard on Monday, but I wondered if you'd like to fly up here for the weekend."

"I'd love to! We'd stay on the boat?"

"Yes, and I've borrowed a car, so I can pick you up at the airport, and we can do some sightseeing."

"Great. I'll see if I can get a flight Saturday afternoon."

"I checked with the airline, and there should be a flight leaving about five-thirty."

"I'll be on it. Should I call you back and let you know what time I'll get in?"

"Fine." He gave her a number. "That's the marina line. If I'm not around, leave a message with whoever answers."

"I will."

"Can't wait to see you."

"I can't wait to see you either."

Catherine started packing that night. She'd booked a flight on Bar Harbor to Boston, then on to Owl's Head in Maine. As she sorted through the wardrobe for the things she'd take, Treasa came running into the bedroom.

"I just found a box on the back steps!" she exclaimed. "You'll never guess what was in it. All the stuff that was stolen from the house. I don't understand. I didn't even get to talk to Rita and Arty. Why did they bring it back?"

Catherine wasn't about to tell Treasa about the Captain's intervention, though she sighed to herself with relief. "Maybe they thought I'd caught on and got scared."

"It's weird," Treasa sighed. "It's not like them."

"Whatever, I'm glad to have it back."

"So am I!" Treasa suddenly noticed the open suitcase on Catherine's bed. "Where're you going?"

"Maine. Peter called. I'm flying up tomorrow night. I won't be back until Monday afternoon. Can you cover the shop?"

Treasa's attitude had been different since her encounter with the

Captain. She agreed without protest. "Yeah, I suppose I could. So he's keeping in touch. Amazing."

"Not so amazing. I told you this was different."

"What are they doing in Maine?"

"Putting the boat up in a yard for repairs."

"We won't be seeing them down here for a while then."

"Did you expect to?"

"No, not really." Treasa tried to make her tone seem indifferent.

The phone rang. Since Treasa was closer, she picked up the receiver on Catherine's nightstand. "Well, hello, Ryan," she said in a minute, sitting down on the bed with her back toward Catherine. "Long time no hear. How're you doing?"

A moment's silence. "Oh, really? No, I'm not busy . . . Meet you here in a half an hour." It was a moment after she'd hung up the phone before she turned to Catherine.

Catherine raised a brow. Treasa's smile contained some of its former self-confidence. "Interesting."

"What? That he called?"

"Hmmm," Treasa said vaguely. "I've got to change."

Catherine watched her sister leave the room. Treasa needed some male company, and Catherine was happy for her.

When her packing was complete, she sat down and put together her last designs and suggestions for the Santa Barbara client and penned a quick note of explanation to Marcie. One of these days, she would have to make a trip out there, though with the shop on Nantucket so busy, she doubted she'd be able to do so until fall. Things on the island would quiet down then.

Rather than leave the Porsche at the airport, Catherine took a taxi from the house the following evening. Her flight and the connection in Boston were both on time. By seven-thirty she was stepping down from the twelve-passenger, twin-engine plane onto the runway at Owl's Head. She saw Peter immediately, waving from inside the fence near the tiny terminal. Hurrying toward him, she felt a warm rush of happiness and sanity as he picked her up in his arms and bestowed on her a welcoming kiss.

"Good to see you, mate," he grinned.

"And you, too." She kissed him back thoroughly.

"Have you eaten yet?"

"Not really. I nibbled a little, but I was too excited."

"I'll take you to a nice waterfront restaurant. And we've got the boat pretty much to ourselves tonight. Jan is off visiting friends. So, tell me all your news," he said as he threw her suitcase into the back of the VW Rabbit he'd borrowed.

They both spoke rapidly, as if trying to make up for lost time. The summer evening was still bright, and as they traveled up Route 1, Catherine caught glimpses of the rugged and rocky pine-covered coast with its many inlets. In the clear air, she picked out the green lumps of the islands that dotted Penobscot Bay, and ahead along the highway, the outline of the Camden Hills, rising directly at the edge of the sea. To either side of the road, predominantly white, shuttered, wood frame buildings, so typical of New Enland, and unspoiled by tacky modernization, were interspersed with fields and small bits of pine and deciduous woodland.

Traffic increased as they approached the town center. "Tourists," Peter explained.

Catherine laughed. "And what does that make us?"

"Righto. Somehow when you arrive by boat you don't think of yourself as a tourist." He steered the car down Main Street. Catherine noticed with pleasure the baskets of geraniums hanging from every lamp post and the window boxes of brilliant blossoms on some of the store fronts. In the center of town, Peter turned sharply right onto a narrow road running alongside the harbor, though it was difficult to see the water itself, except through the alley between the wharfside buildings.

"What do you know—a parking space," he said almost in amazement, as he steered the Rabbit into a tiny slot. "The beauty of compacts," he chuckled.

The restaurant he'd chosen was directly on harborside. They had to wait for a table and went to the outside deck for a drink. The early evening air was growing cool, even in midsummer. Catherine wrapped a sweater over her shoulders as she and Peter sipped their drinks.

Their table gave an unobstructed view of the harbor and the green hills rising at its head. The sun was setting, its last rays focused directly on the harbor, transforming it into a sparkling jewel. The water glowed silver-blue. The hulls of the many boats in the harbor seemed washed in golden white brilliance, as did the buildings behind. A pale moon could be seen in the gradually darkening sky.

Catherine leaned her arms on the table. "This is beautiful."

"Isn't it? Wait until you see the view from the *Escapade*." Peter pointed across the blue, boat-crammed waters. "That's Wayfarers marina. You can just see *Escapade*'s masts and bow, there, fourth down from the end of the wharf."

Although Catherine's eyes followed his motioning hand, she could only guess at the *Escapade*'s location. The long white marina buildings seemed surrounded by a forest of masts along the wharf and up in the yard.

"And I thought Nantucket was mad."

"The Penobscot's a sailing paradise."

"I can see why."

"I won't be seeing much of that this summer, though."

"Do you mind?"

"Are you serious? I love being landbound for a while. What a feeling to be able to stay in one place long enough to get something accomplished for myself."

"I guess I take that for granted."

"I picked up some art supplies this week, but I'll wait until the boat's up in the yard before I get too ambitious." Peter took her hand and held it. "I'm so glad you're here."

"So am I—real glad. I didn't realize how good it would feel to get away! I guess I have been tense with the shop and stuff." Her eyes smiled at him, a smile that he eagerly returned.

Their hands frequently touching, they talked over every bit of news, and more, as they lingered over their dinner at a table by the windows, paying little attention to the other guests in the crowded dining room. The atmosphere was comfortable, with French doors open to the summer night, a high ceiling and old crossbeams, nautical pictures, and a fireplace. The low hum of conversation around them was unobtrusive.

It was dark when they left to walk the dock along the harbor. The gently rippling water mirrored mast and cabin lights and the brighter glow of waterside street lamps and shop windows. Farther up the hillside, yellow rectangles warmly marked the windows of the town's residences and businesses.

They paused on the public landing to view the schooners of the windjammer fleet. The old masts rising in the evening sky reminded Catherine of her views of the Captain's Nantucket. So romantic—of an age when man truly pitted his wits against the elements. She quickly pushed the thought away. She wouldn't allow him to intrude in her time with Peter.

"You're lucky to see the windjammers," Peter explained. "They only come in on Saturday in season and sail every Monday with a new set of passengers. Most of them are genuine old coastal schooners. The *Stephen Taber* over there at the head of the harbor is the oldest, commissioned in the 1880s, if I'm not mistaken."

A roaring rush filled Catherine's ears as they walked farther up the landing. Two wide tongues of foaming water poured down over a natural formation of rocks, mixing with the sea water at the foot of the landing.

"Nice, huh?"

"It's gorgeous! A little bit of everything here."

"Now you know why there're so many tourists."

They continued up to Main Street, then on into the park that sloped, with manicured green lawns, down to the low granite wall marking the harbor's edge. Sitting down on the lush grass, Peter wrapped his arms around around her back, and for thirty minutes they sat undisturbed, in peace with the summer night. Only when the dampness permeated their clothing did Peter rise and pull her to her feet.

"What about a nightcap?" he suggested.

"Fine with me."

"We can stop at Cappy's. My fellow yachties are bound to be there en masse."

He wasn't wrong. As they stepped off Main Street through the door, Peter was greeted by a chorus of calls from those standing three deep around the bar. The tiny restaurant and barroom overflowed not only with people, but with every kind of memento of the sea, from old anchors and brass fittings to lobster traps and buoys. Green glass shades covered the ceiling lamps; every exposed bit of wood was varnished to a high gleam. The whole effect was one of incredible coziness and camaraderie.

Squeezing in at the crowded bar, Peter introduced her to those he knew, not that Catherine could remember any names, so quickly in succession did the introductions come. She doubted anyone would have cared in any case. It was a laughing, merry group. Half a dozen different accents buzzed in her ears.

Peter ordered them each a brandy. Catherine felt a set of arms come around her from behind, as she was lifted bodily six inches off the ground.

"Well, if it isn't Cathy Sternwood," a voice chuckled in her ear.

"Ted!"

"Nope—the bogey man. How're you doing? Welcome to Maine."

When the arms released their hold, she turned and gave Ted a quick hug. "Surprised to see me?"

"I heard a few rumors you might be coming up." He winked. "How's Nantucket?"

"Same as ever. I'm glad to get away."

"We'll show you a good time up here. When d'you get in?"

"A few hours ago. We had dinner at the Waterfront and then took a walk around."

"Like it so far?"

"Sure do."

Peter turned from the bar with a drink in each hand. "Trying to make time with my woman, mate?" He laughed. "Should have known I'd find you here, boozing it up with the rest of the dregs."

"Who me? Drink? I never touch the stuff." With that Ted lifted his glass from the bar and clinked it to Catherine's and Peter's. His handlebar moustache twitched as he tried to suppress a grin. "So how's your sister?"

"Oh, fine."

"Toeing the straight and narrow, eh?"

"Well—"

"Say no more. We've got to find her some work. Listen, Peter, I heard Jimmy on *Drago* is looking for some help. They'll be chartering up here and need experienced fill-in crew for a couple of months."

"Yeah, I told Catherine about it."

"Jimmy's a good skipper, and it's not a bad boat."

"Well," Catherine considered, "I'll tell her, but I won't get my hopes up. She's pretty burned out on boats."

"She may have changed her mind by now."

"Maybe." Catherine had no expectations.

A petite, curly-haired brunette made her way from the end of the bar and, excusing herself, squeezed past them. "Althea?" Catherine quizzed.

The brown head bobbed up. "Catherine? My goodness, I didn't expect to see you here. How *are* you?"

"Just fine. Are you docked in Camden?"

"Only for a day or two."

"Small world, isn't it?" Peter put in. "Where'd you two meet?"

"Nantucket," Catherine answered. "You know Treasa used to be on the *Cherise*."

"Oh, right."

"How *is* Treasa?" Althea asked almost hesitantly.

"Okay." With all the mention of Treasa, Catherine was reminded that her sister had introduced her to these people. She felt a twinge of guilt that she was now so enjoying their company, while Treasa was stuck back on Nantucket minding the shop. Then again, Treasa had made her own bed.

"I'm glad she's fine," Althea continued. "I was sorry she had to leave the boat on such bad terms."

"Bad terms?" Both Peter's and Ted's ears had perked up.

"Oh, nothing important," Althea demured, turning again to Catherine. "Are you here on holiday?"

"For the weekend."

"Well, I do hope I'll see you before you leave."

"I'm sure you will. I'll be staying over at the marina on *Escapade.*"

"Wonderful."

"You know Peter and Ted?"

"For a *long* time. Oh, Peter, I've meant to ask you. Have you heard anything of Karen Bard? Stacy told me she'd hired on as cook on a big powerboat in the Med."

"News to me. Last I saw her was in Saint Martin. She was on a Hinckley, and they were sailing the next day for Saint Bart's., then down island. She didn't seem delighted with the boat."

"Then maybe it's true," Althea mused. And so the conversation went for the next hour with others joining in. New arrivals entered to a chorus of greetings; others left. A good part of the yachting gossip was Greek to Catherine, who didn't know the people or boats mentioned, but she listened with a smile, enjoying the talk of exotic places.

They left Ted at the bar. He said he'd walk back to the boat—he'd be needing the exercise, he figured. Yet he couldn't resist a mischievous wink as they departed. "Not that you two want to see me around for a while. Should I sleep on deck?"

Peter only shook his head and grinned.

The drive to the marina was a short one; a matter of going from one side of the harbor to the other. Peter parked in the lot at the top of the hill and took Catherine's arm as they walked down the paved drive beside the towering hulls of sailing craft hauled up for repairs. They continued across the spotlit yard, past the main marina buildings, and down the dock and the ramp to the boat. The *Escapade* was the third out from the dock, and Peter lent her a hand up the not-so-secure portable steps to the first boat. Catherine felt like she was intruding as they crossed over the decks of the two other boats rafted alongside the dock before they reached the *Escapade*.

"Don't worry about it," Peter grinned. "They expect it, and with us, at any hour."

They paused for a while on deck, and Catherine understood what Peter had meant about the view from the boat. If possible, the scene was even more beautiful from the marina side of the harbor.

Once they were below, Peter immediately pulled her into his arms and kissed her deeply. Catherine sighed with happiness, but later as they lay in Peter's cabin together, she woke from a frightening, all too familiar dream. She'd dreamed that Lucien Blythe was standing over the bunk, gazing down at them. Impossible! Yet it took her a moment to still her racing heart. She cuddled closer against Peter, let the gentle rocking of the boat soothe her as she drifted back to sleep. The Captain couldn't touch her here.

In the morning they sipped their coffee on deck. Streaks of sunlight danced on the harbor waters. The buildings of the town rose opposite, the white steeple of the Baptist Church standing tallest. At the head of the harbor the park glowed like a green gem in its setting of waterfall and pine-covered mountains. Though it was only nine of a Sunday morning, the harbor was coming to life. Residents of the various sailboats moored in the harbor were rowing their dinghies ashore for breakfast; cars were pulling into the public landing, and a steady stream of pedestrians strolled along the dockside near the berthed schooners.

Catherine leaned back on the teak deck and let the sun tickle her cheeks. In a few minutes, Ted joined them, coffee cup in hand.

"How're you feeling?" Peter teased.

"Aside from a slight pain over my left eye, not bad. What are you two up to today?"

"We're not sure."

Ted took a much-needed sip from his coffee cup. "I thought I'd start sanding the rail—"

"Forget it. Take the day off. There'll be plenty of time to start work after she's lifted tomorrow."

"Aye, Aye, Cap. Don't mind if I do. You coming to Mary and Jack's party this afternoon?"

"I'd forgotten all about it. What do you think, Catherine? You up to a party?"

"Why not."

"Should be fun—their parties usually are."

Ted stretched and looked out over the harbor. "Gorgeous day, huh? Nice one for a sail."

Peter suddenly turned to Catherine. "I hadn't thought of it, but how would you like to go sailing today?"

"Well, I'd love to, but aren't you a little sick of it?"

"A little, but it is a beautiful day, and you've never sailed up here before."

"I've never sailed period—except on a sailfish with someone else doing all the work."

Ted shot Peter a look. "You're not thinking of single-handing the *Escapade?*"

"I was thinking of borrowing Jonie's sailing dinghy."

"Yeah, but it's Sunday, and she's probably using it. What the hell. I haven't got anything to do. I sure didn't get lucky last night, and if Cath's never sailed, might as well show her a good time. I'll crew with you. Let's take her out."

"You sure? It *is* your day off."

"No problem. We can go out to Mark Island, have lunch, and still get back for Mary and Jack's party."

"Okay with you, Cath?" Peter asked.

"Fine—great. I just don't want to put you guys out."

"We don't do this for a living for nothing."

"Let's get going, then," Ted urged, "while I'm still willing. Plenty of food and beer in the galley."

In short order they'd removed sail covers and were casting off lines, and with Peter at the wheel, were soon motoring out of the harbor. Catherine sat quietly in the cockpit, watching with interest and staying out of the way of the men. Ted stood mid-deck, and as soon as they passed Curtis Island at the outer edge of the harbor, he started hoisting up the main sail. Peter secured the wheel and went forward to help. As the canvas rose on the mast and filled with wind, the boat heeled over slightly to starboard and immediately picked up speed. The sail secure, Peter returned to the wheel.

"The wind's coming up," Ted shouted back to Peter. "You want the jib, too?"

"Let's try it. We can always reef."

Ted went forward and cranked a winch, and the front sail rolled out like a blind from around what appeared to Catherine to be a tightly strung aluminum tube stretching from bow to the top of the mainmast.

As the jib fluttered out, and Ted hauled it tight and secured it, the boat heeled over further, like a shot. Catherine watched the starboard rail go under water and the previously horizontal deck pitch over to a near vertical. She'd had a mental image of a leisurely cruise, sitting back comfortably as the boat slid smoothly over the waves. Now she grabbed on for dear life to the nearest handhold. She felt herself sliding off the cockpit seat and braced her feet against the opposite one for support. She felt as if she were standing on a ladder, staring directly down at frothing, cold green seas, with nothing between her and them but a few halyards and winches.

They picked up more speed, slicing into the oncoming waves, which, in Catherine's eyes, had taken on the appearance of monstrous rollers. She sat white-faced, trying not to look down. She was afraid of heights and couldn't stand on a tall step ladder without feeling dizzy. And what would happen if she fell overboard? At the speed they were moving, she doubted they could turn to pick her up before she became a victim of hypothermia in the icy Maine waters.

Peter glanced down at her pale, tense face from his position at the wheel. "What's wrong?"

"Ah...I just didn't expect this. I didn't know we'd be going sideways!"

He chuckled with the calm of an experienced sailor. "Too much, eh? Hey, Ted, pull in the jib a bit. Let's level off some."

Catherine was amazed that anyone would be crazy enough to try to navigate up the sheer drop of the deck, but Ted did, without a blink of an eye, grabbing handholds here and there until he was again at the forward winch. With one hand he loosened the line; with the other he cranked the sail in. The boat leveled slightly. "Better?" he yelled back.

"Okay."

Not in Catherine's opinion, but she didn't want to show herself to be a total coward by speaking up. Ted returned to mid-deck and looked up at the mainsail. "What's the wind?" he asked Peter.

"Gusting thirty."

"Think I should reef the main?"

"One for now. We don't want to give Cath too much of a joy ride. This is a bit much if you've never sailed before."

Confirming Catherine's impression that he must be part monkey or acrobat, Ted grabbed for the boom. With one foot braced on the rail, which had reappeared out of the water just slightly, he scrambled up. The boom seemed to hang at an incredibly precarious angle over the chopping waves, but he didn't appear the least unnerved as he grabbed handfuls of sail and yanked down. Folding the canvas over the boom, he tied it down. The mainsail still seemed to loom a mile high, but when Ted was finished, the boat leveled further.

Catherine clung to her cockpit seat with gripping toes and fingers, but she was beginning to relax. Not bad, once you got used to it. She glanced over to Peter. He smiled.

"More comfortable?"

"Much!"

Ted returned and took the seat beside her.

"More wind than we thought," Peter remarked.

"Guess so," Ted eased back in the seat comfortably, although his feet were braced on the opposite cockpit seat as well. "More like the Christmas winds in the Caribbean than summer on the Penobscot." He glanced at the wind gauge. "Still gusting thirty. Not bad—we're doing nearly nine knots. Straight sailing from here—except that it's all to windward." He grinned to Catherine. "Don't worry, the trip back will be a piece of cake compared to this."

"You mean it's not always like this?"

"God, listen to her! None of us would be sailing if it was like this all the time."

"Except those crazy blokes," Peter laughed, "who want to do a whole charter to windward."

"Masochists," Ted snorted.

Despite the comparative leveling of the boat, icy sprays of water arched over the bow to cascade over Ted's and Catherine's heads and down their necks. Catherine soon learned the trick of watching Peter's face as he steered. Each time he narrowed his eyes, she ducked forward, knowing that a few seconds later another dousing was due.

"Focus your eyes on the horizon," Peter told her, probably afraid her bluish color was due to oncoming seasickness, not cold. "Whatever you do, don't look at the deck or the combination of the deck and sea."

"I'm fine," Catherine assured him. "Just keep driving."

That sent both men into peals of laughter.

"I'm going to get a beer," Ted said. "Anyone else want one?"

The thought of putting anything into her stomach at that moment didn't tempt Catherine at all. She wasn't feeling queasy, but why ask for trouble? Peter, however, nodded his head in the affirmative.

Ted moved quickly forward again, raised the hatch and disappeared below, returning with three beers. "Just in case you change your mind," he told her.

An hour later, they pulled into the lee of Mark Island. Catherine sighed as the boat settled to a quiet, easy pace. Her hair was tossled from the winds and wild with dried sea spray that left a salty coating over every inch of exposed skin. Her face glowed rosy from the sun and wind, and she realized she'd had a wonderful time despite her initial fears.

They found a quiet spot to anchor, and when that task was complete, Peter complimented her. "You're a good sailor."

"I am?"

"If you didn't get seasick in that, you're not likely to get sick in anything."

"Well, that's nice to know. I thought I was behaving like a real amateur."

"You were, but you have the makings of a good sailor." He grinned. "I know several *yachties* who would have been puking over the side."

His remarks raised her spirits further. In a moment he and Ted headed below. "We'll get some lunch together."

"Can't I help?"

"Easier for us. We know where everything is. Just enjoy."

Which Catherine did. For the first time she noticed fully the incredible beauty of the scenery—blue waters, green pines, gray-rocked coastline. A green lobster boat chugged in up the coast, idling as the lobsterman snagged one of the bright-colored buoys, attached the line to a motor-driven winch, and hauled the trap aboard. His movements were swift and sure as he emptied the trap, rebaited it, and sent it over the side again, to move off to the next buoy.

Peter and Ted returned to deck with a lavish repast under the circumstances—three kinds of cheese, cold meats, a tin of caviar, crackers, a bottle of chilled white wine.

"You guys do good work!"

"The tip jar's right over there in the cockpit," Ted quipped.

The hours sped by. As Ted had promised, the sail back was very different. With the wind behind them, they eased over the waters as if they were in a bath tub. Late in the afternoon they made their appearance at the party given by old yachting friends of Peter's who had moved ashore to the outskirts of town. There was food and drink in abundance. Catherine was welcomed warmly into the group and never lacked for good conversation and old-fashioned fun as she and

Peter joined in the volleyball game on the back lawn. Laughing and bearing grass stains from lost footing during the game, they returned to the food-laden table and filled their plates.

As the evening wore on, however, Catherine felt her weariness. She settled in a chair on the deck and played quiet observer as Peter chatted with old yachting friends. Something was wrong, and she didn't think it was just her tiredness. The day had been more than pleasant. Peter had been as kind and as much fun to be with as ever. Yet she felt flat—as though there was an empty place inside that couldn't be filled by the activity of the weekend. She found herself thinking of Lucien Blythe, and this time did not elbow the thoughts away. They came so naturally. They seemed to belong.

What was he doing? Was he aware of her absence? Was he tempted to the same jealousy he'd shown when she was out of the house before? She imagined him, pacing the rooms of the house, seeking her out. Was he feeling lonely and deserted?

"You're off in a daze." Peter had come up quietly beside her and squatted down by her chair.

She tried to smile. "Yes, I guess I am."

"You're not enjoying yourself?"

"Oh, no—it's been a great day! Just tired."

"Mmmm, me, too. We can leave in a minute." He studied her face. "You're sure nothing's wrong?"

"No, nothing." How could she tell him what was troubling her, when she wasn't precisely sure herself? Perhaps it was no more than overtiredness.

Ted and Althea drove back with them, and they all sat on deck sipping nightcaps. Ted had them in stitches as he rambled through a succession of sailing stories.

"Remember," he chucked gleefully, "the Thanksgiving we were in Saint George's, Bermuda, and that hurricane came out of nowhere? Hundred-twenty-mile-and-hour winds. Our anchors wouldn't hold. We started dragging backwards. A big roller lifted us, and we looked back to see our stern hanging right over *Fandarko's* bow. You should've seen the expression on their faces! We skidded down the side of her bow, and the anchors finally decided to hold. Peter ran below and drank half a bottle of Maalox. I grabbed a bottle of Lomotil myself. Things finally started to quiet down a little—I mean, the winds were only about seventy miles an hour—nothing serious." He looked heavenward, "And what do these guys decide but to have our Thanksgiving dinner after all—and share it with the crew on

Fandarko. Into the dingy we went, roast turkey, fixings, half a dozen bottles of wine. Solley was cook then. He was more worried about the turkey going overboard than he was about himself. I thought for sure I was a goner. We were only a hundred yards off of *Fandarko*, but the seas were so high we couldn't even see the top of her mast when we were between waves. And there I was, holding on to a pot of yams like they were the goddamned crown jewels."

Peter was laughing so hard, the tears were running down his cheeks.

"What happened? Did you get to eat your dinner?"

"Oh, yeah. After that, we'd better have. Never enjoyed a meal so much in my life—salt water soaked dressing and all."

When Ted walked Althea back to *Cherise* a half hour later, Catherine still felt like lingering on deck, making excuses of wanting to enjoy the beauty of the harbor lights—which she did, but that wasn't the whole truth. Later, in bed, she wondered if Peter sensed the confusion she was feeling. She was afraid to give voice to it herself. It was as if she lived in two different worlds, and they were pulling back and forth upon her with equal intensity. Peter was kind, sweet, wonderful. Why couldn't she feel for him as she felt for Lucien? What ingredient was missing? Why did the mere thought of Lucien still leave her weak? Was it the mystery about him? The feeling she had that they were meant to be one, and eventually *would* be, no matter what she did to fight against the flow of fate?

She stayed long enough the next day to watch the boat being brought up on the rails and into the yard. It seemed immense as it sat in its wooden cradle, its bottom still dripping, its masts reaching high into the skies as the gulls circled and screamed.

Peter drove her to the airport and waited until her flight was ready to board. He took her in his arms for a last, hungry hug. "I'll try to come down in a week or so. Things should be enough in control that I can take a few days off. I hate to see you go."

"Me, too." But her voice was barely audible. She hoped Peter would attribute it to her sadness at parting.

Chapter 20

A blanket of steel gray clouds was shouldering in from the west as Catherine stepped down from the plane and crossed the runway toward the taxi stand.

The first heavy drops spattered the cab windows as the driver swung into Orange Street and shortly thereafter into Catherine's drive. Paying him from the back seat, she sprinted, with bag in hand, toward the back door. The downpour began in earnest as she fitted her key into the lock and pushed the door open.

Barney bounded across the kitchen tiles, whining his joy, wiggling from nose to tail tip and nearly knocking her over with his welcome.

"You'd think I'd been gone a month." She knelt down and hugged the dog, allowing him to coat her cheek with a lavish tongue.

"It would seem that."

She raised her head with a jerk at the familiar voice and saw Lucien Blythe approaching—tall, handsome, dark hair gleaming—displaying one of his flashing smiles that dazzled and lit his face with vibrant life. She was startled at how incredibly happy she was to see him, have him near—like coming home to a warm and cozy fire.

"You had a nice journey—to wherever?" he inquired with raised brows.

"Very nice, Captain." She endeavored to keep her voice steady, but the rest of her was definitely trembling.

"Mmm. Considerate of you to advise me you were leaving."

"I . . . didn't see you before I went . . . it was a sudden trip." She began to rise, and he reached out a hand to help her. His touch was warm, strong. There was such an air of control about him—not egotistical or aggressive—but that of a man who'd known suffering as well as success, and had survived and come out the better for it.

"I know I shall get my nose bitten off, so I won't ask you where you went. I presume to see your sailor."

"I thought you weren't going to ask." She grinned.

He only frowned, then transformed it to a smile. "I'm delighted to have you back."

"It's good to be back."

"Much has transpired here."

"Oh? What?" she asked.

"Although I had no intention of terrorizing your sister, I thought it wise to pay a few visits to her . . . simply as an insurance measure." The Captain's voice was smooth and assured. "I think you will find her remarkably changed."

"How?"

The twinkle was in his eyes. "Totally convinced of the error of her former ways, shall we say?"

"What did you do?"

"Finding myself with her in the lounge one evening, I entertained her at the piano for a short while. From her expression, I do not think she found a great deal of pleasure in my musical abilities. She did an immense amount of alarmed shouting and ran from the room before I could speak to her. I happened upon her in the garden the next day, ready to get behind the wheel of your automobile."

"What! Where did she get the keys?"

"I've no idea, though she had keys in her hand. I walked across the few steps and placed my hand on the top of the door, preventing her from closing it. She paled rather quickly. I suspicioned you did not want her driving your vehicle."

"Absolutely right!"

"I took the keys from her hand and told her that I thought she had caused sufficient trouble. It was time she moved from the house. If she chose not to do so, I would see she regretted it. I have your keys, by the way."

"I'd already told her that she had five days to move out. What did she say?"

"With her mouth hanging open, it was rather difficult for her to speak. In any case, the scenes changed at that moment, and I found myself with my hand gripping thin air, and Pierce walking out of the barn and giving me a strange look."

"Is she still here? Did she open the shop today?"

"Our paths haven't crossed. I've no idea."

"I'll go right down."

"Why the rush?" His fingers tightened on hers, but his eyes were what forestalled her.

"I don't know what she'll do. If she's that scared . . ."

"Then let us go together."

"Together?"

"I've been wanting to take a stroll in your time." He glanced down at himself. "And I believe I am suitably dressed not to cause any untoward attention."

It was true. He was in a white shirt with sleeves rolled up and collar open. His dark pants looked not that much different than modern day dress slacks. There was the possibility they might pass someone she knew, but so what if she was seen walking with a dark-haired, bearded man? If anyone asked, she could say he was a friend visiting from the West Coast. She had another thought.

"What's Treasa going to say when I walk in with you? She'll think the whole thing was a hoax to frighten her away."

"Shall we deal with that when we come to it? I will think of something, and as you said, she may not even be there."

Catherine considered, but for only a second. "Okay. I'm probably crazy, but let's go."

He smiled, beatifically.

As before, they didn't release hands as they left the house. "Shall we drive or walk?" Catherine asked, feeling the lightheartedness of the moment.

"I should love a trip in that vehicle," he answered without hesitation.

"But we can't risk releasing hands."

"It's not necessary to hold hands, I don't believe . . . only to maintain physical contact. My hand on your shoulder should suffice."

"I'll have to slide in from your side." Which she did, awkwardly maneuvering her legs one by one over the gear shift in the low-slung car. Once she was behind the wheel and he was comfortably in his own seat, grinning from ear to ear, he slid his hand up her arm and rested it on her shoulder.

"Will this interfere with you?" he asked.

"Not at all." She smiled, dug in her bag for the keys, put them in the ignition, pumped the gas, depressed the clutch, turned the key, and the engine purred powerfully to life. She allowed it to warm up for a minute. Without glancing over at him, she knew he was watching her with intrigued fascination. Shifting into reverse, she slowly backed out of the drive.

He chuckled. "Marvelous!"

Waiting until traffic was clear, she backed out and started down Orange Street. The rain had ceased; the mass of dark cloud was receding from the skies over Nantucket. A few rays of sunlight trickled through gaps in the clearing canopy. Everything seemed freshly washed and bright—like the aftermath of any summer storm. Except that it wasn't like any summer day. She was driving down the street with Captain Lucien Blythe! His hand was warm on her shoulder, but she chanced a quick look over in any case, just to be sure he was still there. He was, and the grin hadn't left his face. His expression was that of a small boy with a new toy, and Catherine felt her own excited delight in their adventure increasing all the more.

"All these trees!" he exclaimed. "Yet it's quite remarkable that the buildings have changed very little."

"You'll notice more changes in the center of town," she explained. "They had a terrible fire on the island, not long after you left—"

"You're prophesying my future again."

"Not really. It's a fact that—" she stopped herself, suddenly remembering that the historical date for his departure from the island was not all that far in the future either. She let the subject rest. She didn't want to ruin the happy mood between them; nor did she want to think about his leaving. He was soon absorbed elsewhere. They'd stopped at the corner of Main Street, waiting for a break in traffic so Catherine could cross over.

"Good heavens! Where do they all come from? This congestion would put London to shame."

"The ferry," she answered, her gaze concentrated on the line of cars coming up Main Street.

He was turning his head from right to left as if trying to take in every detail of the scene. "I see what you mean. Although the street bears a resemblance to what I remember, all of these structures are new."

His comment made her smile. "New in comparative terms. They're all nearly a hundred years old." Finding a break, Catherine hit the gas and scooted across the cobbles.

"Quite amazing how you operate this machine. I would love to have instructions."

"Not in this traffic, Captain."

"Assuredly not. We might end up forming too close an acquaintance with one of those elms." They both laughed.

"There's my shop to the left, Classics II." As she stopped in another line of traffic, she lifted her hand from the steering wheel to point diagonally forward. "As you can see, it would have been faster to walk."

"But not nearly as amusing."

"Looks like she opened." The door to the shop was braced welcomingly ajar, and Catherine could just make out the hand-painted, "Come In—We're Open" sign in the window.

"One worry off your mind," the Captain consoled. "Quite an impressive little establishment," he added.

Catherine put on her signal light to turn into the private parking area behind.

"I've not had time to think of a plan of action," he said.

"You've been too busy looking."

"Quite true. Why not keep driving for a bit. You know she is here, and if the door is open to business, I doubt she is doing anything nefarious."

Catherine was already in the midst of her turn, but the Captain's suggestion enticed her. Why not show him more of Nantucket? She continued up the side road past her private parking area behind the shop building. "All right, Captain. Where to?"

"You're driving, though I wouldn't mind seeing the docks closer at hand and a bit of the countryside."

"The countryside first then." She wove down the narrow streets, turning this way and that, in a general direction that would take her out of town. The end result brought her to the road to Madaket. She picked up speed as they traveled over the low, rolling moors. Fewer houses dotted the landscape, which basically was composed of scrubby and occasionally mowed fields and tracts of stunted pine. She detoured right down the short road toward Dionis Beach, pausing in the small parking lot behind the dunes so that he could have a glimpse of Nantucket Bay, then turned the Porsche and spun on toward the western end of the island. The land toward Madaket was lower lying and flatter than elsewhere. The first English settlers from Massachusetts had landed there and set up a temporary settlement before establishing themselves more firmly around Capaum Harbor, then moving on to the present location of Nantucket Town, then called Sherburne, when storms closed Capaum Harbor. That original salt water harbor was now a landlocked pond.

His eyes searched everywhere as they drove. "Far fewer farms than I recall," he commented. "There once were sheep roaming these moors. Instead of stands of pine there were hay pastures."

"The economy needed it then. They were more self-sufficient. Most produce and meat is brought over daily on the ferry now. And think what all those sheep and the stripping of the trees did to the ecology of the land—nothing to hold the soil. If I'm not mistaken, the whole island was forested when the first English/American settlers arrived."

"Yes, the English have a tendency to cultivate everything into a garden plot and mold their environment into a facsimile of what they are accustomed to." There was no criticism in his voice; only observation. "But you must know that we have a bustling trade in foodstuffs as well. I am speaking of 1844, of course. A ship of some sort pulls into port nearly every day."

"But there wasn't the dependency on outside grown produce."

"Perhaps not. I've not really thought about it. The food arrives on my table and I eat it. That is Gladstone's province, and I leave him free rein to it. What are those?" he suddenly exclaimed, pointing his free hand to a stand of modern, vertical, wood-sided buildings with huge expanses of glass rising out of the scrub and sandy soil to the left of the road.

"Progress. They're condominiums. Actually, they're pretty well done. At least the builder tried to blend them in with the environment."

"Our opinions differ." He shuddered. "So many of them."

"A lot of people want to live here in the summer."

"And they would ruin the island to do so."

"The zoning on the island is strict."

"Zoning?"

"The laws and regulations governing what can be built where and on what size piece of land. Nantucket keeps on top of the growth and building situation more than most places—fighting to keep the island from becoming another overcrowded seaside resort. You've been to Brighton?" She referred to the resort town on the English Channel first made popular in the early nineteenth century by George IV. The multitude of fashionable had, of course, flocked after him when he'd built his Royal Pavilion, a disjointed, quasi-Oriental playhouse by the shore.

The Captain literally wrinkled his nose. "Don't remind me."

"Well, Nantucket won't become a Brighton—with any luck, or an Atlantic City, or Miami Beach, or even another Cape Cod," she added the last to herself.

She drove through the older section of Madaket, where none of the buildings were nearly as old as Nantucket Town, just precondominium.

"I am not impressed," Lucien said shortly, before she'd had a chance to drive down the sand-strewn road to Madaket Beach. She backed into a convenient drive and headed back, letting the Porsche's engine show a bit of its power navigating the curves of the main road. She wasn't a blatant abuser of safety, but she wanted to give the Captain a bit of unexpected excitement. The car handled like a dream and clung to the pavement in any case, whipping around the corners without her having to lift her foot off the accelerator.

Glancing out of the corner of her eye, she saw Lucien brace his free hand against the dashboard.

"Having fun?" she teased.

"Do you always maneuver this thing so rapidly? You should be on the hunt course on an underexercized, overoated stallion!"

"You haven't seen anything yet." She'd barely touched fifty-five on the speedometer. "These roads are too narrow and highly traveled, or I'd show you what she can really do. I should take you on some of the open back roads in California."

"This will suffice for the moment. You refer to this automobile as 'she.'"

"I think of her like that. Privately I call her the Silver Lady. I've always named my cars, to myself anyway. That way you can yell at them by name when they conk out on the side of the road, or cheer them on when they're taking you through a storm. I've had the Pink Panther, a pick-up bodied Jeep." She saw his bemused expression. "Sort of a small farmer's wagon with a cab and engine where the horses are supposed to be. She was painted bright pink when I bought her—and normally I hate pink—but the paint job was good, so I left her that color. I put pink flowered Contact paper ... wallpaper ... on the door panels and recovered the seats. I loved her back in my college days, but she died—her engine, and I didn't have the money to fix her. I sold her with a tear in my eye. Then I had the Spotted Beetle, a Volkswagen convertible with more prime than paint showing." She noticed his expression. "Forget it. If I try to explain all these details of what everything is, I'll never finish my story. She was spotted white and rust-colored red, in any case. After she died, I had the Brown Bomber, a Granada with a big engine that went miles and miles. She hardly ever let me down. There were a couple of lesser wonders in between. I never had the money to buy a new car, until this one."

"Interesting." He looked heavenward, but he was chuckling. "Much like naming a favorite horse, isn't it? Calling them by name and endowing them with personality does make a difference. My ships each have a personality of their own. *Goddess* is a goddess. She likes to flaunt her superiority over the elements, tease them, in effect. *Sophia,* knowing her worth, rides them with perseverance, points her bowsprit up, and looks down her masts in indignation. The others each have their quirks and foibles and bits of personality, from what my captains tell me."

Catherine's heavy foot on the accelerator had brought them back to town much faster then they'd left it. She headed the car down the narrow streets toward the docks.

Catherine had a feeling the Captain would be disillusioned and disappointed by the modern day docks, but she said nothing. She crawled past the Steamboat Wharf first. In the traffic, she had little choice. The mid-afternoon ferry was arriving, sounding its horn.

The Captain looked out past the wharf buildings to the bulk of the arriving boat. "I begin to understand why there are so many people and automobiles on this island." The cars weren't visible yet, but the crowd of passengers on the upper deck was. Many were waiting in the now bright sunshine, taking advantage of the view of the town until the last minute before going into the bowels of the three-decked ship to retrieve their vehicles.

"An education, but move on." The Captain craned his neck around then forward even as he spoke. "This wharf did not exist to my recollection."

"I think it was built when the steamboats started arriving."

They progressed slowly around the parking lot at the wharf. Easy Street led toward the other wharves, but it was one-way, the wrong way. She stopped, then shot around into a surprisingly vacant parking slot. "We'll have to park here and walk, unless you want to drive all the way around town to pass the other wharves from the right direction. Most of these streets are one-way."

"I shan't mind walking."

He slid his hand from her shoulder, gripped her fingers, and when their hands were firmly entwined, shook his arm as if to loosen the muscles. She hadn't thought how cramped his arm muscles must have gotten after being elevated in one position, holding her shoulder for so long.

They extricated themselves from the car without too much difficulty. She led the way as they left Steamboat Wharf, drawing him through the crowds, feeling an unbelievable excitement to be walking down Nantucket streets with Lucien at her side. They passed the two restaurants to the left of the wharf entrance, turning sharply left onto Easy Street. It was only a short cobbled distance to the Straight Wharf. He gawked at what he saw. Shops selling everything from designer clothing to candy. Art galleries, restaurants, bars, people. They walked along the outer side of the wharf on the honest planking between the back of the shops and the luxury boats.

He gazed around in total confusion. "This is very different. These modern pleasure boats I can understand. At least they have some semblance and shape to what's gone before. But this!" He directed his hand leftward to the shops at either side of the wharf. "There once was commerce here. Hogsheads. Cargo. Men working. This is nothing but frivolity. It escapes me."

"There's commerce here, too, of a different kind."

He made a throaty, barking sound. "Brighton, indeed. It already is!"

"Whaling died in the late eighteen hundreds. Nantucket was a forgotten backwater and lost in poverty. The islanders did the best they could when tourists discovered this place."

He seemed not the least convinced. She steered him around, back toward the head of the dock, empathizing with his shock and dismay and feeling sadness herself. "I shouldn't have brought you here. It's one thing to see it from the study window."

"Nonsense. We're going the next dock down. I want to see where my vessels once berthed."

They followed the wharfside beside the admirably landscaped A&P parking lot. The exterior of the supermarket had been designed with an attempt toward blending in with traditional island architecture. There were no neon or garish signs. Still the Captain shook his head, and taking control now, he led her along.

"There used to be a chandler's up there, to this side of the rope walk, which I'm sure is gone."

"Washington Street," she muttered under her breath.

"Warehouses there," he motioned. "My favorite sailmaker was to the top of this wharf, though I see no sign of his building."

She could sense his frustrated anger. He drew her down the Old Wharf. Saying little, he strode determinedly past the tiny galleries and crafts shops that now predominated the wharf. He walked straight to the end and pointed to several tall, weathered piers.

"Here is where my vessels tied." He glared with disrespect at the lavish cabin cruiser and sixty-foot sailboat presently docked stern-to, their lines tied to the posts he indicated. The luxury accommodations of both, particularly the cabin cruiser, were revealed fully by a glimpse below decks through open companionways.

He swung her around, beat a track back up the wharf. "You were right. I should not have come here."

Once they left the Old Wharf, she directed him back toward Main Street, going behind, instead of in front of, the A&P, one block on Candle Street, two up Main. He seemed to simmer down, though one look at his face told her his emotions were still whirling. They reached the corner of Centre Street and Main. She paused.

After he'd stood unmoving for several moments, his eyes staring at the front of the Pacific National Bank, she said. "My shop's up here to the right."

"That hasn't changed."

"What?"

"The front of the bank."

"It escaped the fire."

"One sanity."

"Are you sorry I gave you this tour?"

That snapped him out of it. He shook his head. "No. I am glad." He ran his free hand through his hair, looked down at her. His eyes seemed almost iridescent blue diamonds. "On to your shop."

"Have you thought of a plan?"

"No."

"Neither have I."

In the end they simply walked through the front door. Treasa was at the counter. There were two people in the shop—one examining fabric samples, the other shelf displays of accessories. Treasa was keeping an eye on them. Since the door was open, she had no forewarning that Catherine and the Captain had entered the shop.

Catherine paused just inside the doorway, the Captain behind her. Their hand holding was hidden behind Catherine's back. They might have been two separate customers entering.

Treasa looked over. Her fingers grabbed the counter edge. She stared past Catherine as if she didn't see her. Her eyes were locked on the Captain. All color had drained from her face. She started backing away in terror.

Suddenly the Captain released Catherine's hand. She swung around, but he was already stepping out of the open doorway and starting up the sidewalk. She expected to see him vanish. Instead she watched him stride up the street past the window in full flesh.

Treasa's gaze followed him with an unrelieved expression of horror.

Catherine finally called out to her. "Hi, Trea."

Treasa jerked, blinked, focused on Catherine, finally seeing her.

"Looks like you've been doing a good job."

Treasa turned her head imperceptibly to glance dazedly at the customers.

"I just got back and wanted to check in," Catherine said. "Everything okay?"

"Yes . . . yes . . ." Treasa's gaze returned to the front windows. "Did you see him?" her voice was high-pitched with nervousness.

"Who?"

"The man who came in right behind you?"

"I got a glimpse of him." Catherine felt uncomfortable with the lie. "Why?" Catherine walked over to the counter. She actually felt sorry for her sister. Treasa was making a valiant effort at pulling herself together. She merely shook her head in answer to Catherine's question.

"Have you done much business?" Catherine hoped the change of subject would snap Treasa out of her terrified state. She was beginning to feel guilty.

"Yeah, quite a bit over the weekend."

"Great. Would you mind watching the shop alone for the rest of the day? I'm pretty tired. I'll take the mail home and sort through it."

"Sure, I guess so," Treasa said numbly. "It's only an hour. I've got some news for you. I've got another job—a sailing job. I'm leaving tomorrow."

"You are?"

"I called Jan this afternoon. He said Peter had heard of something up there."

"Yes. I was going to tell you about it."

"Peter had the captain call me back. The boat's *Drago.* I'll be stewardess. I'll fly up tomorrow. The owners will pay my airfare. The job's for the rest of the season."

"Good for you. Congratulations."

Treasa wagged her head. "I've got to get off this island."

Catherine didn't ask why, only said noncommittally, "It's probably for the best. Are you sure you'll be all right for the rest of the
afternoon?" Catherine was torn between a desire to stay with her
sister, and an equally urgent desire to find out what had happened to
the Captain.

"I'll be fine."

"Okay. I'll see you at home." She went to her desk to collect the
mail, then, with heart nervously pounding, she jog-trotted back to
where she'd left the car parked, expecting to see the Porsche empty.
She couldn't have been more amazed, and delighted, to see the Captain sitting in the passenger seat.

She opened her door, slid in. "You're still here! This is incredible."

"I wondered when you'd get back."

"I was sure you'd be gone."

"I was expecting similar when I walked away from your shop."

"Why did you leave like that?"

"When I saw her expression, I knew I'd done more than enough.
A certain amount of mercy was called for. What did she have to
say?"

"Very little about you, except to ask if I'd seen you. She's taken a
sailing job. She's leaving the island tomorrow."

"Indeed. That's good news." He glanced at her. "Isn't it?"

"Yes, I think it is."

"One other question raises its head."

"*Why* you're still here," she answered, as she fumbled in her
purse for her keys. Her hand was shaking in reaction.

"Quite." His brow was furrowed. "I find myself in the unexpected
position of not being able to leave this modern world of yours,
whether I wish it or not."

"You wish it?"

"Don't be absurd. But I would like very much to understand the
reasons. Drive about for a while before we return to the house."

She did, as he pondered. With no course in mind, she meandered
down various roadways, ending up at a surprisingly deserted beach
somewhere south of 'Sconset. The sun was setting behind them. For
a while they sat silently staring out to the gradually changing colors
of sea and sky.

"Let's walk," he said in a moment.

They followed a narrow track that wove through the clumps of dune grass and down along the top of the wide beach. "I wonder if the house is the key," he mused.

"What do you mean?"

"Perhaps once we have left it in whichever time period, we are glued into that period."

"It doesn't seem logical."

"Our meeting at all is not logical. The fact remains that we are together at this moment—that I did not leave your world when we released physical contact."

Catherine pondered silently. No scientifically plausible explanations came to her mind, yet he was still with her, and they'd never remained together for so long while in the house. "Perhaps you're right," she said. She took his hand and squeezed it, liking the reassuring comfort.

He glanced down at her in surprised pleasure, but she was too deep in her own reveries to notice the look. She only held his hand all the more tightly.

The waves foamed and splashed on the sandy stretch of beach. Due east across the Atlantic was Spain. Up the beach farther rose the sand cliffs supporting 'Sconset. A fraction of a mile up the coast, the sea and the elements had eroded those cliffs, and would continue to do so. The once famous Cliff Path had already been a victim.

They'd walked for over a mile and were all alone but for the gulls. The last sunlight was gone. The world was hazed in twilight. They paused at the base of the cliff in a protected hollow. He suddenly increased the pressure of his fingers.

"This changes our situation drastically, does it not."

Her answer was a whisper. "Yes." That change was what she'd been pondering, realizing the implications of their ability to remain in the same time together. There were possibilities for them now— almost as if they were any normal man and woman, meeting and loving. Almost, but not quite. She'd suddenly seen clearly, too, what had been troubling her in Maine. Her efforts to hold Lucien at arm's length and remove herself from their seemingly futile relationship had been wasted energy. As sincerely as she cared for Peter, she'd been deceiving herself to think he could take Lucien's place.

"This sailor of yours . . . you said you love him."

"I did."

He spun around. "Did? You don't now?"

"I began to discover this weekend that my feelings for him weren't what I thought."

"Why? What caused this change?"

She studied his face, her eyes locked on his. "You. I couldn't stop thinking and caring about you."

"Catherine—"

"It seemed so impossible—you and I from different worlds. You said so yourself. I was afraid . . . so afraid I'd be hurt . . . that it would end . . . that it must . . ."

"And what we've discovered today has changed your mind?"

"It was changed before that. I just didn't realize it."

The wind ruffled his hair, but he stood motionless, his expression as intense as a physical touch. "I know how I feel. I love you—too much to give this up for the risks involved."

His words vibrated in the air. She lifted her hand and touched her fingers to his cheek.

"I've thought about all the impossibilities, over and over," he continued, "and it doesn't matter anymore. One does not dictate these things. I know what I want."

She nodded imperceptibly, her gaze never leaving his. "I want it, too. I've missed you . . . I didn't know how much until now . . . and I don't want to run away from it anymore. I'll face all the risks if we can be together."

She had a sense of inevitability when he lifted his arms and she went into them. For a moment they simply held each other, afraid to let go. She listened to his heartbeat through his shirtfront, sighed when he nestled his lips in her hair. Nothing could change this feeling between them; nothing could supplant it. No other man could bring her such joy, fill her with such warmth, softness, and contentment, yet make her feel so vitally alive.

Deepening violet tinged the sky. Even the gulls had quieted. Only the waves broke the solitary peace in either direction as far as the eye could see. They might have been in any time . . . hers or his, or another altogether.

He took her chin gently in his fingers, urged her head up off his chest. Slowly, tenderly, his mouth covered hers, and as she returned the kiss, they sealed their future. This time there would be no stopping, running, hiding from fate. They would meet it and everything it offered them head on.

His hands pressed into her back as if he couldn't draw her close enough. To touch him, taste him, smell his clean, spicy scent was all Catherine remembered—to feel the arms she'd thought would never hold her again.

He leaned away, stared down at her. Desire smoldered in his blue eyes. His fingers went to the buttons of his shirt, quickly undoing them. He shrugged from the white fabric. The pale moonlight reflected on the planes of his body and his rippling muscles as he bent and spread the shirt upon the sand.

"Lucien—what if someone comes by?" Even as she spoke she knew she didn't care. The hunger she felt for him was too strong.

"Not in this quiet corner . . . and this is our night, Catherine."

His summons was magnetic. She moved toward him. His arms waited. She knew an overpowering yearning as he slowly undressed her, his hands moving wonderingly over her, until her skin, too, glowed pearl-like in the moonlight. He kicked off his shoes, slid off his trousers and stepped from them, then rested his hands on her shoulders and gazed at her.

She sucked in her breath to see his unembarrassed and obvious desire, his superb body—tall, supple, firm. She reeled further when he suddenly drew her against him. She rubbed her cheek against the dark mat of hair on his chest; her fingers over the soft, smooth skin of his back.

"How beautiful you are." The whispered breath brushed her ear. "And how I've waited for this moment . . . you and I, man and woman, with no barriers between us."

She could only nod. She was beyond speech.

He drew her down on his makeshift blanket and snuggled her close against him. As their lips traveled over each other's flesh, their limbs tangled and entwined; their hands touched, explored, lovingly learned the secrets of each other. And the fire between them raged, hotter, more demandingly.

When finally he moved over her, she was trembling. She wanted him desperately—Lucien—loving her as she'd dreamed, fulfilling her beyond any expectation. She drew him toward her, and soon she knew all of that magic. Each thrust, pressing him deeper within her, uniting them, was more exquisite than the last. He was part of her, and she wanted it to go on and on.

"Oh, God, Catherine."

They'd waited so long for this moment. Their bodies throbbed—

cried out for fulfillment, and when it came in shuddering waves, they both gasped in wonderment.

For long moments afterward, they laid in each other's arms, quietly, feeling their completeness. She traced her fingers over his chest, waist and hips. How tiny her own body seemed in comparison. How right it felt to be snuggled in his arms.

He let his lips linger on her brow. "I've never felt this way before, Catherine . . . even with Gwen. It overwhelms. I've wanted you so desperately these weeks, knowing full well I'd be wrong to encourage it. My will power survived the test—until the day your sailor arrived on the scene." His voice roughened. "I felt such jealousy, I wanted to kill. I startled myself. I would have done something desperate, I think, if he hadn't left the island."

She was amazed at the extent of anger in his voice, turned her head to look over at him. "I wasn't trying to make you jealous."

"I know." He sighed. "But did you use him just a little bit to forget us?"

"I did try to forget—but I'd hate to think I actually used him. I was feeling so hurt and rejected after you told me it was over. I thought it was hopeless . . ."

"Yes, with good reason. Not one of my better moments."

"You thought you were doing the right thing. Peter came along after that and helped fill the emptiness. I do care about him. He's a good, kind person. I simply can't love him as I love *you*."

"How thankful I am for that!"

"What now, Lucien?" she said in a moment. "Where do we go from here?"

"Where we would go from here if we were any other man and woman?"

"But we're not." Her voice held the edges of fear. "We don't have any proof this will last."

"We'll find a way. We love each other. This is our beginning. We must believe that."

"I'll certainly try." But she reached over and gripped his forearm, squeezing tightly. "I don't want to lose you."

"Nor I, you."

Unexpectedly he sat up, knelt beside her, slipped his arms under her knees and shoulders, and grinned.

"What are you doing?" she exclaimed.

"Such a beautiful night for a swim. We shouldn't waste it."

"Lucien, I don't swim well enough for ocean surf."

"Then we shan't go in far—and I'll be with you. I *do* swim well enough."

He stood, lifting her in his arms as if she were a feather, and started striding down the sandy slope toward the moon-washed waves. What a vision they made—two naked, silvery figures moving in the shadowy moonlight toward the frothy surf like surrealistic apparitions.

Lucien stepped boldly into the waves, not pausing until the water licked around his waist. He immediately bent at the knees, ducking them both. Catherine gasped as the cold washed over her skin.

Lucien chuckled. "A shock, eh? You'll grow used to it in a moment. Very healthful this."

Her teeth chattered. "If you say so."

He let her drift, floated beside her, then pushed ahead parallel to the beach and motioned her to follow. They swam leisurely together in the shallow water, riding with the up and down motion of the wave crests, occasionally touching hands or legs. There was such a sense of freedom with the water slipping easily over their naked skin. When he paused and drew her close, their wet bodies slid together without friction, like silk. The feeling was incredibly sensuous. Catherine felt her pulse accelerate, the hunger rise inside.

"I want you again already," he said.

"I know," she whispered.

"Right now." He braced his feet on the bottom, secure on the moving sand, and drew her to him in the waist-deep water. She felt his readiness and her own as he lifted her. The water buoyed her weight as she braced her legs around him, and he slowly lowered her, their gazes locked. The heat of him when he entered was all the more intense and exquisite in the cold sea. She gripped his shoulders, clung to him. As a man exultant, he threw back his head and let out a cry of pure joy.

They swam again before he took her hand and drew her toward the shore. "You must be cold."

"Beginning to be."

"Let's get out then before you catch a chill."

Like two children they scampered from the water, up the sandy beach, laughing and shaking droplets of water from their bodies.

Their skin still damp, they struggled into their clothing. He held her then, rubbing his hands over her limbs to restore the circulation and heat.

"Catherine, this night has been beyond description."

"I'm glad I'm not the only one thinking that." She drew down his head and playfully kissed the tip of his nose.

"I do love you!"

"Likewise, my dear, beloved Captain."

Chapter 21

They'd barely gotten back into the house when the phone rang, a jangling annoyance to burst their private bubble. Reflexly, with irritation, Catherine walked across the kitchen and picked up the receiver. It was Peter. She immediately tensed, and dropped her voice. She didn't dare turn to look at Lucien, lest the expression on her face give a clue to her caller's identity.

She was about to tell Peter she'd call back, but he spoke too quickly. "Treasa didn't waste any time about that job. She called this afternoon."

"She told me."

"It looks good for her, and she sounded serious—not doing it for a quirk."

"She wants to get off the island."

"How was your trip?"

"No problems."

His voice grew more intimate. "I miss you already."

"I need to talk to you—" she began, but he interrupted her.

"I've gotta go. Someone wants to use the phone here. I'm calling from the marina office. I'll try to ring you later."

She replaced the receiver and turned quickly, anxious to see what Lucien's reaction to the conversation had been. He was gone.

Her knees went weak in disappointment. She gripped the table edge. How could she have been so foolish as to let go of his hand? She should have let the phone ring. There was so much more they had to say! Everything was different now. What was between them could no longer be lightly brushed aside. They belonged together, and this time their parting seemed unbearable.

Treasa came home shortly thereafter, sober as a judge. "I'm going up to pack," she said quickly as she passed Catherine in the kitchen. "Do you think you could drop me at the airport tomorrow morning?"

Catherine tried to pull her thoughts from Lucien and concentrate on what Treasa was saying. "Sure. What time is your flight?"

"Eight."

"Are you all right, Trea? You really want this job?"

"Yes, I want it, and I'll be fine once I get away from here. There's something strange going on in this house—not just this house, the whole island."

Treasa didn't seem inclined to elucidate, and Catherine wasn't about to press the point.

"You can get someone part-time to help in the shop, can't you?"

"I shouldn't have any trouble. I am glad you're taking this job."

Treasa nodded, but her thoughts had turned inward. As she left the room, she seemed both anxious and jumpy.

Though Catherine willed the Captain to appear again that night in some place of privacy, he didn't. Peter didn't call back either, for which Catherine was almost thankful, though she knew she was only postponing the inevitable. She slept alone, dreaming of Lucien, remembering how his arms had felt. In the morning she drove Treasa to the airport. Both sisters paused just inside the terminal door. So much had happened since Treasa had first arrived on the island; both of them had changed. Impulsively Catherine reached out and put her arms around her sister. In an instant Treasa hugged her back.

"Cath, I'm sorry for everything. I know I pulled some rotten stuff. I'm going to straighten out—I've got to. I'm not looking at things the same way now."

"It's okay. I just hope everything works out for you from now on. I'll be thinking of you, and call if you need anybody to talk to. Take care of yourself."

"Yeah. You, too."

Both pairs of eyes were misty as they parted.

"Let me know how you're doing."

"I will."

"Good luck."

Grabbing up her bags, Treasa headed for the ticket window, walking rapidly, as if afraid to look back.

Catherine turned slowly and walked back outside to the car. Was this really going to be the changing point for Treasa? Had she and the Captain done the right thing in scaring the wits out of her? Would anything short of what they'd perpetrated have worked? She honestly wasn't sure. She could only hope.

Catherine drove directly to the shop, though how she was going to put her mind to business, she hadn't a clue. Her one consolation was knowing Lucien would be working, too, in his own world. Unlocking the front door, she flipped over the "Open" sign, turned on the lights, and went directly to the register to count the opening cash. Once the register was set, she went to her desk at the back of the shop, stashed her purse in one of the drawers, sat down, and examined the stack of mail she'd picked up from just inside the door. A few bills and a good deal of junk mail, which she consigned to the wastebasket. Lifting the ivory-handled letter opener, she began slitting envelopes.

What was she going to tell Peter? Dare she tell him about Lucien? By no rationalization could the fact that Lucien was a man from the past be avoided. To her he was real—flesh, blood, alive, and the man with whom she wanted to spend all her days—but no else would be likely to accept that. Yet she owed Peter more than a cowardly skirting of the truth.

The more she considered, the more confused she became. She rose abruptly and went to the storeroom for a piece of posterboard. With a fat-tipped felt marker, she wrote out, "Part-Time Help Wanted—Inquire Within." She placed the sign in the window where it was readily visible but did not obstruct her window display. She paced the shop, her eye unconsciously inspecting the placement of each piece, checking for dust, yet her mind was far, far away.

It was a quiet morning, and she had some merchandise to unpack. Hauling the carton out of the storeroom, she slit the wrapping tapes and set to work. The pottery she carefully removed from the packing material was the product of a revival of American Indian craftsmanship and design. Each piece was unique. She placed them about the room. To think how her life had changed in just twenty-four hours. What was going to happen now? What of her business? What of Lucien's? What of their separate lives? Would they continue as they were, snatching moments here and there and spending most of their hours miserably alone? The mere thought made her want to cry.

Fortunately the balance of the day went quickly as she helped one customer decide between a Sheffield silver candelabra and a pair of matching early American brass candlesticks. Another customer debated over the purchase of a Queen Anne drop leaf table displayed in the window. Catherine dropped the price twenty dollars and made a sale. Possible future business from the customer would make up for the slight loss of profit.

It was strange to go back to an empty house that evening—Treasa gone and no certainty that Lucien would appear. But how she prayed he would—she missed him. It seemed much longer than twenty-four hours since they'd parted. Of course, she wasn't entirely alone. Barney gave her his usual warm welcome. She let him out into the backyard and saw Marjorie coming up the drive from the street.

"I saw your car," she called, "and thought I'd pop by for a minute. I won't keep you. You're probably fixing dinner."

"I hadn't even thought of dinner yet. Come on in."

Marjorie came quickly up the back steps inside. "Your sister said you'd gone off to Maine for the weekend. Have a good time?"

"Yes, very." Catherine hoped her tumultuous feelings weren't written all over her face.

"Visiting your new manfriend?" Marjorie fairly twinkled.

Catherine managed to nod and hurried on before Marjorie could pursue the subject. "Would you like a drink—a glass of sherry? I could use one."

"Don't mind if I do, but make mine a scotch with one rock. I think this old body can handle a cocktail before dinner."

Catherine took two glasses from the cupboard and deposited ice in each. "Come on into the living room. It's more comfortable."

As Marjorie ambled about the front room, Catherine unlocked the liquor cabinet, made their drinks, and turned on the nearby stereo, which was tuned to a station playing quiet mood music.

"Thanks," Marjorie said as she accepted her glass and took a sip. "Mmm, you gave me the good stuff."

"Saved for special people. Sit down."

They took places on opposite sides of the coffee table. "One of the reasons I dropped by," Marjorie said without preamble, "was to ask if you wanted to go to a lecture with me Thursday night. I think you'll like the topic—ESP. A Dr. Lindquist, who's doing research at Princeton, is speaking. Good credentials. You know I've always been interested in the subject."

"Sounds good. What time?"

"Seven-thirty."

"I'll plan on it." Even as she spoke, Catherine wondered if her disorganized brain would remember the date at all.

Marjorie stared down at the table top as if considering something.

When she looked up, her expression was cautious. "I don't know if I should bring it up, but any more news with your ghost?"

Catherine took a nervous swallow from her glass. This line of conversation wasn't any more comfortable than the first. "I've seen him," she said vaguely. "My sister did, too. She was terrified."

"Oh? But you said you don't feel any menace."

"Treasa has a different attitude about the supernatural. She told me of a bad experience she had in Europe."

"What kind of experience?"

Briefly Catherine repeated Treasa's story.

"I wouldn't fool about with a Ouija board either," Marjorie said sternly. "Some ghosts can be downright evil, but I don't think yours is. If he was, I'd feel something in this house—a discomfort. Not that I'm an expert, but this house feels totally warm and welcoming."

"Yes." Catherine sought frantically for another subject. "Treasa left the island this morning for a new sailing job."

"Well, that must be a load off your mind, not that I don't sympathize with her, but she has to learn to face her problems herself."

"I think she's finally sorting it out. She hasn't had a drink in a week. I just hope she can do it alone. It won't be easy to stay off booze, especially with the yachting life-style."

"She must have friends who'll give her the support she needs."

"The fellow I've been dating found her the job. I know he and his friends would stand behind her."

When Peter called shortly after Marjorie had left, he immediately brought up Treasa's arrival.

"I thought she seemed different," Peter mused. "When I picked her up at the airport, she was very quiet. We all went down to the pub, and I noticed she was drinking plain tonic."

"There's going to be a lot of temptation for her."

"Don't worry. I know her new skipper real well. He's older and as full of common sense as they come. Nice guy in the bargain. She'll be in good hands."

"Thanks. Listen, Peter, I have to—"

"You won't believe how well I'm doing with my painting. I can't wait to show you. I'm going to try to come down for a few days once I get things ironed out with the work on the boat."

Now was the time to tell him—to at least hint to him that things weren't the same for her! But she couldn't get the words past her lips. When she finally hung up the phone, Peter was no wiser to the

situation than he'd been when he called. She hadn't told him she
loved him, but she felt like a wretched, miserable coward!

She was sitting in the living room, still mentally castigating herself, when Lucien appeared. He came quickly across the room and
sat down beside her, drawing her into his arms and giving her a slow
kiss.

"I've missed you," he sighed.

"I've missed you, too! It's even harder now being apart."

"All day long I thought about us," he said worriedly, "seeking a
solution. Unfortunately, my mental perambulations brought me nowhere—except to confirm that I wanted to be with you every second. I left my ledgers on the desk with only a quarter of my work
done. I walked down to the docks, saw one of my brokers, and
wondered what I was doing there when my thoughts were so obviously elsewhere. I was supposed to go to the Macys' tonight. At
the last moment I sent Gladstone with a message."

"Their daughter will be disappointed." Why had she said that?
The mere thought of him with a woman of his own time stabbed at
her.

He grinned. "A touch of jealousy, my sweet? You know perfectly
well their daughter would be disappointed in any case. I have no
interest in her, particularly now! What did you do with your day?"

"Worked—or tried to. I didn't get an awful lot done. This morning I took Treasa to the airport."

"You seem upset—because she left?"

"Actually, I'm relieved about that. She wants to help herself this
time. I'm just feeling so frightened about us. What's going to happen? Where will we go? How can we stay together? What if this
thing that brings us together stops working?"

His arm tightened about her indicating that he, too, shared her
fears. But when he spoke, his voice was deliberately reassuring. "It
does neither of us any good to worry. We'll find a solution. I was
going to play the piano. Come sit beside me."

She knew he was trying to distract her, but she agreed readily
enough. "I always wished I'd continued with piano lessons, but
Treasa was the one with talent."

"I've heard you singing."

"Along with the radio." She laughed. "That doesn't mean I have
much of a voice."

"Quite a sweet one, I thought. Pity I don't know any songs to which we'd both know the lyrics. I'm afraid the popular drawing room songs of my day had no immortality."

She was feeling more lighthearted as they walked arm-in-arm to the piano. He went to lift the keyboard cover and frowned.

"It appears locked."

"In my day it usually is. A quirk left over from my grandmother. I think she must have sensed you around, too, or at least heard you playing."

"Do you? To my knowledge I've honored no one prior to you with my presence. The key?"

"In the bench."

Lifting the lid, he removed the key and used it to release the lock in the satiny wood. Catherine slid down onto the bench beside him. Her hand rested lightly on his lower thigh as he lifted his hands to the keyboard. "What are you in the mood for?"

She considered. "How about Chopin?"

"A waltz, prelude, or nocturne."

"Waltz."

"So it shall be." He paused for a moment, then embarked on the *Grande Brillante*, striking the rapidly repeating opening B flat with his right hand. Soon he swung into the sprightly melody with both. Catherine watched his hands move with unfaltering yet fascinating rapidity over the keys. Could she ever get her fingers to move so quickly? True, she typed, but only efficiently enough to knock off a quick letter or two.

Only one lamp was lit in the room, and the small fire Catherine had started crackled cozily on the hearth. Lucien went from the first waltz into another, then slowed the tempo with a Beethoven piece. Lastly he played a haunting song—one she'd heard him play before and not recognized. The tingling notes sent goose bumps up her arms.

The mood of the music hung in the air—poignant as a soft caress, full of love and emotions that could not easily be given voice to through spoken language.

"I liked that last song the best," she whispered when he stopped.

"As do I, though before now it always brought reminders of Gwen." He turned his head. "Tonight I thought of you when I played."

Another set of goose bumps rose on her arms in the shape of an unwelcome premonition. Would she and Lucien end in tragedy as he and Gwen had?

He read either her thoughts or her expression. "It won't end like that for us, Catherine. We aren't will-less beings—the mere tools of fate. We can create our own destiny, and we will."

"When you say it like that, I believe it . . . but when I'm alone, it's hard not to be afraid. I think that it could end at any moment, and I'll never see you again." Her hands locked around his, drawing strength.

"Then think of me as with you always, whether physically at your side or not. In my thoughts, I will be."

He touched his lips to her forehead, then pulled her convulsively into his arms. If only she could stay there, safe and secure for always.

By unspoken agreement they rose shortly after and went up the stairs together and into the bedroom. Barney's jingling collar announced him a moment later. The dog padded confidently across the floor and with a quick glance at his mistress and the Captain, curled up on the rug beside the bed.

"Must Barney sleep in here as well?" Lucien raised an eyebrow at the contented animal. She knew he was trying to lighten her spirits, and she was grateful.

She smiled up at him. "You know perfectly well he'd be hurt if I put him into the study or the hall. He's one of the family."

"One who must share the privacy of our bedroom, too? Well, I suppose I piteously spoiled my own mutt as a youngster. He was a bird dog, who should have been consigned to the kennels, but spent his evenings sleeping on the hearth rug in my bedroom."

"You have a soft heart for animals, too—admit it."

"Yes, I suppose you've noticed in the way I treat Jeremy and Sarter."

He led her to the opposite side of the bed, took both her hands. "To think that tonight I shall finally share this bedroom with you as I've longed to—as you and I were intended to. Let us made good use of it, my sweet."

They did, and later, as she snuggled against his chest and listened to his heartbeat gradually slow, she knew she was in the place where she belonged, even if everything sane and logical in the present, technologically pragmatic world fought against letting her stay there.

Chapter 22

He was still with her in the morning when they wakened. His warmth came as a surprise as she wakened to the touch of his arm about her waist, holding her from behind. She rubbed her hand lovingly down its length. Her movement wakened him. She felt him start, then lift himself slowly on the pillow.

"What miracle is this?" he teased, but his voice was husky with pleasure.

She rolled to her back, his arm still around her. "Good morning, Captain."

"So formal at such an early hour and in such intimate circumstances?" He grinned sleepily. "I must say I enjoy this. Whose bed are we in—yours or mine?"

Glancing about she saw the telephone on the nightstand, her familiar objects on the dressing table. "Mine."

"Interesting. What time is it?"

She focused on the clock beside the telephone. "Seven."

"I wonder what Gladstone thought—or is thinking—about my lack of appearance in my bed last night? Perhaps he's not discovered me gone yet. I generally don't rise for another half hour."

"Funny to think of servants keeping an eye on you."

"I manufactured quite a tale to account for my whereabouts two days past when we toured the island together, telling him I'd run into an old acquaintance in town, just arrived from a cross-Atlantic journey, and lost all track of time."

"Did he believe you?"

"He made some skeptical noises. I think he assumed my old acquaintance was a female."

"Well, she was."

"Yes, though not like any female Gladstone has ever encountered."

His hand slid up along her midriff to cup her breast and gently fondle it. "We still have thirty minutes before we must go back to our separate realities."

His touch was sufficient to send Catherine's pulses accelerating. "Let's make good use of them, then," she whispered.

"An excellent suggestion."

When they finally rose, Catherine's cheeks had a peachy glow. Lucien's expression bore the same mark of contentment.

"I shall miss you," he said as they sat side by side on the edge of the bed. "Tonight when you return home, try another experiment I have in mind. At precisely six, shall we say, concentrate your thoughts on me. I shall do likewise. Let us see if that is sufficient to bring us together."

"I'll try—exactly at six. What room should I be in?"

"I don't believe it matters, but let's use the study. There's less likelihood of our being interrupted there should we meet in my time."

"The study." Their eyes met, and Catherine felt such a yearning to stay with him—to keep him with her. She could take him to the shop, but she also knew that would present problems in his life. He couldn't simply vanish from his own world for twenty-four hours.

The hands of the clock read precisely seven-thirty. He had to leave. They stood by the bed, naked in the morning light, and embraced, sharing a long, lingering, fervent kiss. With regret in his eyes, he slowly backed away. He'd gone no further than the edge of the carpet when he vanished, a sudden fading of substance as though a television set had been turned off, erasing the image.

That unexpected coming and going still unnerved her. Before going to the closet for her robe, then on into the shower, she glanced down at the bed. The sheets and covers were tossled. Each pillow contained a clear indentation. The heat of their bodies and lovemaking still seemed imprisoned beneath and within the cloth.

Two people walked into the shop that day inquiring about the part-time position. The first, a college-age girl in jeans and T-shirt, struck Catherine as being flighty and irresponsible. Her abrupt manner wasn't one that would encourage sales. Catherine took her name and number and told her she was interviewing others and would get back to her. Later in the day an older woman, a year-round island

242

Jo Ann Simon

resident with grown children, came in. Susan Watts was friendly, cheerful, though obviously a little nervous about the rigors of seeking a job. Catherine liked her immediately, sensing the woman was not only honest, but genuinely enjoyed other people. When she learned through their conversation that the woman had a knack for decorating and in her spare time dabbled with crafts projects, she hired her on the spot to work daily from ten to two and a full day Saturday, which would free Catherine for decorating jobs and antique hunting.

Treasa also called that afternoon. She sounded happy, but sanely sober, which brought Catherine an immense feeling of relief.

"How's it going?" Catherine asked.

"I think I'm going to like this job. The skipper's great. There's one other crew, a young guy who's pretty green, but we get along fine. We'll be chartering, but it'll be different from the *Cherise*. Only a few people at a time, and they're interested in sailing, not in being waited on all the time. Randy does most of the cooking, but I'll help out. We'll be leaving on our first charter tomorrow. By the way, everyone up here says hello. I saw them on the *Escapade* last night. Boy, Peter's really been painting away."

"So he told me. What do you think of his stuff?"

"Great! How's the shop going?"

"I hired a part-time woman today. I think she'll work out fine."

"I'll give you a call in a week or so."

"Okay. Good luck, Trea, and tell everyone up there I said hello, too."

"Peter will probably call you tonight. The owner's flown in for a day or two to see how the work's going. He's keeping Peter pretty busy."

"Tell him no rush. I'll talk to him when he has time."

She really was avoiding the Peter issue, Catherine thought as she hung up the phone, but she was certainly happy for Trea. If only she would hang in there this time.

At six o'clock she was in the study. She'd poured out two brandies in the event there was something to celebrate and placed one on the table by the windows. Brandy seemed to be Lucien's favorite drink. She took a sip from her own glass to still her excited nervousness. She brushed her other hand over the brass telescope on the center of the table, then she closed her eyes and concentrated every thought on the Captain. She pictured his face, his features one by one. She imagined him standing beside her, visualizing him in the homely, low-ceilinged room. She repeated his name to herself, together with a silent summons. Nothing seemed to happen. She felt a growing sense of disappointment.

Then she heard his distinctive, full-bodied chuckle and opened her eyes. He was standing not a foot away along the edge of the semicircular table. "For me?" he inquired, his long fingers covering hers where they still gripped the brandy glass. He winked. "It worked, Catherine."

"It did. I can hardly believe it!"

His fingers remained on hers, and with a subtle movement, he drew her closer, at the same time raising the glass they mutually held. She glanced at it. "I thought we could celebrate our success. There's another glass . . ." She glanced down. But there wasn't. She quickly looked out the window to see the masts in the distance. They were in the Captain's time.

"We shall just have to share this one. To our second victory!"

"And our first?"

"Discovering we can stay together beyond the confines of this house." He raised the glass to his lips, sipped, then extended it to hers. She sipped as well, then smiled.

"This is fun."

"A quaint Americanism. I take it you mean this is enjoyable."

"Quite," she said with all British formality.

He laughed. "Come here, my fair pixie and let me kiss you." He directed the brandy glass to the table, and when it was comfortably settled, drew her into his arms. Their mouths had only just met when there was a quick knock on the door.

"Cap'n."

"Oh, no," Lucien muttered against her cheek. "Gladstone." He lifted his head. "Yes, Gladstone, what is it?"

"A gentleman left a message for you, Cap'n. One of your brokers. Something to do with the cargo."

"Very well, Gladstone. One moment." He looked down at Catherine and spoke in a whisper. "Damnable time for Gladstone to arrive. We can't have him see you. It may break our connection, but you must find some hiding place." He cast his eyes around the room. "There, over in the corner behind that chair." He dropped one more quick kiss on her lips before guiding her across the carpet and depositing her behind an upholstered wingchair that gave fairly ample cover.

"Cap'n?" The servant's voice had grown concerned.

"Yes, yes, Gladstone. I was finishing up some work. Come in."

The servant obviously had every intention of doing that in any case, since the door was already swinging open. Catherine crouched, squeezing herself into the smallest size possible, but Gladstone's back was toward her.

"A boy's waiting below for an answer, Cap'n." Even as he spoke, Gladstone's eyes were surveying the room as if he suspected something was amiss. Lucien took the folded note from the servant's hand and quickly read it.

"Imbeciles. Can't they do anything without supervision? They've got the wrong lot of cargo consigned to us. No wonder they can't find the documentation. One moment, Gladstone, and I'll pen an answer." Lucien went to his desk, and Catherine waited with baited breath for Gladstone to look over in her corner. She heard his footsteps but didn't dare look around the edge of the chair. She could see Lucien bent over his desk as he scribbled.

"There." He turned and handed the paper back to Gladstone. "That should answer their question. Give the messenger boy a coin, would you?"

"Aye, Cap'n. And what about your dinner? When will you be wanting it?"

"Not just yet . . ." That was the last Catherine heard. Suddenly she was gazing at the back of an occasional table that stood beside the much smaller upholstered chair in her own study. The unexpected transition made her jerk and bang her nose sharply against the wood.

"Damn!" she muttered under her breath. "Just when Gladstone was about to leave." Perhaps if she concentrated again, Lucien would do likewise, and they could resume the connection. Her brow furrowed with the intensity of her effort. The table was still in front of her. Her knees creaked. Then she sensed things shifting, turned her head, and saw Lucien coming around the chair with hand extended.

"A close one that," he said as he pulled her to her feet.

"Lucien, before Gladstone left, the connection slipped. I was back in my own study. I concentrated on you again, and—"

"Yes, I had a feeling something of that sort was happening. Once Gladstone was out the door, I concentrated as well. All's well that ends well, as our famous bard informed us. We have about an hour. My good servant will no doubt be back within that time forcing a meal upon me. He grows concerned when I don't eat properly. I dare not carry you to that tempting bed in the next room, but we can at least sit here and converse. And there are some things of mine I've been wanting to show you."

Talk they did, sitting cross-legged on the carpet, sharing the rest of the brandy. How at ease and comfortable she felt with him and with his possessions. What was this incredible reaction that left her soft and warm, yet in the same breath, intensely excited and alive, as if a new world were opening up to her—a world that only he could show her? They seemed interlocking pieces of a puzzle, finally joined.

Lucien showed her some of his treasures from around the world and a current 1844 newspaper. Amazing to see a hundred-and-fifty-year-old newspaper as fresh as the day it was printed.

"They write up the whalers' arrivals as major news articles," she commented.

"They are major to the economy of the island. Each barrel that comes ashore affects the livelihoods of dozens of people, from the ship owners, to the brokers, to the candlemakers, to the crew members, who each get a share of the profits, to the merchants in town who sell to the local populace and reprovision the ships. In the newspapers you gave me to read, the tourist industry figured strongly into newsmaking items."

When the hour was nearly up, Lucien leaned close and kissed her tenderly, letting his lips linger, then looking deep into her eyes. "How I love you—it defies my abilities to describe. This constant parting wears at me more each time."

"It wears at me, too, Lucien. I love you so much. If only there was some way..."

"I have a strong feeling that we shall find it. At least we know now what our powers of concentration can do."

The evening lecture on ESP several nights later proved more than interesting to Catherine. The words of the speaker tied in to her own communication with the Captain. Dr. Lindquist stressed that the ability to communicate mentally had gone dormant over the millennia because of the strength of other human senses. By focusing and channeling the mind's substantial energy flow, such things as precognition, telekinesis, and thought transfer could be within any person's power. Provided, of course, they were open to the possibility.

She felt Marjorie nudge her gently during the lecture, and later the older woman spoke with excitement. "Your ghost—he's left behind a tremendous amount of energy in your house. You, for some reason, have been able to tap into that energy."

"Perhaps."

"You must be sensitive."

"You've seen him, too."

"Only brief glimpses, and at the time I'd been thinking about the old stories and the portrait you found in the attic."

"I don't know if ESP has anything to do with it."

"Not ESP, but the energy! You must let me bring that lady I know to the house, and see what she discovers."

"No, Marjorie, I'd rather not just now." In fact, Catherine had no intention of letting anyone in the house to investigate the Captain. What they had was precious—it was *hers*. He'd be furious as well. Marjorie's suggestion had the effect of silencing any further confidences Catherine had considered making. As an afterthought, she added: "You haven't told anyone about the Captain, have you?"

"Only this one particular friend of mine."

"Please don't."

Marjorie seemed to understand. "I don't go around divulging confidences, and my friend would never say anything. We all know how some people feel about anything remotely supernatural."

Although Catherine concentrated all her thoughts on the Captain that night as she prepared for bed, he didn't appear. She remembered then that he'd said he had business out of the house that evening. What business? Dinner at the Macys', where the Macys' daughter could work her charms? And what had brought that image to mind? She was in a sorry state indeed if she was becoming a victim of jealousy!

Her dreams were filled with Lucien. She woke once thinking he was actually beside her. He wasn't. The other half of the bed was empty and undisturbed. Yet, as she fell back to sleep, she dreamed of him again. He was dressed formally, as he'd been the first night she'd seen him. He was standing to the side of an ornately furnished room and was deep in conversation. He was speaking with a pertly pretty young woman. She wore a modestly cut satin evening dress with puffed sleeves and long, belled skirt. Her auburn hair fell in clustered ringlets from either side of a center part. Her features were animated, and there was no mistaking the look in her eyes as she gazed up at Lucien.

Catherine felt a heavy weariness when she rose in the morning. Neither a brisk shower nor three cups of coffee alleviated her feeling of inertia. It had been only a dream, but she was suddenly remembering comments Dr. Lindquist had made about precognitive dreams.

Once she reached the shop, she was able to put much of her

uneasiness from her mind. Susan arrived at ten, and Catherine continued with her training. The woman was working out wonderfully. She'd been working only five days, but already was at ease and confident.

She and Catherine rearranged the front window display, using some of the Navajo accessories, during a lull in the brisk afternoon business. Susan volunteered to stay an extra half hour until the task was finished. At four-thirty Catherine started tallying up the daily receipts. She was double-checking her tape when a masculine voice brought her head up with a jerk.

"Hey, mate, those figures must be good news."

"Peter!"

"Surprised you, did I?"

She managed a nod. "I had no idea . . . you didn't say . . ."

"Thought it would be more fun this way. The owner left this morning, well satisfied. I hopped on the first plane I could get. I took a cab in from the airport. The shop looks good." But his eyes were only for her, and they were devouring her face at the moment. He came around the counter. "No welcoming kiss?"

He didn't wait for her to respond, only draped an arm about her shoulders and pulled her close. The resulting kiss was far more emotion-filled on his part than hers. She felt horrible. Why hadn't she told him on the phone? Why had she procrastinated?

He lifted his head and smiled, misinterpreting her cool reaction. "Not the place for kissing, is it? What would your customers think?" His eyes were bright with his own delight at seeing her.

She pulled herself together, tried to smile.

"When are you closing?"

"I was just cashing out now."

"Okay. I'll make myself invisible while you finish." He gave her shoulder a squeeze, moved out from behind the counter to stroll nonchalantly around the store.

She forced her mind back to the figures, but what was she going to do? He would obviously expect to stay at the house. What would Lucien think? What would Peter think if Lucien suddenly appeared? She no longer had a choice. She had to speak to Peter before the evening was over, but the thought sent her stomach into a knot.

Peter whistled quietly as she counted the cash in the drawer, deducted the amount of the day's sales, and balanced on the nose. She extracted the amount of that night's deposit, made out a deposit slip, stuck the whole in an envelope, and locked the register.

"All set," she said, "except for the lights and locking up."

She wondered if her nervousness showed as they left the shop and walked up to the corner, where Catherine dropped off the envelope in the night deposit slot at the bank. Her mind was working furiously. She wished she was the kind of person who could make light, mindless conversation. Instead her mind had gone blank.

"Shall we go out to dinner tonight?" Peter threw into the gap.

"Yes . . . I guess."

"I brought along a canvas I want to show you."

"You've got one finished?"

"All but for the touches. A seascape, but with a difference."

"Show it to me at the house."

They walked up Orange Street, Peter carrying the conversational ball. His spirits were so high, he didn't seem to notice her introspection. At the house Catherine sent a silent message to Lucien *not* to appear. Of course, that wouldn't necessarily work. Peter slid his bag and the thin packing box containing his canvas onto the floor of the kitchen and leaned over to pet Barney. "Remember me, mate? Been a while." Peter straightened and seemed about to come over and wrap his arms about Catherine.

In panic she went to the cupboard. "Would you like a drink before we go out?" Should she tell Peter now, or wait until they were in a restaurant?

"A drink sounds fine. It's good to be back here." He picked up the packing box as he followed Catherine from the kitchen to the living room. "This house has a good feeling."

"Yes . . . I know. How's everyone in Camden?"

"Busy. Treasa was doing real well. They came in from the first charter, and she was still straight as an arrow."

"She sounded happy when she called."

"Seemed so, too."

As Catherine poured the drinks, Peter removed his canvas and set it on the fireplace mantel. "What do you think?" he asked as she turned. His expression was a boyish combination of pride and uncertainty over her reaction.

She studied the painting. It would have been difficult not to. It drew the eye and was better than any of his sketches. With brush strokes and colors that gave an impression rather than an exact depiction, he'd caught the feel of the coastal rocks and waters in a way that touched all the senses.

"It's better than good, Peter," she said finally, her voice slightly hushed. "It's incredible. And why do you think you need finishing touches? It's perfect the way it is."

"Not too rough?" He gazed at his work critically, but was obviously pleased with her comments.

"That's part of its appeal. You won't have any trouble selling it—for a good price."

"You've just made my day completely." He grinned. "I was going to take it around to a couple of the galleries in Camden, but I wanted to get your opinion first. Now I have more confidence."

"You should never have doubted yourself." She walked over and handed him his drink, her eyes still on the painting, her quandary at talking to him for the moment forgotten.

Peter sat down on the couch and patted the cushion beside him. "Relax. You seem all uptight."

"Just haven't wound down, I guess."

"Well, I'll help you do that."

Catherine sat and took a nervous sip from her glass. "Peter . . ."

Before she got another word out, he reached over and gripped her shoulder. "It's good to see you." Leaning forward, he touched his lips to hers. "I've missed you. Phone calls aren't enough. I want to wait out the season before I leave the boat, but after that . . ."

Nervously, Catherine glanced up over Peter's shoulder, trying to formulate the words she must say. She still cared for Peter—enough to want to spare him unnecessary pain.

Lucien walked through the doorway and stopped in his tracks. His eyes went back and forth between Peter and Catherine. Peter's back was to the doorway, thank heavens. He noticed nothing. Lucien took in everything, however: Peter's hand on Catherine's shoulder; their close proximity on the sofa. His expression went from startlement, to shock, to white-lipped anger—or was it pain? He spun on his heel and strode from the room. She had to go after him and explain. She sought desperately for an excuse.

"I . . . I think I just heard someone at the back door. Excuse me a second." It was lame, but what could she do? "It might be Marjorie. She stops by." She was off the sofa before the last words were out of her mouth. She caught a glimpse of Peter's bewildered frown. Hurrying out into the hall, she looked up the staircase. If he'd gone that way he would still be climbing. The staircase was empty. She hurried through the sitting room, then the dining room. Finally she burst into the kitchen. He was nowhere in sight. There was no sign of him in the yard either. Already gone. She felt sick. If only he hadn't jumped to conclusions but stayed nearby long enough to hear what she had to tell Peter.

She went back to the living room. Peter craned his neck around. He was still frowning.

"It must have been the wind blowing the screen," she said with an effort at glibness.

"There isn't any wind. Catherine, what's wrong? I've sensed it since I got here. You're not acting like yourself. It's almost like you don't want me around."

She paced the floor. "Peter, I don't know how to tell you this, but I . . . I don't feel the way I did. It's not that I don't care, but things have changed. I guess, well, that I'm not ready to get so serious."

He sat stock still, his mouth slightly open. He snapped it shut. "I don't understand! A few weeks ago in Camden, everything was fine. You were a little quiet, but—"

"I was quiet because I was thinking things through, trying to decide if I was ready to get as involved as you were."

"You're trying to let me off easy. It's another man—"

"No, not exactly." That wasn't quite a lie.

"Not *exactly?* What does that mean?"

How could she explain without telling him about the Captain, who wasn't a man in terms that Peter would understand. She sat down beside him. "Peter, please, I don't want to hurt you. I do care about you. I think the world of you. It's me. I'm just not ready. I'm confused. I'm sorry," she finished inadequately.

Closing his eyes, he remained silent for a second. She saw his throat convulse as he swallowed. In a moment his eyes flicked open. "You've thrown me for a loop. I don't believe it! Why didn't you say any of this on the phone when we talked?"

"I tried to. I just didn't know how. Peter, I was wrong. I know it. It's nothing you've done. I feel awful." Her tone reflected that emotion.

He groaned, took a long swallow from his drink as if he suddenly needed it. He set the empty glass down on the table and rose. "So what now? Do you want me to stay out of your life?"

"No. I'd like to stay friends. It sounds so hollow—so inadequate. You're probably feeling pretty bitter about me at this moment."

"Probably is right! I also feel like a regular jerk. Why didn't you give me any warning?"

"I was wrong—totally. I would have told you if I'd known you were coming down, not that I'm trying to make excuses."

He swung from her, stared up at his painting. "I painted that with you in mind, you know. The day we sailed."

"I'm sorry." She was beginning to sound like a broken record, but what else could she tell him?

"I'm not looking for pity," he said sharply. He took a huge breath as if steadying himself. When he spoke again, his voice was tightly controlled. "I suppose we can stay friends. Considering what I went through with Mary Jane after our divorce, I never had much use for people who became enemies because the love wasn't there anymore." He turned back toward her. The look on his face made her want to cry. His tone was sarcastic. "Pardon me if this takes time to sink in. This changes my plans, obviously. I may stay on with the boat."

"But your art?"

He shrugged.

"Peter, don't give that up because of me."

"I've some thinking to do before I make any decisions." He looked at her long and hard. "Your mind's obviously made up."

She nodded.

"There doesn't seem much else for us to say, then, does there? I might as well shove off."

"Where are you going? You'll never get a room on the island on such short notice. Stay here. Treasa's room is empty."

"Somehow I don't think that's the thing. There's a late flight off the island. I'll see if I can catch it. I have friends in Boston if I can't connect on to Maine." Every word was clipped, cold.

He moved around the coffee table. She was on her feet in an instant, her throat choked. She hadn't thought ahead to this parting. She sought for something to say to make it less painful. Nothing came.

"I'll get my bag," he said, when she remained mute. He started from the room.

"Your painting . . ."

"Keep it. Sell it for me, if you want. Whatever. You know where to find me 'til the end of October."

She hurried after him as he went down the hall. In the kitchen he went for his bag and slung it over his shoulder.

"Peter. . ."

Briefly he turned, an instant's flash of hope on his face.

Her eyes were wet. Her lips trembled. Unable to speak, she quickly shook her head.

"See you around then, mate. It's been lovely." With his bitter angry words hanging in the air, he walked out the back door, letting the screen slam behind him. She rushed to the door, looked out to see him disappear up the drive. Her face crumbled. She leaned weakly against the door jamb and sobbed.

Chapter 23

Four days had passed since Peter had left, and Catherine had spent them in misery. Her misery was doubled by the fact that Lucien had stayed away as well, and she knew it was deliberate on his part. She knelt on the ground weeding the perennial garden, feeling acutely lonely and morbidly sorry for herself. In the blink of an eye, the garden was transformed from her weedy patch to the Captain's luxuriant one.

She looked up as Lucien's shadow crossed over her. She didn't know what she felt—relief, joy—or anger that he'd left her alone so long.

His blue eyes flashed over her. "I'd like an explanation," he said without preamble.

Catherine straightened, put her hands on her hips. She took immediate exception to his autocratic tone. "You've waited long enough!"

"You have a way of bringing one up short when one least expects it. What was *he* doing in my house?"

"*My* house, and his name is Peter. You have no reason to refer to him in that sneering way."

"How else should I react when I see you two cooing on the sofa together? You might at least have warned me he was coming."

"I didn't *know* he was coming. And if you hadn't rushed off like you did—"

"Oh? I was to stay, make a fool of myself?"

"I was about to tell him I wouldn't be seeing him anymore."

That stopped him.

"And it wasn't easy. It's not pleasant to hurt someone who cares about you. Peter happens to be a very decent person, and it upset me to break it off with him. Now you have the nerve to stand there and yell at me after you jumped to conclusions, stomped off in a fit of anger, and ignored me for days!"

He shifted uneasily. His color heightened with a trace of embarrassment. "This is true? You broke off with him?"

"Yes!"

"I apologize. I didn't realize." He looked at his feet.

"You might have waited to let me explain."

"I'm sorry. My wretched temper."

"It was a rotten way to break it to him, too, after he'd come down here to surprise me."

Lucien's face softened. He knelt down beside her and rubbed a consoling hand down her arm. "Forgive me. I've been behaving like a boor. I did deliberately stay away from you."

"I know."

"There were several times when I felt the connection forming and let it go." He paused. "I suppose my anger was accentuated because a few evenings before I saw you with your friend, Peter, I had told Lucinda Macy that I had no feelings for her other than friendly interest, and could have none in the future. The news devastated the poor girl. She ran from the room in tears. It was my fault for not setting her straight long past. I won't be invited back to the Macys' for some time, not that it matters."

"You were at the Macys' the other night? Which night?"

He seemed puzzled at her question. "Let me see . . . last week . . . Thursday, I believe."

"I dreamed you were there! I saw you talking to a very pretty young woman—auburn hair in ringlets. She had on a satin dress with puffed sleeves and wide skirt."

"That description would fit Lucinda." He studied her. "You dreamed this?"

"Vividly. I saw you talking in an ornately furnished room. The expression on her face was pure adoration. The dreams kept me up half the night. I'd been to a lecture on extrasensory perception and precognition, and thought that had something to do with it."

"Interesting. Another tie."

"Pardon?"

He shook his head, abruptly changed the subject. "Let us take a walk."

"Where?"

"Around my Nantucket. I owe you some frivolous enjoyment

after my boorish behavior, and I see you are more or less appropriately dressed."

Catherine had worn a long, cotton print summer skirt for gardening. The skirt was old, but the length of the hemline was correct even if it wasn't exactly fashionable for his day. The early evening had been unseasonably cool, and Catherine had thrown a sweater over her shoulders.

"Put that on, too," he indicated.

"Where are your servants? Won't they see us?"

"It's their evening off, and since they are likely spending it in the waterfront pub, it's doubtful our paths will cross."

Catherine felt a growing excitement as they left the grounds hand in hand. Her previous walk with the Captain had shown her only a small section of Orange Street. That night they continued on to Main Street. Catherine's senses spun as they paused on the corner and she looked up and down the nearly treeless street. What a difference the elms had made. Only a few buildings seemed obviously familiar, one being the Pacific Bank. The other storefronts bordering the street were basically of wooden construction. Instead of the automobile and pedestrian congestion of her day, the center of town was quiet. A few wagons and carriages lined the streets, horses dozing or stomping. A pedestrian or two wandered along the sidewalks, which were constructed of boards in some sections.

As they approached the docks, her nose was assaulted by strange smells—a rank, unidentifiable one that she guessed might have something to do with crude whale by-products; more familiar ones of tar, horsedroppings, overripe fruit or vegetables. Lucien explained that it was inevitable that some spoilage occurred during the long sea voyages. The brick building at the bottom of Main Street was also familiar. She recognized it as the Pacific Club, but the sign read Rotch Warehouse. The pedestrians on and around the docks were predominantly male. A few surprised glances were cast in her direction, but Lucien gave back a scowl of his own, and the staring eyes were quickly averted. The looks probably had something to do with her attire, Catherine realized. Her print skirt was rather loud for Quaker taste. She wasn't wearing a hat or bonnet, and her blond hair hung free and shining to her shoulders.

"*Sophia* is in," Lucien informed her, "though moored out until there is space at the dock for her. You can have a glimpse of her in any case." He took her to the end of the wharf. Hogsheads and barrels were piled high to either side. Above and beyond them rose the majestic masts and rigging. Lucien found a gap between two vessels whose bowsprits and brightly painted figureheads protruded over the wharf. Catherine hadn't expected them to be quite so big, and the tide was in, so they were riding high beside the dock.

"There she is," Lucien spoke with barely suppressed pride, "directly in front of you, the three-master."

Catherine nodded. From the distance, the vessel appeared sleeker of line than some of the others moored nearby. She could easily visualize Lucien commanding from her decks.

In a moment he took her away from the docks, and they wandered down side streets, crossing town at Centre Street.

"That's where my shop is!" she exclaimed. "It doesn't look the same, does it?" The building she was gazing at was now strictly a residence. There was a narrow, neat sidewalk in front, but the road had yet to be cobbled.

Lucien only smiled and led her forward, down winding lanes, past Quaker houses that hadn't changed much over the years. They stopped at the Cliff Road, which was not much more than a sandy, double-rutted track. No elegant summer homes graced the cliff with its view over Nantucket Bay—only beach grass and wild roses. The light wind off the Bay fluttered her skirt, lifted her hair away from her cheeks. A pinkish light remained on the western horizon, and one star twinkled in the darkening sky.

"Lovely spot, isn't it?" Lucien asked quietly.

"Lovelier than in my time. With all the private homes, the public rarely gets a glimpse of this."

"The price of growth and progress. Pity." His arm tightened around her. "I have been thinking all during this walk. Do you regret, Catherine, having given up your other gentleman?"

"I regret hurting him. It's not as though I didn't care about him."

"But you no longer love him?"

"I love him as a friend. If it hadn't been for you, it might have been different for Peter and me."

"I never intended to put you in this position—you know that. Here am I, a man from another time, making demands upon your emotions. It seems irrational to even consider it." He hesitated, still staring out to the Bay. "But I can't let you go—I can't freely give you up."

"And I don't want you to! Lucien, don't you know how much I care. I love you enough to do what my common sense tells me is crazy."

Swiftly he turned toward her. He brought his hand up to her face and caressed her cheek. He drew her against his body and held her as if she were a precious thing. And she melted into his arms, so glad to have his warmth and his love. The heat and hunger between them seared, untempered by the wind that coursed past, whipping at their hair, pulling at their clothing.

"Ah, Catherine," he sighed. "What are we going to do to see this love fulfilled? I can no longer live without you."

"Nor I without you."

The late summer days sped away, their love growing with every one. They were bright, sunny ones for Catherine, even when it poured down rain. Labor Day came and went, marking the end of the mad bustle of summer tourism and the beginning of cooler evenings. Business in the shop was still excellent, as older tourists who had no school-age children arrived. This new wave of visitors was also more inclined toward expensive purchases.

Treasa called right after Labor Day. She'd just gotten in from a long charter and had heard Catherine and Peter had broken up.

"Why?" she asked almost angrily.

"I just wasn't ready," Catherine prevaricated.

"I know I said yachties were a waste of time—here today, gone tomorrow—but Peter's turned out different. He's a real basket case since you split up, Cath!"

"I'm sorry. I really am. I never meant to hurt him. It hurt *me* to do it."

"I don't understand you at all. He's such a great guy. Why don't you give it another chance?"

"I can't—not now." Catherine felt close to tears. "Tell him I said hello."

"You think that's going to make him feel any better?"

"Has he been painting?"

"Yeah—great stuff. But Ted said he wouldn't go near his paints the week after he came back from seeing you. The guys all talked to him and finally got him going again."

"Is he staying on the boat?"

"I don't know. He hasn't said anything to me."

Catherine changed the subject. "How's it been going with you?"

Treasa fell for the ploy. "Super. I love the skipper. He's great to work for, and the charterers have basically been a good bunch. It's different this time and going real well."

"When will you be finished up?"

"I'm not sure yet. We'll keep chartering for a while, as long as the weather stays warm."

"I'm glad you called. You sound wonderful!"

"I feel pretty wonderful!"

Catherine was thrilled over the turnabout in Treasa. If only she didn't feel such sharp twinges of guilt over Peter.

The hours Catherine and Lucien spent in her world were truly joyous—no one in the house but themselves; no one to question or explain to. They went for frequent trips beyond the house, testing their theories. As yet nothing had occurred to separate them once they went beyond the perimeters of the property. And at home together, they shared a loving peace. He was thoughtfulness itself, sometimes surprising Catherine, as he adjusted without complaint to the greater equality of the twentieth century male/female relationship. He understood her need to put extra hours into her business. He listened to her political views with interest—not that he always agreed with her opinions, particularly when she criticized the attitudes of his own era and chastised him for having been so unconcerned about the plight of his generation of women.

"And why should I have considered it?" he asked with a grin. "My mother never complained. In fact, she was positively happy with her life. Gwen never complained either, though she was a free spirit in a different sense. And, of course, I was away from England so much, entirely in the company of men . . . aside from those evenings when we went ashore." His eyes twinkled.

"I can imagine what went on. A dozen lust-crazed men descending on town."

"Nothing compared to when an Admiralty ship gave shore leave."

"That hasn't changed today either."

He continued to pour over her modern magazines and books, and with his sharp intelligence digested new theories and facts with incredible agility. His only weakness as far as she was concerned was the television, which he found fascinating, right down to the mind-deadening commercials. He'd suddenly break out in roars of laughter at women going into ecstacies over their spotless laundry.

"I've never seen you do that," he said afterward.

"You're not likely to either."

"The amazing thing is that every product advertised produces the same response. Do the makers of these commercials actually think people believe them?"

"They must. They also must have a very low opinion of the average human intelligence."

In the end they compromised with television by watching the public television stations where, even he admitted, the quality of the programming was higher, and Catherine wasn't driven to distraction by constant commercial breaks.

Their hours in bed together became more frequent, as if fate was conspiring on their side. Long, love-filled nights became the rule, rather than the exception, and their loving was exquisite. With Lucien, Catherine found a fulfillment that had been rare before. Because of her own nature and a morally prudent upbringing, abandoning oneself to passion had been an unconscious taboo for her, leaving her more an observer than participant in the sexual act. Except with Lucien. Any expression of their love seemed natural and totally intended. He had the power to free her from herself, and with his help, Catherine discovered physical joys she'd only imagined possible.

Catherine drifted along in total bliss, trying not to think ahead, only savoring every moment with Lucien. They had a few close calls when one of Lucien's servants nearly blundered into them.

"Gladstone had a chat with me yesterday," he chuckled, though there was a tiny crease between his brows. "He wanted to know what I was up to. Said he knew I was sneaking a woman into the house.

"'A woman?' I said to him with some amazement."

"'I saw her,' he said, 'flitting out of the study when I brought your supper.' His face was screwed up with all the reproach he'd have shown if I'd brought a woman aboard ship. I simply laughed and told him that perhaps he needed spectacles.

"'Nothing wrong with my peepers,' he told me, but thankfully he let the subject drop. We shall have to be more careful. I can't see Gladstone accepting the story of a ghostly visitor, and worse yet, he might get in his cups and mention my female visitor to his cronies at the pub."

"You know that my neighbor, Marjorie, has seen you—up on the walk, in the garden. She knows your history, too. She happens to believe in the possibilities of ghosts—or at least believes there are a lot of phenomena science hasn't explained—but I worry about what her reaction would be if she knew how much we see of each other and how close we actually are."

"Risks we must take," he said. "It's worth it, is it not?"

"It's worth it."

A few days later Catherine came down the back steps of the house. She'd left her checkbook at home and had come to collect it

before going around to island antique shops looking for postsummer
sales. She was preoccupied as she crossed the lawn to the Porsche,
digging in her bag for her keys. She came up short as she reached the
spot where her car should have been and instead nearly collided with
an open, two-seater carriage, actually resembling a fancy pony cart.
Lucien's horse was harnessed between the shafts. He stomped restlessly, his black coat gleaming in the sunlight.

For an instant Catherine stood gaping. Her initial thrilled reaction
was tempered by the fact the Lucien's groom would be around. She
couldn't be seen. She started to back away, when Lucien came out of
the barn. He walked straight toward her, grinning his delight.

"What do you think?" he asked. "Smart little equipage, isn't it?
Pierce just picked it up, and I was about to take it for a trial run. Now
you can join me."

"Pierce," she said in a nervous undertone. "Where is he?"

"At the moment, shuffling some bales of hay in the back of the
barn."

"What if he sees me?"

"Then climb up quickly, and let's be off."

All thought of antique hunting fled from Catherine's mind as she
did as Lucien instructed and stepped up into the cart. Lucien jumped
in beside her and picked up the reins. He slapped them over Sarter's
back, and they started forward. They'd almost reached the end of the
drive when there was a shout from behind them.

"Cap'n, before—" The male voice choked off abruptly.

Pierce has seen me, Catherine thought. Instinctively she squeezed
down into the narrow floor space in front of the seat. Lucien continued forward as if he hadn't heard his groom's call, but the instant
they were out of sight of the house, he burst into roaring laughter.

"What's so funny?" she snapped.

"If only you could see yourself. You look as if you'd been caught
with your hand in the master's cash drawer."

"Well, he saw me! What was I supposed to do?"

"He probably thought it even stranger that you suddenly ducked
down out of sight." His eyes were dancing. "Come up off the floor.
You're safe now."

Catherine slid back up on the seat, dusting off her knees. "You
think it's so funny, but what are you going to tell him?"

"Oh, I shall think of some tale—a poor waif coming down the
drive and asking if she might have a lift across the island."

"He'll never believe that."

"It's my problem. Don't worry over it. Enjoy this glorious day."
He turned Sarter into a side lane. "My, this cart handles nicely. We
should be able to get up to a good clip—nothing to compare to your
automobile, of course."

As they left the cluster of town, Catherine did relax. Sarter trotted
briskly down the sandy roads. The air was crisp; the sky was a brilliant blue with only a few white puffs of cloud; the moors were
turning crimson. The breeze caressed both their faces and tossled
their hair.

"This is so different from riding in a car," she exclaimed.

"You mean to say you've never ridden in a open carriage?"

"I went on a hayride once when I was ten, but otherwise, no."

"Extraordinary. Then again, I suppose it's not. Well, enjoy."

"I intend to."

They went all around the island as he gave her a tour of the places
that hadn't been easily accessible during their walks. 'Sconset looked
to be precisely what it was—a working fishing village. The landscape was dotted with farms and sheep pastures. The view seemed
endless with so few trees, particularly when he drove to the crest of
Alter rock, tied Sarter to a scrubby pine, and took her hand to walk
about. There were farm houses in the distance, and the sea all
around, but Catherine felt a sense of peaceful solitude, as if she and
Lucien were the sole occupants of a private haven.

He seemed to feel similarly from the expression on his face as
they paused near a cluster of wild rose bushes and Catherine plucked
at the brilliant red rose hips.

"I want you," he said throatily.

Catherine nodded her agreement, and he led her to a protected
spot behind the bushes where the grass was mossy soft. Slowly they
undressed each other, touching each other's bare flesh with loving
caresses. There was a freedom to their actions. Away from the house,
in the open sunshine and sweetness of nature, they had no fears of
sudden separation. She marveled in the magnificence of his body—
tall, strong, his need for her so clearly and firmly evident. Her hands
wandered over his chest, his back, his hips, his belly, finally soothing over the soft, hot velvet of his erection. There was no embarrassment between them, no self-consciousness.

Moaning, he drew her down onto the grass and proceeded to kiss
every inch of her, lingering in the warm thatch between her legs until
she cried out her satisfaction. She wanted to return the favor, but
instead he pulled her onto his lap so she faced him with her legs

wrapped around his back. As they both watched, he entered her, slowly, tantalizingly, bringing both of them to a searing pitch of arousal as they saw their oneness become a fact. For long moments, his hands eased her back and forth as he clutched her hips. His pleasure was etched on his features and reflected in his haze-filled eyes. His body was tense with the control he was exerting over himself. Then the pleasure became too intense. He drew her toward him, pressing deep once, twice, and the third time crying out. Shuddering, he drew her against him in a vise-like grip. She buried her face in the hollow of his neck and pressed her lips to the throbbing vein in his throat, overcome by her own intense reaction.

"God, how I love you!" he choked. "I'll never let you go."

But there were hours of worry, too. They were both growing more and more conscious of the facts that no argument could deny. Catherine had the deeds to prove that in 1846 Lucien Blythe sold the house on Nantucket and did not return.

"Old tales and rumors are more often than not exaggerated, Catherine," he mused.

"But I have the written deed."

"Yes, but where could I have disappeared to with my booming business? It needs more thought. And at the moment fate seems to be working in our favor in giving us more and more time together."

In the following early autumn days, they experimented with longer and longer periods away from the house, in both time periods. But they had absolutely no answers as to where Lucien had gone after 1846. The uncertainty began to wear on Catherine. The date seemed to hang ominously, a warning that they could one day be separated—forever.

"This won't do," Lucien admonished one evening as they walked back to the house in the gathering dusk. "I won't see you moping around with a worried frown. We must try to enjoy what we do have. The fact that I sold this house does not mean the end for us."

"True."

They entered the kitchen. Catherine closed the curtains before switching on the light.

"Before we ponder this any further," Lucien ordered, "we shall have a light meal—one of those tin-wrapped things—and then I shall play for you."

Simply seeing his smile was enough to lift her spirits. She went from freezer to counter to stove, Lucien lightly holding her arm and following. Their inability to release contact for any length of time within the house was always a frustrating problem. It left them feeling as though they were Siamese twins.

Dinner was finally in the oven, and Lucien sat at the table beside her sipping a glass of wine as they waited for the food to heat. Catherine took only one sip from her glass, then set it down. The wine wasn't settling well. She felt queasy and knew it was nerves. Too much tension and uncertainty.

Lucien was watching her face. "You look pale all of a sudden."

She wagged her head. "I'm fine."

"I see you're not going to relax. Let me see those old deeds."

They went to the sitting room, and she removed the book that contained the packet of deeds.

"Do you want to see them all?"

"Only the ones pertaining to me."

She found them. He sat down in the chair to read. She stood behind, her hand on his shoulder.

"Yes, I remember well the day I signed this in Obed Starbuck's office. Only five years ago. Strange to see the paper so aged and yellowed." He went on to the other deed, which Catherine couldn't help seeing as a death sentence. He slowly shook his head. "Very strange. The firm mentioned here as representing my estate is the legal firm I used in London. They still handle various documentary work for me in connection with the shipping business. I'm puzzled. My brother is executor of my estate. If I had died—and listen to me, speaking in the past tense—he would have seen to the liquidation of my assets personally, and he does not use this firm in London. You also notice that this deed does *not* state, 'from the estate of the deceased Lucien Blythe, Esquire'? Quite a puzzle. Do I return to England and for some reason have my solicitors handle the sale of this property?" His hands, still holding the deed, fell to his lap.

"Don't even *talk* about death!" she exclaimed.

"I obviously have no desire to do so, but we must consider all possibilities. I still own extensive land holdings and a house in England," he added thoughtfully in a moment.

"I didn't know."

"The estate where Gwen and I were to live. It's leased at the moment. Considering my feelings when I left England, it never occurred to me I might return there one day."

"You think that's where you went then?"

"Perhaps. How hard to predict what my actions will be two years down the road." He refolded the deeds, and turning in the chair, handed them to her. "Perhaps because of you, all my original plans changed, and you come with me."

"Do you have any relations—descendants—alive in England now?"

"And how would I know that?"

"Silly question, but maybe I could find out. Your brother had children. Perhaps there's a present day Blythe who would know your history. Maybe this law firm is still in business." Her voice rose on a thread of hope. "How would I go about finding out?"

"I can tell you their original address. Whitefriars Street, off Fleet."

"And your family home—what was the name of it?"

"Oak Park, near Waltham, Hampshire, but I think you are catching at straws."

"We won't know unless I try."

"It is something for us to think about."

Catherine's nervous stomach quieted after dinner. When they went into the living room to sit side by side on the piano bench, she leaned her head on Lucien's shoulder as he played. "I love you," she whispered for no reason.

"I love you, too . . . with all my heart."

Later, he paused in the bedroom before they undressed and impulsively pulled her close, burying his lips in her hair. "To think I am here now in the twentieth century, holding you, loving you, when my own past is a mystery. What shall I do if I lose you?"

Hardly had the words passed his lips, when he vanished. No longer did she feel the pressure of his arms, or the substance of his chest beneath her cheek. She lifted her head in panic. There was absolutely nothing in the spot where he'd stood instants before.

Her feeling of horror and shock stunned her. She reached for the arm of the chair and collapsed into it. They'd been touching. Never before had he vanished when they were touching! Their premise about physical contact had just been seriously undermined.

A feeling of urgency prodded her actions the next morning. She'd slept hardly at all, but the painful wakefulness had left her time to plan exactly what she would do that morning. When Susan arrived at the shop at ten, Catherine left for the library. She'd already penned a letter to Lucien's former solicitors, though she really didn't have much hope. For the firm to have remained at the same address for over a hundred years and still have records going back to a client of the 1840s seemed a remote possibility. She had more hope in writing to Oak Park, but there again, the estate may have gone into other hands. She left the shop and brought both letters to the Post Office, sending them certified air mail.

In both she'd stated that she now owned the house previously owned by Lucien Alexander Blythe. She was researching the house, which was of historical value, and urgently required information on Captain Blythe after he'd left the premises.

She'd had one other thought during her sleepless night, and her next stop was the library, where she sought out a book of British peerage. She found a thick volume on the research shelf, not a current edition, but still possibly helpful. Thumbing to the Bs, she paused. What had his brother's full title been? She remembered Lucien saying he was an earl, but earl of what? Simply Earl Blythe? She found a listing under Blythe: Fifth Earl (Jonathan Terrance). He'd been born in 1888 and had died in 1915 without issue. From the number of military honors listed, she surmised he'd been killed in the First World War, the last of the earls.

The paragraphs below his name listed earlier holders of the title, and from that list she knew she had the right family. A John Edward was listed as the third earl, having inherited his title from his father, Edward Alexander, in the eighteen thirties. Within the paragraph pertaining to the second earl, Edward Alexander, she read: "Issue, John Edward, third earl; Lucien Alexander."

The peerage listed only title holders and did not trace their various untitled progeny. The last earl had been an only child, but his father had had two sisters, who had perhaps had offspring. There was every possibility that Blythe descendants were alive and well in England at that moment, but if not at Oak Park, where? And would they have records of the family history? She was sure there were other avenues for research. If she turned up nothing with either of her letters, perhaps she could hire a genealogist.

With that thought in mind, she returned to the shop and sent out a prayer that she'd see Lucien that evening.

Chapter 24

Before she went home that evening, Catherine stopped next door at Marjorie's.

"Isn't this a nice surprise. Come in."

"I won't stay long, but I wanted to ask your advice on something."

"You're not interrupting anything. Evan went to the mainland today and won't be back for another hour. Sit down. Coffee? A drink?"

"A drink would be fine, but make it a light one."

As Marjorie extracted a bottle of scotch from one of the lower cupboards and poured two drinks, Catherine took a seat at the round pine table in the middle of the spacious kitchen. The room was welcoming and homey, with pine cabinets, beamed ceiling, country print curtains, and a comfortable clutter giving evidence to the many projects Marjorie had going at the same time.

Marjorie sat down next to her, moving a pile of paperwork to the far side of the table. "I'm helping with the annual Historical Society pamphlet," Marjorie explained. "So how have you been? I haven't seen much of you except for a wave over the fence."

"I've been busy, as usual. I wanted to ask you, Marjorie, if you had any suggestions. I've decided to do some research on the Captain. I've always wondered what happened to him after he left the house."

"Something new going on that you haven't told me?" There was a subtle, probing look on Marjorie's face.

"I'm just curious."

"Maybe you're better off leaving well enough alone."

The comment caught Catherine by surprise. She shot Marjorie a look. "Why do you say that?"

"I don't know . . . a feeling. Now that your sister is gone, and you're not seeing that young man—he seemed like such a nice fellow, too—you're alone too much over there. I'm worried about you, particularly with a ghost roaming around. It's easy to get caught up with history and the past, but you can get carried away as well. You're young. You should be out with people, getting involved with other things."

"I am, all day at the shop."

Marjorie removed her wire-rim glasses and absently polished them with one of her shirttails. She seemed to relent. "I'll ask around at the Historical Society, maybe get some clues of where and how to look for information like that. You know so few facts about him before and after he came to the island. The deeds say nothing except that he was from England—that would be like tracing a needle in a haystack, I think. Perhaps you could find something by tracing his ships in the old port records."

Marjorie replaced her glasses. "But I really am begining to think it's not wise for you to get too engrossed in Captain Blythe."

"You thought it was fascinating," Catherine said, puzzled. "Why the sudden change?"

Marjorie shrugged. "I'm not quite sure myself. Put it down to an old woman's eccentricities if you like, but I'm uneasy."

The evening was chilly, reminding Catherine that cold weather would soon be upon the island. The streets were emptying. There were fewer cars each day, although a number of tourists favored the glorious autumn days when the moors were awash in scarlets and golds and rich umbers, and the air was clear and crisp. Homes around the island were being boarded up for the winter. Some shops and restaurants had closed for the season, and more would close after the Christmas holidays.

The chill had penetrated the house, and she brought in an armload of firewood from the barn, carried it upstairs to the study, and stacked it in the fireplace. The wood was dry, and a fire was soon blazing on the hearth. She stood looking up at the portrait, thinking of Lucien—frightened over the ramifications of the previous night's separation.

She felt hands on her shoulders and turned swiftly, wrapping her arms around him. "Lucien! What happened last night?"

He gripped her tightly. His voice was grave. He'd obviously spent the day worrying, too. "My love, I don't quite know. I can only guess that because I was thinking with dread of our separation, we did in fact separate."

"It's never happened before."

"It would seem we must screen out all negative thoughts. We must think always that we *shall* remain together." He tangled his fingers in her hair, gazed down at her anxiously and kissed her hard, as if the kiss would seal them together. Drawing her to the chair by the fire, he sat down and pulled her onto his lap. His arms circled her, and he touched his lips to her brow. She felt the soft tickling of his full beard against her cheeks.

"You've lit the fire," he murmured. "A good night for it. We belong in this setting, Catherine—cozy, secure, together, quietly talking as we sip a brandy, reviewing the events of our days. Why must we be faced with these worries?"

Her lips sought the bare skin of his neck above his collar, but his new uneasiness hung in the air, infecting her. "I sent those letters today," she said in a moment. "To your old attorneys and to Oak Park."

"Mmmm." It was a thoughtful sound. "We shall have to wait and see."

"I also looked up your family in a book of peerage."

He craned his head to look down at her. "And?"

"The last listing was for the fifth earl, who died in 1915 without heirs. Though that doesn't mean there aren't any other family members alive."

"True. The title would have to pass through the male line. Nineteen-fifteen," he mused. "What would that make the last earl—my great-great-nephew? My brother was the third earl."

"He was in his late twenties when he died. I think perhaps he may have been killed in the First World War from the number of military honors he received."

"So our only hope of finding a Blythe descendant is through the female line."

"And it will probably be weeks before I hear back."

"We must both have patience."

Although they sat for hours in front of the fire, Lucien occasionally rising to throw on another log, their conversation was dampened by the fresh worries they both felt. It was the most somber evening they'd spent together.

At least nothing separated them that night. Before bed, they showered together—a novel experience for Lucien, who hadn't known the luxury of indoor plumbing. He thought it a delight to stand beneath the spray of hot water, and urged her into the shower whenever they found themselves in her frame of time in the evening hours. As she turned on the taps, he watched her with twinkling eyes—a twinkle that forewarned of a bit of mischief.

As soon as they were both standing beneath the spray, he took the soap and began lathering her body, slowly, a smile on his lips. His hands smoothed over nearly every inch of her, with a particular object in mind. He didn't cease his labors until she was trembling.

"You're a tease," she whispered.

"Yes, but I have a wonderful ulterior motive."

She took the soap from his hand and began her own delightful journey over his flesh. As she sudsed his back and torso, she marveled again at his firm, hard muscles, the broadness of his shoulders. Bending, she lathered his legs, working ever upward.

His eyes were half closed, his breathing deep. "Do you know what you do to me? How good that feels?"

"Precisely my intention."

The shower poured down unheeded until finally Lucien gasped and pulled them both under the spray. Lather still clung to their bodies as he turned off the water and climbed from the tub, drawing her after him. He lifted her in his arms and strode quickly from the bath into the study, where, kneeling down before the fire, he lowered her to the carpet. He followed, leaning over her, his damp skin hot against her own.

"I can't wait another second. I must have you."

"Come," she moaned, needing him just as badly.

Yet, with all his need, he entered slowly, prolonging the pleasure for both of them, until he could stand it no longer and pressed deep and hard.

Later, they snuggled tight under the bedcovers, almost afraid to move lest one or the other of them slip away.

At seven-thirty the next morning they parted, with as much reluctance as ever. Gladstone would soon be knocking on Lucien's door.

"Damn Gladstone. Damn it all," he said under his breath.

As she stood in the shower alone an hour later, she felt an overwhelming sadness. *Why?* That unanswerable question over and over. She rinsed under the hot spray, turned off the taps, and stepped out onto the bath carpet. Reaching for a towel, she was overcome by a sudden vertigo. She grabbed for the edge of the bathroom sink and stood gripping it until the unnerving sensation passed. It did within a few moments, only to be succeeded by twinges of nausea. She took several deep breaths, stared past her pale face in the bathroom mirror. Was she coming down with the flu? But this wasn't the first dizzy spell she'd had. She'd felt odd before in Lucien's company after they'd been together in either his world or her own. Was it possible her body was reacting to that movement back and forth in time? It obviously wasn't a natural phenomenon. There was the strain, too, of their always having to maintain physical contact while in the house, the uncertainty of never knowing when they would meet. Yet he didn't seem to be experiencing the same sensations. Or, if he was, he was keeping it to himself.

She had tea that morning instead of coffee, and by the time she arrived at the shop, she was feeling a little better, determined to fight off any illness with sheer force of will. The shop was busy, leaving her little time to think, and she spent several hours at a client's home, consulting on the decorating job she would be doing for them over the next month. Feeling exhausted when she got home, she lay down on the living room couch for a few minutes. The few minutes became a few hours, and she didn't waken until close to ten. She made herself a sandwich, and still feeling groggy, decided to call it a night. Her system was obviously under stress. Should she tell Lucien? No, she decided. It would pass, and she didn't want to cause him any additional worry.

When the alarm went off the next morning, she had to drag herself out of bed. There was no sign of Lucien. He hadn't joined her during the night, but considering the way she felt, it was just as well. She ran for the bathroom and vomited into the bowl. She felt like death. She should stay home in bed, but Susan wouldn't be in until ten. Like an automaton, she showered and dressed, deciding to open the shop and leave for a few hours' rest after Susan arrived. Yet by ten-thirty she was feeling well enough to stay at her desk, and when she saw Lucien that night, she was feeling marvelously improved, though apparently she didn't appear so to him.

"Why are you so pale?" he asked almost immediately.

She kept her voice light. "I haven't felt too great the last few days. You haven't been feeling odd, have you?" she added in a moment.

"Odd? No. My health seems perfect. What's wrong? Why do you ask?"

"I must have the flu. I thought maybe you'd caught it, too."

"Perhaps some fresh air would do you good. Let's go for a walk . . . or are you up to it?"

"I'm fine at the moment."

He seemed to believe her, and they headed away from the house to meander through the narrow streets of twentieth-century Nantucket. With most of the tourists and summer people gone, they encountered few others, and the solitude gave them the opportunity to concentrate on their personal dilemma and future. Only the increasing chill in the autumn air sent them back to Orange Street two hours later. It was dark by then, but Catherine had left the back light burning, and it sent out a warm glow over the backyard. They'd rejoined hands as they'd approached the house, and his fingers felt warmly reassuring as they headed up the drive. As they rounded the back corner of the house, Catherine saw Marjorie's back porch light burning across the low fence. In the next moment, the older woman stepped out of her kitchen door. She was looking in their direction, though might not have noticed them where they stood partially hidden by Catherine's back stoop and railing.

Catherine jumped back behind the cover of the house, dragging Lucien with her.

"What is it?" he questioned.

"My neighbor. I think she may have seen us. If she didn't, she will when I take you in the back door."

They both heard Marjorie's call. "Catherine, is that you?"

Lucien groaned.

"She may come over and investigate if I don't answer. She worries about me, and she knows who you are."

"Then we must part here. Kiss me. Think of me when you climb into bed."

"I will." Their mouths met quickly, crushingly, then he stepped away. Catherine walked forward, around the house, into the glare of the back light. Marjorie was still standing on her porch. She waved a hand in greeting as she saw Catherine.

"I thought that was you. Silly, but I always worry about prowlers with you alone in the house. You are alone, aren't you? I thought I saw someone—"

"Just me," Catherine called before Marjorie could speculate further. She knew the ruse about prowlers was just an excuse on Marjorie's part. "I dropped my keys on the drive and went back to look for them."

"You found them?"

Catherine lifted her key ring in the air.

"Ah, good. Well, good night." Marjorie retreated toward her kitchen, but Catherine knew she watched protectively until Catherine was safely in the house.

A close call, Catherine thought, flicking on the kitchen light as Barney ambled over to greet her. *Had* Marjorie seen Lucien before they'd darted around the house?

By the end of the week, Catherine began to suspect that she was suffering from something other than the flu. But what she was beginning to suspect made her feel faint. She went to the calendar and sought to trigger her memory. When had she had her last period? It was after Peter, of that she was sure. Why hadn't she kept better track? Yes, of course . . . the day she'd met with Mrs. Walters . . . she'd had such terrible cramps. She reached for her appointment book in her bag, found the appropriate entry, went back to the calendar, and counted.

She sagged into the chair beside the kitchen table and started shaking. Eight days overdue. She was never late. Twenty-eight days as regular as clockwork. She and Peter had taken precautions, but with Lucien, she hadn't thought.

Why hadn't she thought? Because he was a ghost? Oh, God, how could she have been so stupid? When he was with her, he was as much a man as any other. There was nothing ghostly about him— quite obviously!

She wanted to convince herself there was another reason for her lateness, her dizziness, her queasiness. The conviction didn't come. She was pregnant with Lucien's child . . . pregnant by a ghost—if not a ghost, a man who lived a hundred and fifty years in her past!

What were they to do now? Until she was sure, she couldn't tell him. She didn't want to put that burden on his shoulders until she had no shadow of a doubt. In the morning she would pick up a pregnancy test at the pharmacy. And that night, if she felt his arm come around her in bed, she would say nothing of her fears.

Her hands were shaking as she followed the test instructions in the bathroom at the shop the next morning. She stared at the resulting ring in the vial, then looked at the instructions again, hoping she'd read them incorrectly. She hadn't. The test was positive.

The phone rang out in the shop, and Susan knocked on the bathroom door.

"Catherine, there's a call for you from your Santa Barbara shop."

"Yes. Be right there."

As she flushed the results down the toilet and dropped the test package in the wastebasket, she wondered how she would get through the rest of the day coherently.

She waited for him that evening, casting every thought in his direction, willing him to appear. She'd mentally rehearsed the words she would say, if she could remember them when the time came. She was so afraid of what his reaction would be. He might be furious at her carelessness, but why should he be? Women of his age hadn't been encouraged to use birth control—on the contrary. He wouldn't expect it of her, and he'd certainly never seemed concerned about her conceiving. Perhaps he hadn't thought it a possibility himself?

She looked up quickly at the sound of the piano. A fire was burning on the living room hearth. She felt, rather than saw its glow. A candelabra was lit atop the piano, and he was playing Brahms.

His blue-eyed gaze caught hers across the room. "I thought that might bring you." He smiled slowly.

She dashed off the couch to slide down on the bench beside him before the connection broke. Her fingers gripped his muscled shoulder as if it were a lifeline.

He raised his brows and his eyes twinkled teasingly. "Is it my music, or are you making certain we don't part?"

"Both."

"Hmmm, something in your tone tells me we have things to discuss."

"I'll talk to you as you play."

His expression grew worried, but Catherine didn't notice. She stared at his rapidly moving fingers, then the candles. She'd had all the words worked out, but now they didn't come. How she loved his music. She'd raided her grandparents' collection and had given him the sheet music of some more modern composers—modern to him —Tchaikovsky, Brahms, Rubinstein, Liszt. He'd obviously been practicing.

While she hesitated, he finished the Brahms and went smoothly into Rubinstein's *Romance*, lyrical, aptly suited to its title.

"I love this piece."

"I thought you might." He paused. "You were going to say?"

Her gaze went back to the candles. It was easier to speak looking at the dancing flames than at the possible expressions on his face.

"I . . ." she stumbled, started again. "You know I haven't been feeling well for the past week or so."

His hands momentarily stopped.

"Keep playing."

He did.

She licked her lips. "I thought it was the flu. I felt tired, queasy, but the queasiness seemed to pass by mid-morning . . . sometimes recurred at dinner. I checked the calendar yesterday. I'm eight—no nine—days overdue. I took a test this morning. Lucien, unless all of that is wrong . . . I'm pregnant."

His hands did stop that time, on a broad chord. The sound echoed in the room. She chanced a look at him. He was staring at her.

"Pregnant. Mine."

She nodded.

"I never thought." His voice was hushed.

"Neither did I."

"Do you know what this means?"

"I do, Lucien, and it scares me to death."

His arms came around her. "You have no doubts."

"I haven't been to a doctor, but no, not really."

"History *is* repeating itself. Gwen, now you!"

"Don't say that!"

"I didn't intend to. My thoughts were speaking aloud. My fears are speaking aloud. It won't be the same this time. I won't allow it to be the same." His arms were warm bands around her. "I love you."

"I love you, too."

"Catherine, I would have spared you this. I should have."

"It takes two . . . and we can't go back." Where was she getting the presence of mind to be so pragmatically logical, she wondered?

"No, we cannot . . . and that leaves the future. What are we to do about that? We *must* find a way to remain together! I can't bear to lose you . . . you and our child."

"If we were normal people, Lucien, would you be happy now?"

"I *am* happy, except for the circumstances of our future. Did you think otherwise?"

"I wasn't sure."

"I'm stunned, shocked—but to think we've created a life . . ." He stared at her. "We've drifted along not knowing our future, yet I've known I wanted you for my wife—wanted this progression of things. I feel so powerless now to think there may be nothing I can do to protect you—that we may simply be pawns on a board." He took a breath. His mind was obviously churning, seeking some solution. "One thing is very clear. We are gong to have to walk away from this house in one or the other's world, start a new life, and pray no quirk of fate interferes again."

"Would it work?" she asked breathlessly. "We've only tested it for a few hours."

"Do we have a choice?"

"No."

"We must take the risk, Catherine. Remaining as we are offers an even greater risk."

"There are so many people who would be affected in either of our lives."

"An unfortunate truth, but if we plan things carefully..."

"Whose world?" How strange to even discuss the possibilities of moving into one century or another at will. She loved him beyond anything she'd ever felt before, but she hadn't truly looked ahead to this actuality. What had she been waiting for? A miracle that would require no sacrifices, no dangers, on either of their parts? She lifted her head to look about the room—his room. These were the things she would have to become accustomed to, but not in this house. They had to leave this house. She had her business, her friends, her sister to consider as well; and Lucien a shipping enterprise, family in England.

He hadn't answered her question, but she pressed on. "Maybe history has already told us something. You do leave this house, and your attorneys in England handle the sale."

"Yes, I can imagine myself having them represent me in something of that nature. I did so when I left England and turned the leasing of my properties over to them. I can also see myself feeling bitter hatred for this house, this island, if I should lose you."

They sat facing each other on the piano bench, their hands gripped together between them. "We shall stay together, you and I, and our child." His eyes flickered with the blue light that always seemed to spark from his portrait when the sun shone upon it. "I won't allow history to repeat itself."

She looked down at his hands and ran her thumbs over the backs of his fingers where they held hers. She noticed how the black hairs sprang up from his tanned, weathered skin. How masculine his hands were; how strongly and beautifully shaped. How she loved and needed to feel those hands touching her, caressing her body, giving her moments of comfort and joy in all circumstances. "I can't live happily without you."

"Nor can I without you. We'll find a solution."

"Play for me again?"

"If you like."

"When I listen to you play, I feel like everything's as it should be . . . that we're normal people with nothing extraordinary to fear."

"Then I'll play for you the rest of the night." He let his fingers move through the melodies of Brahms, Tchaikovsky, and Liszt, pouring emotion into every note, telling Catherine without saying a word of the turmoil he was feeling—and of his love for her.

While he played, her arm slid down to encircle his back. The last bars of "Liebesträume" rang in the air. He swung around on the bench, dragging her against him. She laid her head on his chest and silently cried.

"It will be all right," he soothed. "We won't be parted."

Chapter 25

An increasing quality of desperation threaded their conversations. Would it work? Would they be able to remain together in one or the other's time? And when should they make the attempt to leave the house together for good? Each of them had matters in their separate lives to be put in order.

It was all Catherine could do to keep from falling apart and to keep her business on an even keel. Lucien was feeling a similar strain.

"Gladstone barked at me this morning for my recent short temper," he confessed as he and Catherine sat together in front of the study fire. "And he was right. I've been a bear. Too much on my mind." Barney came across the room and curled on the carpet by their feet. "I go from one plan to another, to another—in the end, cast them all away. I feel impotent! I want to protect you. I don't know how."

The worry lines were evident on his face. Catherine reached up a hand to smooth them away, but the same worry was reflected in her features, made worse by the fact that she was still plagued with morning sickness and an overwhelming feeling of exhaustion.

"I went to a doctor today," she said quietly.

He waited, staring down at her.

"He's sure I'm pregnant, though it's early for a physical examination to be conclusive. But with all my symptoms, and the pregnancy test. He took some blood samples. I'm anemic. He gave me some iron pills and said I should be feeling less tired over the next few days. Otherwise I'm healthy."

"Did he ask about the father?"

"From the information I'd given his receptionist, he knew I wasn't married. He only asked if I intended to have the baby. If not, I should act as soon as possible."

"I don't understand." Lucien frowned.

"Abortion is legal now. If I didn't want the child, I could abort it."

"I see . . ."

"I wouldn't do it, Lucien."

His answering sigh held relief. He added somberly, "It would be another alternative for you."

She shook her head. "Not your child."

He rose, and holding her hand, took a step to the hearth and dropped another log on the fire. "One plan I considered," he said as he returned to her, "would be for us to leave the island on one of my ships. The *Goddess* is due in two weeks' time. We could board her as she's set to sail. I have the house in England. We could live there."

"Two weeks? Why can't we just leave now? I can't stand this waiting and not knowing."

"You have to put your affairs in order, and it seems the most logical approach. Remaining on this island otherwise in my time might present difficulties. That is, if you want to live in my world. Compared to yours, it is sadly lacking in conveniences, and medical care is primitive." He rubbed his brow. "That is what holds me back. Both Gwen and our child might have been saved in this world—at least Gwen."

Catherine silently agreed. She surmised that Gwen had died of hemorrhage. The thought did scare her. But she'd rather face *it*, if there were no other alternatives, than face living without Lucien. "You don't want to remain in the twentieth century?"

"I didn't say that. I could adjust, anachronism though I would be—"

"And I wouldn't be an anachronism in your world?"

He smiled. "Perhaps I think of myself more in that capacity, since I would be the dumb fool in a technological society. And from what I've read, we might have more difficulty explaining me away. You all seem so well documented and accounted for. More importantly, what would I do to make a living? The days of sail are gone."

"Only commercial sail. Pleasure sailing is a tremendous business."

He made a face. "Push a button to raise a sail? Hmph. I could do it, of course, but again we have the problem of documentation. Who shall I say I am? Even in my day, captain's papers were required."

"There might be ways of getting your papers—at least modern identification. We could find a way."

"Illegally, of course."

"Well, how could you avoid it?"

"Yes, imagine the reaction of the scientific community should they get their hands on me, a man born in 1810 and still thriving. God awful. I'd no doubt be put in a cage for analysis and study."

Catherine didn't laugh. She could imagine just such a thing happening. If not a cage, at least a scientific or government research facility. Imagine the impact on man in his quest for immortality, longevity. A ghost come to life!

"We could avoid that happening," she said. "We could go to California. I still have my apartment there. We could tell people we'd met on Nantucket. We just wouldn't say how. You'd moved to the States from England. No one would question it." She paused. "And I'd have less to lose if we stayed here—oh, I don't mean materialistically. I'm frightened about living in a time when women had no rights, no real freedom. I wouldn't be able to vote, own my own property after marriage, run my own business."

Now it was his turn to pause. "It's so important to you? Losing the right to vote I can understand. But I would take care of you, see that your every need was met. I won't be an autocratic husband."

"Lucien, you know I don't simply want to be taken care of. I want to be an equal partner. A relationship for me has to be fifty-fifty. I could never be a pampered wife and mother. I've learned too much of my abilities. I have to make use of them."

He was silent as he stared into the fire. "I've admired you for those very qualities. Strange that I didn't think of what the loss of them would mean. I can promise in writing that whatever we have will be ours equally, so there is never a question."

"Oh, Lucien, I don't know why I'm being so demanding and picky. I'd put up with anything if it meant staying together!"

"So we have two alternatives. Which shall it be?"

"Will we have a choice? On the day we decide to leave, we won't know what world we'll be meeting in."

"We could leave both options open—be prepared in either case. Or we could wait until we meet in the world we wish to remain in."

"I'd rather leave both options open."

"So be it. We will make preparations. And we can't tell anyone what we are planning."

"They'd try to stop us."

"Undoubtedly they would, or think we're mad. I shall revise my will, leaving my shipping business to my brother, with the contingency that none of those in my employ suffer sudden and undue hardship. John is not a sailing man, but he is an excellent manager."

"I'll make a will, too, though there's only my sister."

He pulled her against him. "This talk of wills is depressing, is it not."

"But we're not talking of death."

"No . . . both our lives." His hand slid to her stomach. "And a third. Let us set a date now. Shall we settle on the *Goddess*'s arrival in the middle of November?"

"I'm so afraid to wait that long."

"We've had nearly six months since our first meeting, and to try to leave the island on other than one of my vessels would be risky. Ah, Catherine, it's not that I don't want our future settled. I would see it settled now, this moment, if it were that easy. We could walk from this house this instant, into your world, but my conscience would plague me for the havoc I'd left behind in mine. And I have nothing with me—no cash or valuables to help see us through. We've come this far. I can't help but believe we *will* find our happiness. More and more I feel that we would never have been brought together at all if we weren't meant to *remain* together."

As he took her into his arms, she wished she shared his firm conviction that two weeks was not too long to wait.

"We'll use these next two weeks to smooth the way for the rest of our lives. And I'll be here to give you comfort. I love you," he whispered fervently in her ear.

"And I love you."

The next morning he wasn't with her when she woke, but she felt no undue alarm. She'd see him that evening. If only she could still the horrible anxiety inside. He was right—they'd had more than six months together. Why should she suddenly be so desperately afraid of waiting a few weeks?

She felt like she was living in a world of surreality. She went to her lawyer and had a will drawn up. She was acquiring assets, she told John. A will seemed a sensible thing. John agreed and also agreed to her suggestion that there be some stipulations that would prevent Treasa from liquidating everything and frittering away the money. She wanted to enchance her sister's new sense of responsibility, not undermine it with the prospect of a windfall.

Catherine began instructing Susan in the full responsibilities of running the shop, using as an excuse probable trips she would be making to the West Coast over the winter. The other woman raised no question and caught on quickly.

Treasa called to say she'd be staying on the boat for at least another month. She'd be delivering the boat as far as Florida, and there was a possibility of her staying on. She sounded happy, excited, and admitted there was also a new man in her life—a real nice guy this time.

"I met him on one of the charters," she explained. "He was one of a group of businessmen from New York. He's flown up twice, and I'm going down next weekend to New York. He's a stockbroker. Can you believe me with a stockbroker?" Treasa laughed.

"I think it's great."

"Keep your fingers crossed for me!"

"I will."

"Peter's been asking for you," Treasa added on a more serious note.

"Tell him I said hello. How is he?" Peter suddenly seemed part of a life she'd lived in another dimension.

"He's painting. He's sad, but he doesn't talk about it."

"I never meant to hurt him, Trea, you know that."

"Yeah. So does he, I guess. Well, I better go."

It occurred to Catherine that this might be the last conversation she had with her sister. "Trea, I'm sorry about everything that happened over the summer. I'm sorry I never understood you after Mom and Dad died."

There was a moment's silence at the other end. "I'm sorry, too. I was a shit . . . whether you understood me or not. But why are you bringing it up now? It's in the past. It won't happen again."

"Right." Catherine swallowed. "Take care of yourself. I love you."

Another second's silence. "Love you, too."

Her eyes burned when she hung up the phone. Was it possible she'd never see Treasa again—or any of the other people who'd been her dear friends . . . Marcie, Marjorie. What should she tell Marjorie? Should she say good-bye?

The iron pills had helped. She didn't feel as tired, but now there was another anxiety. She hadn't seen Lucien for three days. As she put together a bag of her most precious belongings, she thought of him constantly. Yet those thoughts weren't working their usual magic. Perhaps it was because he was busy too, getting ready.

And three days wasn't so long actually. There had been longer stretches when they hadn't met, and it had all been fine. She'd keep busy. The waiting wouldn't seem so long. She bought enough iron and vitamin pills for her whole pregnancy. Another day passed. She marked it off on the calendar. She went through the house, consigning to memory the cherished things she soon might never see again. She raked leaves in the backyard, finished teaching Susan the intricacies of running the shop.

A letter arrived from England, from the present owners of Oak Park. They were very sorry they couldn't assist her in her search for facts. They'd purchased the main manor house and several surrounding acres thirty years before from a land developer. The balance of the property had been divided and sold separately, and part of the land was now a housing estate. They knew the manor house had once been in the possession of the Blythe family but could give her no historical details, since they knew none themselves. If there were any Blythe descendants, they were not personally acquainted with them. All very polite; all very much a dead end.

The letter left Catherine with a hollow feeling in her stomach, a hollowness that increased a few days later when her letter to Lucien's solicitors was returned. The envelope was marked, "Not at this address. Current address unknown."

More days checked off on the calender and still no Lucien. Where *was* he? Why hadn't he made even a brief appearance. She needed him so badly! What was wrong! She tried to suppress her fears, but her panic was growing. She'd wake up in the night soaked in perspiration, calling out for him. She sat in the study, staring at his portrait; sat on the piano bench, fingering the keys.

They shouldn't have waited these two weeks. Why didn't he come? How could it be ending already? They had so much to give each other. Were they not going to be allowed the chance? The thought was unbearable! It was the nightmare she'd not allowed herself to consider. But it *was* possible. Fate might already have interceded.

She had their child . . . the proof and gift of their love. Would she be left to raise that child alone? Was she prepared for raising that child alone? Of course, she would do it. She already loved the tiny seed of life within her. She would find a way, but it wasn't what she wanted! She wanted Lucien to be with them.

On the fourteenth day, she climbed to the widow's walk and gripped the railing made damp from fog. The cold wetness permeated her clothing, stuck tendrils of hair to her cheeks. The *Goddess* would be docking now—that very day! She willed the scene before her eyes to change, so that she could glimpse the tall wooden masts rising from the fingers of fog. She willed it with such intensity her temples throbbed, her whole body shook.

"Oh, Lucien," she cried to the evening sky, as tears streamed down her cheeks, "Lucien, come to me! Don't let it end now!"

Chapter 26

From the widow's walk the Captain watched the *Goddess* cross the bar and ease through the harbor toward the docks. His heart felt like a leaden weight in his chest. For fourteen days he'd waited in agony, at first not believing; then, finally, he was forced to see the bitter truth for what it was. It was finished. They would meet no more. The woman he loved had been taken from him again with all the finality of death, as had their child. Why? Why was he being so punished? Perhaps he should take consolation in knowing that Catherine and their child still lived, but how small a slice of peace that when he would never see them again. His pain was so overwhelming, it left him dazed, unable to think, unable to function.

He'd tried so desperately to force a connection—concentrating his thoughts on her until his whole head ached; standing beneath his portrait, knowing it formed some link. He'd sat at the piano keyboard for hours, paced the garden, lain dreaming of her in bed during nearly sleepless nights. He'd held on to a shred of hope until the last moment, but seeing the *Goddess* arrive, knowing they would have been sailing away to happiness on her decks, he felt the last glimmer fade away. If they were going to meet again, they would have met by now.

"Don't let it end this way!" he cried, lifting his face to the gray November sky. "Hear my call! Come to me!"

His voice broke. The cold air numbed his hands, reddened his cheeks. The tears that rolled unheeded from his eyes were warm against his skin, but he felt neither their warmth nor the chill. He stared as his ship drew up to the dock and her mooring lines were secured. He saw Perry and the crew moving about her decks. He remembered the day he'd arrived in Nantucket and the pain he'd been suffering then. It seemed as though the five intervening years hadn't passed at all. He mourned again—this time even more devastated. Why, why, why? he asked himself. There seemed no logic or rational reason for the hurt life was bringing to bear upon him!

Hardly aware of what he was doing, he turned from the rail, and with the steps of an old and disillusioned man, descended from the roof. What was Catherine doing? Was she experiencing the same horrifying grief as he was? Was she feeling misused and abused by fate? Was she crying out for him, as he cried out for her? And it would be worse for her. She had their child to raise alone. What would she do? To whom could she turn? Oh God, how he yearned to be with her! He couldn't allow the second love of his life to face bearing their child alone. The thought of Catherine meeting the same end as Gwen nearly brought him to his knees.

He refused to leave the house, even to check the *Goddess*'s cargo. In the next days messengers traveled continually between the docks and the Orange Street house. He could barely put his mind to penning the necessary answers. Perry came up to the house, concerned.

"You're ill," he said almost immediately, after Gladstone had shown him into Lucien's study. "You should call a physician."

"My ills are nothing a physician can cure."

"What has happened? Last time we put in, you were in fine fettle."

Yes, Lucien thought, that had been two months before, and he and Catherine had been blissfully in love. He shook his head. "Personal worries."

"Not over business. The profits made this last passage alone should put a smile on your face."

"Not business. Something I shall have to sort out myself."

"You worry me," Perry stated flatly. "I haven't seen you look like this since you left England."

"Yes . . . not since I left England." Lucien finished off his brandy with a long swallow. "Don't let my state concern you, Perry," he said after a moment. "There is nothing anyone here can do."

Perry's expression was far from happy when he left a half hour later. He took Gladstone aside in the downstairs hall.

"What's troubling him?" he asked the servant. "If he'd not always been in such perfect health, I'd say he was seriously ill."

"I don't know, Cap'n," Gladstone said heavily. "These past few weeks he's gone about looking like death itself. Won't talk about it."

"Another disrupted affair, do you think?"

"Haven't noticed him paying court to any lady, though there's been some strange goings on here. I know I've seen a woman about the house who runs off whenever I show my face. Pierce has seen her, too, but the Cap'n denies it."

"Perhaps that is it then, though such clandestine behavior seems out of character for Lucien."

"Well, I'm hoping he'll snap out of it. He's not one to be kept down."

Lucien, however, didn't snap out of it. He roamed about the house a lost soul, vague, haggard. His face was pale and dark circles ringed his eyes from lack of sleep. He barely ate, and his trousers hung loosely from his hips. In the evenings he stood for long hours on the widow's walk, or sat in the study staring vacantly at the fire and drinking too many brandies. By day he paced the rooms of the house and the garden. He never left the premises, nor did he seem tempted to put a saddle on Sarter's back and head out for the rides he'd so enjoyed in the past.

Gladstone's worry became grave concern. The captain was wasting away, all interest in living gone. When he came to the study to collect another barely touched dinner tray, he knew he must speak.

Lucien sat in the armchair, fingering a strange-looking magazine, making no attempt to read, simply holding the printed matter as if it were a precious possession.

Gladstone cleared his throat. "Cap'n, it's time we had a word."

Lucien stared at the fire, giving no response.

"Cap'n, you can't go on like this. You don't sleep. You don't touch your meals. You'll be ruining your health."

"It is my health, Gladstone." Lucien slowly turned his head toward the servant, unconcerned.

"Please, Cap'n, this isn't like you. Even when you were in such a state five years ago, you didn't behave like this."

"Pour me a glass of brandy, would you, Gladstone?"

"And you've been drinking altogether too much of that grog!"

"It eases the pain."

"What pain? Tell me what it *is* that's troubling you, Cap'n! It's been twelve years now we've been sharing the same quarters—"

"Yes, and after twelve years you should know when I want to be left alone. Please go, Gladstone. I don't wish to talk at the moment."

"Cap'n, I'm not—"

"*Gladstone.*" For a brief instant Lucien's eyes flashed with some of their former spark. It was sufficient to make the servant turn toward the door, but as soon as he was out of the room, the Captain's eyes returned to a study of the fire and became filmed by a dull haze.

"Oh, my love," he whispered, "I miss you so. If nothing else, may that thought reach across time to you. May you have the strength I now lack and find a way to raise our child in health and happiness. Never forget me or what we shared, but you must find a new life without me . . . for our child's sake . . . and your own."

Chapter 27

She had to face the cruel, unrelenting facts. She'd lost him. Whatever had brought them together had ceased to exist. Yet Catherine clung to the slim shred of hope that it wasn't too late; that it wasn't over. For four days she'd called in sick to the shop. She had to be there, in the house, when he arrived. But she waited through those tortured hours in vain. With every passing hour her desperation grew.

She fingered the miniature he'd given her, staring down at his youthful face. She had so few possessions of his to remember him by. The miniature, the portrait, the sea chest—so little to cherish and to prove his existence, as if it all *had* been a dream. But she had his child—irrefutable proof of their love.

When there was a sharp knock on the screen door, Catherine glanced up. Marjorie stepped briskly into the kitchen. The dim, glazed look in Catherine's eyes was enough to put a row of worried creases in the older woman's brow.

"Something is terribly wrong, isn't it?" Marjorie said softly. "I've debated for days whether or not to interfere, but it's obviously time someone did. What's troubling you? What can I do to help?"

The genuine concern in Marjorie's tone cut through a layer of Catherine's stupor. She blinked her eyes and, as if in slow motion, motioned Marjorie to sit down.

"Now, what's happened?" Marjorie asked. "Some bad news? Your sister?"

"No, not Treasa. Much, much worse."

"Whatever it is, you must talk about it."

"Yes, I should talk. I can't deal with it alone anymore. I'm pregnant, Marjorie." Her voice had the quality of a sleepwalker.

"Oh, dear girl!" Marjorie quickly reached over and gripped Catherine's hand. "No wonder you've seemed so distraught. But I thought you and your young man had broken up . . . oh, I see . . ."

"No, I don't think you do. It's not Peter's. It's not any living man's. It's Lucien Blythe's."

Marjorie flinched as if she'd been stung. "No. Catherine, that's impossible!"

"It's not. I haven't just seen glimpses of him around the house. We've been meeting and talking to each other for months. It's strange to explain, but he isn't really a ghost. When we're together, he's as real and alive as any man."

Marjorie eyes were wide behind her glasses.

"Sometimes he'd appear in my time; sometimes I'd be in his time, his world. I've walked the streets of 1844 Nantucket with him. I've seen his ships. He's seen modern day Nantucket. He gave me this." She turned the miniature toward Marjorie. "It's of him when he was a boy."

Marjorie took the miniature, studied it. "Catherine, you're in shock. Ghostly energy possibly does exist—assuredly it must, since I've seen the ghost myself—but what you're describing is beyond belief. Perhaps with the trauma of discovering you were pregnant—"

"No, I haven't dreamed it, if that's what you think. I'm not crazy. It happened. He was real. At first neither of us believed it was happening either. I truly thought he was a ghost, but when he talked, and I touched him . . . he was real. Our meetings were something we couldn't stop from happening."

"And with all the contact," Marjorie said in a whisper, "you fell in love."

"Yes . . . very much in love. I was afraid at first, and there was Peter, but after a while, I knew it wasn't Peter I loved, but Lucien Blythe. We began to believe that fate—whatever—had intended us to meet. He'd had a tragic love affair before he came to Nantucket. That was why he came. Her name was Gwen. She died having their child. The child died, too. He was away at sea and hadn't even known she was pregnant." Catherine's voice faded into a painful sigh.

Though Marjorie's face was pinched and white, she squeezed Catherine's hand more tightly. "Keep talking, Catherine. You need to."

In a second Catherine did. "When we were in the house we needed to be in physical contact to stay together, most of the time, but then we discovered that if we left the house together, we could walk out into whichever world we were in and stay together until we returned to the house. The house was the key. When I discovered I was pregnant, he was afraid history was repeating itself. We made plans to leave the house together—in his world or mine—and not come back. We set the date . . . I haven't seen him since. We were going to leave five days ago. I guess history has repeated itself."

Marjorie was silent. She pressed the fingers of her free hand to her brow. "This is almost beyond me. I don't know what to say. I've had these feelings something very unsettling was happening, and one early evening, I thought I saw the two of you together on the widow's walk. At the time I tried to convince myself my eyes or the light were playing tricks on me." She shook her head. "A living ghost . . ."

"I don't know what to do, Marjorie. I keep hoping . . ." Slow tears ran down her cheeks. "But I'm so afraid."

"There's no question that it's Lucien Blythe's child?"

"None."

"Oh, what a tangle. It's just beyond understanding. If anyone else had told me this story, I wouldn't believe them."

"It's the absolute truth."

"You I *do* believe, but what advice can I give?"

"I'll just keep waiting. I can't let myself think we'll never see each other again."

"Have you ever gone without meeting for such a long period of time?"

"No . . . this is the longest."

"He may never come back. It's a horrible thing for me to tell you, but unavoidable."

"He *must* come back! We love each other—and the baby!"

"Catherine, you're numb with shock, but consider what you're saying. You can't cling to a hope that may never be fulfilled. Not only for your sake, but for the child's, you must make some alternative plans—go forward as if he's not returning."

"I can't!"

"Unfortunately, you must. Heavens," she added helplessly, "I know how difficult all this is. You love him. You're carrying his child, but he's not a normal man—at least not one from this dimension. Think of your child. You must provide for its well-being. Because of that new life, you have to carry on. You're not alone. You have Evan and me. We'll help you in any way we can."

Catherine dropped her head in her hands. "Marjorie, I can't think of it being over—I can't!"

"Perhaps it isn't, but you have absolutely no assurances of that. You have to go on living. He'd want you to, wouldn't he?"

"Yes . . ." she choked, "he'd want me to."

Marjorie rose from the table. "I'm going to make you a cup of tea. And have you eaten?"

"I'm not hungry."

"You can't afford to get run down. I'll fix you something, and then we'll talk some more."

Marjorie's scurrying figure was vaguely comforting to Catherine. The older woman busied herself fixing eggs and bacon and toast from one of her own homemade loaves. When Marjorie set the hot food on the table, Catherine did manage to eat. They talked quietly about Catherine's future, about Lucien and all Catherine had learned from him. It was a release to speak about him and describe to Marjorie all their wonderful hours together, but only a salve for Catherine's pain.

"I think you should come over and stay with Evan and me for a while," Marjorie said as she cleared off the table.

"I can't leave here. This house is our connection."

"Being alone here isn't good for you."

"He still may come back. I have to wait!"

The tight set of Marjorie's lips showed she wasn't happy about Catherine's decision, but she conceded. "All right. But I'll stop by every night to check on you. You may think I'm interfering, but I wouldn't rest otherwise."

After Marjorie had left, Catherine went upstairs to the study. With a single lamp burning, she stood in front of the portrait and sobbed. How good a likeness of him it was, capturing his internal vigor as well as the physical planes and shadows of his face. How she loved him! How shattering was the thought of living without him . . . of never seeing or touching or talking to him again! She didn't think she could bear it.

But if nothing else, the logic of Marjorie's advice did settle in Catherine's subconscious as the days passed. She wouldn't give up hope, but for the child's sake as well as her own, she had to hold herself together. Lucien wouldn't want her to lose everything. If only she could concentrate. Lucien's face kept flashing in front of her eyes. Was that a sign? But the house was as empty as ever—echoingly so.

After Lucien, nothing would be the same. She would never look on life again with the same perspective. She, who'd experienced something that most people would consider impossible, could never go back to dealing with life as she had before. She barely understood the depth and breadth of the change within her. Her decorating business seemed inconsequential; and material luxuries that had always brought her pleasure seemed mere fripperies. What did any of it matter when she'd touched something far beyond? But she would need money to support their child. She couldn't let everything she had slip away for lack of interest.

If Lucien could speak to her now, what would he tell her to do in his absence? She ran her hand over the gleaming wood of the piano, thinking of him. The back door opened. A voice called for her.

For an instant she froze, her heart pounding against her ribs even as she stood rooted to the floor.

"Catherine! Are you here?"

She was engulfed by a wave of disappointment. It wasn't Lucien. But what was *Peter* doing here?

She heard his footsteps coming up the hall. He stepped through the doorway to the living room.

Seeing him again left her with the strangest sensation. Her fingers gripped the piano.

There was no question of the expressions rapidly crossing his face—relief, joy, doubt over his welcome.

"Hello, Catherine."

"Hello, Peter."

"I didn't mean to barge in on you," he said quickly, anxiously. "But I had to see you, Catherine . . . talk to you."

She stared at him, and he seemed to pull together all his reserves of courage. He spoke rapidly.

"I'm done on *Escapade*. I've come to the island until I decide where I'm going from here. I haven't been able to forget you. I couldn't leave without giving it one last try."

As she motioned him to the couch, she felt strange, as if she was disconnected and walking through someone else's dream. Her whole being had been so wrapped up in Lucien . . . still was. She knew the impression she was giving, but couldn't help it.

They sat down on either end of the couch facing each other. He slid his hand nervously over his jean-covered knee and spoke with the same nervousness.

"I've been doing well with the painting. The gallery in Maine's sold half a dozen and want more. By the way, thanks for the check you sent for the one I left here."

"It sold within three days."

"I hadn't expected so much."

"It was worth it." She knew she was being cold, brittle, but it wasn't deliberate.

"Catherine, I've been doing a lot of thinking the last couple of months. What we had was too good to throw away. I understand you don't want to be committed, but I had to talk to you. I've taken a room on the island for a few weeks. I'd like to see you."

Slowly she wagged her head.

"I'm not asking anything," he pleaded, "except to talk. I've missed you. I still love you—" Impulsively he slid across the couch and took her hands.

"No, please, stop, Peter," she said in panic. "I can't return that kind of love anymore."

"There is someone else." His face fell.

"There was."

"Why are you being so cold? Is it because of me coming here uninvited?"

She shook her head. Her lips trembled and she pressed them together.

"If it's not my being here, then what? This other bloke . . . did he hurt you?"

"It's nothing I can talk about."

"Catherine, at least let me be your friend."

"Please, Peter . . ." It was too much. She couldn't explain to him. She couldn't think of it without tears rising from the depths of her grief and fear.

Immediately his arms came around her, and he brought her head to his chest.

His arms felt so comforting. How desperately she needed a safe haven . . . for just a little while. Eventually her sobs quieted into soft hiccups, and all the while, Peter held her, his hands rubbing gently over her back.

"Better now?" he whispered.

"Yes."

"Talk to me. What's happened to make you so unhappy?"

She hadn't intended to tell him, but suddenly the words were out of her mouth. "I can't see you again. I can't offer you anything. I'm pregnant."

"Obviously not mine," he said after a moment.

"No."

"Did he leave you because of it?"

"No." She couldn't tell him about Lucien. Instinctively she knew Peter wouldn't accept such a thing.

"But he has left you."

"He may come back."

"May? Who is this bastard?"

"No one you know."

"You're still in love with him."

"Yes."

"What are you going to do?"

"Have the baby."

"All by yourself—without help?"

"I'll be all right." She lifted her head from his chest. "I shouldn't have told you. It's not your problem."

"Catherine, I care about you. You're in trouble. I want to help you."

"You can't. There's nothing you can do."

"There is. I'm not leaving you alone. I'll stand by you—even if it's not my child."

"Peter, you're making it worse." Her throat was closing. "It wouldn't be fair."

"Let me decide what's fair. You don't love me the way you did, but you don't hate me."

"I love you as a friend, but that's all I can give."

"Think about it."

"Peter . . . no."

"Just think about it. I'm going to get a drink. You could use a sip or two yourself. Still keep it in the same place?"

She nodded.

Gently he slid his arms from around her, rose and walked to the liquor cabinet. She watched him, undone, unable to think. She shouldn't have told him. She'd complicated matters totally. He'd meant what he said about protecting her, and he would, short of her forcing him out of her life. Or was all of it intended to happen? Was his protection precisely what she needed? If Lucien wasn't coming back, was this what he would have wanted her to do?

Peter returned with his drink. She didn't protest when he sat down close beside her and put his arm around her waist.

"Take a sip."

She did, but only a small one. He took a swallow himself. "We have a lot more to talk about," he said. "Then I'll make us some dinner."

"Peter, you can't stay here."

"We'll talk about that, too."

As if to take her mind off her own worries, he talked about his painting and what had been going on in Camden. Only as their conversation wore on did he ask how she was feeling, if she'd seen a doctor. Rundown and emotionally weakened, she didn't fight off his solicitousness, but when he probed further about her child's father, she clammed up.

"Why are you trying to protect this man?" he demanded angrily. "Obviously he's a sot."

"He's not a sot, but it's nothing I can explain. Leave it be, Peter."

Reluctantly he did, and shortly thereafter they went to the kitchen to get together something for dinner. The task wasn't easy. Catherine had been too upset and distracted during the last days to buy groceries. He finally found the makings of a salad and some canned soup. While Catherine prepared the salad, Peter went out to the barn for firewood. Through the window she saw him start crossing the lawn, then pause and look toward Marjorie's. He redirected his footsteps toward the fence between the two houses. Catherine sidestepped to get a better view from the window. In the porch light she saw Marjorie and Peter talking, quickly and seriously from the expression on Peter's face. A few minutes later Peter turned and continued on to the barn, and Marjorie stepped back into her kitchen.

"What were you talking to Marjorie about?" Catherine asked as Peter returned with an armload of wood.

He hesitated, seemed a bit uncertain, then spoke quickly. "She was just wondering who I was. Said she likes to keep an eye out with you living here alone. Of course, she recognized me when I went over."

Yes, that sounded like Marjorie. Catherine said nothing else as Peter went on into the living room with the wood. After their dinner, however, he suddenly spoke up. "I want you to come down into town with me tonight—stay at my place. Don't worry—there's an extra bed."

"I'm staying here."

"You shouldn't be in this house alone."

"Why?" Her eyes darkened with suspicion.

"You're too upset. You need someone around." But his cheeks had flushed slightly as if he were hiding something.

"I appreciate your worrying about me, but I'm staying. It's my house."

"Then I'll stay with you—in one of the other bedrooms. Don't say no. My mind's made up. At least for tonight."

It wasn't worth arguing with him. His features were set with determination. Yet she felt there was more motivating him than simple concern. What had Marjorie said to him?

At ten o'clock they went upstairs. He'd been kindness itself all evening, making no romantic overtures. He'd behaved more as a caring older brother, keeping Catherine sufficiently distracted that she had little time to dwell on herself. Catherine showed him to Treasa's former room where the beds were made up. As she glanced at the beds, she thought of the nights she and Peter had shared one together. She remembered the feel of his body and his always tender lovemaking. They'd been a good combination in bed, but she couldn't think of that now. So much had happened since.

Before she turned to leave, he put an arm around her shoulders and gave her a light kiss. "Sleep well. I'll be right here if you need me."

He was only making a thoughtful offer.

"Good night."

She knew he watched as she crossed the hall to her bedroom. How strange to have him there. How strange to have someone else in the house again after all her nights of private agony. When she'd changed into her nightgown, she didn't go straight to bed. Quietly she opened the door to the study. The light from her bedroom lamp filtered in as she walked to a spot beneath the portrait. The familiar, beloved features were easily visible despite the dim light. The blue eyes gazed down, bringing a tearing pain to her breast. Would she ever gaze on that face again in the flesh? Once again she remembered the last words he'd uttered to her.

"I love you, too..." she whispered, "forever. Please come *back*."

Chapter 28

Somehow the days passed. Somehow Catherine got through them. She barely admitted to herself that it was easier with Peter nearby—but it was. And Marjorie was there, too, as a staunch support. Catherine went down to the shop for a few hours each day, overseeing and doing the books. Anything else was unnecessary since Susan had things well in hand. The daily traffic had slowed to a trickle. Catherine contemplated closing the shop altogether for the winter. Without realizing it, she was beginning to think ahead to a life without the Captain.

Peter busied himself with his painting, using his rental rooms as a studio. None of his persuasions worked in getting Catherine to leave the house, so he returned to Orange Street every night, sleeping in Treasa's room. Though Catherine could see the love in his eyes, he didn't press her for more than she could give. Subtly, by slow degrees, she was healing under his influence, accepting him, sincerely grateful for his help. She cared for Peter. She might even have been able to love him again, if it hadn't been for Lucien Blythe.

Afternoons, Marjorie stopped by for a few minutes' chat. She was quick to note the gradually improving color in Catherine's cheeks and didn't hesitate to mention it."

"It's good that Peter's here. A godsend for you."

"It's only temporary."

"Why?" Marjorie quizzed patiently. "He loves you. He wants to stay. He told me he wants you to marry him."

"I couldn't, Marjorie."

"Because you're carrying another man's child?"

"Yes . . . and because I don't love him the way he loves me. I love Lucien . . . it's a feeling that never goes away."

"You always will love him, but the hard fact is that he's gone. The chances of his reappearing now are so small." She sighed. "I don't mean to hurt you, but you have an opportunity with Peter to begin again. He's willing to accept the baby. He's here now, and he's a real and living man."

"He's told you a lot, hasn't he?"

"Only because he cares. He's torn apart to see you like this, to have you reject him."

"You haven't told him about the Captain!"

"It's not my place. I don't know if he'd believe me if I did. I *have* inferred to him that this house carries bad memories for you."

"Why? And it's not so! When I think of the times Lucien and I—"

"That's just it," Marjorie interrupted. "You're not going to begin to put all that behind you while staying in this house and being constantly reminded."

"I don't want to put it behind. It happened." Catherine dropped her hand to her abdomen. "I have our child."

Marjorie looked over with sad compassion.

That night Catherine's sleep was tormented by dreams. In them, Lucien was beside her, smiling, his arm around her as they walked through Nantucket, sat by the study fire, and on the piano bench together as she listened to him play. He was beside her in bed, his arms coming around her in loving embrace. He was with her in a re-enactment of every happy and sad moment they'd shared. Her mind was filled with vivid images . . . so real. She heard his voice . . . heard him calling her. She rose, following the voice speaking silently to her brain. He was there, nearby. He'd returned. Her feet carried her to the study. She stood in the center of the room, relishing the feeling of closeness, and of joy. Then the images in her mind suddenly changed. The smile vanished from Lucien's face. The color drained away. His body sagged and slowly wilted to the floor, diminishing in substance until it was only an image on a painted canvas— without life.

She screamed, her hysterical cries rising in her throat without volition, vibrating, echoing, though she stood stock still, like blanched white marble. The door from the hall crashed open. Light flared into the darkness. Peter bounded across the carpet and grabbed her cold body, enfolding her.

"Catherine! What in God's name! Catherine!"

His brisk slap across her face finally roused her. She stared at Peter uncomprehendingly.

"What's wrong, Catherine? What happened?"

Slowly she turned her head toward the portrait. Her whole body began to shudder.

He pulled her close, but his eyes followed hers. "Were you dreaming? Was someone here?"

"I . . . don't know."

"Why are you staring at that painting? Who is he?"

She didn't answer.

For several seconds he started at the portrait as well, then he abruptly turned her away and led her forcefully from the room, across the hall to his own bedroom. "That's it. I'm getting you out of this house." He spoke through clenched teeth as he sat her down on the edge of the bed and chafed his hands over her frozen limbs.

"It's not the first time you've cried out in your sleep. Almost every night I hear you calling. Who is it you're calling? The baby's father?"

She couldn't speak. Lucien was once again in front of her eyes, crumpling onto the carpet. Had she seen it or dreamed it? And if a dream, it could only symbolize one thing—Lucien's death.

"You're staying here with me," Peter ordered. "I'm not leaving you alone. Come, get under the covers. You're freezing."

Sapped of all strength, filled with an unbelievable pain, Catherine allowed Peter to guide her into the bed. He slid in beside her, wrapped strong arms around her, and held her close to his body's heat. Vaguely, dimly, she heard his murmuring voice. "Forget him, Catherine. I'm here with you. I love you."

In the morning he gave her no time for protest or thought; not that she was capable of either. She'd slept not at all after wakening in the study. She'd been aware of Peter's arm and hard body beside her, and when he'd kissed her and had moaned softly to himself, she hadn't turned away.

Without even waiting to make a cup of coffee, Peter bundled Catherine and Barney out of the house. "I'll come back for your clothes, but you're coming down to my place, the sooner the better."

From his small but cozy rooms on India Street, he telephoned Marjorie. Catherine listened with half an ear to his side of the conversation as he briefly explained the situation.

"Marjorie's going to bring your things down here," he said after he'd hung up. "It'll be easier."

Catherine merely nodded.

"Come on. While the coffee's brewing, I'll show you around, such as it is. It was furnished, so I won't take credit for any of this." He motioned to the overstuffed sofa and chairs filling the small front living room, to the side of which was a minuscule kitchen. "I've been using this big back bedroom as a studio. The light's good." An easel holding a partially finished canvas stood near the double back windows. Other paintings were propped against the walls and on the dresser top, drying. The double bed had been pushed to the far side of the room and obviously was of secondary importance to the work area.

"I'll have to do a little cleaning up," Peter added with a touch of embarrassment.

Catherine was gazing at the drying canvases with the first spark of interest she'd shown since they'd arrived. "These are better than the one you gave me."

"You think so? I'd like to believe I'm improving with practice. I've added some new material since I've come to the island."

Her gaze stopped on a painting braced against the side of the dresser. Peter awkwardly stepped between her and the painting, but she walked around him for a better look. "When did you do this?" she asked in hushed tones.

"A little here, a little there . . . from memory. But it's not finished."

"It's good."

"I thought so. I was going to surprise you with it."

He'd painted her against a background of windswept sand dunes and beach grass, catching her face just as she turned to look back over her shoulder. The feel was of animation, happiness—her own happiness. How long ago that seemed.

"Is that how I really looked to you?"

"Yes." He waited for a moment. "Let's finish the tour." Leading her through the second doorway off the living room, he indicated a smaller bedroom. "You can sleep here." It was neat, with pink-flowered wallpaper, white bedspread, sanded wood floor, but decorated without imagination.

"I thought while we're here," Peter said as though reading her thoughts, "that you could put your talents to work—brighten things up. I haven't done anything to the place except use it to paint."

"Maybe," she answered, but unconsciously she'd already been adding small touches—a few throw rugs, curtains in an accenting color, a brighter spread.

They sat at the narrow breakfast island dividing the kitchen from living room and sipped their coffee. She was aware of Peter worriedly studying her when he thought she wasn't looking. Marjorie arrived with Catherine's clothes not long after. She bustled in through the door. Peter took the two bags from her and put them in the extra bedroom.

"I took what I thought you'd need," she explained to Catherine. "It's a good idea you're out of there," she added, patting Catherine's hand.

Later Catherine heard Marjorie and Peter talking quietly from the other room. She picked up only bits and pieces. "Ah, the portrait..." Marjorie said. "You think that's it... bad dream... yes... other man... gone... better here... call me for anything."

All through the day Catherine felt disjointed and vague. Dream or not, perhaps it was a sign that she should start rebuilding. In the same breath, she grieved. She still couldn't believe Lucien dead or gone forever.

Peter coaxed her out of the house for dinner, to a quiet table at Jared Coffin's. There were other diners, but the crowd was nothing in comparison to the summer months.

"Are you feeling better?" he asked when they'd finished eating.

"A little."

"Good." He didn't bring up her dream again, or the house, or the memories. They left the restaurant and collected Barney and went for a walk, bundled in heavy sweaters against the evening chill. She was genuinely tired when they returned to his rooms, and much of the tension had drained away, leaving an odd peace—perhaps acceptance.

She went into her room, changed into her nightgown, and came back out to use the tiny bathroom stuck between the two bedrooms. Peter was standing by the front window, staring out. He twisted around.

For a long moment she returned his intense look.

"I want you to leave the island with me," he said.

"I can't leave."

"Marry me, Catherine. I want to take care of you. Let me."

Marjorie's words suddenly sprang into Catherine's mind, but she shook her head. "I can't... not yet."

Disappointed though he was by her refusal, Peter's attitude was one of patience. He cosseted her. His only request was that she not go back to the house, and because she was still so numbly inert, she didn't protest.

"Peter, I can't give you back the love you're giving me," she told him.

"It doesn't matter for now."

"It will."

"We'll worry about it then—if that time comes."

Drifting along, she occupied her hours, sometimes watching him paint, which he said he didn't mind. She brought back some things from the shop to brighten the apartment—a couple of hooked throw rugs, vases of silk flowers, a handstitched quilt to cover the tattered upholstery of the couch. At the five-and-ten she purchased some inexpensive curtains and hung them in the living room and spare bedroom. Peter needed the studio windows open to all the light he could get. She took Barney for long walks, but heeding Peter's orders, she never went near Orange Street. She wanted to, she yearned to, but she managed to convince herself, at least partially, that Marjorie and Peter were right. Put the memories behind. Don't remind herself of the pain; of what it had been and all she'd lost. Her encounter with Lucien had been wonderful and glorious, but only an encounter . . . a thing out of time to treasure for the rest of her life. It was over. Yet she missed him, so very much.

Thanksgiving came and went. She and Peter celebrated quietly at the apartment, sharing the responsibilities of cooking the turkey and fixings. Catherine would have forgotten the holiday altogether, if Peter hadn't reminded her and tried to infuse her with some enthusiasm. "I've always liked this American holiday," he told her. "We should have something like it in Australia." During their meal Catherine had honestly tried to smile and be cheerful—Peter deserved something other than her glum, silent looks. Thanksgiving. What did she have to be thankful for? She had her growing child; she had her memories of Lucien and all they'd shared; she had Peter, who loved her and was willing to accept her as she was. She glanced over to him, and when their eyes met, she felt that love like a warm, invisible caress. Why couldn't she return that feeling? Marjorie and Evan had come later in the day for drinks and dessert. Evan was as good-naturedly quiet as his wife was loquacious. The rest of the day had passed pleasantly, comfortably, with no demands placed upon Catherine, but she knew she was being treated like a fragile china doll and handled with kid gloves. She felt pangs of guilt for causing these wonderful people so much worry, but she couldn't come fully alive.

Catherine paid her scheduled visit to the doctor. All was well. He was pleased her morning sickness was gone. "You seem troubled," he said to her as she was about to rise from the chair near his desk. "Is something worrying you? Have you had second thoughts about having this baby alone?"

"No, I haven't changed my mind. I want the baby very much. And I'm not all alone."

He nodded. His eyes were knowing and seemed to say more than his words. "I'm here any time you need to talk."

She left his office thinking of Lucien and aching afresh.

One sunny and unusually warm December day, Marjorie came and took her out to lunch, suggesting a small restaurant in 'Sconset that was still open.

They sat at a window overlooking a garden where frost-browned leaves were all that remained of the flower beds. The tree branches were bare and grayish, but a fire blazed behind them lending a cozy warmth to all. They dipped their spoons into hot bowls of soup.

"You're feeling better, dear?" Marjorie asked. "Adjusting?"

"I try."

"Peter's such a good man."

"I know he is—too good." Catherine looked down at the table.

"You deserve someone like Peter."

"I can't give Peter what I should. Whenever I try, I feel as though Lucien's standing there between us."

"Give yourself time. It's only been a month and a half."

Catherine's fingers unconsciously gripped the spoon.

"You'll heal, dear," Marjorie added softly. "We all do, no matter how tragic the event. The human spirit is amazing in that."

"I don't want to heal, Marjorie—that's what bothers me. I just want him to come back."

"He can't, dear. You have to accept that. You will."

She shifted slightly in her chair, brightening her voice, moving away from the painful subject. "What are your plans for Christmas? It's so lovely here on the island."

"I don't know . . . I hadn't really thought. We'll stay here I guess. Peter has no family in the States, and I got a letter from Treasa saying she was spending the holiday with her new boyfriend in New York."

"Ah, how are things going for her? Is this new boyfriend nice?"

"I haven't met him, but from what she says, yes. He's different from the others—a stockbroker. They've been seeing each other for a few months. It sounds like it might be serious."

"Good for her. If you don't have any definite plans, why don't we all get together for Christmas dinner?"

"Fine. I'll tell Peter."

"His painting's going well?"

"Yes, but most of the galleries are closed here this time of year. He wants me to leave the island with him after the first of the year . . . find a place near Boston."

"I think that's a good idea."

"I can't leave, Marjorie."

"You can always come back, you know. And the house will be fine. I'm checking it. You were thinking of closing the shop for the season anyway."

"Yes." But her answer was wavering and indecisive.

Chapter 29

Marjorie had invited them for a late dinner on Christmas Day—at four-thirty. It was already dark when Catherine and Peter walked up Orange Street to the Schmidts' front door. In the dim street light Catherine saw the outline of her own house only a half dozen yards away. The front was reflected whitely, while the other contours of the house faded into the darkness. The windows were blank, dark, unwelcoming; the house seemed abandoned. Catherine shuddered. Peter stepped protectively to her side as if to block her view. "I don't think this was a good idea," he muttered under his breath.

Marjorie quickly opened the door to their knock. Her round face was glowing.

"Merry Christmas! Come in. Evan's got his punch all ready, and the fire's roaring. My, it's gotten cold." She quickly shut the door behind them and took their coats, hanging them in the hall closet. Evan Schmidt stepped around the doorway to the living room on the right and motioned them in with a wide smile.

"Wouldn't be surprised if we had snow tonight," he said, as he accepted the two packages Peter handed him.

"Fine by me." Peter grinned. "First time I've spent a whole winter in the North. For under the tree." He nodded to the gifts.

Evan deposited them by the six-foot fir in the corner decorated, unsurprisingly, in antique ornaments collected by Marjorie over the years, and then went to the punch bowl on the coffee table. While he ladled out a cup for Peter and Catherine, Catherine glanced around the Federal-style room. It was formal, yet warm with the glow of antique woods, cream and burgundy wallpaper, complementing upholstery and a huge Persian carpet. Marjorie had hung a garland of holly and pine over the fireplace, and bowls of green and red candles decorated every tabletop. Involuntarily Catherine looked toward the two windows that faced her house. The lined drapes were pulled firmly closed across them.

"Sit down," Marjorie said, as she bustled into the room. "We'll eat in about twenty minutes, and then after dinner we can open our gifts." She picked up her own cup of punch from the table and lifted it. "Cheers."

They chorused the toast and all sat down to chat.

"What a treat." Marjorie beamed. "I so enjoy good company for Christmas. How's the painting going, Peter?"

"Real well. I have a bunch of canvases ready to go."

"Not much market here for them in the winter."

"No, I'm going to take them over to the mainland."

At his words both he and Marjorie glanced to Catherine, but she was lost in thought and didn't notice.

Marjorie eventually headed toward the kitchen for the food.

"Can I help?" Catherine asked.

"No. You just enjoy yourself. Nobody in the kitchen tonight but me."

They moved into the dining room on the opposite side of the hall. The oval Hepplewhite table was set with Marjorie's best Aynsley china, crystal, candles, and a jolly Santa in his sleigh as a centerpiece. Evan carved the turkey as Peter expertly uncorked and poured the wine.

"My, you're good at that," Marjorie commented.

"I ought to be," he laughed, "I've poured enough glasses of whatnot for charterers."

"I thought you were Captain."

"No one escapes lending a hand from time to time."

Halfway through the meal Catherine began to feel strange. Not ill, not the light-headedness she'd often experienced in her pregnancy, but a feeling of disassociation, as if only part of her were there in the room with her friends. She tried to shake the feeling away. The others were talking and laughing and didn't seem to notice her silence. She took a small sip of wine, forced herself to eat, but it was a mechanical action. Part of her was being drawn. Drawn where? Next door, she knew, to her house. But it was only the memories—all the pain-inducing memories.

Throughout the rest of the meal she found concentration difficult. She felt impelled to rise and walk out the front door. Of course, she didn't. Marjorie or Peter would have stopped her from going next door in any case.

When they were opening gifts in the living room, Peter became aware of her distraction. She felt his touch on her shoulder and realized she'd been staring toward the drape-covered windows. On his face she saw puzzlement and worry.

"Oh, how marvelous!" Marjorie exclaimed, as she pulled the wrappings from Catherine and Peter's gift. "You know I've always wanted one of these old etchings of the harbor. Where did you find it?"

"In an old house on the island," Catherine explained. "I put it away in the shop months ago to give to you."

"Well, I'll cherish it. It will hang right there over the mantel."

Catherine forced her mind back to her surroundings as she opened her own gift, a scrimshaw pendant on a silver chain, a genuine relic of the whaling days. She was truly touched. "I don't know how to thank you, Marjorie, Evan."

"I thought you would get much more use out of it than I've ever done." Marjorie's cheeks bore rosy spots of pleasure.

After the men opened their gifts—Peter a set of expensive brushes, Evan a gold pen and pencil set—they ended the evening with coffee and fruitcake. The strange compulsion came over Catherine again, to be followed by a draining sense of empathetic grief and loss—someone else's grief; someone else's loss. She felt dazed and disoriented by the time Peter helped her into her coat, and pulled herself together only long enough to warmly hug and thank Marjorie and Evan.

She was silent on the way home, despite Peter's efforts at conversation. When they arrived back at the apartment and removed their coats, he drew her over and sat her down on the couch.

"What's wrong? What happened to you tonight?" His voice wasn't harsh, only deeply concerned.

"I don't know." Her own was somewhat hushed. "I just felt so strange."

"Strange how? Ill?"

"No . . ."

"It's that house—it's being so close to it. There's something wrong with that house. What is it? Tell me," he pleaded. "Tell me what happened there."

She only wagged her head. Her motion could have been interpreted either as no, or that nothing had happened.

"Cath, I've been wanting to talk to you. I've found a place outside Boston. My friends arranged it—the lower floor of a house,
four rooms with a bit of a garden. He says the neighborhood's decent
and convenient. We can have it as of the middle of January. It's a
good base for the winter, close enough to the galleries so that I can
sell my stuff. I've saved quite a bit from my days on boats. I've got
plenty to take care of us. You wouldn't have to worry about a thing
until the baby's born." He gripped her hands tightly, willed her to
look at him. "Marry me, Catherine."

He saw her hesitation and quickly added, "You've seen how well
it's gone with us this last month. We get on together. We can make it
work. And God knows I love you."

"Peter, please . . . you know I can't marry you."

"Why? Not that nonsense about the baby not being mine. You
know it doesn't matter to me. The baby's part of you, and I'd love it
as if it was my own."

"You might change your mind. To have a living reminder of—"

"You—that's all."

"Oh, Peter . . ." She started to crumble. "I'm just not ready."

"All right. I understand. I won't push you into marriage until you
are ready, but come and live with me anyway, until the baby's born.
Then, if you decide . . ." He let the sentence hang, then spoke in a
firmer voice. "But I'm not leaving the island if you don't come
along."

"I couldn't bear to leave the island forever."

"It wouldn't be forever. We'll be back. Say yes, Cath."

Peter was wonderful, kind; she cared for him. It had to be obvious that Lucien wasn't coming back, and she had a terrible fear that
she would fall apart if she was all alone. She made her decision
desperately, impulsively.

"Yes," she sighed. "I'll go."

"Thank God." He pulled her against him, kissing her hair. "I love
you so much. I'll make you happy."

She closed her eyelids against the tears behind them. *I think
you'd want to do this, Lucien,* she said silently. *I pray you would.*

Peter suddenly leaned away. "I nearly forgot. I have another gift
for you."

Catherine was unconsciously trembling at the commitment she'd
just made, but Peter didn't seem to notice as he resumed his seat. He
handed her a small box.

"I bought it with hopes," he said as she ripped off the paper.

She opened the box to find a ring, a large opal in an elegantly simple white gold setting. She gasped. "Peter, I couldn't."

"It's not an engagement ring . . . only a token of how I feel. Wear it in friendship if you'd rather think of it that way."

She allowed him to slip it on her finger. Consciously or not, he put it on the fourth finger of her left hand.

"It's very beautiful, Peter," she said softly, "but in friendship only. I can't make any permanent commitments."

"I'm not asking you to, now."

New Year's Day came and went. Catherine made herself believe that what she was doing was the right thing. She made herself believe simply by not allowing herself to think of the alternative. Marjorie stood beside her like a rock when Catherine told her of their plans. It made it easier to have a wiser, older friend constantly reassuring her that she was correct in the action she was taking.

"I know how you feel," Marjorie sympathized, "but you'd only pull yourself to shreds staying here. Get away. Get a new lease and perspective on life. You're in safe hands with Peter. He loves you. He'd never hurt you."

"And I'll try not to hurt him." But would that be possible? Could she ever return all the love he offered so freely?

Peter glowed. His bright, almost continuous smile lightened every corner of the apartment, which otherwise would have seemed dreary on certain gray January days. A light dusting of snow fell on the island, only a few inches, but Peter coaxed her out in it with boyish delight.

"Well, you know I haven't seen much of this white stuff in my life," he teased with a twinkle. "Let the novelty wear off."

Though she'd lived in California for so many years, Catherine still vividly remembered her childhood winters in New England, sledding, skating, skiing. She could understand his enthusiasm and entered into it by helping him build a snowman in the Atheneum square. Unfortunately, a warm spell a few days later turned the white into a grayish slush.

Catherine closed the shop for the season. Susan worked with her in packing away merchandise, throwing dust covers over furniture and racks of fabric samples.

"I'd like you to come back the end of April and open up," Catherine told her, "unless you'd rather find a year-round job."

"No, I love working here. I can use the winter to get some things done around the house."

"Wonderful. I'll stay in touch."

Catherine also called Marcie on the Coast to tell her she'd be off the island and that she'd call with her new phone number. Of course, Marcie wanted her to come out to Santa Barbara. Without being specific, Catherine hinted at a new man in her life and said she'd think about it. From all indications, Marcie was doing a fabulous job of managing Classics. Catherine wasn't physically needed there, though now that she knew she was leaving the island, she yearned to see the shop and her Santa Barbara friends again.

She and Peter started packing. He was adamant that she mustn't go to the house on Orange Street to collect anything. As he'd been doing all along, he arranged with Marjorie to pick up those things Catherine wanted. It annoyed Catherine, but she understood that he was prompted by worry over her, not by an imprisoning protectiveness.

Time went too quickly. The day before they were to leave for the mainland, Peter dug his camera out of the already packed bags and asked to borrow the Porsche.

"I want to go over to the other side of the island and get some shots to back me up on those paintings I've started. I might be a while. You're welcome to come, but from the looks of the weather, it's going to be pretty cold. I'll probably be tramping about."

"No, you go ahead." She dug in her purse for the car keys and handed them to him. "Why don't you take Barney along. He needs the exercise. I'll get all the boxes ready to go."

"Sure you don't mind?" he asked, rubbing his fingers down her cheek.

"No. Have a good time."

He chuckled. "I don't know how much fun it's going to be. I'll probably come back feeling like I'd just done a watch in a howling winter gale." He dropped a kiss on her lips, tucked the camera inside his foul weather jacket, and grabbed Barney's leash. The dog immediately came bounding over, tail wagging in excitement.

"See you in a bit," he called, as Barney pulled him through the door and down the stairs.

Catherine turned and went to the bedroom for the carefully packed boxes of Peter's canvases. She started moving them into the living room, standing them beside the rest of the things to be taken on the ferry. As she worked, she was suddenly overcome by a feeling of emptiness. She tried to shrug it off, blaming it on the fact both Peter and Barney were away from the apartment. She started back to work but found herself drifting to the window to stare out at the street.

It truly was a dreary day, overcast, with a piercingly damp fog whisping up from the harbor to hang about the barren tree branches and lamp posts and leave the brick sidewalk dark red and shiny with moisture. In the distance she heard the regular eerie blare of the fog horn near the harbor's mouth.

Tomorrow all of this would be behind. She'd be settling into a new house, a new life. She and Peter . . . to return, who knew when . . . probably after her baby was born.

Her feeling of emptiness grew more intense. She was seized by an incredible impulse to go to the house on Orange Street once more. To say good-bye; to prove to herself that it was over. She couldn't leave without doing that, could she? But did she dare go back? Would being there and seeing all the things that reminded her of Lucien make the hurt all the more crippling? Or did she owe it to Lucien? Did she owe both of them one more—one last—chance?

The question was decided for her. Some other power had taken control of her will as she moved from the window, took her coat off the peg near the door, put it on. Descending the stairs to the street, she walked out into the misty chill. Her feet followed a course they knew so well, across town, toward Orange Street. While something unexplained spurred her on, her own inner protective mechanisms told her not to hope. Nothing would happen. If he'd been meant to return, he would have long since, before she'd left the house. She would walk through the rooms, remember one last time, tell him good-bye, and leave.

She thought of Marjorie and all her well-meant advice. She knew that if the older woman saw her, she'd try to stop her from entering the house. Detouring around an extra block, Catherine approached the house from the opposite direction, away from Marjorie's. The fog enveloped her as she walked up the drive, but still she was nervous about being seen. She'd forgotten her purse and keys. She reached under the back stoop for the key she always kept hidden there. Swiftly and quietly she mounted the back stairs, inserted the key, and slipped inside. How good it felt to be back, to see the familiar rooms and furnishings. She walked slowly through each of the downstairs rooms, pausing at the piano, lovingly touching the keys, remembering Lucien's beautiful music, his smile, his eyes laughing over at her. And sometimes not laughing but speaking with another intense emotion.

Reluctantly she left the piano, then with purpose climbed the stairs, walked through her bedroom and into the study.

His room. It would always be Lucien's room to her. She didn't dare turn on a light, but went to stand by the windows. Her view of the harbor was hindered by the fog. She could barely see the rooftops below on Union Street. Her small back yard looked deserted and neglected. "Ah, Lucien," she thought, "remember the times we stood here together . . . the first time I viewed your harbor . . . the first time we made love." She felt tears gathering in her eyes, her throat closing. She swung from the windows and walked to his portrait, gazing up.

"I still love you," she whispered. "You know that. I'd never leave if I thought—" Her voice cracked. "If I thought you'd come back. I'm doing what is best for our child. I'm doing what I think you'd want me to do. I hope I'm right."

The blue eyes of the portrait seemed to flicker, but she knew it was her imagination, wishing him there beside her so badly. Suddenly she questioned her wisdom in coming to the house. It was only making things worse for her. Peter and her new life seemed of another world. But they weren't. They were the real world. She fingered Peter's ring, slid it up and down, drew it off and held it in the palm of her hand.

Once more she let her eyes meet his in the portrait. Minutes passed. "All we had together," she sighed. "Where are you now? Are you feeling the same ache as me? Lucien, why, why did it have to be like this?"

The tears were coming again. Her pain was unbearable. She had to leave before the ache tore her apart. In agony she looked out the study windows one last time and finally faced the irrefutable facts. It *was* over. She and Lucien would never be together again. She must think of her child and Peter. He'd be coming home soon, looking for her. Her eyes glazed with tears.

"Oh, Lucien, my beloved Captain, you'll always be a part of me, but . . . good-bye . . ."

Wretched with loss, she began to turn. Her eyes caught on a shadow in the mist-veiled yard below. She stopped, stared. Gradually the shadow took form. Peter's ring fell from her hand and clattered to the table top. In the next instant Catherine was running from the room, down the stairs, across the kitchen and through the back door.

He was standing in the midst of the small lawn, shoulders slumped. His features were ravaged by grief and hopelessness. The emptiness in his soul reached out like an aura around him.

"Lucien!"

He lifted his head. His eyes focused on her, first with disbelief, then uncertainty. Then his face lit with incredible joy.

"I'm not dreaming! It is you!"

He started forward. She rushed across the damp lawn toward him, running into the loving warmth of his arms as they swept around her, nearly crushing her. He lifted her in the air, held her tight against his chest. Her hands gripped his neck, tangled in his hair as her lips lavished kisses on every inch of his face. "Lucien—Lucien—Lucien." She couldn't stop repeating his name.

"How I feared! Oh, Catherine, I'd nearly given up hope. But then today I felt you so close. I've waited here by the house all day, praying to a God I don't believe in, begging for this!"

"And it's happened! We're together again."

"This time nothing is going to part us." He crushed his mouth on hers in a kiss that left them both breathless, shaking.

She stared at his face, devouring it, feeling dizzy and mad with joy to be gazing into his blue eyes once more. "These days have been a nightmare. I've missed you so terribly. Nothing would have been the same without you—"

"I know," he choked. "I know too well. But those days are over, Catherine. It's not going to end. We *shall* be together. I love you—so much."

"And I love you!"

He smiled, radiantly, and she glowed in the reflected warmth and happiness. Once more he brought his mouth down hard on hers as if to make up for all their days of agony. Then he wrapped his arm tight about her waist.

"Come, my love. Our future's awaiting us."

"Yes. Our future!"

Their eyes meeting in a loving bond, their hands locked together, they turned, started down the drive, and walked away from the house on Orange Street into the enveloping mist.

Epilogue

"The answer's here, isn't it? This is where they found my ring."

"Yes, Peter, I think it is." Marjorie walked into the study, her eyes automatically going to the portrait.

"Tell me. She can't have just disappeared without a trace."

"I understand how much you loved her. I understand how hurt you are—you especially." Quietly she turned to look at him. "But if I told you what I think is the truth, you wouldn't believe me."

"Why wouldn't I believe you? What are you trying to hide? She may be in danger."

Marjorie considered. "Perhaps, but not a danger you or I can do anything about."

"I don't understand."

"Maybe someday I'll feel I have the right to explain. She didn't mean to hurt you, Peter. This was just the way it was intended to end."

His eyes, too, went to the portrait. "It has something to do with him, doesn't it?"

"Almost certainly, I think."

"Who *is* he?"

"Another sea captain."

Peter closed his eyes as if he couldn't stand anymore, spun around, and strode from the room. She would go talk to him and try to give him some kind of comfort . . . what comfort there was to give.

She stood a moment longer below the portrait, then spoke quietly. "And I didn't think you'd come back. Good luck . . . to both of you."